Mary Catharine Ferguson

Sir Samuel Ferguson in the Ireland of His Day

Vol. 1

Mary Catharine Ferguson

Sir Samuel Ferguson in the Ireland of His Day
Vol. 1

ISBN/EAN: 9783337322564

Printed in Europe, USA, Canada, Australia, Japan

Cover: Foto ©Andreas Hilbeck / pixelio.de

More available books at **www.hansebooks.com**

SIR SAMUEL FERGUSON

IN

THE IRELAND OF HIS DAY

BY

LADY FERGUSON

AUTHOR OF 'THE IRISH BEFORE THE CONQUEST,'
'LIFE OF WILLIAM REEVES, D.D., LORD BISHOP OF DOWN,
CONNOR, AND DROMORE,' ETC., ETC.

WITH PORTRAITS

IN TWO VOLUMES

VOL. I.

WILLIAM BLACKWOOD AND SONS
EDINBURGH AND LONDON
MDCCCXCVI

PREFACE.

THE conviction that it is not easy for a wife to estimate justly the lifework of her husband has, in combination with other feelings, made me shrink from the effort, which friends have urged me to make, of writing a biography of Sir Samuel Ferguson.

Nine years have now elapsed since his death. I would hope that after so considerable an interval of time it may be possible for me to revert to the past with necessary aloofness, and write of him without undue partiality.

I feel also that—however incompetent in a literary sense—no one else could be so cognisant of

> " That best portion of a good man's life—
> His little, nameless, unremembered acts
> Of kindness and of love,"

as one who had the high privilege of his companionship during thirty-eight years of happy married life.

It will be my endeavour, to as large an extent as

possible, to let Sir Samuel Ferguson speak for himself. His own writings, and the letters of his friends, will best illustrate his character and opinions. In these will be evidenced his many - sided genius, and his manly, noble, and chivalrous personality. These gifts he devoted throughout life to the service of his country; and it may be that the utterances of a patriot — frankly outspoken and absolutely disin- terested — may appeal not alone to his compatriots, but also to a wider audience.

Beyond the circle of his friends and immediate ac- quaintances Sir Samuel Ferguson was known in many ways: to some as the poet who sought to make the tales of ancient Ireland familiar in the Ireland of to-day, and beyond the Irish Sea; to some as the translator into verse of the Confession of Saint Patrick; to some as the methodical official, keeper and ar- ranger of the Records of Ireland; to some as the painstaking inquirer in regard to Oghams and allied questions; and to some as the author of such humor- ous pieces as "Father Tom and the Pope" and "The Loyal Orangeman." In this biography I hope to show the varied powers, and the diligence which made each of these part of his lifework.

My acknowledgments are due, and are hereby ten- dered, to Dr J. J. Digges La Touche, for his kind- ness in drawing up the statement of my husband's services in connection with the Record Office, given in the twenty-sixth chapter of this book—" His Work as Deputy Keeper of the Records of Ireland." Also to Mr R. Macalister, who selected for my use ' Transactions ' of the Academy required for chapter twenty-five—" His Work as a Member of the Royal Irish Academy."

I desire to express my gratitude to friends who have read large portions of my manuscript, and have aided me by their counsel; to Dr Ingram, President of the Royal Irish Academy ; and Sir Thomas Grainger Stewart, Professor of Medicine in the University of Edinburgh. Also to my brother, the Rev. Robert Guinness, Vicar of Market-Harborough, to whom, with the surviving members of my husband's family and of my own, I desire to dedicate this book.

M. C. FERGUSON.

CONTENTS OF THE FIRST VOLUME.

SIR SAMUEL FERGUSON.

CHAPTER I.

1810–1886.

THE EVENTS OF AN UNEVENTFUL LIFE.

> " There is a history in all men's lives,
>   Figuring the nature of the times deceas'd :
>   The which observ'd, a man may prophesy,
>   With a near aim, of the main chance of things
>   As yet not come to life ; which in their seeds,
>   And weak beginnings, lie intreasured.
>   Such things become the hatch and brood of time."
>   —SHAKESPEARE.

SAMUEL FERGUSON, youngest child of John Ferguson and his wife Agnes, was born in Belfast on the 10th of March 1810, in the house of his maternal grandparents in High Street.

" My grandfather Knox," wrote Sir Samuel in afterlife, " was a practical astronomer, a man of science. He contributed distinguished papers on optics to the ' Transactions of the Royal Society,' and was, I believe, the possessor of the first private observatory in Ulster." Mr Knox's wife was a lady of good position, eldest daughter of Mr Anthony Horsman.

Samuel Ferguson of Standing Stone, in the county of Antrim, the paternal grandfather of Sir Samuel Ferguson, had by his wife, Hessy Owens, a daughter and six sons, amongst whom he left a good estate, around and including the little town of Parkgate, Co. Antrim. The Ferguson property was situated in and about the valley of the Six-Mile Water, which empties itself into Lough Neagh near the town of Antrim. Here stands one of the earliest of the Irish round towers, and not far distant may be traced the remains of the royal fort of Rathmore — Moy-Linny. The region is dominated by the moat of Donegore. This fine earthwork is a conspicuous object in the landscape. It commands an extensive view over a rich and undulating country to Lough Neagh, with its expanse of waters and boundary of distant mountains. To the north rise the Connor Hills and the wedge-like mountain of Slemish. At the base of the moat, or rath, stands the pretty church of Donegore. Here, on its lower slopes included in the churchyard, is the burying-place of the Ferguson family, and in this plot of ground repose the mortal remains of the Poet and Antiquary who is the subject of this biography. He lies amid scenes endeared to him from childhood, and often described by his pen. He sleeps among kindred dust on an Irish green hillside.

The Ferguson family came from Scotland early in

the seventeenth century. They believed themselves to belong to one of the oldest of the Highland clans, " Mhic Fhearghuis " of Athole. The crests are identical—a Scottish thistle with a bee sucking honey from "the symbol dear." The motto is " Dulcius ex asperis " (sweeter on account of the asperities). The immediate progenitors of the Fergusons migrated to Antrim from south-western Scotland.

In a ' Historical Notice of the Parish and People of Donegore ' it is stated that its

original members were colonists from Scotland, who came over, encouraged by an Act of Parliament passed in 1605. They were chiefly from Ayrshire, Dumfriesshire, and Wigtownshire. . . . The largest holders of land were the Adairs, Agnews, Fergusons, Gillilans. . . . The first of the Adairs, Fergusons, and Shaws came over as officers in the Scottish army soon after 1640. The first of the Owens and Williamsons came at a later date, probably attached to the army of William the Third. . . . It may not be out of place to mention here the names of three families long connected with Donegore, some of whose descendants have risen to distinction. These are the Fergusons of Thrushfield, from whom is descended [the late] Sir Samuel Ferguson of Dublin ; the Millers of Rathmore, from whom is descended the late William Kirk, M.P. for Newry ; and the Marshalls of Dunadry, from whom is descended the present [Master of the Rolls] Andrew Marshall Porter.

It has been frequently observed that the intellectual faculties in men of genius are derived from the mother. All the children of John and Agnes Ferguson—three sons and three daughters—had an unusually high average of mental power. Mrs Ferguson was a beautiful woman—even at a very advanced age her finely cut features were handsome; but her chief attraction was her intelligent conversation. While her children were young it was her habit to read with them the books she loved. The plays of Shakespeare, the poetry and novels of Scott, Milton, Burns, Byron, Shelley, Keats, stimulated their youthful imaginations. Her daughters, who married young, in afterlife wrote both in prose and verse. Her sons were all able men, and throughout life reverenced their mother.

Looking back on his early days, Samuel Ferguson subsequently wrote :—

During my childhood the family resided at Cider Court, near Crumlin, and afterwards at The Throne, near Belfast, and Collon in Glenwhirry, where I received those impressions of Nature and romance which have more or less influenced all my habits of thought and sentiment in after-life. I received my education first at the Old Belfast Academy, and afterwards at the Belfast Academical Institution, and in Trinity College, Dublin, but never graduated, and held no academic rank till the honorary degree of Doctor of Laws was conferred on me in 1865 by the University of Dublin after the publication of the 'Lays of the Western Gael.'

It was Samuel Ferguson's fate to be thrown on his own resources from boyhood. His father, who had not been brought up to any profession, had run through his property before this his youngest child had completed his education. It became necessary for him to support himself. This he did with his pen while studying for his profession as a barrister, and before he was of age he accomplished literary work of considerable merit both in prose and verse. He was but twenty-one when he contributed to 'Blackwood's Edinburgh Magazine' one of the most popular of his poems, "The Forging of the Anchor." It attracted the attention of Professor Wilson—the "Christopher North" of the 'Noctes Ambrosianæ'—who read it to that literary coterie.

"But is 'The Forging of the Anchor' your own, Kit?" asks Tickler, on hearing it.

"I wish it were," is North's reply. "But the world will yet hear of the writer. Belfast gave him birth, and he bears the same name with a true poet of our own Scotland—Ferguson. 'Maga' will be proud of introducing him to the world."

A visit to Edinburgh in 1832 brought the young poet into personal intercourse with William Blackwood and his family, and with Professor Wilson, Thomas Aird, and other eminent men of letters in the northern metropolis. Introductions given by them made him known in literary and artistic circles in London, and added to his enjoyments while residing there during the prosecution of his legal studies.

It was not till he had attained his twenty-eighth year that Ferguson was called to the Bar of Ireland in Trinity Term 1838. Thenceforth his home was in Dublin, and his primary object the pursuit of his profession. Yet every moment that could be spared from law was given to poetry and literature. Under these labours his health gave way; and he spent a year—

1846 — on the Continent, which restored him to strength, and added largely to his knowledge of history, archæology, and art.

On his return to Dublin Ferguson made the acquaintance of his future wife, the eldest daughter of Robert Rundell Guinness of Stillorgan. They were married in 1848, and after a time settled permanently in 20 North Great George's Street in that city.

The succeeding ten years were busily occupied with professional and literary work. He became a member of the North-East Circuit, and enjoyed a fair share of practice in all departments. His leisure hours and many of his holidays were devoted to the study of Irish antiquities and the production of poems dealing chiefly with the early history and legends of his country. Thus occupied, and surrounded by hosts of friends, these years went by most happily.

In 1859 Ferguson was called to the Inner Bar. As Queen's Counsel he earned for himself a good position. He retired from the practice of his profession in 1867, to become the first Deputy Keeper of the Records of Ireland.

To any man of intelligence the organisation of a new department must be of great interest. To Ferguson the work was fascinating. He formulated what he conceived to be the best methods for every detail of the office work. And he took pains, while meeting the great ends of his office, to consider every detail. Even mechanical arrangements were planned by himself, and the organisation became so complete as to earn the highest praise from those who knew the difficulties of classifying documents in such a way as to render them accessible for consultation at any moment. Apart from all such matters, he was full of personal interest in the individuals of his staff. They were as members of a family of which he was the head. Their welfare, and that of all his workmen, was dear to him. He regarded them with unfailing kindness and consideration.

These years brought many recognitions of his services. He received the degree of LL.D. *honoris causâ* from Trinity College, Dublin, in 1865, and the honorary membership of the Society of Antiquaries of Scotland—a number limited to twenty-five—in 1874. And, in acknowledgment of his services to the State, Ferguson received in 1878 the honour of Knighthood. In 1881 he was elected President of the Royal Irish Academy, a distinction which he highly valued.

In the Chair of the Academy, which in Ireland corresponds to the Royal Societies of London and of Edinburgh, he manifested all his wonted enthusiasm and tact. Not only did he contrive to make original contributions to its Transactions, but by well-timed encouragement stimulated the work of others. In March 1882 he delivered his address as President of the Royal Irish Academy, and held the chair during the remaining years of his life.

But neither the Academy's duties nor any other led to the slightest relaxation of his work at the Record

Office—his latest Reports being marked by the same minute accuracy which characterised the earlier volumes. Although many of those he loved had passed away, he was still surrounded by faithful friends, and his holidays as well as his work brought him much enjoyment. Not the least agreeable of these absences from home was that of April 1884, when he represented the Royal Irish Academy at the celebration of the tercentenary of the University of Edinburgh, and was one of those to receive the honorary degree of LL.D. There he made new friends and renewed old friendships.

Early in 1886 his health began to fail, and by slow degrees his bodily powers became more and more enfeebled. The 8th of April was the last day he spent at the Record Office. He did not then realise the serious nature of his illness, but hoped that he would have strength to preside at the festivities in May, when the Academy was to celebrate its centenary by a banquet at which the Lord Lieutenant and other magnates were to be entertained. Sir William Stokes and Dr Gordon, Ferguson's medical attendants, though refusing to expose him to the shock of hearing that his illness — failure of the heart — left no hope of recovery, told his wife. She made the necessary arrangements with Dr Ingram— then Vice-President and now President—who took the chair and did the honours of the Academy dinner. In his speech Dr Ingram thus referred to the absent President :—

I regret, and I am sure you all join in the feeling, that the distinguished poet, man of letters, jurist, and antiquary who presides over this Academy is not present at our centenary celebration, and that we shall not hear from his lips the weighty and well-chosen words which we have so often heard from him when he occupied our chair. More still than his absence we lament that illness should be the cause of it. We tender to Sir Samuel Ferguson our hearty sympathy, and we ask him to take as a solace in his retirement, which we trust will be of very short duration, the assurance that he is not merely honoured and admired in this Academy, but is the object of a warm feeling of affection on the part of all who have been admitted to his more intimate friendship.

On the evening in which the Lord Lieutenant and the Countess of Aberdeen, with the chief citizens of Dublin, were to be entertained at a conversazione, Ferguson insisted that his wife should be present to receive their Excellencies and other invited guests at the Academy House. She attended, not without reluctance, for he who was so inexpressibly dear to her was very ill. On the arrival of the Viceregal party she accompanied the Lord Lieutenant and the Countess of Aberdeen to the seats of honour prepared for them. Lord Aberdeen courteously inquired for the health of the President, and expressed his regret for Sir Samuel's illness. "I hear much of him on all sides," he continued. Then, suddenly stopping, he turned to Lady Ferguson, looked her in the face, and in a tone which told how much he was struck by it, said to her, "But they are all so fond of him!" And so it was. Love was the sentiment he inspired in all who knew him—not only in those nearest to him, but also in his domestics, his dependants, his friends, and even those with whom he came but casually in contact. The benignity of his nature, its kindliness and tenderness, endeared him to many besides his intimates. Wherever he went he diffused an atmosphere of sunshine—the sunshine of the heart, which draws forth all the fragrance and sweetness of which human nature is capable.

As the summer advanced he removed to Howth, and there in the much - loved and familiar ground, with the utmost sweetness and calm resignation, he contemplated the approaching end of his life in this world, enjoying to the last the beauties of nature, the society of those he loved, and the comforts of an unclouded faith. His life slowly ebbed away, and on the 9th of August he was with us no more.

On the 12th of August the funeral procession—one of the most numerously attended ever seen in Dublin— left 20 North Great George's Street for St Patrick's Cathedral. The coffin, covered with laurel and floral wreaths, was received at the entrance by the Dean and officiating clergy, including the Archbishop of Dublin. Then followed the officers and members of the Royal Irish Academy, bearing their mace draped with crape. The mace had been that of the Irish House of Commons. The staff of the Record Office, including even its workmen, were present, and the Cathedral was filled by relatives and friends of the deceased, and by 'many of the humbler classes, former servants, and others to whom his kindness

had endeared him.   To them, at the conclusion of
the service, the Archbishop of Dublin (Lord Plunket)
delivered the following address :—

While these strains of comfort are still ringing in our ears,
I desire upon my own part, and, I think I may say, upon the
part of all here present, to pay a last tribute of respect and
affection to the memory of our dear friend who has been taken
to his rest.   I have grave doubts, and I daresay they are
shared by many in this Cathedral, whether it be right, or
wise, or considerate, that a funeral service should always be
accompanied by a funeral address.   Very often I feel that
we should leave our solemn and beautiful service to speak
for itself.   But there are times when the instincts of our
hearts, and, I may say, when the instinct of a nation, claim
some further utterance ; and if ever there was such a time,
I believe that the present occasion is one.   For, do we not
all feel that by the death of our dear brother departed in the
Lord, we have all of us, as Irishmen, suffered an irreparable
loss ?   In whatever light we may regard the character of him
who has been taken from us,—whether as a Scholar, a Poet, a
Patriot, or a God-fearing Servant of his Master,—we must all,
I repeat, feel that Ireland has suffered a loss which it will
be impossible to repair, and which cannot be confined merely
to those who belong to any one class or any one creed
amongst us !   The whole land suffers for it !
I have spoken of our dear brother as a Scholar.   He was
a man of general culture and of varied learning.   But, as
we all know, his chief eminence was attained in the department of antiquarian research.   I need scarcely refer to
the fact that, as a token of appreciation in this respect,
he was given, and retained to his death, the highest honour
that Science and Learning could bestow in this land upon
those who are worthy of it.   He died the President of
the Royal Irish Academy.   And I have only to refer to
the many valuable papers which he read before that body
in order to remind those who need to be reminded that
he has enriched the literature of archæology with many

precious stores for which we, as Irishmen generally, should be for ever grateful.

I have spoken of him as a Poet; and here, I doubt not, my words find an echo in the breasts of those who have read and learned to prize his poetical works. He had, as we all know, the passion and fire of the genuine poet, tempered at the same time by great tenderness and purity. Above all, there was in his poetry that spirit of wild romance and playfulness, that combination of pathos and humour, which specially characterise the productions of Irish song.

There is, however, among his poems, or rather his poetical translations, one legacy which we who meet together in this Cathedral ought specially to prize — I mean the last paper which he read before the Royal Irish Academy, upon "Patrician Documents"—a paper containing a wonderfully beautiful translation of those works which all learned men attribute, as genuine, to the great founder of Christianity in this land. This translation is one that we must all treasure, and we should all thank God that before our dear brother was taken from us he left us such a legacy.

I have spoken of him as a Patriot, and if ever there was one who was an Irishman to his very heart's core, it was Samuel Ferguson. His was a pure, single-minded, disinterested form of patriotism. He embraced within it a love for all his fellow-countrymen, to whatever class or creed they might belong; and, keeping apart from political bitterness, the one thing he longed for was the prosperity and peace of his native land.

I now approach a more sacred aspect of our dear friend's character—his social and domestic relations; and I would not touch upon them at all were it not that by overlooking them we would miss one of the special traits of his character. I allude to his courtesy — a courtesy marked by a singular refinement and polish. And yet it was not only polish. For, as those who knew him were well aware, it was the outcome of a generous, considerate, and kindly nature. What he said with his lips, and what was expressed by his countenance, was felt and meant by his heart. As to his attitude towards his friends and those who were nearest and dearest to him, I may say there is just one word which expresses it, and that is—Love. It was simply a continual outwelling of an unselfish, deep, and fervent love!

A few moments remain for me to speak of that most sacred of all aspects in any man's character—his relations with his God. It would be a painful thing if, after having described the other features of our dear brother's character, I were obliged to be silent upon this point. Thank God, that is not necessary. Our dear friend was not demonstrative as regarded his religious convictions. He was free from any taint of sectarian bigotry. He had a large heart, and great breadth of thought. He had a repugnance, I would almost say an excessive repugnance, to certain dogmas—not essentials of Christianity — which he considered to be due merely to the invention of man. But withal he had a simple, earnest, manly, and at the same time child-like faith in God, and a true and genuine appreciation of his dear Saviour's love and work. He was a man of a very reverent disposition. It was my privilege, not long before his death, to administer to him the memorials of our dear Lord's death, and I can never forget how, notwithstanding my dissuasions, he, at great physical inconvenience and pain, knelt to receive the emblems of his Lord's Death, showing his appreciation of the solemnity of the holy rite in which he was engaged.

Nor was this religious temperament merely the result of declining years, or the fear of approaching death. Many of you here present may have read the beautiful poem which he composed nearly thirty years ago, recording a visit of his to Westminster Abbey, where he says—

> "Amid the tombs of England's dead
> I heard the Holy Scriptures read."

In the poem he speaks of "the comfort of the Holy Book," and of "the Gospel's joyful sound." He expresses the great enjoyment that he felt in listening to the strains that rose upward within the venerable pile, and yet he does not forget the humbler churches of his native land. He says—

> "Yet hold not lightly home, nor yet
> The graves on Donagore forget ;
> Nor grudge the stone-gilt stall to change
> For humble bench of Gorman's Grange.
>
> For in that Presence, vast and good,
> That bends o'er all our livelihood,
> With human kind in heavenly cure,
> We all are like, we all are poor.
>
> Enough for Thee, indulgent Lord,
> The willing ear to hear Thy Word,
> The rising of the burdened breast,
> And Thou suppliest all the rest !"

That is the outpouring of a yearning heart—a heart whose craving, too, had been supplied !

No wonder that one who thus, in the days of health, was able to look up reverently to his heavenly Father, and to find his wants supplied by Him—no wonder, I say, that when he felt that death was drawing near, he awaited with fortitude the end. No murmur of impatience during the long months of his last sickness escaped from his lips. There was a courageous readiness to depart. At one time he called to his bedside the one that was dearest to him, and said, " Be brave, dear wife, we shall be reunited !"

His last words—and let us treasure them in our hearts—were these, spoken in a whisper which could scarcely he heard, —" All is well ! All is well !" Oh, what brave words to hear from a dying-bed ! Oh, what comforting words to ring again and again within a bereaved and lonely heart !—" All is well !" May every one of us, whether in health or in sickness, in the fulness of life or at the approach of death, be able to say, " All is well !"

And now, dear brethren, whatsoever is earthly of our dear brother will be taken presently from this Cathedral, and to-morrow will be laid amongst " the graves of Donegore," which he has celebrated in song ; and if you ask me, meanwhile, as the prophet's messenger asked of the Shunammite, " Is all well with our brother?" my answer to you is the answer given in our brother's own words, "All is well!"

At the conclusion of these tender words, and of the "service high and anthem clear" in the national Cathedral, all that was mortal of Sir Samuel Ferguson was conveyed to the family burying-ground in the county of Antrim. The procession to Donegore was accompanied by the Bishop of the diocese and many other mourners. Here, at the grave, the service was completed by the Bishop, his old and faithful friend William Reeves, in "hope of the resurrection to eternal life," and the spot is marked by a simple tablet:—

SACRED TO THE BELOVED MEMORY OF

SIR SAMUEL FERGUSON, KNT., Q.C., LL.D.,

DEPUTY KEEPER OF THE RECORDS OF IRELAND,

PRESIDENT OF THE ROYAL IRISH ACADEMY,

WHO DIED ON THE 9TH OF AUGUST 1886,

AGED 76 YEARS.

CHAPTER II.

1810–1847.

DOMESTIC AND FAMILY LIFE—EARLY YEARS.

> " How happy is he born and taught
> That serveth not another's will ;
> Whose armour is his honest thought,
> And simple truth his utmost skill !
>
> .   .   .   .   .   .
>
> Who hath his life from rumours freed,
> Whose conscience is his strong retreat ;
> Whose state can neither flatterers feed,
> Nor ruin make oppressors great.
>
> .   .   .   .   .   .
>
> This man is freed from servile bands
> Of hope to rise, or fear to fall ;
> Lord of himself, though not of lands ;
> And having nothing, yet hath all."
> —SIR HENRY WOTTON.

THE circumstances of Ferguson's early life leave little record of his domestic and family relationships. His father's home was broken up when he was still a boy, and his brothers and sisters were so much his seniors that they were launched before he began to play his part in life. Still there are some facts worth recording. His father was a handsome and vigorous man, but his habits were extravagant. He dissipated

his fortune with astonishing rapidity, and left his
family to fight the battle of life for themselves. His
mother was prudent and self-denying, and although
a beautiful and intellectual woman, was content to
lead a retired life, devoted to her domestic duties.
She was exact and honourable in money matters,
and retained the esteem of family and friends. She
lived to an advanced age, and died in 1861 in her
youngest son's house, of which from the time of her
widowhood she had been a frequent inmate. Samuel
Ferguson, admirable in this as in his other relationships, showed her the tenderest consideration. One
letter only, written to her in the summer of 1860 from
Circuit, remains to exhibit his character as a son.
His family circle, which at the time included his wife's
brother and sister-in-law—very dear to him, as were
all her relatives—were spending the summer at Marine
Cottage, Howth.

ARMAGH, *9th July.*

MY DEAR MOTHER,—I hear with much pleasure from
my dear Mary that you are well, and beginning to feel yourself at home at Howth. I know no more healthful or agreeable place during the summer months, and am truly happy
to think that you are still able to enjoy the beautiful face
of Nature which sea and land now present to you at all
times of the tide and of the day. I suppose by this time
the meadow in front of the house is cut, and the fresh green
after-grass beginning to appear. You will be able to walk
out on the height and sit under the shadow of a haycock,
looking over the sea on one hand and up to the Hill of
Howth on the other, and still be within sight and hearing
of the house and of the children playing on the strand. You
now have plenty of society, as I hear from Mary. Richard's

Lizzie is so frank and cordial a person, that if you retain your old perception of character, I am sure you will love her. Indeed I cannot imagine a happier society than you ought to be; and I am deeply thankful to God, who has permitted you in your old age the opportunity of enjoying life so tranquilly, and so much in accordance with your own love of the country and of the society of friends. I daresay you will find yourself soon able to extend your walks, for the Howth air is very invigorating; and as soon as you are able for it, I would advise you to get out on the sands in front of Mr Kane's, where you will enjoy a delightful sea-breeze, and perhaps be able to return by Mr Kane's house, where they will be very glad to see you. Now good-bye, old woman, and rest assured that we all wish to make you happy, and that I am always your affectionate son,

SAML. FERGUSON.

Samuel Ferguson's earliest recollection was of the departure for the West Indies of his eldest brother. William Owens Ferguson was a high-spirited youth, with a passion for adventure. Instead of settling down to mercantile pursuits, he volunteered for military service under General Simon Bolivar in the South American War of Independence. In the early part of the century the misgoverned colonies of Spain shook off her yoke, under the leadership of Bolivar. The young volunteer rapidly rose to the rank of colonel, and became aide-de-camp to the Liberator, who selected him for command in expeditions requiring energy and military capacity. Of these, one of the most remarkable was William Ferguson's forced march across the Andes from Peru to Venezuela with 120 men only, who rode night and day in order to check the revolt of General Paez in the northern provinces during Bolivar's absence in Peru. The Liberator felt the importance of securing the wavering allegiance of Columbia and Venezuela by promptly communicating the intelligence that he was on the march to chastise Paez. This was the task which he confided to his gallant young aide-de-camp. On approaching by a forced march the frontier of the revolted province, Ferguson found his small detachment broken down from fatigue. He halted them for a day's rest for men and horses, and rode on alone. He arrived towards night at the frontier town, and boldly entered the Governor's quarters, where he announced himself an avant-courier of the Liberator. This functionary, who was sitting over his wine with his staff, informed him that Bolivar had been superseded by Paez, and that he—Ferguson—must consider himself a prisoner: meantime he invited him to take wine and biscuits. In the conversation that ensued at table, Colonel Ferguson learned that on the following morning the revolted troops, 2000 strong, were to arrive at Barquisimeto, a neighbouring town. He addressed himself to the group of officers, pleaded the claims of Bolivar on their allegiance, and influenced twenty-five of them, whom he persuaded to mount and ride through the night to Barquisimeto. Early on the following morning they reached the place and dashed into the principal square. Here they observed a group of gentlemen unarmed and in conversation, who were evidently personages of importance. These they surrounded and at once arrested. Then leaving some of his party to guard his unarmed prisoners, Ferguson with the rest charged the flying crowd and surprised the barracks. Thus possessed of the arms and ammunition in the place, Colonel Ferguson issued his orders to the municipal authorities, and directed them to provide quarters and rations for his force, whose arrival he hourly expected. Paralysed with terror, and believing the twenty-five officers to be the advance-guard of a formidable army, they obeyed; and before the 120 wearied men appeared to undeceive them, Ferguson had read to the populace Bolivar's proclamation, and had induced them to reconsider their position and pledge themselves to the cause of the Liberator. He then despatched messengers to the neighbouring towns, commanding their levies to present themselves next day at Barquisimeto, to whom he would supply arms and ammunition. These prompt measures were successful. In two days Colonel Ferguson had assembled and armed a force outnumbering that of Paez. The rebel general was compelled to retreat. He ultimately submitted to Bolivar, whom Ferguson joined at Caracas, and there received the warm thanks of his chief, to whom he had rendered by his daring and gallantry this vital service. The incident is recorded in the official statement of the services of Colonel William Ferguson of the Columbian army:—

By a subsequent order he got command of the vanguard of the army that marched on Venezuela, with only 120 men of the Battalion Paya. He occupied in two days all the west, the defence of which consisted of four battalions of regular militia, eight squadrons of cavalry, and four pieces of artillery—all of which force he caused to espouse the Government cause by his movement on Barquisimeto, which place he took by surprise. He then occupied San Felipe, Nirqua, and Araure, and forced the division which had invaded Barinas to capitulate.

Colonel Ferguson lost his life on the 28th of September 1828, at the early age of twenty-eight years, heroically defending his friend and chief in a military revolt at Bogotá. He was honoured with a public funeral, and lies in the Cathedral of Santa Fé de Bogotá. His journals, medals, autograph letters of General Simon Bolivar, are still treasured by his family. The statement of his services is as follows: "He served in the Battalion of Rifles of the Guards—Staff of the North Battalion Carthagena—Battalion Voltigeurs of the Guards—Staff of the Liberator." Colonel Ferguson took part in most of the campaigns and battles of the War of Independence.

Not long before his death, William Owens Ferguson, in a letter to his sister, observes: "In one thing I believe few families have the advantage of ours—affection and tender interest amongst its members." This amiable quality existed among them although early separated by circumstances.

Samuel Ferguson's second brother, John, a handsome, accomplished, and honourable gentleman, was also considerably his senior. So were the three sisters, who all married young, and thus had little influence on his life in childhood. As William's death made John head of the family, he came in for such remnants of the property as had not been dissipated by their father's extravagance. John married in early life Miss Matilda O'Donnell, and eventually settled in the Co. Antrim, and had a family of seven children by her.

The most intimate companions of Samuel Ferguson's childhood were his cousins Alicia and Hessy Gunning, daughters of his father's only sister. They spent much time at Tildarg, the home of their uncle Thomas Ferguson and his wife Rachel Owens of Brecna Hill, who at that time were childless. After a married life of upwards of twenty years a son was born to them, who grew to manhood, married, and died leaving children; and that branch of the family is now represented by two sons, of whom the elder, Thomas, a young poet of much promise, is author of a volume, 'Ballads and Dreams,' published in 1885.

Of the sports of Samuel Ferguson's boyhood, fishing seems to have been chief. He has described an adventure—the attempted " knieving " of a salmon—in a note to his story of " The Wet Wooing " :—

" Knieving trouts " (they call it tickling in England) is good sport. You go to a stony shallow at night, a companion bearing a torch ; then, stripping to the thighs and shoulders, wade in ; grope with your hands under the stones, sods, and other harbourage, till you find your game, then grip him in your " knieve " and toss him ashore.

I remember, when a boy, carrying the splits for a servant of the family, called Sam Wham. Now Sam was an able young fellow, well-boned and willing, a hard-headed cudgel-player, and a marvellous tough wrestler, for he had a backbone like a sea-serpent : this gained him the name of the Twister and Twiner. He had got into the river, and with his back to me was stooping over a broad stone, when something bolted from under the bank on which I stood, right through his legs. Sam fell with a great splash upon his face, but in falling jammed whatever it was against the stone. "Let go, Twister!" shouted I; "'tis an otter, he will nip a finger off you." "Whisht!" sputtered he, as he slid his hand under the water; "may I never read a text again if he isna a sawmont wi' a shouther like a hog!" "Grip him by the gills, Twister," cried I. "Saul will I!" cried the Twiner; but just then there was a heave, a roll, a splash, a slap like a pistol-shot: down went Sam, and up went the salmon, spun like a shilling at pitch-and-toss, six feet into the air. I leaped in just as he came to the water; but my foot caught between two stones, and the more I pulled the firmer it stuck. The fish fell in a spot shallower than that from which he had leaped. Sam saw the chance, and tackled to again; while I, sitting down in the stream as best I might, held up my torch, and cried, "Fair play!" as shoulder to shoulder, throughout and about, up and down, roll and tumble, to it they went, Sam and the salmon. The Twister was never so twined before. Yet, through cross-buttocks and capsizes innumerable, he still held on; now haled through a pool; now haling up a bank; now heels over head; now head over heels; now head and heels together; doubled up in a corner; but at last stretched fairly on his back, and foaming for rage and disappointment; while the victorious salmon, slapping the stones with his tail, and whirling the spray from his shoulders at every roll, came boring and snoring up the ford. I tugged and strained to no purpose; he flashed by me with a snort, and slid into the deep water. Sam now staggered forward with battered bones and peeled elbows, blowing like a grampus, and cursing like nothing but himself. He extricated me, and we limped home. Neither rose for a week; for I had a dislocated ankle, and the Twister was troubled with a broken rib. Poor Sam! he had his brains discovered at last by a poker in a row, and was worm's meat within three months; yet, ere he died, he had the satisfaction of feasting on his old antagonist, who was man's meat next morning.   They caught him in a net.   Sam knew him by the twist in his tail.

Ferguson's delight in fishing — a taste which remained with him till late in life — is expressed in one of his earliest ballads.   "Willy Gilliland" tells of an ancestor who fled in Covenanting times from Scotland to Ireland, and was dependent for his sustenance on his skill with the rod in the Glenwhirry river :—

It was a summer evening, and, mellowing and still,
Glenwhirry to the setting sun lay bare from hill to hill ;
For all that valley pastoral held neither house nor tree,
But spread abroad and open all, a full fair sight to see,
From Slemish foot to Collon top lay one unbroken green,
Save where in many a silver coil the river glanced between.

And on the river's grassy bank, even from the morning grey,
He at the angler's pleasant sport had spent the summer day ;
Ah ! many a time and oft I've spent the summer day from
    dawn,
And wondered, when the sunset came, where time and care
    had gone,
Along the reaches curling fresh, the wimpling pools and
    streams,
Where he that day his cares forgot in those delightful dreams.

The Covenanter was tracked by his foes, his horse captured and conveyed to Carrickfergus.   Its recapture by Gilliland is the subject of the ballad.   From him was descended Ferguson's great-grandmother, Ellen Gilliland.

Ah ! little thought Willy Gilliland, when he on Skerry side
Drew bridle first, and wiped his brow after that weary ride,
That where he lay like hunted brute, a caverned outlaw lone,
Broad lands and yeoman tenantry should yet be there his own :

Yet so it was ; and still from him descendants not a few
Draw birth and lands, and, let me trust, draw love of Freedom
    too.

Samuel Ferguson, then keeping his terms at Lincoln's Inn, in a letter written in May 1832 to his
brother John, tells of his recent visit to Edinburgh,
where the young poet had been cordially welcomed
in literary circles. This epistle shows him to have
been not a little proud of his reception among the *élite*
of the Modern Athens :—

I have been reproaching myself for the last two months for
not writing to you [he says], and have gone on procrastin-
ating till I am now past the power of apology, although still,
I hope, within the security of pardon. . . . I am beginning
to be confirmed in my suspicion that I am a promising young
man and a favourite. I must take care not to let myself be
overcome with vanity ; but there is little fear of that. . . . I
spent ten days delightfully in Edinburgh, receiving every kindness and compliment that I could have possibly desired.
Wilson asked me to Ambrose's, where I had a "nox Am-
brosiana," and introduced me to his family, with whom I
spent two very pleasant evenings.

Blackwood had me at his house almost every day, and sent
me round the country in his carriage—to Roslin, Hawthorn-
den, the Pentland Hills, &c. He is very desirous that I
should continue a regular contributor, and of course you have
heard how handsomely he paid me for the "Wet Wooing."
Wilson complimented me very highly on that, particularly on
the "Canny Courtship," which you will be glad to know
went round most of the Scotch papers. I was very much to
blame in not having an article in the last number, but it was
hardly possible for me to do anything till I got quietly settled
in lodgings here ; and indeed even then it was not till I shut
myself up for a week and was "not at home" to all comers
that I could get up the needful for next month : if it should

appear, I will get what will bring me home decently through some part of the country that I have not yet seen. I wish very much to get home by Scotland, where young Blackwood is anxious that I should join him in a walk through the Highlands. If not, I may possibly go by Dublin. . . . I must get myself introduced to Lockhart and Hunt (who has my manuscript still) before I leave town if possible, both being in their opposite ways men of high character. By the bye, I am to be taken to a conversazione at Kensington Palace some night, given by the Duke of Sussex' private secretary, Mr Pettigrew, where I will see all the Whig worthies. The Duke himself is generally there, and many men of great distinction. . . . I had a very delightful evening with George Cruikshank looking over the original sketches of his drawings. He showed me the process of etching a copper. I had a letter to him from Mr Blackwood. Campbell has been very kind. He introduced me the other day to Lady Caroline Drummond—a great old *dust*. . . . She is a red-hot Tory. . . . All's up for the present with the Tories. The Lords are impotent, defunct, contemptible. The King is badgered, fevered, miserable. The People of substance are kept from their trade and the Beggars are on horseback. The insolence of the Mob-orators is only equalled by the ungoverned atrocity of the press, and the Whigs are already quailing before the devil they have raised and cannot lay. The Bill is sure to pass in all its unmitigated harshness towards the old system. The new one may in the course of time prove simpler and cheaper, no doubt, but it is a terrible thing to contemplate the overthrow of one great and long-established scheme of Society in order to allow another to be set up for trial on its ruins—which, if unsuccessful, must lower us from the first to the third or fourth rate in the scale of nations. . . . So you see to what a philosophical conclusion I have brought my honest endeavours to make up for my bad behaviour to you, my dear brother. God grant us all fewer troubles, for we have had enough—and so I think have you had of my yarn.—Ever affectionately yours,

S. FERGUSON.

Ferguson, who from this time forward was a frequent contributor to 'Blackwood's Magazine,' had no opportunity of renewing his personal intercourse with the great publisher.   More than half a century had elapsed when he revisited Edinburgh to receive the honorary degree of LL.D. conferred by its University on the occasion of its Tercentenary celebrations in April 1884.   He embraced the opportunity to renew old friendships, and on a bright afternoon called with his wife at Charlotte Square to visit Miss Blackwood, the daughter of the friend who had shown him so much kindness fifty-two years before.   He had known her then as a young lady, and though he had never met her since, the memory of ancient kindnesses made him seek out her home.   It so chanced that he and his wife entered the drawing-room unannounced.   They had reached the middle of the room before Miss Blackwood was aware of the presence of visitors.   She rose from the fireside, and in a moment, holding up, and then holding out, both hands, said, " Oh, Mr Ferguson, 'The Wet Wooing'!"   She laughed heartily, and continued, " I shall never forget the reading of that story to my father.   He sat in this very chair in which I am now seated, and on that stool I read to him your MS. Oh, how we enjoyed it! Redrigg's 'Canny Courtship'!" and Miss Blackwood again laughed with infectious hilarity at the remembrance of her own and her father's mirth.

Ferguson's artistic faculty showed itself from early life.   He drew and etched with accuracy, and had a fine eye for colour, but lacked technical instruction.

His sketches from Nature were full of feeling, revealing his sense of her loveliness and charm. He could also, with pencil or pen and ink, produce a good likeness of the human face divine. Yet in a short poem, "The Sketcher Foiled," which appeared in the 'University,' July 1836, he records his failure to depict the features of "Laura":—

> With trembling hand I strive to trace
> The fairy lines of Laura's face;
> But Laura's lip and Laura's eye
> My utmost powers of art defy.
> Whence comes the failure, maidens tell:
> Ah me, I feel the cause too well;
> I feel *that* image ne'er will part
> From where 'tis graven—on my heart!

This seems a confession that "Cupid had clapped him on the shoulder"; and it is not improbable that the "Laura" was his much-loved cousin Hessy Gunning. They were playfellows in childhood, and in early youth had launched together on the Drumadarragh river, which flowed through Tildarg, the bluebells whose course down the stream were to be emblems of their future destiny. Whatever may have been the feelings of the youth, the girl, it would seem, had for him a friendly affection only. She married early, and settled with her husband, Mr Cassels, in Australia. He—the rejected cousin—wrote a touching little poem entitled "Hopeless Love," a lyric full of tenderness, yet without a trace of the bitterness of spirit a rejected suitor feels when he has been misled by the heartlessness or coquetry of her whose love he sought :—

HOPELESS LOVE.

Since hopeless of thy love I go,
Some little mark of pity show,
And only one kind parting look bestow.

One parting look of pity mild
On him, through starless tempest wild,
Who lonely hence to-night must go, exiled.

But even rejected love can warm
The heart through night and storm ;
And unrelenting though they be,
Thine eyes beam life on me.

And I will bear that look benign
Within this darkly-troubled breast to shine,
Though never, never can thyself, ah me, be mine.

Ferguson's chivalrous and high-souled nature is revealed in another lyric, " Mary's Waking," which in its original form bore the name of " Laura " :—

MARY'S WAKING.

Soft be the sleep and sweet the dreams,
And bright be the awaking,
Of Mary this mild April morn,
On my pale vigil breaking :
May weariness and wakefulness,
And unrepaid endeavour,
And aching eyes like mine this day,
Be far from her for ever !

The quiet of the opening dawn,
The freshness of the morning,
Be with her through the cheerful day,
Till peaceful eve returning

Shall put an end to household cares
  And dutiful employment,
And bring the hours of genial mirth
  And innocent enjoyment.

And whether in the virgin choir
  A joyous sylph she dances,
Or o'er the smiling circle sheds
  Her wit's sweet influences,
May he by favouring fate assigned
  Her partner or companion,
Be one that with an angel's mind
  Is fit to hold communion.

Ah me! the wish is hard to frame!
  But should some youth more favoured
Achieve the happiness which I
  Have fruitlessly endeavoured,
God send them love and length of days,
  And health and wealth abounding,
And long around their hearth to hear
  Their children's voices sounding!

Be still, be still, rebellious heart;
  If he have fairly won her,
To bless their union I am bound
  In duty and in honour.
But, out alas! 'tis all in vain;
  I love her still too dearly
To pray for blessings which I feel
  So hard to give sincerely.

Shakespeare has told us how bitter a thing it is
to look into happiness through another's eyes. Yet
though the struggle be great, victory is possible to the
generous and unselfish nature. The strength gained
through conflict may not alone ensure peace, but give

power to aid and comfort others. An illustration of this occurred on the 13th of November 1876. On that evening Ferguson returned at an unusually late hour from a meeting of the Royal Irish Academy. The servants had gone to bed, but his wife had not retired. Sir Samuel told her that the meeting had been a stormy one, and that Isaac Butt, who desired to be elected a member, had been black - balled. He was very sorry for Mr Butt, for he knew that eminent lawyer's mortification would be great when he read in next morning's paper of his rejection by the Academy. Ferguson took up his pen. A few minutes sufficed to write the following sonnet. " I think," he said, as he read it to his wife, "it might console him to receive this in the morning before he gets his daily paper. I will go now to his house and drop it into his letter-box." He did so, and received next day a few touching and grateful lines from Mr Butt. The sonnet ran thus :—

TO MR BUTT

(ON THE RESULT OF THE BALLOT AT THE ROYAL IRISH ACADEMY,
13TH NOVEMBER 1876).

While the Academy, refusing to submit itself to the control of the Department of Science and Art, even at the peril of losing its annual vote, had laid its case before the House of Commons by petition, and stood in its extremest need of support from parliamentary and public opinion, Mr Butt, whose membership ought to have been deemed an honour and advantage at any time, was proposed as a member, and rejected.

Isaac, the generous heart conceives no ill
   From frank repulse. The marriage-suit denied
   Turns love to hatred only where 'tis Pride,
Not true love, woos : Love holds her lovely still,

Let sharp Remembrance bring what stings it will;
  And when he sees her children by her side,
  For her, for them, for him with them allied,
Blessings and prayers the manly breast will fill.
Lovely she stands though she has said thee nay,
  And sad expectance clothes her brow in gloom,
  While guardians tyrannous withhold her dower:
Now show the soul's magnanimous assay,
  And when her day in that High Court shall come,
  Plead in your old love's cause with double power.

The subsequent correspondence of Ferguson and his cousin, separated by space and never destined to meet again in this life, though evidencing cordial interest in each other's wellbeing, has no trace of the pathos of unrequited love. Mrs Cassels wrote in 1846 to tell her cousin that her marriage was a truly happy one,—"knowing the interest you take, and how much pleased you would be to hear that I am in the enjoyment of both health and happiness; and if I had all my friends out here, I would not have a wish ungratified." In a letter written to Sir Samuel Ferguson in 1884—when Mrs Cassels was a widow and a grandmother—she says, "When you and I used to amuse ourselves throwing pebbles into the brook below Tildarg, we little thought that we should be so far separated." In his reply, dated March 29, he gives details of his career during the years that had passed, and of his married life, assured that in all that concerned his happiness his cousin would sympathise :—

20 NTH. GREAT GEORGE'S STREET,
29th March 1884.

MY DEAR HESSY,—I have kept your affectionate and very welcome letter a long time by me, feeling that you would expect I should tell you a good deal about myself, and being readier to write about any other person's history.´ I have been fortunate in life in having one of the best of wives, and in attaining to a social position which has quite enough of dignity and distinction for my highest ambition. I wish for the sake of others I was richer, but enjoy the additional blessing of being content to share what I have and thank God for what is left. We have no children, but a tribe of nephews and nieces, and grand nephews and nieces, numbering about eighty, and I suppose cousins near a hundred. My wife was Mary Catherine Guinness, of a very widely connected Dublin family, the heads of which have been the great brewers of Dublin for many generations.

She is a woman of great intellectual culture, whose conversation is much appreciated by men of ability, and what with works of usefulness and benevolence, and keeping up her correspondence, besides attending as she does to all domestic affairs, accounts, and hospitalities, is as busy a creature as can be. She is now sixty, and I am seventy-four. I am Deputy Keeper of the Public Records in Ireland, having given up my practice at the Bar owing to ill-health about sixteen years ago. The apprehended break-down did not take place, and although ailing, I continue able for the discharge of my duties. My salary is £800 a-year; but the office suits my tastes, and I do not repine at the loss of the prizes which I left behind me. Molly and I, with one of our nieces, go next month to Edinburgh, where the University is to celebrate its third centenary, and proposes to confer an honorary degree of LL.D. (amongst many others) on me. I attend as representing the Royal Irish Academy, of which I am President.

I have kept a corner, dear Hessy, to say I remember as well as if it were yesterday how you, Alicia, and I threw the bluebells from the little bridge below Tildarg into the Drumadarragh river, to watch their course down the stream and augur our future from their progress. Dear Alicia lived a tranquil and, I believe, a happy life. You have the happiness of being surrounded by your grand-children : I have told you how my bluebell has floated so far in its progress to the sea. It is sweet to recall the days of our youth. I know you will remember the same with pleasure.—Yours, dear Hessy, most affectionately, SAML. FERGUSON.

CHAPTER III.

1825–1844.

SCHOOL FRIENDSHIPS AND EARLY LITERARY WORK.

> "Greatness and goodness are not *means*, but *ends!*
> Hath he not always treasures, always friends,
> The good great man? Three treasures—Love, and Light,
> And Calm Thoughts, regular as infant's breath ;
> And three firm friends, more sure than day and night,
> Himself, his Maker, and the Angel Death."
> —COLERIDGE.

FERGUSON had throughout life the happiness of possessing warm and constant friends. To them, though not demonstrative in manner, he was ever faithful and attached. How highly he valued this precious gift of God is evidenced in his writings, and is thus expressed in his epic "Congal":—

> Thou who givest to men wives, children, riches, fame,
> And rarer than the worth of wives, and which the wealth tran-
> scends
> Of fame, as fame the worth of gold—who givest a man his
> friends,
> I thank and praise Thee.

Amongst my schoolfellows and youthful associates in Belfast [wrote Sir Samuel Ferguson in after-life] were the late Mr John Maclean, afterwards the London millionaire, and [the late] Lord O'Hagan. We three used greatly to affect the society of another young Belfast man, Mr George Fox, son of a widow lady resident in North Street in that our common native town. Mr Fox, to judge of him by the influence he exercised on the minds of two at least of our coterie, will be recognised as a man of singular ability and attractiveness of conversation. His discourse, indeed, possessed a fascination equal to all that I have heard ascribed to that of Coleridge. Under these influences my poetic faculty, which had already shown itself in the ballad of "Willy Gilliland," acquired strength for the production of the "Forging of the Anchor," published in 'Blackwood' in May 1832. We had formed a private class for the study of Irish. The early history of Ulster had already seized on my imagination, and the "Return of Claneboy," a prose romance which I contributed about that time to 'Blackwood,' may be regarded as the first indication of my ambition to raise the native elements of Irish story to a dignified level ; and that ambition I think may be taken as the key to almost all the literary work of my subsequent life.

Mr George Fox probably died at an early age. He lost his mother, and left Belfast to push his fortunes in British Guiana ; and no doubt succumbed to its unhealthy climate. His youthful friends heard no more of him. They spared no efforts, through a long series of years, to learn his fate. When Ferguson in 1864 published his "Versions from the Irish" in his 'Lays of the Western Gael,' he would not include one of the best among them, as he considered George Fox entitled to share in the authorship of "The County Mayo," and when almost fifty years had passed since his early friend

had been heard of, and he, in 1880, published his
'Poems,' the volume bore this brief but touching
dedication—

GEORGIO,

AMICO,

CONDISCIPULO,

INSTAURATORI.

Time had not obliterated the memory of his friend,
nor the affectionate regard he bore him.   Perhaps they
have greeted on that farther shore—

"Where tempests never beat nor billows roar."

Tennyson has imagined the musings of the man
passed in the race of life by his early companion.
The career of the "divinely gifted" man, as depicted
by the poet, worthily describes that of Lord O'Hagan.
The friendship between Thomas O'Hagan and
Samuel Ferguson, commenced in boyhood, remained
unbroken till death.   Both were devoted to their
country and to its literature; and though they differed
in creed and politics, they had so much in common
that their friendship suffered no diminution.   O'Hagan
rose rapidly in his profession, and became in 1868
the first Roman Catholic Lord Chancellor of Ireland.
Two years later he was raised to the peerage under
the title of Baron O'Hagan of Tullahogue.   His
elevation made no change in his manner nor in his
friendships.   Kind-hearted, affable, unassuming, all
who knew him intimately rejoiced in his success.
His career was honourable, for he reached his high

position without sacrificing his convictions or swerving from his principles.

Lord O'Hagan was an orator, eloquent, impassioned, and dignified. Noble and exalted sentiments were enforced by a graceful delivery and a musical voice.

The irony of Fate was evidenced in his experience, as in that of many others. With each success came a crushing sorrow. The death of his wife, son, and three of his daughters, left him nearly heart-broken, though an object of envy to some on account of his rapid attainment of station, power, and influence. The happy marriages of the only surviving children of his first family—one to Colonel John M'Donnell, and the younger to Mr John O'Hagan, a rising barrister, afterwards Judge and head of the Land Commission—seemed to break the spell. After some years Lord O'Hagan remarried, much to his own happiness, Alice, daughter of Colonel Towneley of Townley Hall, Lancashire. The birth of a son and heir to his peerage was a source of great delight not only to the parents, but to their numerous friends. In reply to the congratulations of Ferguson and his wife, Lord O'Hagan wrote :—

Your most kind and cordial note gave me great pleasure, but I could not answer it until now. Accept my best thanks for it, and thank Sir Samuel on my behalf. I have had shoals of letters from every quarter, but I know how to value at its especial and peculiar worth such genial sympathy as yours.

The evening of Lord O'Hagan's life was made bright and happy by the birth of two daughters and a second son.   He died on the 1st of February 1885, honoured and beloved, and was deeply lamented by his attached friend and former schoolfellow.

The study of Irish pursued by O'Hagan, Fox, and Ferguson had considerable influence on the future career of the young poet.   It was his pleasant task to turn into verse the literal translations which were the outcome of their labours.   These are contained in a series of papers contributed to the 'Dublin University Magazine' in the April, August, October, and November of 1834, entitled "Hardiman's Irish Minstrelsy." The poems from the Irish possess in their English dress much of the *aroma* of their originals.   From the prose of these articles a few citations are here given.   They show the hopes and aspirations of Ferguson for his native land :—

Oh, ye fair hills of holy Ireland, who dares sustain the strangled calumny that you are not the land of our love ?

> "Sweet land of the bee-abounding hills,
> Island of the year-old young horses,
> Soil of the heaviest fruit of trees,
> Soil of the greenest grassed pastures,
> Old plain of Eber, harvestful,
> Land of the ears of corn and wheat,
> Land of heroes and clergy,
> Banbá of the golden-haired damsels,
> Land of blue running pure streams,
> And of the gold-rich fortunate men."

Who is he who ventures to stand between us and your Catholic sons' goodwill ?   .   .   .

The only emulation between us shall be in the honest endeavour of each to benefit and protect the common object of our affection ; and, scorning the rancour of low rivalry that would contend with misrepresentation, detraction, or suppression, we will be the first to tell to the world what genius, what bravery, what loyalty, what pious love of country and kind, have been vindicated to the mere Irish by Mr Hardiman, in his collection and preservation of their national songs. . . . We will not suffer two of the finest races of men in the world, the Catholic and Protestant, or the Milesian and Anglo-Irish, to be duped into mutual hatred. . . . Let it first be our task to make the people of Ireland better acquainted with one another.   We address in these pages the Protestant wealth and intelligence of the country, an interest acknowledged on all hands to be the depository of Ireland's fate for good or evil.   The Protestants of Ireland are wealthy and intelligent beyond most classes, of their numbers, in the world ; but their wealth has hitherto been insecure, because their intelligence has not embraced a thorough knowledge of the genius and disposition of their Catholic fellow-citizens. The genius of a people at large is not to be learned by the notes of Sunday tourists.   The history of centuries must be gathered, published, studied, and digested, before the Irish people can be known to the world, and to each other, as they ought to be.   We hail, with daily-increasing pleasure, the spirit of research and liberality which is manifesting itself in all the branches of our national literature, but chiefly in our earlier history and antiquities—subjects of paramount importance to every people who respect, or even desire to respect, themselves.   Let us contribute our aid to the auspicious undertaking, and introduce the Saxon and the Scottish Protestant to an acquaintance with the poetical genius of a people hitherto unknown to them.

The second essay contains the following :—

Seven hundred years of disaster, as destructive as ever consumed the vitals of any country, have each in succession seen our people perishing by famine or the sword in almost every quarter of the land ; yet at this day there is neither mountain, plain, nor valley that is not rife with generations of the unextinguishable nation : long may they walk upon our hills with the steps of freemen! long may they make our valleys ring with the songs of that love which has thus made them indomitable in defeat and ineradicable in a struggle of extermination!

The third essay thus continues the theme :—

Loyalty, in its usual sense of attachment to the sovereign, is the extreme extension of the patriarchal principle ; loyalty, in its literal sense of attachment to the constitution, or loyalty to the existing law, belongs to a new order of sentiment where reason and interest assume the places of veneration and affection. . . . Ireland, longer and later than any other European country, has continued under the operation of patriarchal principles inseparable from that shepherd state by which Dane and Norman alike found her divided and devoted.   Had these principles been permitted to attain their legitimate extension, the nation might have been united and independent ; but, hindered by the very vigour of their own growth, those seeds of a legitimate loyalty ran to waste in the wild and thorny entanglement of factious clanship, instead of shaping themselves into the simple strength of individual monarchy— the briery cover of a thicket, instead of the broad protection of a royal oak.   To us who feel the blessings of a representative government, the principle of an individual despotism is hateful in theory, as our ancestors have shown it to be intolerable in practice ; but even such a government we must prefer to anarchy. . . . Alas that a nation glowing with the most enthusiastic courage, moved by the tenderest sympathies, and penetrated by a constitutional piety as devoted as profound, should so long have misapplied these noblest attributes of a high-destined people!   What material for an almost perfect society does the national genius not present?   Instinctive piety, to lay the only sure foundation of human morals and immortal hopes ; constitutional loyalty, to preserve the civil compact inviolate ; legitimate affection, to ensure public virtue and private happiness ; endless humour, to quicken social intercourse ; and last, and, save one attribute, best, indomitable love of country, to consolidate the whole.

Another friend whom Ferguson attracted in early youth, and by whom he was profoundly influenced, was George Petrie, LL.D.,

> "Archæologist, painter, man of letters ;
> As such, and for himself, revered and loved."

Perhaps he is most generally known by his researches on the Round Towers of Ireland and his essay on Tara Hill.   The charming personality of Dr Petrie, his kindness, his gentleness and refinement, endeared him to all who had the privilege of his friendship.   It was characteristic of him that among them he was ever spoken of as "dear" Petrie.   He was beloved as a father by the younger men, being their senior by many years.   He loved Ireland, and rendered her native music enchantingly on his violin.   But he played only to a sympathetic audience.   Ferguson was in his twenty-third year when he wrote the following letter to Dr Petrie :—

BELFAST, 10*th* Sept. 1833.

I have just finished a careful perusal of the 'Rerum Hibernicarum,' and have extracted everything from the Annals that I recognise as referring to my pet county [his native Antrim].   Pray make my respects to O'Donovan, and tell him I have begun Irish, and have translated all I want of Hardiman.   I'd like to know his reasons for supposing the Lagan to be the "Cassan line," as he states in the 'Penny Journal.'   If you come through Belfast again, you must have a sight of a splendid cross in the possession of a Mr Blair near this.   It isnot an *Irish* antiquity, though, but a thing of wonderful beauty and curiosity.   The inscriptions are in *Runic* characters, and on its case there is some beautiful enamel painting. I don't know the date, for, to tell the truth, I can't read the inscriptions. You can't conceive anything so fine as the carving of the woodwork of the cross. Pray, do you know whether the inauguration of Irish kings was uniformly by placing the foot in a track of its shape; or did they ever employ the *hand?* My reason for asking is, that I think what is generally called the *Giant's Chair* on the top of the Cave Hill has been a crowning-stone. But instead of the impression of a foot, I find on one of the arms of the seat a hole, to all appearance artificial (vulgarly called the *Giant's snuff-box*), which is just the shape of the inside of a glove and fits the right hand pretty exactly. The stone in which it is, seems to have been brought thither. The others appear part of the rock. If that was the O'Neills' crowning-stone in Lower Claneboy, they must have had a fine view on the coronation day. . . .

I have begun an extract of *all* the Abers, Invers, Bels, Ballies, Kens, Pens, Pits, Beths, Camberses, and Lans, in Domesday, the Returned Inquisitions, the Irish do., the Rotuli, Hundredmen, the *valor beneficiarum*, the Rolls — in fact all I can scrape together; and the first result—viz., the comparative number and relative position of the Abers and Invers, in red and blue upon a map of Scotland—is *beautiful.*—Ever, dear Petrie, faithfully yours,

SAML. FERGUSON.

P.S.—I have a great design on hands just now of firing a *boomerang* off the mouth of a mortar!

In the autumn of 1834, Ferguson, who had been visiting the counties of Kildare, Carlow, and Kilkenny, received the following letter from Dr Petrie:—

21 GREAT CHARLES STREET,
October 7, 1834.

MY DEAR FERGUSON,—I feel greatly obliged for your truly interesting letter, which gave me a particular pleasure, not only from its matter, but also because I was anxious to hear where you were and what you were about. . . . . I read your third paper on the Hardiman Minstrelsy with particular pleasure and interest, and think it the best of the three.   .   .   .

The church of Killeshin was not unknown to me, though I never saw it.   Last year I sent Wm. Morrison the architect to sketch and measure it for me, a commission which he executed with his wonted skill and judgment, but he did not copy the inscriptions as well as you.   These inscriptions are of great importance, not only in settling the age of this beautiful church—the twelfth century—but also of many others in Ireland of the same style, respecting which we should otherwise be in the dark.   The tradition respecting the destruction of the tower is not correct.   It was maliciously destroyed more than a hundred years ago by Colonel Wolsely, one of Cromwell's creatures, the ancestor of the present Sir R. Wolsely.

If I can manage to spend a day with you in Carlow before the month is over, I will write to you.

While you are on the spot, by no means neglect to visit the old church of Ullard, which is somewhere near you.   It is in the same style as Killeshin, and may perhaps have inscriptions on it.   I have not seen it, but have heard enough to excite me prodigiously.

For heaven's sake see it, and tell me and draw me all about it.   If you should happen to go to Kilkenny town, it would be worth your while to visit Freshford, the ancient Achadur of St Lactean, where you would see one of the finest doorways of the Saxon or Lombardic style in Great Britain.   It has a long and perfect Irish inscription, and is of the eleventh century.   You should also visit St Mullins on the Barrow, the cemetery of the Kavanaghs, and get the best account you can from the natives of the *scene* at the interment of the last chief and first heretic of the name.   .   .   .

There is also a fine Norman castle in your neighbourhood, built by the Hacketts of Fitz-Hacketts to keep in check the Byrnes, Tooles, and Cavanaghs; it is called, I think, Castle More.   I wish also you would try to discover the ancient Dinree of Milesian and Pagan times.

Excuse this scrawl, and believe me ever, my dear Ferguson, most faithfully yours,   Geo. Petrie.

On the following day Ferguson replied from Clashganny, sending drawings of Ullard, which he had visited on receipt of Dr Petrie's letter of the 7th October :—

CLASHGANNY, *October* 8, 1834.

MY DEAR PETRIE,—Only think of my being within sight of Ullard, and knowing no more of it than that one end had been converted into a ball-alley! I crossed the Barrow in half an hour after receiving your letter, and poked away at the ruins till five o'clock. Now that I have dined, I sit down to describe you this very interesting antiquity, and send you all my drawings of it, which I have hastily run over with pen and ink. Don't you think I improve in my etching? I must get a lesson from you in foliage, and then I think I could not be at a loss so far as walls and ivy go. No inscriptions remain, although from the disposition of the detached frieze above the doorway I have no doubt there was a pious claim upon the reader for some soul's benefit. The doorway, as you will perceive, is in the same style with that of Killeshin, but not so elaborate, and much more decayed. . . . The partition pointed arch is evidently contracted by the introduction of a more modern although semicircular one. The difference of the masonry is as observable as that of the style. . . .

My next subject is a cross, of one side of which I send you an accurate drawing. The stone into which it is mortised is highly ornamented on the side I give, and the people speak of an inscription, but I saw nothing of the kind, and I had a sharp look-out.

What do you think of the harper? I protest it is a true copy; but if it be a harp he plays, how could the strings be fastened, as they would seem to be, on such a frame? Bunting would be highly tickled—he gives a cithara in his first volume not unlike the shape. . . .

Do try to come down. The country looks beautiful, and the scenery here is enchanting. My brother desires me to say he will be very happy to see you here, if you think of making a day to St Mullins or Ullard.

There is a large rath near Burris called Dunroe.   I have no
data for finding Dinree.—I am, dear Petrie, ever truly yours,
S. FERGUSON.

In reply Dr Petrie assures his young friend—

You are certainly an admirable fellow—I say it soberly and
without any joke.   Your letter describing Ullard and the
accompanying sketches are equally excellent, and when I give
you a few lessons in foliage, which with the blessing of God I
will most assuredly do, you will be a first-rate sketcher as well
as antiquary. .   .   .
I delayed writing to you till I had read your 4th "Hardiman."   I got it last night, and have gone through it with
intense interest and pleasure.   It is superior in interest and
merit to all its predecessors—and probably the very highest
article that the U. ['University Magazine'] has yet put forward. .   .   .
In your list of towns which had mints in the fourteenth
century . . . you have given the public an excellent condensed
notice of the progress of coinage in Ireland.   .   .   .
I have only time to add, Long life to you, my honest fellow!
You are certainly destined to do great things for Ireland, and
are worth a whole regiment of such fellows as Ledwich and
Vallancey.

Ferguson contributed to the 'University' a Memoir
of Petrie in 1839, and in the following year noticed
the 'Dublin Penny Journal,' then edited by his friend.
In 1845 he reviewed his great work on the Irish Round
Towers.   From this a few extracts may be given :—

But in giving the question, for the first time, its full and
final solution — showing that the towers were regular parts
and members of those aggregations of characteristic buildings
which constituted the early ecclesiastical establishments of
this country—Mr Petrie found himself among other subjects
of inquiry, till now wholly undreamt of, and infinitely more

interesting to the philosophic antiquary than any refutation of the false theories of the towers, or any demonstration, however complete, of their real origin and uses.   He therefore passed from the specific demonstration of these portions of our early Christian architecture to a general investigation of the whole subject, which is unquestionably the richest and most interesting field of inquiry that modern research has discovered, in connection with the spread of Christianity in the west of Europe, giving us an insight, altogether unhoped for, into the lives and habits of our early ecclesiastics, and into the state of arts and letters in Ireland, during the six centuries preceding the Anglo-Norman invasion.

.   .   .   .   .   .

His original profession of a painter, making him personally familiar with every local remnant of antiquity, has, more effectually than probably any other course of preparation could have done, conspired with his subsequent scholastic pursuits, enabling him to identify a multitude of localities hitherto unknown, as well as to transfer to his text the most accurate and elaborate representations of his subjects.   He is also the first who has submitted his original authorities from the Irish text, vouchers never adduced by any other writer, but as abundant in Mr Petrie's essays as are his own comments. And, which is a still greater excellence, Mr Petrie has brought to his inquiry extreme caution, pure candour, and all the temperateness of an accurate and calm scholar.

Petrie and Ferguson contributed each an essay introductory to 'The Ancient Music of Ireland' by Edward Bunting.   This gentleman had devoted himself from his nineteenth year to the patriotic task of collecting, arranging, and thus preserving to his country its national music.   Mr Bunting's first volume, published in Belfast 1796, contained sixty-six Irish airs never before printed.   Seventy-five additional airs were collected in 1809.   His third volume, containing one hundred and fifty-one melodies, appeared in 1840. Mr Bunting was stimulated to these efforts by a gathering of Irish harpers assembled in Belfast in 1792, in response to an invitation given by residents in that town.

BELFAST, *December* 1791.

Some inhabitants of Belfast, feeling themselves interested in everything which relates to the honour as well as the prosperity of their country, propose to open a subscription which they intend to apply in attempting to revive and perpetuate *the ancient music and poetry of Ireland.*   They are solicitous to preserve from oblivion the few fragments which have been permitted to remain as monuments of the refined taste and genius of their ancestors.

In order to carry this project into execution, it must appear obvious to those acquainted with the situation of this country that it will be necessary to assemble the *harpers,* those descendants of our ancient bards, who are at present almost exclusively possessed of all that remains of the *music, poetry, and oral traditions of Ireland.*

It is proposed that the harpers should be induced to assemble at Belfast (suppose on the 1st of July next) by the distribution of such prizes as may seem adequate to the subscribers; and that a person well versed in the language and antiquities of this nation should attend, with a skilful musician to transcribe and arrange the most beautiful and interesting parts of their knowledge.

An undertaking of this nature will, undoubtedly, meet the approbation of men of refinement and erudition in every country.   And when it is considered how intimately the *spirit and character of a people* are connected with their national poetry and music, it is presumed that the Irish patriot and politician will not deem it an object unworthy his patronage and protection.

Dr Petrie contributed to Mr Bunting's work a memoir of an ancient Irish harp preserved in Trinity

College, Dublin; and Ferguson an essay on the antiquity of the harp and bagpipe in Ireland. In this were included some fruits of his linguistic studies, for he had versified from the Irish the words of four of the pieces selected by the harpers for their competition. Six of them were blind, yet all appeared happy and contented, "convinced of the excellence of the genuine *old Irish music*, which they said had existed for centuries, and, from its delightful melody, would continue to exist for centuries to come." O'Neill, one of the harpers, with tears coursing down his cheeks, called them "the dear! dear! sweet old Irish tunes."

In noticing the more remarkable pieces and melodies of Mr Bunting's collection, Ferguson dwells on the " Neaill ghubh a Dheirdre," which he says is " perhaps the oldest piece in the collection; for the story of the Death of the Sons of Usnach, in which the Lament occurs, ranks in antiquity with that of the 'Children of Lir,' and refers to a period considerably anterior to the Ossianic era. It is hard to say in what particular part of the story the interest lies, which has taken so strong a hold on the imaginations of the people. It would appear, however, to consist mainly in its frequent examples of magnanimity and fortitude, and in the high idea which it gives us of ancient honour." This story, "which hath never been varied during many hundred years of constant tradition, and which hath delighted more princes and nobles and honourable audiences than any other story of Milesian times," dominated Ferguson's imagination from youth to age.   His literal translation, with the lyrics versified, constitutes the first tale in 'Hibernian Nights' Entertainments.'

Nearly half a century later, in his 'Poems,' Deirdré, its heroine, forms the central figure in a drama called by her name.   Her story is a sad one.   A lovely girl, brought up in seclusion by the orders of King Conor MacNessa, who designs her for his future wife, Deirdré meets a lover Naisi, eldest of the sons of Usnach. They wed; and, accompanied by his brothers, fly to Alba [Scotland] to escape the vengeance of the Ulster king.   They establish themselves on the shores of Loch Etive, where to this day traditions are rife associated with their names.   An island in the loch called Eilean Uisnachan, the remains of a dun or fort also so named, and the *Coille nāish*, or wood of Naisi, are still pointed out in the vicinity of the beautiful loch, where, so many centuries ago, the exiles made their sylvan home.   Conor, desirous to recall them, sends Fergus MacRoy with a guarantee of safety.   Notwithstanding the apprehensions of Deirdré, her husband decides to return to Ulster.   Deirdré's " Farewell to Alba," translated from the Irish by Ferguson in 1834, is as follows :—

> Farewell to fair Alba, high house of the sun,
> Farewell to the mountain, the cliff, and the dun;
> Dun Sweeny, adieu! for my love cannot stay,
> And tarry I may not when love cries away.

Glen Vashan! Glen Vashan! where roebucks run free,
Where my love used to feast on the red-deer with me,
Where rocked on thy waters while stormy winds blew,
My love used to slumber, Glen Vashan, adieu!

Glendarō! Glendarō! where birchen boughs weep
Honey dew at high noon o'er the nightingale's sleep,
Where my love used to lead me to hear the cuckoo
'Mong the high hazel-bushes, Glendarō, adieu!

Glen Urchy! Glen Urchy! where loudly and long
My love used to wake up the woods with his song,
While the son of the rock,[1] from the depths of the dell,
Laughed sweetly in answer, Glen Urchy, farewell!

Glen Etive! Glen Etive! where dappled does roam,
Where I leave the green sheeling I first called a home;
Where with me and my true-love delighted to dwell,
The sun made his mansion, Glen Etive, farewell!

Farewell to Inch Draynach, adieu to the roar
Of the blue billows bursting in light on the shore;
Dun Fiagh, farewell! for my love cannot stay,
And tarry I may not when love cries away.

The Lament which his heroine sings in his drama of
"Deirdré," published in 'Poems,' 1880, is pitched in
a different key:—

> Give me my harp, and let me sing a song;
> And, nurse, undo the fastenings of my hair;
> For I would mingle tresses with the wind
> From Etive-side, where happy days were mine.

I.

> Harp, take my bosom's burthen on thy string,
> And, turning it to sad, sweet melody,
> Waste and disperse it on the careless air.

---

[1] Son of the rock—*i.e.*, Echo.

II.

Air, take the harp-string's burthen on thy breast,
And, softly thrilling soulward through the sense,
Bring my love's heart again in tune with mine.

III.

Blessed were the hours when, heart in tune with heart,
My love and I desired no happier home
Than Etive's airy glades and lonely shore.

IV.

Alba, farewell !   Farewell, fair Etive bank !
Sun kiss thee ; Moon caress thee ; dewy stars
Refresh thee long, dear scene of quiet days !

On reaching Ireland, Fergus is detained at Dun-
severick, and the cavalcade continue the journey to
Emania (Armagh) under the safe-conduct of his sons.
Conor violates his pledges. The sons of Usnach are
slain, and Deirdré, who scorns to survive her husband,
thus bemoans his death :—

> The lions of the hill are gone,
> And I am left alone—alone :
> Dig the grave both wide and deep,
> For I am sick, and fain would sleep !
>
> The falcons of the wood are flown,
> And I am left alone—alone :
> Dig the grave both deep and wide,
> And let us slumber side by side.
>
> The dragons of the rock are sleeping,
> Sleep that wakes not for our weeping :
> Dig the grave, and make it ready ;
> Lay me on my true-love's body.

Lay their spears and bucklers bright
By the warriors' sides aright ;
Many a day the three before me
On their linkèd bucklers bore me.

Lay upon the low grave floor,
'Neath each head, the blue claymore ;
Many a time the noble three
Reddened these blue blades for me.

Lay the collars, as is meet,
Of their greyhounds at their feet ;
Many a time for me have they
Brought the tall red-deer to bay.

In the falcon's jesses throw,
Hook and arrow, line and bow ;
Never again by stream or plain
Shall the gentle woodsmen go.

Sweet companions ye were ever—
Harsh to me, your sister, never ;
Woods and wilds and misty valleys
Were, with you, as good's a palace.

Oh ! to hear my true-love singing,
Sweet as sound of trumpets ringing ;
Like the sway of ocean swelling
Rolled his deep voice round our dwelling.

Oh ! to hear the echoes pealing
Round our green and fairy sheeling,
When the three, with soaring chorus,
Passed the silent skylark o'er us.

Echo now, sleep, morn and even—
Lark alone enchant the heaven !—
Ardan's lips are scant of breath,
Neesa's tongue is cold in death.

Stag, exult on glen and mountain;
Salmon, leap from loch to fountain;
Heron, in the free air warm ye,—
Usnach's sons no more will harm ye!

Erin's stay no more you are,
Rulers of the ridge of war;
Never more 'twill be your fate
To keep the beam of battle straight!

Woe is me! by fraud and wrong,
Traitors false and tyrants strong,
Fell clan Usnach, bought and sold,
For Barach's feast and Conor's gold!

Woe to Eman, roof and wall!
Woe to Red Branch, hearth and hall!—
Tenfold woe and black dishonour
To the foul and false clan Conor!

Dig the grave both wide and deep,
Sick I am, and fain would sleep!
Dig the grave and make it ready,
Lay me on my true-love's body!

The last stanzas of Deirdré's lament, as conceived by her poet, no longer in the trammels of a translator, are as follows :—

IX.

Oh, greedy grave-dug earth, that swallowest
The strength and loveliness of all that lives,
Thou shalt not always hide from hopes immortal
The coldly-hoarded treasures of thy clay!

X.

A day shall come, the May-day of Mankind,
When, through thy quickening clods and teeming pores,
The sunward-mounting, vernal effluences
Shall rise of buried loves and joys reborn.

XI.

Dig the grave deep, that, undisturbed till then,
They rest, past reach of mortal hate and fear;
Past the knave's malice and the tyrant's anger,
And past the knowledge of what rests for me.

XII.

Dig the grave deep.   Cast in their arms of war,
Cast in the collars of their hounds of chase,
To deck their chamber of expectant slumber,
And make the mansion wide enough for four.

Many contributions from Ferguson's pen appeared about this time in ' Blackwood '—" An Irish Garland," " The Fairy Well," "Songs after Beranger," and a vigorous rendering of the " Death Song of Regner Lodbrog" included in a prose article on the Scandinavian hero.   This essay contains also a rendering of a little poem on his native isle by St Donat, better known under his Latinised name of Donatus, Bishop of Fiesole, A.D. 844.   Prose stories,—republished in 'Tales from Blackwood,' — " The Forrest - Race Romance," " Nora Boyle," " The Return of Claneboy," and " An Adventure of Shane O'Neill," were written before the young author had attained his twenty - fourth year.

Of these the two last named have been republished in ' Hibernian Nights' Entertainments ' (Messrs Sealy, Bryers, & Walker, Dublin), with other historical tales which appeared in the ' University Magazine,' 1833-34, " The Captive of Killeshin," "Corby MacGillmore," and " The Rebellion of Silken Thomas."

The revolt of the Fitz-Geralds in the reign of King Henry VIII. is the subject of the last-named story. It contains rhythmic utterances of intense power and passion, which are supposed to be uttered by the Bard of the Earl of Kildare. One is a denunciation of the traitor who has betrayed his stronghold of Maynooth to the besiegers. It is followed by a touching lament over the " mighty Gerald " lying dead in the Tower of London, deprived in his last moments of the ministrations of those who loved him. The extremes of hate and execration, of tenderness and devotion, are powerfully expressed, and are quite marvellous as the work of so youthful a writer.

In a very different style is Ferguson's " Inaugural Ode," written for the opening number of the ' Dublin University Magazine,' January 1834 :—

> Oh ! friends, be firm, and gather to one head
> Under our banner.   Though a slender band,
> And the breached rampart rocks beneath our tread,
> Yet bold and loyal here we make our stand,
> For God's dear love and sacred Ireland.
> .   .   .   .   .   .
>
> Here in our battle's vanguard have we planted
> The flag of freedom on the rock of ages.
> .   .   .   .   .   .
>
> Stand for the cause of patriots and sages,
> Nor heed the traitor's praise, nor flatterer's smile,
> So as ye serve the truth and your loved native isle.
> How dear we love our fair and famous island,
> Let the unbidden tears which ever rise
> With dewy valley green, or azure highland,
> As first they open on our longing eyes
> After a sojourn under other skies,

> Witness!—Let each loch, river, glen, and grove,
> Which we have sworn and sought to immortalise,
> Witness, how dearly all earth else above,
> Thee, land of song and sighs, lorn Ireland, we love!

The sources of this love are alluded to in a sonnet which appeared in the 'Magazine' in February 1834, "Athens: by Samuel Ferguson, Esq." It was the first of his productions to which the young author put his name. It concludes with these lines:—

> Temple and tower, and tale heroic told
> In her own tongue, can give the natal soil
> Claims unimagined on her conscious son;
> Yet I, methinks, so love my barbarous isle,
> That more I could not, though each nameless Dun
> Had been an Areopagus of old.

These lines are surpassed in poetic charm by two lyrics which closely followed—"The Forester's Complaint" and "The Fairy Thorn." A critic—himself a poet—the late Mr Justice O'Hagan, has observed that the former "has that indescribable charm of tenderness and delicacy (*molle atque facetum*), the charm not only of feeling but of finish, which, if we do not deceive ourselves, is found more amongst the poets of Ireland than elsewhere. Still more tender and pathetic is 'The Fairy Thorn.' The superstition on which it is founded is Ulster-Irish, and it possesses no Gaelic colouring in the language, but yet how Celtic it is in its dreamy and mystic supernaturalism! A presence not of earth pervades and breathes from the sinking twilight."

The fairy people carry off to the " land of thought "
one out of a group of girls who have ventured to dance
around the Sacred Tree :—

But solemn is the silence of the silvery haze
    That drinks away their voices in echoless repose,
And dreamily the evening has stilled the haunted braes,
      And dreamier the gloaming grows.

And sinking one by one, like lark-notes from the sky
    When the falcon's shadow saileth across the open shaw,
Are hushed the maidens' voices, as cowering down they lie
      In the flutter of their sudden awe.

For, from the air above, and the grassy ground beneath,
    And from the mountain - ashes and the old Whitethorn
      between,
A Power of faint enchantment doth through their beings
      breathe,
    And they sink down together on the green.

  .   .   .   .

Thus clasped and prostrate all, with their heads together bowed,
    Soft o'er their bosom's beating—the only human sound—
They hear the silky footsteps of the silent fairy crowd,
    Like a river in the air, gliding round.

No scream can any raise, no prayer can any say,
    But wild, wild the terror of the speechless three—
For they feel fair Anna Grace drawn silently away,
    By whom they dare not look to see.

They feel their tresses twine with her parting locks of gold,
    And the curls elastic falling as her head withdraws ;
They feel her sliding arms from their trancèd arms unfold,
    But they may not look to see the cause :

For heavy on their senses the faint enchantment lies
    Through all that night of anguish and perilous amaze ;
And neither fear nor wonder can ope their quivering eyes,
    Or their limbs from the cold ground raise,

Till out of night the earth has rolled her dewy side,
  With every haunted mountain and streamy vale below;
When, as the mist dissolves in the yellow morning tide,
  The maidens' trance dissolveth so.

Then fly the ghastly three as swiftly as they may,
  And tell their tale of sorrow to anxious friends in vain—
They pined away and died within the year and day,
  And ne'er was Anna Grace seen again.

The description here given of dawn, when "out of night the earth has rolled her dewy side," was penned forty-one years before Tennyson painted for our delight a companion picture. He gives us in "In Memoriam" the doubtful dusk, the breeze which said

  "'The dawn, the dawn,' and died away;
    And East and West, without a breath,
    Mixt their dim lights, like life and death,
  To broaden into boundless day."

On a winter. evening, long ago, when a few chosen friends were with him, and had gathered around the fire, listening to the storm which raged without, Sir Samuel was called on to repeat one of his poems. He recited "The Fairy Thorn" in an eerie tone which made it most impressive.

I remember well [he continued] the night I wrote it. I was in London keeping my terms; and long after midnight, when all was silent in the great city, and in the house in which I lodged, I projected my thoughts into fairy-land and felt its mystery and awe. When the poem was completed, my imagination was so excited that I still felt as under a spell. I could hardly move. At last I shook myself free, and with an effort got into bed. Next morning I could not explain to myself the supernatural terrors of the night, nor the impression made on my mind.

Ferguson has himself placed on record the influence which Petrie exercised over his mind in directing him to antiquarian studies.

These tendencies [he wrote] were strengthened by the intimacy which sprang up between me and the late Dr George Petrie, then engaged in the preparation of materials for the projected Ordnance Survey Memoir. In Petrie's study I formed the acquaintance of O'Donovan, Curry [then without the O], and Mangan, and in the parlour of the Editor of the 'University,' of Stanford, Waller, Butt, the O'Sullivans, and later on of Wilde.

Petrie infused his own spirit into his staff, and thus, in the words of his biographer, formed " a school of archæology from which sprang men whose subsequent works have done so much for the history, the literature, and the language of ancient Ireland."

Mr Wakeman, one of the workers who assembled in Dr Petrie's house, has given a graphic description of the men who daily met there, and their labours :—

How well do I recollect my first sketching journey, when employed on the intended Ordnance Memoir. Dr Petrie was the head of that particular department of the Survey to which I was attached. In the little back-parlour in Great Charles Street we used to meet daily : by we, I mean John O'Donovan, Eugene Curry, Clarence Mangan, P. O'Keefe, J. O'Connor, besides two or three more. The duty of the office was to collect every possible information, antiquarian or topographical, about that particular portion of the country which was at the time being surveyed. All sorts of old documents were examined, old spellings of names compared and considered.

O'Donovan and Curry, even then the first Celtic scholars of the age, settled the orthography of the towns, villages, baronies, or other divisions of land, so that the Ordnance maps might be as correct, in a literary sense, as they undoubtedly were as surveys.   At the same time Petrie's great work, 'Ecclesiastical Architecture of Ireland,' as also his admirable essay on the 'Antiquities of Tara Hill,' were being completed.   Indeed, we lived in such an atmosphere of antiquarianism that a thousand years ago seemed as familiar to us as the time when we first donned breeches.   For my own part, I felt as if I had a personal acquaintance with Niall of the Nine Hostages, or Con of the Hundred Battles (or bottles, as poor Mangan humorously misstyled the hero), or with Leogaire, who would not mind the exhortations of Saint Patrick, but insisted on being interred, sword in hand, in his rath at Tara, with his face turned to the east, as bidding defiance to the men of Leinster.   Petrie, as head of the office, superintended every-thing ; and the mass of antiquarian and topographical infor-mation collected far exceeded the expectations of the most sanguine.   .   .   .

I should like to dwell a moment on the scene of that very happy time when we used to meet in Dr Petrie's back-parlour. There was our venerable chief, with his ever-ready smile and gracious word ; there poor Clarence Mangan, with his queer puns and jokes, and odd little cloak and wonderful hat.

It was in that office Mangan penned his since famous ballad, "The Woman of Three Cows," and I verily believe the com-position did not occupy him half an hour.   Mangan was a man of many peculiarities.   .   .   .

At this time O'Donovan was about thirty years of age.   As in the case of almost every man who has risen to distinction, he was an unwearied worker, never sparing himself, and evidently holding his occupation a labour of love.   With all employed in the office he was a general favourite, and in the intervals between his most serious business would often give us some of his experience as a traveller, telling his tale in a rich emphatic manner peculiarly his own.   .   .   .

At the time I write of, Eugene Curry had really commenced

that course of application to the illustration of ancient Irish history which has gained for him the proud appellation of the Chief Brehon and Lexicographer of Ireland.   He too belonged to our staff, and during the summer-time was engaged chiefly in travelling, and collecting information about old names and places for the use of the Ordnance authorities.

Such were the workers who, under the guidance of Petrie, investigated all existing remains on Irish soil, both Pagan and Christian, illustrated the topography of the land, and the orthography of ancient names of baronies, townlands, and parishes.   This great and comprehensive scheme, which included the geology, products, and social condition of the people, was due to Captain Larcom, R.E., who in 1828 directed the proceedings of the Ordnance Survey from Mountjoy, Phœnix Park, near Dublin.   He was made Census Commissioner in 1841, and Under Secretary for Ireland from 1853 to 1868, when this true friend to Ireland retired from its public service, and died at Heathfield, Hants, in June 1879.

An incident told by Sir Thomas Larcom to the present writer is so characteristic that it is worth recording :—

When I first came to Ireland [said Sir Thomas], and found that my life would be chiefly spent there, I thought it desirable that I should learn Irish.   Soon after my arrival I was walking down Sackville Street, and read over the door of a large house, The Irish Society.   It was open, and I walked in. I mounted the stair without meeting any one, and seeing before me a baize-covered door, pushed it open, and found myself in presence of a group of gentlemen seated round a table.   I apologised for my intrusion, and explained my object.

I heard in return that the Committee of the Irish Society, whom I had interrupted, desired to convert the people to Protestantism by giving them the Scriptures in their native tongue.   One of the gentlemen told me he could recommend a thoroughly qualified Irish teacher, but added that he was imperfectly acquainted with English.   He wrote on a sheet of paper the name and address of John O'Donovan.   I sent my servant to the address with a request that O'Donovan would call on me next day.   I was at breakfast when my note was put into my hand, and I was told that the bearer was in the hall.   "Show him up," I said, and O'Donovan, in peasant garb, entered the room.   I asked him to sit down and share my breakfast, and proposed that he should do so two or three times a-week and undertake to teach me Irish without requiring me to write exercises, as I had no leisure for study.   He consented.   I found him a very able man, a thorough master of the language.   Under his instructions I made considerable progress.   But it soon occurred to me that if I should teach him English it would be a better arrangement.   Accordingly our positions were reversed.   As we took our tea and toast I instructed him, and in due time placed him on the staff of the Ordnance Survey, where he did such valuable work for the country.

The first of the Ordnance Survey Memoirs appeared in 1839.   Its subject was the county of Londonderry. In Captain Larcom's introduction to the volume he thus writes :—

A perfect map, with a perfect memoir, should constitute the statistics of a country : such a combination has been attempted in the Survey of Ireland, and though it is not to be assumed that perfection has been attained, no pains have been spared to fulfil the enlightened intentions of the Legislature.   Geography is a noble and practical science only when associated with the history, the commerce, and a knowledge of the productions of a country ; and the topographical delineation of a county would be comparatively useless without the information which may lead to and suggest the proper development of its resources.

In Stokes's ' Life of Petrie ' we learn that the work "was hailed with unmixed satisfaction by all classes in the country, not only on account of the intrinsic merits of the memoir, but as an earnest of the nature of the great work which was to illustrate every county in Ireland in the same manner. . . . Irishmen of all sects and parties felt that in the completed work they would have, for the first time, the materials for a true history of their country. But these hopes were not to be fulfilled."

The British Association, by its distinguished member, Dr Romney Robinson, appealed to the then Government in favour of the continuance of the work :—

The memoir was suspended without the slightest attention being paid to the memorial of the British Association, which I had the honour of laying before you on Saturday, which was the expression of the sentiments of at least two thousand highly informed persons from all parts of the empire, whose intellectual rank entitled them to some consideration.

Sir William Rowan Hamilton, President of the Royal Irish Academy, also memorialised the Government in the name of that body, the *élite* of the educated classes in Ireland :—

In the prosecution of the Ordnance Survey of Ireland, it appears that, in addition to the usual details of such works, much valuable matter has been collected. The desire of enlarging our knowledge as to the productive resources of the country has caused the collection of a vast quantity of information respecting its geology, natural history, and statistics, while the necessity of fixing on some sure basis the orthography of the maps has led to the accumulation of a treasure of antiquarian research which is doubly precious from the perishing character of its materials and the total neglect that previously attended such inquiries.

The Academy, as specially including these pursuits among the objects of their institution, welcomed the appearance of the 'Memoir of Derry' with a satisfaction too soon checked by the abandonment of that plan of publication in which the materials of every kind, relative to the same locality, were brought together and exhibited in one view. Since, however, they find that a separate publication of the geological part of the Survey has been permitted, they venture to hope that the public will not be deprived of the remaining matter—in no respect less important, in some respects far more interesting.

From Ferguson's article in the ' University,' 1844, on the Ordnance Survey Memoir, we learn that when Sir Robert Peel became Prime Minister he appointed as Commissioners Mr Young, Captain Boldero, and Lord Adare, to take evidence and report on such points of inquiry as he considered it right the Government should be acquainted with before they took any final step in a matter of such importance. It contains the following passage :—

Much light has been thrown on the literary and ecclesiastical history of Ireland by Archbishop Ussher, Sir James Ware, and Colgan, while the topographical and monumental antiquities have had but meagre notice. The subject is therefore unexhausted, indeed almost untouched ; and no inquirer, until the officers of the Survey commenced their labours, has ever brought an equal amount of local knowledge, sound criticism, and accurate acquaintance with the Irish language to bear upon it. There are at present more monuments of early antiquity existing in Ireland than in England. Some districts are particularly rich in them; but from the injuries of the weather, neglect, and the increase of cultivation, they are rapidly disappearing.   So that if Irish antiquities are to "escape the shipwreck of time," it would seem they must do so now or never; the best possible opportunity for collecting the materials presents itself; there are at hand admirable instruments for the task in Mr Petrie and his assistants, trained, as they have been, in the orthographic department of the Survey: such persons are of rare occurrence, and the limits within which the Irish language is spoken are year by year becoming narrower.

Ferguson thus appeals to the British public in his article :—

Is Great Britain, the most powerful and wealthy nation in the universe, the most illustrious for her bravery and spirit of enterprise—for her skill in mechanical arts and manufactures —for the capability of her sons to reach the highest point of human excellence in every intellectual exertion,—is, we say, such an empire to continue for ever, from the want of Government support, inferior to many others of limited power in its attention to the general diffusion of knowledge of all kinds amongst its people, and particularly of those classes of knowledge which give loftiness and dignity of thought to a nation, and without which wealth only becomes in the end the cause of national corruption, debasement, and decay?

With reference to his own country he thus concludes :—

Is it not a delightful spectacle, now perhaps for the first time exhibited in Ireland, to see Irishmen of all parties and creeds, the most illustrious in rank and the most eminent in talents, combining zealously for an object of good to their common country? and may we not take it as an auspicious omen of the happiness and peace yet in store for us, and which must follow as an inevitable result of the continuance of a unity thus happily begun?

The hopes thus expressed were not realised.   The Government stopped the publication of the Ordnance Survey Memoir on the scale on which it had been commenced.   It was concluded with maimed proportions, its staff broken up, the cost being deemed too great.   The MS. letters of O'Donovan have been deposited in the Library of the Royal Irish Academy, and may there be consulted by students interested in the topography and antiquities of the land.

CHAPTER IV.

1832–1882.

EARLY FRIENDSHIPS AND EARLY LITERARY WORK (*continued*).

> "For a' that, and a' that,
>   Our toils obscure, and a' that;
> The rank is but the guinea's stamp,
>   The man's the gowd for a' that!
>
> .   .   .   .   .
>
> Then let us pray that come it may—
>   As come it will, for a' that—
> That sense and worth, o'er a' the earth,
>   May bear the gree, and a' that;
> For a' that, and a' that,
>   It's coming yet, for a' that,
> That man to man, the warld o'er,
>   Shall brothers be and a' that!"
>   —BURNS.

FERGUSON was on terms of affectionate intimacy with Dr Stokes and his family, and was a frequent guest at his hospitable house, 5 Merrion Square North, and, during the season of summer, at Stokes's country-house, Carrig Breac, Howth.

William Stokes was in his day one of the foremost physicians of the world. He was a rarely gifted man, a man of genius, and yet eminently practical. A lucid writer, a profound and most accurate clinical observer, he was early recognised as a master in his profession. But he was also a skilful practitioner, at once full of kindness and sympathy, observant of every symptom, and rich in resource. At the bedside he inspired confidence, and often affection. As a teacher he was constantly followed by crowds of admiring students. Like most men of real power, he had many interests and pursuits outside of his profession. He was a lover of music and of art, a keen archæologist, a true lover of his country. The tenderness of his nature and his brilliant wit and humour were only manifested on occasion. His manner was often abstracted, but his domestic affection and his love for his chosen friends never failed. It was not everybody that could win his friendship. Ferguson enjoyed with him a close and unbroken intimacy till the death of Dr Stokes in January 1878.

Mr James Pim, the introducer of railways into Ireland, and projector of the Atmospheric Railway, was also a kind friend to the young poet, who entertained for him a grateful regard; as also for Mr George Smith, the eminent publisher of the 'Annals of the Four Masters,' a monumental work ably edited by Dr John O'Donovan.

In a letter written to Sir Thomas Larcom, then at Heathfield, Ferguson thus speaks of Smith, Petrie, Pim, and Stokes:—

I was one of the dinner-party at George Smith's when the publication of the 'Annals' was determined on, and I remember the faces of all present, from the gentle exaltation of Petrie to the shrewd lines of speculative intelligence round the eyes of Smith, and the large, sympathising satisfaction of the mouth of Pim. I would wish to see as many of the old faces assembled again as Fate will permit. George Smith is still enjoying the vital air, laden with the perfume of his greenhouses and the pure salt of Killiney Bay, at his retreat at Ballybrack. Stokes is for the present confined to his sofa, but I trust that we shall see him again, ere long, able to mingle in the van of the march.

On the death of Mr Smith, Ferguson wrote as follows of the "illustrious band of men of mind and action" whose friendship he had shared and enjoyed:—

The death of Mr George Smith reminds me of the gradual disappearance from this scene of an illustrious band of men of mind and action who made the second quarter of this century a memorable period in social progress in Ireland. About one half of them are now gone, including Hamilton, Petrie, Todd, M'Cullagh, and Pim. Larcom and Robinson and Stokes survive. No stronger force of scientific and literary ability ever existed together in this country. Hamilton, a pure mathematician, metaphysician, and poet, looked out from his intellectual observatory over all the realm of mind and matter. He stood so high that all who looked up at all saw and recognised his pre-eminence. James Pim, then junior, in introducing our first line of railway, conceived within prudent realisation the largest views of social advancement due to the locomotive and the electric telegraph. He was a man of ardent imagination ; not poet himself, but the associate not only of engineers and accountants, but of poets, and inspired with an enthusiasm as energetic as theirs, but an enthusiasm compounded with sagacity, that exerted itself in the production of works of mechanical and industrial organisation. He was a great diviner of the capacities of men. As Petrie saw and cultivated the power of O'Donovan and Curry, so he developed the latent workmanlike ability of Dargan.   Larcom, then Lieutenant or Captain, with the statistical genius of Petty combined the higher political economy that we now call sociology, in its most human and sympathising applications.   Every development of a self-respecting patriotism that could advance and elevate a people had its place in his Economics.   In speaking of Petrie educing the literary ability of O'Donovan, it might be questionable whether Larcom should not have been named as the nurturer of Petrie.   But the truth is, that where great and congenial minds are brought together, such as Pim's, Stokes's, Larcom's, Petrie's, it is impossible to say from which intellectual centre the electric agency proceeds.   The power— or rather the involuntary capacity—of imparting enthusiasm is one of the greatest gifts of great men.   It is a distinguishing characteristic of Stokes.   No one has more largely diffused a noble energy among those with whom he has come in contact; and it is a remarkable fact that he and Robinson of Armagh, who with our Provost have been selected by the advisers of the Emperor of Germany for the extraordinary distinction of the Prussian Cross of Merit, have all their lives been the associates and intimates of men of the poetic temperament. All the men named, and many more who might be named, in the high walks of thought and practice, were the friends and intimates of George Smith.   He had his faculty of discernment as well as they, and when he met a man of capacity, knew him as infallibly, and attracted as well as was attracted to him.   He associated with them not merely as a publisher, but as a sympathiser in all their aims and aspirations.

Sir William Rowan Hamilton, spoken of by Ferguson as standing so high " that all who looked up at all saw and recognised his pre - eminence," was Andrews Professor of Astronomy in the University of Dublin, Royal Astronomer of Ireland, and President of the Royal Irish Academy between 1837 and 1846.   Professor Sedgwick has described him as "a man who possessed within himself powers and talents perhaps never before combined within one philosophical character." As inventor of the Calculus of Quaternions he took high rank in the hierarchy of Science. He was hardly less distinguished in the world of Letters, and was a poet of no mean excellence. From the early age of three years Hamilton was remarkable for his attainments. He could then read English, and before he attained his eighth year was master of three languages. To these he added within the next two years Hebrew, Persian, Arabic, and Sanscrit.

Sir W. R. Hamilton died at the Observatory, Dunsink, on the 2d of September 1865, at the comparatively early age of sixty years. His friend Professor De Morgan said of him that "in exact science he will be the Irishman of his day and of that to come, just as much as his namesake was in mental speculation the Scotchman."

Robinson of Armagh, a dear and lifelong friend to Ferguson, was physically, intellectually, and spiritually a great man. In later years the magnificent head and flowing beard of Thomas Romney Robinson, D.D., recalled Michael Angelo's statue of Moses in the church of S. Pietro in Vinculi at Rome. The Jewish lawgiver as conceived by the sculptor, with the glory of his sojourn on Sinai illuminating his face, might have been chiselled from Dr Robinson's massive and intellectual features. The astronomer of Armagh was a giant, a king of men even to look upon. Eminent in every department of science, there was no realm of divinity, history, literature, or poetry that Robinson had not made his own. His memory was marvellous: poetry and prose were recited by him with equal facility. If the amazed listener asked how it was possible to recall with perfect accuracy words read years before, he would reply that he never forgot what he had once studied with care. In conversation he was brilliant, and would illustrate and enrich from his accumulated knowledge any topic which might be started. It was said that, at a conversazione given by the British Association, Robinson was pointed out as "a man who knew everything." "Introduce us," said the incredulous listener, "and I wager half-a-crown I shall find plenty of subjects of which he will be ignorant. But first let me hear who he is." "He is a Doctor of Divinity," was the answer, "a man of science, the head of the Observatory at Armagh, an ex-Fellow of T. C. D., and the author of a volume of poems written when but twelve years of age." The introduction was effected, and the doubter having started various subjects, on all of which he found Dr Robinson thoroughly informed, artfully led the conversation to cock-fighting. But to his astonishment the divine proved quite familiar with the jargon of the cock-pit. The discomfited questioner produced his half-crown, handed it to the winner, and telling of the wager he had made, begged to be informed how a grave and reverend senior had acquired this unlooked-for knowledge. "It has been my habit," said Dr Robinson, "to enter into conversation with those in whose company I find myself. If they take no interest in my topics, I encourage them to expatiate on their own. I found myself at a dinner-table seated beside a country gentleman with whom I had no interests in common. I acquired from him my knowledge of the slang of cock-fighting."

When Ferguson, in March 1882, heard of the death of his revered friend, he wrote thus of the great man who had passed away, full of years and honours :—

Alas! I hear this morning of the death of Romney Robinson. Noble old man! what becomes of *his* genius? Does it go into some common stock, some intellectual reservoir whence the brains of little men are filled? Surely such faculties can no more perish than heat or light or motion? When a great learned man dies, much learning dies with him if it be not so.

John O'Donovan, already named with Eugene O'Curry, James Clarence Mangan, and others, as workers in the topographical and archæological departments of the Ordnance Survey in Petrie's parlour, was a man of marked individuality. His intimate acquaintance with old as well as modern Irish, his knowledge of ancient MSS., of the pedigrees of old families, his laborious application to the work of a scribe as well as a decipherer of ancient learning, made his services of inestimable value. Larcom had early discovered his capabilities, and had doubtless widened his literary horizon before placing him in the position which enabled him to do such splendid work for Ireland. His country owes to O'Donovan not only his services while on the staff of the Survey, but his monumental work, the translation, enriched with illustrative notes from his stores of knowledge, of the 'Annals of the Four Masters.'

The Four Masters were Brother Michael O'Clery, and his kinsmen Cucogry and Conary O'Clery, and Ferfeasa O'Mulconry, who compiled the Annals of their country up to the year 1616. These were transcribed in the Franciscan convent at Donegal, and dedicated to Fergal O'Gara, Lord of Moy O'Gara and Coolavin, in the county of Sligo, by Brother Michael in words worthy of commemoration :—

In every country enlightened by civilisation, and confirmed therein through a succession of ages, it has been customary to record the events produced by time. For sundry reasons, nothing was deemed more profitable or honourable than to study and peruse the works of ancient writers who gave a faithful account of the great men who figured on the stage of life in preceding ages, that posterity might be informed how their forefathers have employed their time, how long they continued in power, and how they have finished their days.

The guardian of the monastery in 1636 thus comments on the recently compiled Annals :—

How prophetic were the just apprehensions of that chief compiler, "that if the work were then neglected, or consigned to a future time, a risk might be run that the materials for it should never again be brought together." Such, indeed, would have been the sad result. . . . What a solemn lesson, then, is here given us of the necessity of giving durability, while yet in our power, to the surviving historical remains of our country, and thereby placing them beyond the reach of a fate otherwise almost inevitable! To me it appears a sacred duty on cultivated minds to do so.

John O'Donovan's letters, written in minute but clear handwriting, are full of dry humour. In a letter to Ferguson commenting on his reviews of "Etruria Celtica," which appeared in 'Blackwood,' April 1845, and "O'Connor's Irish Brigades," 'Dublin University Magazine,' May 1845, O'Donovan relates an adventure of the historian of the Brigades, Matthew, seventh son of Denis, son of Charles O'Conor of Belanagare, which befell him when, a penniless youth, expelled from the Irish College at Rome in consequence of his refusal to become a priest, he was arrested in France during the Revolution as a spy. Matthew had the good fortune unexpectedly to meet with a kinsman in the French service, whose treatment of him is amusingly narrated. Many scions of Irish Roman Catholic families — "Wild Geese," as they were called—had been for some generations in foreign service, having followed into exile the House of Stuart.

8 NEWCOMEN PLACE, NORTH STRAND,
April 22, 1845.

DEAR FERGUSON,—The anecdote you allude to I often heard from Mr O'Conor himself, but I cannot bring to mind the name of the town where he was taken up, nor indeed the year; but calculating from certain data, I would say that it was the year 1787. Mr Matthew O'Conor was the seventh son of Denis O'Conor of Belanagare, who was the son of the venerable Charles O'Conor, the antiquary. He was born in the year 1772, and died in the seventieth year of his age. He was sent to the College of Saint Omer's when very young, where his brother, Dr Charles O'Conor, the translator of the Annals, who was eleven years older than he (Matthew), had been placed several years previously. At the age of fourteen the eldest of the boys was asked (according to a rule of the College) whether he would be a *prêtre*—*i.e.*, presbyter,—and the boy answered in the affirmative, although he had no such intention, his ambition urging him to a loftier station, say that of a *prætor*, though he afterwards turned out a *prater ;* and even while at college, he, with wonderful precociousness, wrote several articles in a Roman Journal in the Italian language against the President of the College.   However, when the age of ordination had arrived, he was called up with several others to receive the dignity of *prêtre ;* at the hearing of the which he grew pale with rage and annoyance at being caught in such a trap ! cold sweat oozed through every pore, and he exhausted his rage on his younger brother by giving him a most merciless licking for no reason !   However, as his word of honour had been pledged, he submitted to his destiny and received the sacerdotal order *against his will !* He might have foreseen that he had no *vocation*, and that his future conduct would not be much in accordance with the humility of the Gospel, or with the rules prescribed for obeying a plebeian hierarchy ! He therefore gave vent to his angry feelings against the Irish Bishops ; and when he contended (*nolo Episcopari*) for the Bishopric of Elphin, he told the priests that indeed it would be no great honour to him to be Bishop of Elphin, who ought rather to contend for the kingdom of Connaught !   His letters of Columbanus are worth more than all the exploits of Turlough the Great or Charles Crovdherg.

The younger brother, Matthew, when he completed his fourteenth year in the College at Rome, was asked if he would be a *prêtre*, and he answered boldly in the *negative ;* upon which he was immediately turned out, and left to the mercy of a few shillings of pocket-money which he chanced to have. With these few shillings he faced home in the midst of the French Revolution !   Passing through or by the town of —— in France, he stopped to look at an esplanade ; but wearing the Italian dress, he was taken up as a young spy !   He could not speak French, but he told them in Italian and English that he was an Irish boy who ran away from the Irish College at Rome.   One of the officers present recognising the Connaught *brogue*, came over and asked, "Who the devil are *you?*" "I am the seventh son of Denis O'Conor of Belanagare. My father sent me to the Irish College at Rome, but they turned me out when I said I would not be a priest." "Damn your *sowle!* you young rascal, have you any money?" "I have two shillings and no more." "Your brother Roderic is stationed at ———. He was taken the other day and nearly murdered for not tearing the *fleur-de-lis* from his coat; but don't you go near him. I am D. M'Dermott of Coolavin, your first cousin, and I will give you a couple of crowns, which I can badly spare. Go home directly, and do not linger in France." Master Matthew returned to Connaught, but his father was so enraged at his conduct that he did not condescend to see him for three years afterwards; but at the importunities of his relatives he consented to get him bound to an attorney in Dublin. While serving his time Matt. never wished to hear a word about Rome or the Irish College; and when asked, "Mr O'Conor, didn't you see the Pope?" "Yes, sir." "What sort of a man is he?" "The Pope is a fine man, sir;" and stooping his head, he would go on with the transcription of his pleonastic document stuffed with *inania verba* (*vain* and *insignificant* expressions), in which, though he found little intermixed for thought, he still preferred them to the legends of the 'Breviarium Romanum.' He was called to the Bar in the year 1819, when he was in his forty-sixth year; but having a very sound knowledge of law, he got on well, though he never was a brilliant speaker. He left his children an estate of about £5000 per annum, besides twenty thousand in the Funds. His father left him but very little. I have the probate of his father's will, which I will send you if you have any fancy to see it.

I read the article about "Etruria Celtica" in 'Blackwood's Magazine' with great interest, and feel satisfied that it has "demolished" Sir Guy Ollgothach's quackery. If not, he is incurable! I send you a proof of my last attack upon him, in which I introduce the Punic Speech in Plautus to show that it is very improbable that the Phœnician was mo-no-sylla-bic—i.e., *greater - noble - seed - day - little.*   I think that this amounts to something like real argument, though he never thought how much it stood in his way.

I am most anxious to know if O'Conor has given any account of the Kavanaghs in his "Irish Brigade."   My grandfather was the second cousin of the Kavanagh who passed out to Bohemia, where he became Baron of Gniditz.   His name was John Baptista Kavanagh, and he was the son of the "renowned warrior" Brian na Stroak Kavanagh of Drummin who fought at the Boyne and Aughrim, and who had his cheek cleft in a duel with one of William's officers at the Boyne, and from the seam of the wound in his cheek he received the appellation of *na Stroak.*   There was another relative of my grandfather's a captain in the French service, named Morgan or Murrough More Kavanagh, who was one of the largest men in Europe. I often conversed with old men who saw him in his old age after returning from France.   While in the service he came over to Ireland to send out " *Wild Geese,*" and during his stay in Ireland he often stopped with my grandfather.   My grandfather's uncle was also in the French service, and was taken prisoner at Waterford in the year 1739, when my grandfather was present in the nineteenth year of his age ; but he was afterwards ransomed, and I often heard that he left a family in France, but I have not been able to learn where. His name was Edmond O'Donovan, and was the son of Cornelius by Rose Kavanagh, the aunt of Brian *na Stroak,* who was son of Edmond by Catherine Gall de Burgo of Gaulstown in the county of Kilkenny.   But I suppose O'Conor doesn't give any lists of officers.—Wishing you every success, I remain, your most sincere well-wisher,

J. O'DONOVAN.

At a subsequent period Ferguson, engaged on his poem " The Cromlech on Howth," refers to O'Donovan's account of Athairne, the bard who cursed the Leinstermen.   The following brief but lively correspondence ensued :—

MY DEAR O'DONOVAN,—Your reference for Athairne is 'Book of Ballymote,' fo. 77, p. 2, col. 6, at p. 17 of "The Tribes."

It's my opinion that the sons of Ir (*i.e.*, the Clan Rury—*i.e.*, the men of Ulster) may yet be the means of emancipating the Milesians.—Yours ever faithfully,

SAML. FERGUSON.

JOHN O'DONOVAN, ESQ.

On the reverse side of this little note O'Donovan replied,—

MY WORTHY FRIEND,—Mr Curry says that the story of Athairne is not given in the 'Book of Ballymote,' and that Athairne did not actually hurl the red bolt of his satire against the Leinstermen; he only *threatened to do so.* I suspect that I took my quotation from Hardiman's statute of Kilkenny, where he refers to the satirising of Leinster. The witherer of grass and corn crops of Leinster was poet to Niall of the Nine Hostages, and lived much later than Athairne of Howth.—Yours ever sincerely,   JOHN O'DONOVAN.

P.S.—The story of Athairne is in the 'Book of Leinster' in the College Library; I think Curry has a copy of it *in extenso.* Athairne was a ruffian! The race of Ir are those of whom St Malachy complained to St Bernard. *Scoti sumus non Galli!*

The Bishop of Down and Connor wrote to Master Camden to tell him that the inhabitants of his diocese were as stubborn and intractable then as they [were] in St Malachy's time.

J. O'D.

On another occasion Ferguson received a characteristic note from O'Donovan. It was to this effect :—

I understand that the mad poet who is my next-door neighbour claims acquaintance with you. He says I am his enemy, and watch him through the thickness of the wall which divides our houses. He threatens in consequence to shoot me. One of us must leave. I have a houseful of books and children, he has an umbrella and a revolver. If, under the circumstances, you could use your influence, and persuade *him* to remove to other quarters, you would confer a great favour on yours sincerely,   JOHN O'DONOVAN.

Ferguson's review of O'Donovan's 'Annals of the Four Masters' appeared in the 'University' in March and May 1848. A few passages may be given from these articles :—

A general history of Ireland is not what we at present require. . . .
The histories we now want are particular and local; such as, it is true, would furnish no material for large philosophic inductions, but such as will enable us to know one another and the land we live in, and every spot of it; that such knowledge may beget mutual confidence and united labour, and that we may strive to advance our own and our country's fortunes here in the place assigned to us in the world, quite regardless of what others, who are not concerned in our relations, may think or say respecting the meagreness or barbarism of the material we have to work on.
The style of these writings is meagre, and the subject of them such as, in this stage of social progress, is usually deemed barbarous. But they are the same sort of events, only told with greater certainty of time and place, as those which fill up a good part of the heroic period in classic history; forays and cattle - spoils, which may be deemed ignoble, or otherwise, as the herdsman is a clown or a Prince Paris; and murders, which may excite our loathing or admiration, as the deed is perpetrated by a vulgar stabber or an Orestes. We dare say, had it been the policy of any party in ancient Greece to win the thoughts and affections of the Greeks from their own country, so as to make them a safer provincial dependency of some earlier civilised neighbouring nation—Syria, say, or Egypt—this sort of argument or expostulation would have been very often employed by them. Where is the use of tracing back the barbarous tra-

ditions of the house of Atreus—a series of rapes, incests, parricides, and treacherous butcheries?   Why waste your time on idle enumerations of the pedigrees of Inachus? on nonsensical tales of satyrs and sea-monsters? or on trifling questions of how long such or such a robber in the mountains of Attica lived before or after the return of your Heraclidæ? Turn your thoughts to Egypt, such persons would say,—the glorious actions of Sesostris are something, indeed, worthy of the study of men of enlightenment.   The sources of the Nile, and the causes of its overflow, you may investigate with profit and delight.   The various genera and species of plants and animals are to be seen at Memphis.   Indulge no more the idle dream of being Greeks—North-west Egyptians, methinks, would sound more proper, &c.   Had such representations been made to the Greeks, and had the Greeks acknowledged the wisdom and prudence of adopting that course, the Memphians might, perhaps, have been obliged by them with the same sort of services as Rome obtained from them in later times; but we should have heard nothing of Euripides, Sophocles, or Æschylus—the men who, out of that barbaric material, made the literature of the world. Our cattle-spoils and hostings, our family pedigrees, and royal and princely successions, are as precious to us now as theirs were to them then.   We will treasure them as they did ; and the time may yet come when our Egypt herself will thank us for having cherished the seeds of a new literature, after her own may possibly have fallen to decay.

From the fabulous period, down to the arrival of the Anglo-Normans, these particular annals, along with those of Ulster and Innisfallen, have already been given to the curiosity of the select objects of his bounty by the late munificent Duke of Buckingham, who published them up to this point, with Dr Charles O'Conor's Latin translation and notes, under the title 'Rerum Hibernicarum Scriptores Veteres.'   We would pray the great lords and magnates of the present day to reflect how infinitely greater has been the return in real renown which this nobleman has secured to himself and his successors by that act of splendid liberality, than if he had expended ten or a hundred times the same amount on any of the ungrateful *barathra* which we see, from year to year, swallowing up princes and their revenues. What is it, we would respectfully ask some of those noble and fortunate persons, to buy the applause of the race-course, or the excitement of the hazard-table, at the cost of whole estates, and sometimes of entire patrimonies, in comparison with the cheap purchase, at the cost of a few weeks' or even days' revenue, of the fame of having contributed the first foundation-stones to a nation's history, and the satisfaction and solace of having won a nation's thanks, and the sympathies of all the educated classes of a nation, for them and for theirs, to the third and fourth generation? May the clouds which lately lowered over Stowe soon be altogether dispersed; may it never be necessary to afford us the opportunity of purchasing those national heirlooms (precious though they are to us, and eagerly as we know the learned of Ireland court the opportunity of acquiring them) which it was lately rumoured would be brought under the hands of the auctioneer; and may the Irish at large learn to appreciate great services to their name and nation as well when rendered by an English prince in England as by their own poor brethren at home. *O si majoribus nostris tales contigissent moderatores!*

When Ferguson wrote thus on the Stowe MSS. he little thought that it would be his own good fortune to secure for his country those manuscripts from the Stowe Collection which were concerned with Ireland. Yet so it was. Years later, when about to start for the Pyrenees and northern Spain, where he proposed to spend his vacation, a paragraph appeared in the newspapers which changed his plans. It was announced that the Government were about to purchase this celebrated collection for the nation. Sir Samuel —at this time Keeper of the Records of Ireland and

President of the Royal Irish Academy—at once re-solved to remain within reach of London. Instead of going abroad he went to Buxton, and as soon as the purchase was effected went to London and pressed on the Lords of the Treasury the claims of Ireland. These claims were conceded. The Irish part of the collection, including an ancient MS. with its decorated case, known as the Stowe Missal, is now deposited in the Library of the Royal Irish Academy.

In his second article on the 'Annals of the Four Masters,' Ferguson points out to his countrymen of the upper classes how inferior they are in taste, erudition, and above all in patriotic spirit, to their predecessors. He suggests that had they been "better Irishmen" the chasm between them and the people would not have been so great as it has become, nor would the landed gentry have fallen into their present helpless and humiliating position. They have lost touch with their fellow-countrymen, and now find themselves powerless and isolated.

So long as the populace are set against the gentry, and the gentry, attaching themselves to external associations, refuse to know their own country and its people, that state of things must continue; for no power of laws or government ever will or can make the people of Ireland other than Irish; and the more the minds of the upper classes are withdrawn, and fixed on external attachments, the wider and deeper must be the chasm separating those who ought to be united, and the more deplorable and humiliating the weakness inseparable from that division. And, in returning to the position whence they ought never to have departed, our gentry have to make no retrograde movement in civilisation. Their grandfathers, better Irishmen, were also better scholars, and more polished men. Base caricaturists have made money, and gained a kind of spurious reputation, by defaming them ; reckless humorists have recommended themselves to the scornful laughter of English readers by exaggerating their peculiarities, and drawing ludicrous pictures of the state of society which prevailed among them ; but men who judge them by the legitimate evidences of their acts and monuments—by their mansion-houses, their libraries, their collections of painting and sculpture — by the works written by them, and published amongst them, and for them— and by the testimony of contemporary competent judges, know for a fact that society has not advanced in Ireland— that the spurious civilisation of little economists and quibbling logicians is not an improvement on the solid and elegant acquirements, and constitutional and legal learning, of the Irish noblemen and gentlemen of the last century.

O'Donovan died in 1861. A noble poem on "The Dead Antiquary" was sent to Ferguson by its author, the Hon. T. D. M'Gee, from Montreal. In this M'Gee alludes to the elegy pronounced on O'Connell by D. F. M'Carthy, and to Ferguson's "Lament for Thomas Davis":—

"Far are the Gaelic tribes, and wide
Scattered round earth on every side
    For good or ill ;
They aim at all things, rise or fall,
Succeed or perish—but through all
    Love Erin still.

Although a righteous heaven decrees
'Twixt us and Erin stormy seas
    And barriers strong,
Of care, and circumstance, and cost,
Yet count not all your absent lost,
    Oh land of song !

Above your roofs no star can rise
That does not lighten in our eyes,
    Nor any set
That ever shed a cheering beam
On Irish hillside, street, or stream,
    That we forget.

No artist wins a shining fame
Lifting aloft his nation's name
    High over all ;
No soldier falls, no poet dies,
But underneath all foreign skies
    We mourn his fall !

  .   .   .   .   .

Though haply still by Liffey's side
That mighty master must abide
    Who voiced our grief
O'er Davis lost ; and him who gave
His free frank tribute at the grave
    Of Erin's chief ;

Yet must it not be said that we
Failed in the rites of minstrelsie,
    So dear to souls
Like his whom lately death hath ta'en,
Although the vast Atlantic main
    Between us rolls !

Too few, too few among our great,
In camp or cloister, Church or State,
    Wrought as he wrought ;
Too few of all the brave we trace
Among the champions of our race
    Fought as he fought.

  .   .   .   .   .

He toiled to make our story stand
As from Time's reverent, runic hand
    It came, undecked

By fancies false, erect, alone,
The monumental arctic stone
    Of ages wrecked.

  .   .   .   .   .

With gentle hand he rectified
The errors of old bardic pride,
    And set aright
The story of our devious past,
And left it, as it now must last,
    Full in the light !

  .   .   .   .   .

Happy the life our scholar led
Among the living and the dead—
    Loving, beloved ;
'Mid precious tomes, and gentle looks,
The best of men and best of books,
    He daily moved.

Kings that were dead two thousand years,
Cross-bearing chiefs and pagan seers,
    He knew them all ;
And bards, whose very harps were dust,
And saints, whose souls are with the just,
    Came at his call.

  .   .   .   .   .

He marshalled Brian on the plain,
Sailed in the galleys of the Dane,—
    Earl Richard too,
Fell Norman as he was, and fierce,
Of him and his he dared rehearse
    The story true.

O'er all low limits still his mind
Soared Catholic and unconfined,
    From malice free ;
On Irish soil he only saw
One state, one people, and one law,
    One destiny !

> Spirit of Justice ! Thou most dread
> Author divine, whose Book hath said
>   The Just man's seed
> Shall never fail for lack of bread,
> Oh, let the flock his labour fed,
>   Thy mercy feed !
>
> Inspire, O Lord ! with bounteous hand,
> The magnates of the Irish land,
>   That being so moved,
> As fathers of the fatherless,
> They shield from danger and distress
>   His well-beloved.
>
> And teach us, Father, who remain
> Filial dependants on that brain
>   So deeply wrought,—
> Teach us to travel day by day
> By honest paths, seeking alway
>   The ends he sought ! "

Of James Clarence Mangan, whose "Woman of Three Cows" was, as we have seen, produced in Petrie's parlour, it is enough to say that his Irish and German Anthology, as well as the few sad original poems which do not profess to be translations, prove him to have been a man of poetic genius. His "Dark Rosaleen," his "Lament for the Princes of Tyrone and Tyrconnell," and his rendering of "O'Hussey's Ode to the Maguire," are intensely passionate and of high imaginative power. He does not pretend to be a literal translator. Of the "Ode to the Maguire," Ferguson wrote :—

There is a vivid vigour in these descriptions, and a savage power in the antithetical climax, which claim a character almost approaching to sublimity. Nothing can be more graphic, yet more diversified, than his images of unmitigated horror— nothing more grandly startling than his heroic conception of the glow of glory triumphant over frozen toil. We have never read this poem without recurring, and that by no unworthy association, to Napoleon in his Russian campaign. Yet perhaps O'Hussey has conjured up a picture of more inclement desolation, in his rude idea of Northern horrors, than could be legitimately employed by a poet of the present day, when the romance of geographical obscurity no longer permits us to imagine the Phlegrean regions of endless storm, where the snows of Hæmus fall mingled with the lightnings of Etna, amid Bistonian wilds or Hyrcanian forests.

Poor hapless Mangan has told his sad personal story in the piteous poem which he calls " The Nameless One " :—

> " And he fell far through that pit abysmal,
>   The gulf and grave of Maginn and Burns,
> And pawned his soul for the devil's dismal
>   Stock of returns.
>
> But yet redeemed it in days of darkness,
>   And shapes and signs of the final wrath,
> When death, in hideous and ghastly starkness,
>   Stood on his path.
>
> And tell how now, amid wreck and sorrow,
>   And want, and sickness, and houseless nights,
> He bides in calmness the silent morrow,
>   That no ray lights.
>
> And lives he still, then ? Yes ! Old and hoary
>   At thirty-nine, from despair and woe,
> He lives, enduring what future story
>   Will never know.

> Him grant a grave to, ye pitying noble,
>   Deep in your bosoms !   There let him dwell !
> He, too, had tears for all souls in trouble,
>   Here and in hell."

Clarence Mangan died in the Meath Hospital on the 20th of June 1849.

Eugene O'Curry, like O'Donovan, was versed in the Irish language. He also was a man of simple and homely ways. Like the " dead Antiquary," who pre-deceased him by one year only, O'Curry did valuable work by transcribing and making known the ancient lore of Ireland. He became Professor in the Catholic University. The lectures he delivered while he filled that chair, on " The Manuscript Materials of Early Irish History," entitle him to be called the Historiographer of his country. On O'Curry's death in 1862 M'Gee wrote an elegy, from which a few stanzas are here cited :—

> "Alas ! that rite should now be claimed,
>   O world ! for one we least can spare ;
> Whose name by us was never named
>   Without its meed of praise or prayer !

> An *Ollamh* of the elect of old,
>   Whose chairs were placed beside the king,
> Whose hounds, whose herds, whose gifts of gold,
>   The later bards regretful sing ;
> Ay ! there was magic in his speech,
>   And in his wand the power to save,
> This sole recorder on the beach
>   Of all we've lost beneath the wave.

Who are his mourners?   By the hearth
  His presence kindled, sad they sit;
They dwell throughout the living earth,
  In homes his presence never lit;
Where'er a Gaelic brother dwells,
  There heaven has heard for him a prayer;
Where'er an Irish maiden tells
  Her votive beads, his soul has share."

CHAPTER V.

1834-1886.

LITERARY WORK AND FURTHER FRIENDSHIPS.

> "I love all that thou lovest,
>   Spirit of Delight !
> The fresh Earth in new leaves drest,
>   And the starry night ;
> Autumn evening, and the morn
> When the golden mists are born.
>
> I love snow and all the forms
>   Of the radiant frost ;
> I love waves, and winds, and storms,
>   Everything almost
> Which is Nature's, and may be
> Untainted by man's misery.
>
> I love tranquil solitude,
>   And such society
> As is quiet, wise, and good."
>   —SHELLEY.

WHILE Ferguson was studying for the Bar, he spent some time in London, and devoted his spare hours to the library of the Archbishop of Canterbury at Lambeth and the reading-room of the British Museum. In papers which appeared in the 'University' in January and June 1837, under the title of "Curiosities of Irish Literature," he extols the perfect arrangements for the convenience of students afforded in these great libraries :—

Everything in this noble institution is on a scale of grandeur and munificence that makes it a delightful subject to turn to, after even the best of our establishments at home.   Good character your only introduction—a million and a half of books and manuscripts at your command—a reading-room, commodious and comfortable as the best apartment of a large hotel, expressly for your occupation — numerous and intelligent porters to bring the books or manuscripts you have selected from the catalogues, to your table, and to remove them when no longer required, to their proper shelves in the immense depositories within—surrounded by several hundreds of the first scholars and writers of the age,—you sit, without the outlay of a single farthing, the enviable possessor of means to knowledge which could not be purchased for ten millions of money.   Nor is this all: the officers of the establishment, men of high attainments, and of the most obliging manners, are ready to assist the inexperienced investigator by pointing out the proper course of study, and, if they find him diligent, by perhaps bringing him acquainted with other inquirers engaged on the same class of subjects.

But perhaps an equally delightful resort for the lover of manuscripts—and for the lover of the middle-age antiquities of Ireland, beyond comparison the most delightful in existence—is the palace at Lambeth.   Here, under one roof with the Lollards' tower, overlooking the full, broad Thames, with the hall and abbey of Westminster rising, grand beyond expression, on its farther bank—the aged elms of Bird Cage Walk, rustling with breezes from Richmond, under your window—the spirit of antiquity pervading the air you breathe—the genius of the constitution present in the very space around you,—to sit, as we have sat on a warm day in summer, turning over the autographs of Sidney and Sussex, and the impetuous Perrot, (swearing great oaths in his very dispatches)—of the politic Chichester and the severe Mountjoy—of Desmond, and the White Knight, and Florence M'Carthy — of " We, Shane

O'Neill, from our camp at Knockboy," of Sorley Buy Mac-Donnell from Dunluce, and great Earl Hugh himself from his castle of Dungannon—then turn to the annals of Friar Clynn, or the Book of Howth, and mix again with the De Burghos and the Mortimers, the Laceys and the De Courceys of Norman times—or from narrative to have recourse to representation, and study native arms and costumes in the plans of battles and sieges, or trace our ancient topography in the plots of towns and castles or forfeited countries of rebel lords beyond the Pale, —to spend the hot mornings thus under the shadow of antiquity, and in the evenings to stroll about the precincts of the seat of Government—the Horse Guards, the Admiralty, the Treasury, the State Paper Office,—it is enough to make a man a lover of history, and a reverer of the constitution for ever after.   To the distinguished prelate in whose keeping those treasures of literature are deposited we would here pay our tribute of grateful acknowledgments, as well on our own part as on behalf of all our countrymen who have experienced his liberal permission of access to them.   The same obliging disposition characterises the keepers of all the stores of learning in London.

Ferguson's intense delight in these opportunities of study, of which England may well be proud, no less than of the scholars so trained who have devoted their labours to the elucidation of her history, made him feel, perhaps the more deeply, the contrast as concerns his native land.   There is mingled grief and indignation in his utterances on this topic:—

There is a species of national self-knowledge as conducive to public respectability as individual self-knowledge is to personal self-respect.   This knowledge of the country we inhabit, too many of our educated men have only upon hearsay.   The causes of this want of information, which in any other country would be considered a disgraceful species of ignorance, are chiefly these: first, a prevalent impression that there is no history of Ireland yet written; secondly, a feeling that if such a history were written its study would not be necessary to a liberal education; and thirdly, a dastardly fear of looking former times in the face, which is, of all other motives to ignorance, at once the most congenial and the most infatuated. It is true there is no adequate compilation of the existing materials for a history of Ireland; but the case was the same in England up to a comparatively recent period; yet it is impossible to point out any time since England had an historical existence in which her educated classes were deficient in knowledge of their country's history. The fact that no history of Ireland is taught in our schools (an instance of self-abasement unexampled in the practice of any country of Europe) gives more than plausibility to the second argument; and we admit it is too true that an Irish gentleman may be ignorant of his own country's history when he dare be ignorant of no other branch of what is called a good education. But the time for that dashing disclaimer of acquaintance with an unfashionable subject is past. The subject is no longer one of choice or caprice; it has become the weapon of argument on topics of vital interest, and must be studied in self-defence, or those who neglect it must abandon the contest. Whether a man seek for change or for continuance of existing institutions, he must ground a great part of his reasonings on historical example. Many unpalatable truths must be encountered, many cherished prejudices must be abandoned on both sides, before a fair or an effective use of such materials for argument can be expected. . . . If we transfer our inquiry from private individuals to public institutions, we shall find the same subject of complaint, though in a less degree. A library is here a vital part of the body politic of each, and in every library there are of course some works on the history and statistics of the country. But in no one whatever is there a perfect collection. A perfect collection of printed books relating to Ireland does not exist— there is not such a thing to be found in the whole world; and probably in the whole world there is no other civilised country which has the same shameful tale to tell.

" It had been part of my ambition," Ferguson subsequently wrote, "to compile a history of my native county of Antrim, and in my studies and researches for that purpose at the British Museum, Lambeth, and elsewhere, I had become familiar with the more recondite sources of Historical and Record Learning." Although he did not carry out his project, yet the time and labour thus spent in acquainting himself with original sources were by no means wasted. He became familiar with records, rolls, inquisitions, and other historic material, and long afterwards applied with good effect in the service of the public the knowledge thus acquired.

The young Irish law-student, in a previous paper published in the 'University Magazine,' January 1834, speaks of London, its citizens and its public buildings :—

Let no one suspect us of not venerating the English character and not loving the society of Englishmen. We believe the English gentleman to be one of the finest and best fellows in the world—calm, courteous, discreet, manly, candid, and generous.

He had previously been describing his own countrymen, and his "delight in their witty company at home and abroad." But he could not admire the architectural taste at that time conspicuous in London. "Paint and stucco, split plaster pilasters and garret windows peeping out of sculptured pediments, tawdry attics, and Agrigentan columns of lath and plaster," "dislocated abortions of vile taste ; of yellow stone, with pot-metal pillars." But for its ancient and venerable buildings

Ferguson had unbounded admiration. He thus records his impressions of Westminster Hall :—

Over the echoing field of stone you tread like a ghost, for the cold and solemn dread that inhabits around and above you weighs down on your diminutive consciousness, as if the dusk void were compact of shades of kings. You do not think at first that you never before saw so huge a hall; but you think that you never before felt yourself to be so near the measure of a span. Your eye will presently enlarge its apprehension, and the enormous beams of yellow chestnut (for they are not of Irish oak) will lean out magnificently into the dim distance, from side-wall to side-wall, then meeting under the roof-ridge, high as many a church steeple; the vast windows, through which, were they the arches of a bridge, the greatest barge on the Thames might row with all her flags afloat, nor rub a single oar-blade or pennon-end, will open on you, widening as you gaze, till you think they might admit sunshine enough to enlighten chaos; but the obscure light between is still dim in undispersed shadow, and still extending its grey boundaries before you, till you begin at length to understand how knights of old found "ample room and verge enough" within its listed precincts for their chargers' career, when the splinters of broken lances used to leap high as the heads of those carven cherubim, and the trumpets of pursuivants at arms awakened the forgotten echoes sleeping in all the airy corners of the roof. But, grow the hall as it will, you have not partaken in the enlargement, you are still a pigmy, nor will you be yourself again till you get out of the giant's house. Let us then enter one of these oaken and studded doors lately pierced in the side-wall, for you are now in a fit frame of mind to approach the fountain of law.

Ferguson was especially happy in his descriptions of scenery. His delight in Nature was intense. He was familiar with her varied aspects in his own beloved land, and he knew Ireland thoroughly. No holiday on foreign soil gave him the same fulness of enjoyment as rambles nearer home. He explored her historic scenes, her antiquities, and her scenery with the enthusiasm of a lover. He found the society of her people, whether gentlefolk or peasants, congenial. And in the good old days the Irish peasant was, in truth, a delightful companion. Hospitality, courtesy, delicacy and refinement of feeling, tact, as well as wit and humour, characterised him. Of late years these virtues have been under eclipse, from the lessons of distrust and discourtesy which have been sedulously inculcated. But the clouds are breaking, and the sun of good-humour and kind-heartedness will shine forth, and again make the Irish peasant what he was of old, an innate gentleman.

Ferguson commenced his series of papers on the "Attractions of Ireland" in the 'Dublin University Magazine' of July 1836. They were continued in the September and December numbers of that year. They gave a graphic account of the country, its scenery, places of historic interest, and of society in Dublin, and were followed by a statistical article entitled "The Capabilities of Ireland," which appeared in the 'University' in January 1837. A few extracts will illustrate his treatment of each of the topics discussed in the "Attractions of Ireland." Here also appeared his verses on an Irish peasant, "The Pretty Girl of Loch Dan," who showed hospitality to him and to Carleton when they rested at her cottage during their walking tour in the county of Wicklow.

We will now suppose our tourist, in addition to his qualifications as an engineer, endowed more or less with the eye of a painter and the heart of a poet. For such a man all nature abounds with enjoyment; but nowhere, we venture to say, will that enjoyment be obtained by such a man more fully, more expeditiously, more cheaply, or more safely than in our own country—nay, at our own capital. Of all the northern capitals, Dublin indeed seems to us the best situated in this respect; for while the city itself stands in a plain as rich and cultivated as high civilisation can make it, a single day's march will bring an active citizen where he may roam about the length of a summer morning, not only out of sight of the habitations of men, but in full view of the eyrie and within hearing of the scream of the eagle. . . .

The lingerer by lakes and rivers has only to encounter a single morning's drive to enable him to float at ease above the haunts of the char in the clear bosom of Lough Dan, or to cast his line across the deepest pool of the Vartrey, the Avonmore, or the Liffey; while he who delights to expand his chest with vigorous inhalations of the mountain air, may start from Nelson's Pillar at sunrise, and breathe as pure an atmosphere as encircles the summit of Mangerton itself, on the head of Kippure, before persons keeping ordinary hours have sat down to breakfast. . . .

It was a lovely morning, and though I had seen Glendaloch so often before, I now saw a thousand new beauties. The lakes, ruffled by the fresh morning air, were as blue as sapphire; the rocks in the clear atmosphere rose majestically near; every leaf was glistening with dew, the woods quite quivering with song; and oh, the verdure of the greensward; the gurgle and gush and musical clamour of the running waters; the verdurous coolness of the ravine with its glimmering pools and snowy cascades, and crossing and dancing shafts of sunshine under the breezy canopy of leaves! And then when we had emerged from the thickets of Poolanass, and had got out upon the open side of Derrybawn, between which and Lugduff our way lay into Glenmalure—oh! then, the exulting sense of freedom, the limbs' spontaneous play, the lungs that crow like chanticleer, the animation and the expansion and the rapture! Who can walk the heather without feeling this, and more than this? Who that can walk the heather on such a hill as Derrybawn, and that in one day's march from care and Dublin, would not sometimes feel his heart enlarge with such sensations!

But there is a higher species of local attraction with which Ireland abounds, and which we must not pass unnoticed. We mean the interest which particular spots derive from historical or poetic association. Poetically classic ground does not, alas! occur with us, as on the shores consecrated by a Shakespeare and a Scott. The spots are in comparison very rare where the traveller can stop and say, Here is the locality of such a chapter or of such a scene. This rock, that ruin, yonder glen, are the very objects on which the memory of the poet dwelt while realising these passages which have now given them as it were a new existence. . . .

We have the authority of Sir Walter Scott for saying that the county of Cork alone abounds in more unwrought romance than all Scotland. Ireland is at the present moment the richest mine of historical and romantic material in Europe. It is not in coarse burlesques on national humour, nor in frivolous representations of passing events or characters however vivid, that justice is to be done to such materials. A Hume, a Dugdale, and a Scott, would have here enough to do to exhaust even the now accessible portion of the mine. It is in such a country that the man of really solid acquirements will find local associations most agreeable. They have not yet lost their freshness; they are only a few who can enjoy them; there is the charm of an almost independent discovery attached to each. The Rock of Cashel, to a man of respectable historical attainments, is one of the most intensely interesting scenes in the United Kingdom. Such a man among the comparatively humble ruins of Holycross will enjoy more of the genius of the place than under the fretted aisles of Melrose itself. To a contemplative and philosophic spirit there is not, perhaps, in Europe a more congenial spot than the desert graveyards of Clonmacnois, where still stand, some of them in dilapidation and some of them in ruin, the nine churches "built by the kings and petty princes of these parts for their places of sepulture,

who, although at perpetual wars in their lives, were contented
to lie here peaceably in death." The roads travelled by Patrick
are still in being; the bells handled by him may still be
touched and listened to—the same tones that rang in the ears
of pagan princes still sounding the advent of the Gospel to our
own!   From the palace of Aileagh and the cell of Columbkill
at Derry, to the walls of Limerick and Kilmallock, and the
towers of Waterford and Hook—from Glendaloch to Loch
Derg, and from Inniscatha to Downpatrick, length and breadth
ways—the island is full of touching recollections and inspiring
hopes.   Here it was that King Brian defeated the Danes;
there the Norman conquerors first set foot on Irish soil.   In
that wood prince Hal received knighthood from the sword of
the ill - fated Richard; in yonder castle he lay imprisoned.
There is the scene of an exploit of Raleigh; here are memorials of Spenser and Sir Philip Sidney.   What shall we say of
the Kildares, the Desmonds, the O'Neills, the Ormonds? or
how shall we restrain ourselves if we attempt to do but passing
justice to the memories of our other warriors and patriots, the
lights of succeeding days, summoned up as they are by heroic
monuments in almost every field?

A meeting of the Royal Irish Academy, presided
over by the Provost of that day, Dr Bartholomew
Lloyd, is next described.   He was the father of
Humphrey Lloyd, who afterwards filled the same
exalted position, and was no less eminent as a man
of science.   Dr Humphrey Lloyd and his accomplished
wife subsequently presided over the hospitalities of the
Provost's house with dignity and graceful courtesy.

This is a meeting of the Royal Irish Academy.   The
Provost of the University presides.   His son, the distinguished
Humphrey Lloyd, sits near him.   That animated individual
with the eager eye and broad forehead, who is reading the
formula from the demonstrating board, is Sir William Hamilton,

the illustrious mathematician and astronomer.   This intelligent-looking personage, whose countenance combines so much gravity and liveliness, is the Archbishop of Dublin.   There is Petrie—he with the Grecian brow, long hair, and dark complexion—the accomplished antiquary; and here is Pim, the introducer of railroads into Ireland.   Here sits the scientific Portlock, with Apjohn, our leading chemist; and this is Stokes, the great physician of the lungs. . . .   But who are these who have just entered : one with a light step, huge frame, sharp Irish features, and columnar forehead; the other lower in stature, of a paler complexion, large featured, with the absent aspect of a man of learning?   They are Carleton, author of the 'Traits and Stories of the Peasantry,' and Anster, the translator of 'Faust.'

The Archbishop of Dublin here described was Richard Whately, D.D., a Churchman of the "Broad" school, a logician, a wit, a man of genius and of great benevolence, but widely severed by temperament and opinion from the clergy whom he came to Ireland to rule over.   Ferguson's estimate of his character appears in the following suggested epitaph :—

> Here lie I, Richard Whately,
> Archbishop of Dublin lately,
> Who, for the amelioration
> Of the ignorant Irish nation,
> Coming hither with much vain knowledge,
> Have learned in these poor people's College
> Some things have been a boon to me
> Were heretofore unknown to me.
> > I taught quibble,
> > And learnt the Bible;
> > I brought ability,
> > And took away humility.

Archbishop Whately's theological views were undoubtedly much modified in later years.

Carleton, with the "light step and huge frame," himself sprung from the people, has, beyond all other delineators of Irish character—except, perhaps, Miss Edgeworth, before his day, and Miss Jane Barlow in recent years—given truthful and touching portraits of Irish peasants, pictures instinct with humour, pathos, and vivid individuality. No reader can ever forget his "Poor Scholar"; nor Miss Barlow's "Widow M'Gurk," to whom she has introduced us in her 'Irish Idylls.' Ferguson, always ready to render such services as were in his power, was in after-years helpful to Carleton and his family. Long after her father's death Miss Carleton wrote to thank him for his "great kindness":—

I feel it difficult to express to you how truly grateful my sister and I feel for your exertions on our behalf. We have learned from Mr Bourke how you have worked for us, but we did not need this testimony to confirm our belief in the kindness of your heart and your desire to aid us.

Dr Anster, "with the absent aspect of a man of learning," was an early friend, and in later years a very agreeable neighbour, to Ferguson. He had a cultivated wife and charming daughters, and a pleasant and hospitable home. Many agreeable evenings were passed there, and the Anster family were frequent and welcome guests when Ferguson, as a married man, could offer his friends musical parties, dances, and other social enjoyments in his own house. It is generally understood that the most poetic translation of Goethe's masterpiece would never have been given to the world but for the energy and devotion of Miss Anster. Her father wrote on scraps of paper, and it was her labour as amanuensis that evolved order and sequence out of the chaos of his literary workshop.

Although Ferguson wrote much in prose, yet it is as a poet that he hoped to be remembered. His earliest compositions were in verse. "Light and Darkness," produced at a very early age, shows traces of the influence of Shelley on the writer's mind. It deals somewhat ambitiously with "Chaos and Eternal Night," and was not included by its author in the volume of his works collected in 1864. It appeared in 'Blackwood' in 1832, after he had made his mark by the "Forging of the Anchor." The originality, vigour of expression, and imaginative glow of this latter poem are marvellous, when it is remembered that when it appeared Ferguson was only in his twenty‑second year. The "Forging of the Anchor" has found its way into many anthologies, has been published with illustrations by Messrs Cassell & Co. in 1883, and some of its stanzas set to music by Sterndale Bennett and performed at a Norwich Festival.

"Captain Bey," a humorous ditty, also belongs to this early date, and was not republished by its author. But some lively prose writings which appeared in 'Blackwood' in May 1837 and May 1838 have been again and again reprinted in 'Tales from Blackwood.'

"The Involuntary Experimentalist" narrates in a minute and matter-of-fact way the supposed scientific observations of an imaginary sufferer who is described as having fallen into a vat in a distillery during a great conflagration which actually occurred at the time in Dublin. "Father Tom and the Pope; or, A Night at the Vatican," is a humorous *skit*, suggested by a controversial encounter on a Dublin platform between Father Tom Maguire, a well-known priest of that day, and Mr Pope, a clergyman of the Church of Ireland, champions respectively of their opposing faiths.

Sir W. R. Hamilton, in a letter to Professor De Morgan, asks the mathematician—

Did you ever read in 'Blackwood' the article entitled "Father Tom and the Pope; or, A Night at the Vatican"? If so, you cannot have enjoyed it as I have done, who am an Irishman. . . . What I invite you to do is, to tell me *which* was the Protestant and which the Papist. If you had ever spent, as I once did, a night—the richest night of my life— with *Father Tom*, you could decide at once.

To these polemical contests Ferguson was carried, somewhat against his inclinations, by two lady friends, desirous of his conversion to Roman Catholicism. Mrs Fitz-Simon and Miss Mary O'Mara would take no denial, and in courtesy he felt himself bound to obey their behest, and take care of them at these stormy meetings. The married lady was the eldest daughter of O'Connell, and wife of Christopher Fitz-Simon of Glancullen, Clerk of the Hanaper. She was an accomplished and charming woman, most engaging in manner. She is said to have had more of her father's genius than any of his children. To the close of her life she was a frequent guest in Ferguson's house, as he and his wife were also at Glancullen while the agreeable and hospitable circle remained unbroken. Christopher Fitz-Simon was a genial and kind-hearted host, and in their mountain home, surrounded by their large family, there was ever a welcome for friends and relatives, and count-less attractions to draw them thither. Miss O'Mara, a connection of the Fitz-Simons, was a brilliant and witty lady of the old school. She as well as others of the household were quite as much French as Irish, both in language and manner and mode of life. In the penal days Roman Catholic families of their social rank were frequently educated abroad, so great and galling were their disabilities at home. Mr Fitz-Simon's father — who had landed property in the county of Wicklow as well as among the Dublin mountains — when riding with other gentlemen of position to meet the High Sheriff of the county on some state occasion, was mounted on a very fine horse. One of the party admired the animal and asked its value. Its rider stated that he had bred it himself, and valued it at £200. The Protestant —so-called gentleman—drew from his purse a five-pound note, handed it to Mr Fitz-Simon, and said, "You are a Papist, and are not entitled to have a horse exceeding five pounds in value: that animal is mine." Such was the law in the penal days. It is not surprising that its owner in disgust left Ireland. His son, the husband of O'Connell's daughter, only returned to his native land and his property after Catholic Emancipation had been won by the Liberator in 1829. Having thus suffered for their religion, it is needless to say that the family were devotedly attached to their Church, and did all in their power to bring others to the same way of thinking. After the publication of "Father Tom and the Pope," Mrs Fitz-Simon doubtless looked on her friend Ferguson as hopeless, and solaced herself with the plea of "invincible ignorance." However that may be, she remained throughout life a true and affectionate friend, and wrote occasional poetry to and of him, of which the following adaptation of "John Anderson, my Jo," may serve as a specimen :—

"Sam Ferguson, my friend Sam, when you I first did know,
My locks were like the berry brown, that now are like the snow ;
I was not very old then, *you* some years younger still,—
Both climbing up the sunny side of Life's steep toilsome hill.

Sam Ferguson, my friend Sam, in calm and windy weather
We've wandered many a pleasant day among the mountain
    heather ;
But the pleasantest of all were those when you had by your side
The gentle, good, and gifted one you chose out for your bride !

Sam Ferguson, my friend Sam, since then I've learned to know
How fleeting is the happiness bestowed on us below !
But I raise my thoughts with fervid faith and trembling hope on
    high,
And pray that SHE, and *you*, and I, may meet there when we die !"

Nothing can be more at variance with the truth than the idea entertained by some that poets are unpractical men, incompetent to deal with the facts of daily life. They *are* poets by the predominant gift of imaginative insight. So Shakespeare tells us, and few will dispute the statement—

> "And, as imagination bodies forth
>   The forms of things unknown, the poet's pen
>   Turns them to shapes, and gives to airy nothing
>   A local habitation and a name."

But is not the man of science, the discoverer, the inventor of each practical appliance of knowledge, of necessity possessed of the same gift ? He, too, must in mental vision body forth the forms of things unknown before he can turn them to shapes for the furtherance of human progress. In his many-sided mind Ferguson afforded an instance in point. He was throughout life practical. Even when discussing contemporary poets in an article on the 'Dublin Penny Journal' ('Dublin University Magazine,' January 1840), in which he desires to express his "admiration —any less strong expression would not convey our meaning"—of poems contributed to the Journal by Sir Aubrey de Vere, the Rev. James Wills, and James Clarence Mangan, he thus emphasises the essential value of fact :—

In reviewing the whole progress and prospects of Irish literature, there is no event to which we would be disposed to attach so much importance as an effectual revival of that taste for *facts* which prevailed in the times of Ware, of Davis, and of Ussher. It is a most prejudicial error to suppose that matter of fact, however the term may have been abused, is necessarily dry or uninteresting; on the contrary, there can be no true romance, no real poetry, nothing, in a word, that will effectually touch either the heart or the imagination, that has not its foundation in experience of existing facts, or in knowledge of facts that have existed in times past. . . .

It is this enlarging of our portion of space, of time, of feeling, that is the true source of all intellectual pleasure. In poetry we extend the bounds of our feelings and imagination; the minor drama widens the circle by embracing new varieties of individual character; the historical drama and the epos, in addition to this, make other centuries and distant generations our own; science, to crown all, charters us the denizens of other worlds,—and all this doubling and trebling, and infinite multiplying of the shares of time, and space, and feeling, originally placed at our disposal, is the result of the observation and recording of facts. . . .

What we have to do with, and that to which these observations properly point, is the recovery of the mislaid, but not lost, records of the acts, and opinions, and condition of our ancestors—the disinterring and bringing back to the light of intellectual day the already recorded *facts*, by which the people of Ireland will be able to *live back*, in the land they live *in*, with as ample and as interesting a field of retrospective enjoyment as any of the nations around us.

Two papers on Robert Burns appeared in the 'University,' January and March 1845. Ferguson thoroughly appreciated the genius of the Scottish bard, with whose dialect he was familiar. Throughout his life he could repeat, and keenly enjoy, the poetry of

> " Him who walked in glory and in joy,
> Following his plough along the mountain-side ";

and he dwells on it in his review with contagious enthusiasm.

Burns asks for no classical recollections, no associations of learning; enough for him to have been blest with the happiness of feeling Nature—enough for him to have experienced the sweetness of love, the glow of patriotism, the aspirations after fame.   No man whose breast has ever owned a spark of poetic feeling can read this exposition of Burns's youthful raptures without being thrilled to the soul with keen delight :—

> "I saw thee seek the sounding shore,
>   Delighted with the dashing roar ;
> Or, when the North his fleecy store
>   Drove through the sky,
> I saw grim Nature's visage hoar
>   Struck thy young eye.
>
> Or, when the deep green-mantled earth
> Warm cherished every floweret's birth,
> And joy and music pouring forth
>   In every grove,
> *I saw thee eye the general mirth*
>   *With boundless love.*
>
> .   .   .   .   .
>
> To give my counsels all in one,
> Thy tuneful flame still careful fan :
> *Preserve the dignity of man*
>   *With soul erect,*
> *And trust the universal plan*
>   *Will all protect.*
>
> .   .   .   .   .
>
> Then never murmur nor repine ;
> Strive in thine humble sphere to shine ;
> And trust me, not Potosi's mine,
>   Nor king's regard,
> Can give a bliss o'ermatching thine,
>   A rustic bard."

In these delightful stanzas, rising and culminating as they proceed, until, towards the conclusion, they attain a pitch of beauty as lofty, perhaps, as any other poet has ever risen to in the English language, Burns rapidly sweeps away all the gloomy impressions made by his earlier reflections—the atmosphere grows clear around us—the walls of the spense spread and widen—the roof springs aloft—and, when at last the Muse binds the holly round his beaming brow, we see before us, instead of the weary and careworn thresher, eaten up with indigence and self-censure, the poet, conscious of the dignity of his office, rich in the rewards of enthusiasm, and radiant with the light of pride and joy.

During the same year, 1845, Ferguson wrote, with full appreciation of its high quality, of the poetry of Elizabeth Barrett Browning, and noticed Leigh Hunt's and the Rev. J. Wills's poetical works. He likewise contributed other articles to the ' University' and ' Blackwood,' the most important of which were those spoken of by O'Donovan in the letter already cited. In an autobiographical fragment he wrote in later years of this period of his life :—

My call to the Bar in 1838 withdrew me from these agreeable literary pursuits for some years ; but in 1845 an occasion arose for my appearing once more as a contributor to the ' University' in a letter addressed to Mr Hallam on a subject needing acquirements of a somewhat rare kind at that time in Ireland. The new Houses of Parliament had then been built, and it had been proposed to decorate them with effigies of the most prominent defenders of the national liberties. These, it was thought, would be best selected for the House of Lords from amongst the Barons whose names appear as witnesses to Magna Charta. The number of signatories exceeding the number of niches to be filled, the Committee, of which the Prince Consort was chairman, and Mr Hallam secretary, undertook the office of selection. The feeling towards Ireland embodied in that first form of the æsthetic movement initiated amongst us under these auspices, may be judged of by the fact that one of the most prominent of the signatories, Henry de Londres, Archbishop of Dublin, was excluded, and his place given to John, Bishop of Gloucester, on the frankly avowed ground that being but an Irish Prelate he had no business there. I dealt very quickly with the right of the Committee, which I denied, to "villipend" the Queen's Irish subjects in a matter of commemoration affecting the whole United Kingdom. And from records and authentic history, chiefly drawn from the pages of Prynne and Rymer, I showed that while De Londres had been one of the signatories to this instrument, he had not been signatory to, but, on the contrary, had stood alone in protesting against, another charter executed by King John, and to which every man of the number preferred before him had given the sanction of his hand and seal, to his and their eternal dishonour—namely, the infamous deed of grant of England to the Pope, and acceptance back of the premises as feudatories of the See of Rome. Not only had De Londres with tears of indignation refused so to alien the liberties of his country, but, when all England lay under interdict, he had been the only cleric of Episcopal rank found manly enough to continue religious ministrations to his flock. Numerous writs and King's letters drawn from forgotten repositaries testified to his eminence as an administrator and public servant. My expostulation wound up with a bold demand for a reconsideration of the report of the Committee, and the admission of De Londres to his rightful place in the foremost rank of the defenders of British independence.

Mr Hallam, in a letter to the 'University' in reply, made the least lame excuse he could for the blunder, and De Londres' effigy was elevated to its niche where it now stands, first on the right hand entering the House of Lords.

This was a triumph of which Ferguson was proud, the more so that Sir Robert Peel, in an autograph letter, had stated that there were " great difficulties in the way of carrying the suggestion into effect."

Ferguson's literary work had a wider range than Ireland and her politics. His imagination travelled far afield, though his heart, untravelled, fondly turned to home. His contributions to the 'University' in

1849 included a poem on Hungary, a review of 'Fergusson on Fortification,' a notice of Bastiat's 'Popular Fallacies,' and a paper on Physical Geography, " The Air," November 1849.   From this, as it gives evidence of his " sense of Nature's bonnie scenes," and his pious reverence for the God of Nature, a few passages will be given :—

Man's place on the earth—the scene of all the manifestations of life, animal and vegetable—seems to lie in a wonderfully narrow compass, when we compare the thin envelope of air to which our existence is limited with the bulk of the earth on the one hand, or with the abysses of space on the other. . . .

But confined in bodily presence though he is within these boundaries, man darts his intellect into the worlds beyond, weighs his own planet against the sun and planets of the external abyss, calculates the law which prescribes their motions and periods, and of the wandering host of heaven makes guides and sentinels for his own paths over the desert and the oceans.   .   .   .

There is no capacity for ideas of magnitude and grandeur in our nature which the aspect of the mountains actually seen by us does not fill.   .   .   .

Small therefore, relatively to the great world of the *Cosmos*, as the objects and phenomena may be which are transacted immediately around us, they are infinitely great and majestic to us, who, in truth, can comprehend nothing greater, however we may argue that there are things to which the greatest of these are little in comparison.   The delight which we feel in participating in Humboldt's emotions, when he stands to contemplate the falls of the Orinoco, or the cone of Chimborazo, is a complete pleasure, not to be added to by anything in its kind.   Coleridge's hymn in the vale of Chamouni fills all our capacity for the adoration of God in His works, and leaves us nothing to desire in additional height for the mountain, expansion for the vault of heaven, or rapidity or force for " Arve and Arveiron fiercely glad."

It is, however, the characteristic of knowledge, that the more we know the greater delight we have in perceiving so much more to be unknown; and they are the Newtons and Humboldts of the world, who, in the evenings of lives of philosophic toil and triumph, can best bow themselves with Job before the demands of the Divine interlocutor; or, with hearts of understanding, extol the praises of the God of Nature, in the language of that oldest and best philosophy spoken by the Psalmist: "O all ye works of the Lord, bless ye the Lord; praise Him, and magnify Him for ever!"

Perhaps Ferguson's acquaintance with natural history may have originated in his friendship with the late Professor Edward Forbes, F.R.S., born in 1815, who died in 1854. Professor Forbes was an ardent student of natural history. His 'History of British Star-fishes,' his 'Geological and Palæontological Map of the British Isles,' and his 'Distribution of Marine Life,' added to his high reputation, and in 1841 he was attached to a scientific expedition sent to Asia Minor. In the following letter to Ferguson, Professor Forbes urges him to take up the subject, and review the 'Travels in Lycia,' in which the work of the expedition is detailed:—

Your picture of Ireland is a very sad one, and I fear too true. My duties will oblige me before this month is out to be a spectator of the sad scene, out of which, sad as it is, I trust good is predestined to grow. Ireland will rise phœnix-like from the ashes of its dead. A fearful regeneration, truly.

Thanks for the article on Thomas Davis. It chimes in completely with my own sentiments, and I rejoice to see justice done him in a quarter whence justice is doubly grateful.

The not sending of the 'Travels in Lycia' to the 'University' was an oversight. I had ordered it to be sent, and when

I went to my publisher on Saturday he believed it had been, but found, on looking, that he was in error! I should like much to see you take up the subject in the 'University.' The book is simply a mass of facts, but facts pregnant with curious considerations. In writing it we have abstained from the poetry of the subject, however tempted. By the by, if you do write, give your countryman Graves justice for his services in promoting discovery in the Levant. His merits have been lost sight of by all the reviewers.

Among Ferguson's early friends were two of his fellow-townsmen, Sir Joseph Napier of the North-East Bar, who afterwards became Lord Chancellor of Ireland, and Sir James Emerson Tennent, who, after the passing of the Reform Bill of 1832, represented Belfast in Parliament. Mr Emerson, who took the name of Tennent on the death of his wife's father, and was made a Baronet, was a D.L. of Fermanagh, in which his house of Tempo—said to have been the " Castle Rackrent " of Miss Edgeworth's novel — is situated. He wrote much on Eastern topics; the most important of his works, ' The History of Modern Greece from its Conquest by the Romans, B.C. 146, to the Present Time,' was published in 1830. Tennent was Secretary to the India Board, Colonial Secretary and Lieutenant-Governor of Ceylon, and at a later period Permanent Secretary to the Board of Trade. He died in 1869. On receiving the first collected poems of his early friend in 1864, Sir J. Emerson Tennent wrote from London :—

I have read your charming volume with great relish and satisfaction. Along with your natural perception of poetic beauty, and your rare power of harmonious versification, you display a knowledge of Irish history and tradition which to me is as instructive as it is agreeable.   It was most kind in you to think of me, and I acknowledge it *gratefully*.

66 WARWICK SQUARE, PIMLICO,
LONDON, *Feb.* 10, 1867.

MY DEAR FERGUSON,—Gout, which pinned me to my bed, has been the cause of long delay in acknowledging your kind letter and congratulations.   I *value* the latter, because I know they are and must be sincere.   Few people now living have known me so long as you have, and the great regret in that long vista that we have lived so little together and met so rarely.   It would be a great gratification to me if this summer I could induce you to come and see us at Tempo?   Is there a likelihood of it?   We shall be there for many months, say July till November, and you can choose and name your own time.   Do say yes.—Faithfully yours,

J. EMERSON TENNENT.

Among the correspondence preserved by Ferguson are letters written between 1840 and 1848 by an intimate friend, Dr Robert Gordon of Bellaghy, who died at the early age of forty-two at Castle Dawson. It is a one-sided correspondence, for none of Ferguson's letters are extant, with the exception of an imperfect copy of a rhymed epistle, a New Year's greeting for 1845. What is noteworthy in the friendship of these young men is its high moral and intellectual tone.

MY DEAR FERGUSON,—God bless you for your good letter. . . . O to be earnest, truthful, loving—so would the world grow green again (and it will) and "the wilderness blossom as the rose." . . .

You rejoice me, I speak seriously, by saying you are doing.

To be and *to do*. O Ferguson, these little words contain the sum of all man's destiny. . . . Write to me and take counsel with me, for yours is to me a voice crying in the wilderness. . . .

I think there are men—nay, I know—now living and breathing, who are equal to great things; you, I know, are one: many more I know: to say I am, would be perhaps vain, but I would cut my throat with my own lancet if I did not feel other thew and brawn in me, than appears in the "water-flies" who usurp the pools and eddies of the modern mind. Moreover, I know there is a desire and an appetite and a capacity far and wide for brawnier food than the meagre dishes of the day can offer. . . .

There is always wanting the one something to make this life the Perfect Paradise it never was intended to be. Action in the field we feel suited to our powers, and moral purity, a strong will, and a clear conscience, are the sword and shield against the universal enemy. With them pitiful, physical privations are lighter than vanity; without them, wealth and power and all the baubles of the round world are jingling burdens, and grievous as life itself. . . . Were it but to eat pulse and drink water—what is that?—a wholesome diet making the blood run cool and pure, with cheerful mornings and sound sleeping nights. . . .

How we fret ourselves for shams and figs' ends, when some quiet hour we shall close our eyes and sleep and awake to them no more, but to the great Real Scene, the home and bourne of every noble thought and every precious feeling, the world where thought and feeling shall be action, faith lost in substance, hope in fruition ! . . .

I know not why, but I would fain press all this on you; for you are strong, and I would have you strike some stroke that will reverberate adown the vista of Time. Will you, Ferguson ?   R. H. GORDON.

The mountain men would strike you. A singular intelligence is in the faces of this variety of men—a very peculiar and patriarchal look distinguishes the elders. But they are so simple, and yet so intelligent. When the day comes that will un-bigot and educate our natives, they will rank high in the mental scale : there is a pensiveness, almost touching, in some of their faces and voices, and a certain gentleness of manner indicative of a high degree of feeling and sensibility. I know not how or where it is, but you don't find it in the Scotch. They are hearty and have feelings very deep too, but there is a rude, big-footed, corn-trampling air about their very crutches which is quite absent from the native Irish. . . . You ought to write a great book, and no man will be more delighted to read it than yours heartily,   R. H. GORDON.

BELLAGHY, *25th December* 1842.

MY DEAR FERGUSON,—I am extremely obliged by your kind letter and for your trouble ; as we said at school, " I'll do as much for you again if it comes my way." . . .

The man who thinks and feels for *party*, call him as you may, may be a good man, a conscientious man, and willing to serve his country or his kind, but he is only a pioneer and subordinate instrument in the service of mankind. He has not arrived at that region in intellect which lies beyond local and temporary feelings and enmities and interests, from which above the smoke and noise he can overlook a wider horizon and think and see for man.

In all party the evil is and has been, that men having strong convictions, feelings, and views, regard them as *alone* not only truth, but *the* truth and the *whole* truth ; whereas others have their convictions equally forcible and *incomplete*. A man should never write history who cannot realise to himself the motives, beliefs, and views of opposing interests, and give the like credit to all who sincerely act in accordance with them. . . .

We claim to live in an era of great civilisation and enlighten-ment. I don't believe it. We live in an age of great physical science ; but that is a low sphere of human advancement. We act to each other now as they did of old,—not so well often. What weapons we have are used for wounding and bruising our brethren. We pursue the same wretched idiotcy, which, overlooking Love, the only principle of social weal, splits us into *units* and forbids *unity*. . . .

We have not yet arrived at Godhead! We have no prerogative of infallible opinion! another man's opinion, sincerity, and earnest inquiry, being equal, are as well entitled to respect as mine; and the wisest and best have differed. . . .

How are you? Gaussen, whom I saw a few days ago, tells me you are very busy and working hard. Will you turn out a "lawyer" exclusively? If most to your desire, I rejoice at it. But do not forsake the green old ways; do not belie the spirit within you.—Yours heartily, R. H. GORDON.

It was the grey dawn before the sun got up. I stood on a hill, and every bough and blade of grass about was jewelled with the frost, and stood as if carved in gems and marble, so beautiful and still. The hills lay against the sober sky and dreamed. I saw a [stretch] of ground round which ran an old fringe of trees—it had some nameless affinity with my heart, and O but the tears were sweet that ran as I gazed on it! Then uprose the sun among unspeakable glories, the unswerving God, to run his race, and long lines of gold and pearl laced the Eastern hill, and all Loch Beg was one sunrise fountain, and I stood as it were transfixed. . . .

A philosopher you'll try to be—a poet. Why, a poet is a philosopher, and a true poet the truest philosopher, and a true poet is Samuel Ferguson. Do, do, and gain blessings. Nature is wise: who loves her loves and finds exceeding wisdom, light from the fount of light, through no devious channel polluting the stream it carries. Be a poet again to us. Shake off old Drowsihead, put out your arms and wrestle as you did ere now,

> " When hard by icy lands
> You wrestled with the sea-serpent upon Cerulean Sands."

A music that has rung in my ears for many a year is there. Once more, " Ring out, ye crystal spheres," as Daddy Milton saith. You are older now, more thoughtful, wiser: so deeper still, like green-sea floods, the ocean stream will roll.

When I came back from days and hours spent where I have leisure to feel and think, I repel our pseudo-society, and know sadly how human soul and substance is here wasted, worn, lost, to *no end.*

O dream (if a dream) of holy living, once the paradise of my heart.   O Hope, O Faith, O Love, leave me never, however, crucified : there is a home for ye.   Bear me witness, blue sky and sunset, and quivering tree and speaking stream, and the green dell, and thou Imperial Ocean, and thou life within me answering to them, No surrender.

To-day—glorious of all glorious days—I strode forth at 7 A.M. into the Spring, ankle-deep in May flowers, green grass, violets, daisies, and amaranthine whins, under such a firmament as gives the earnest of Heaven to the eye and the substance to the heart. . . .

To-day I got my fingers on the fine poesy you sent me long while ago, dear Ferguson, and of which I have since heard or seen naught.   Why?   I read it with great delight : I know your hand better now (for allow me to say you are a little illegible), and, by the soul of Amanda, you wrong her to let it lie unseen.   In that piece there is much ore of feeling, imagination, and harmony.   Sing, sing, for I have forgotten the trick of it.   Yet did I oft " organ " to the vales and hills.

> " The round earth everywhere
> With crowded beauty burns ;
> Still from the earth or air
> Or ocean's secret urns
> The disappointed soul unsatisfied returns, "

and I feel it now as I did not before.   That stanza is worthy to stand beside some lines which have long fascinated me, an old sea-rover and sea-dreamer—

> " Or haply, in a cove
> Shell-strewn, and consecrate of old to some Undine's love,
> To find the long-haired mermaidens, or hard by icy lands
> To wrestle with the sea-serpent upon Cerulean Sands. "

Beautiful ! softly lapsing as a summer wave.

"Amanda," which Dr Gordon so much admired, seems never to have been completed. A few imperfect stanzas are alone forthcoming. These are in the metre of Shelley's "Skylark." The exquisite music of this and others among Shelley's lyrics delighted Ferguson's ear. These he would often recite with expression and feeling.

The poet seems to have been a wise adviser of his friend, and encouraged him to literary effort. Gordon published in the 'University' occasional essays under the signature *Coul Goppagh*.

My dear Ferguson [wrote Dr Gordon in 1844],—I had yours to-day. It is a pleasant thing for you that you can keep a mind so interested about those things. I freely confess that all old visions of Ireland have faded from me, and the philosophy of my present state is that all men and all nations have the same ultimate and perpetual interests. The destiny of Ireland is one with that of the future world, and material progress following quick on intellectual and moral improvement will abolish national exclusiveness and make mankind one. The greatness of England is a mechanical and material force ; commerce and the competition of wealth supports a bulky Power ; . . . but the narrow sphere of old Greece, and in a period nearer the infancy of history, can well compare in its productions of intellect with the long story of England. Plato, Archimedes, Euclid, Homer, Xenophon, Aristophanes, Sophocles, Lucian, Æschylus, Socrates, Demosthenes, are names which for ever can challenge the future, and few of whom we can equal. Shakespeare only can cry quits. Newton was a great man, but Euclid was before him, and the originator of the very means by which he thought. Remember Homer, and Socrates, and Plato—ah ! no—national emulation is but as schoolboys in a class. Man was born for the universe. . . .

I do not by any means undervalue your efforts or ideas. I only say that enthusiasm has faded from my mind. . . . *N'importe.* How are you? Why do you "lie on chares" and write illegible lines? What is your article you call, as well as I can read, the "Welshmen of Tuesday" ["The Welshmen of Tyrawley"] in last 'University'?

As already observed, the only letter of Ferguson's which is forthcoming is "A New Year's Epistle to Robert Gordon, M.D.," dated the 1st of January 1845 :—

> A Guid New Year I wish you, Gordon.
> Hech ! Forty-four has been a hard ane,
> And on our backs has laid its burden
>   Wi' pressure fell ;
> Still, hae we had our orra guerdon
>   Within oursel',
>
> To haud us up, and reconcile us
> To that sour Madam Fortune's malice,
> Wha o' the Muse has aye been jalous
>   Sin' auld blind Homer
> Beggit his bit amang Greek billies
>   Revolting from her.

To these high-spirited young men, too proud and right-minded to marry for money, and not able themselves as yet to make an adequate income, nor "gleg eneuch to see the wife to choose," though their hearts yearned for a home and the sweet voices of wife and children within it, nothing remained but to content themselves with "The Muse," who, though bringing little of "warld's gear," demanded no expenditure of cash. It is pleasant to record that within a few years both Gordon and Ferguson had found "the wife to choose," and to a modest extent the ways and means for simple house-keeping. Dr Gordon married, in 1847, Miss Hill of Bellaghy Castle. A young family sprang up around the wedded pair—alas! too early severed by death. Mrs Gordon, whose health was fragile, died, to the inexpressible grief of her husband, in her twenty-seventh year. He followed her to the grave when only forty-two. Ferguson married in 1848. His union was a long and happy one, though Providence withheld from the wedded pair the precious gift of children.

> And bonny bairns to grace the country,
> You canna hae thae sweet wee gentry
> Without the wifie and the pantry
>   And hoose and a'.
> That, reckonin' up my sorra' inventry,
>   Won't suit ava'.

Under these untoward circumstances nothing remains for the poor young men but to console themselves with the poetic gift which each of them was conscious of possessing. The Muse is thus apostrophised :—

> Oh bonny hizzie, braw and gaucie,
> Thou minds me I was young and saucy
> When first adown Life's sunny causey
>   I steppèd fain,
> And thocht nane ither like the lassie
>   I thocht my ain.

> Thou was the Muse, my bonny thing,
> That first did plume my fancy's wing,

And raised me frae the miry ring
        O' warldly wark,
Up through the heaven o sang to spring
        Like ony lark.

And bonny were the lays we sung
In thae bricht days when I was young,
And thou wast fairer than the tongue
        O' mortal man,
Or tongue 'twixt lips o' angels hung,
        Could speak or ken.

Yet yesterday it seems nae mair,
And thou was blyther than the air,
And all around thee fresh and fair
        And kind and sweet :
The vara grun' did greener wear
        Beneath thy feet.

Since then I hae seen mony a face,
And mony a form o' youthfu' grace,
And mony a lassie high in place
        Weel to gang wi';
But, och, I never saw the lass
        I looed like thee !

But—odsake, man !—I maunna bore ye
Wi' this auld everlastin' story
O' birkies wha frae dreams o' glory
        And love awauken,
To find themselves by Chrônus hoary
        Half owertauken—

And, hech ! eld's hirplin' up belyve,
For, for a lad that's yet to wive,
And born intil this bizzin' hive
        In aughteen-ten,
This aughteen hunner forty-five
        Is brawly *ben*.

And in thae five-and-thritty seasons
O' greetin's, mitchins, learnin' lessons,
Dreamin's and coortin's, tears and kissin's,
      Fechts and sae forth,
What hae I dune, bune ither messens,
      O' guid on Earth?

Whaur's a' the visions I hae painted?
Whaur's a' the braw sangs I hae chaunted?
Whaur's a' the bletherin' hopes I've vaunted
      O' fame and gain?
And whaur's the precious life I've panted
      Awa' in vain?

Fient haet o' me can either tell
Or guess; but here I am mysel',
As fou o' sperit as a *stell*,
      And gleg as ever
At head-wark or the random spell
      O' clishmaclaver.

And, aiblins though at times mislasted
Wi' grievous thochts o' moments wasted,
Auld frien's estranged, and green hopes blasted,
      As birkies will
When the mid line o' life they've crossed it,
      I'm happy still.

For ilka day I'm growin' stranger
To speak my mind in love or anger;
And, hech! ere it be muckle langer,
      You'll see appearin'
Some offerin's o' nae cauld haranguer
      Put out for Erin.

Lord, for ae day o' service done her!
Lord, for ane hour's sunlight upon her!

> Here, Fortune, tak' warld's wealth and honour,
>   You're no' my debtor,
> Let me but rive ae link asunder
>   O' Erin's fetter!
>
> Let me but help to shape the sentence
> Will put the pith o' independence,
> O' self-respect in self-acquaintance,
>   And manly pride
> Intil auld Eber-Scot's descendants—
>   Take a' beside!
>
> Let me but help to get the truth
> Set fast in ilka brother's mouth,
> Whatever accents, north or south,
>   His tongue may use,
> And there's ambition, riches, youth,
>   Take which you choose!
>
> But dinna, dinna take my frien's;
> And spare me still my dreams at e'ens,
> And sense o' Nature's bonny scenes,
>   And a' above;
> Leave me, at least, if no' the means,
>   The thocht o' love!
>
> Adieu, my boy: the nicht's worn through,
> Aurora's beasts are yokit-to,
> And through the pouthery mornin' dew
>   Come, micherin' keen:
> We'll see what stalls they'll hae in view
>   Next New-Year's e'en.

The latest letter from Dr Gordon is a lively one, written not to Ferguson but to a lady—a mutual friend —probably in 1845. It was sent to Ferguson, at that time about to visit the Continent in search of health.

Gordon's half-real, half-assumed contempt for his friend's antiquarian tastes, expressed in this note, recalls Burns's description of Captain Grose :—

> "He has a fouth o' auld nic-nackets ;
> Rusty airn caps and jinglin' jackets,
> Wad haud the Lothians three in tackets
> A towmont guid ;
> And parritch-pats, and auld saut-backets,
> Before the Flood."

DEAR MISS MACDOWELL,—I thought you might be glad to hear I had a letter from Stokes, who says there is nothing seriously the matter with Ferguson. He says he was much cut up, or cut *down* (if you choose), by an attack of inflammation, and it was thought desirable for him to rest from his labours.

M'Glashan tells me that same Sam is writing "a book "—I only trust it is not about Henri de Londres or Ireland in any shape ; he is regularly mad about that, and would fall down and worship the head of a staff like Jacob (was it Jacob?) if it were only dug out of some dirty Irish bog. Ireland is a downright bore among a circle of very wise fellows in Dublin, of whom Ferguson is not the least sinner, who pay their vows to a lot of old spikes and rusty nails and the lids of decayed teapots, which they stick in a dark place called R. I. Academy, and adore under the titles of spears, arrowheads, and trusty shields. God convert them.—Very truly yours,   R. H. GORDON.

A sympathetic notice of Dr Gordon appeared at the time of his death in a Belfast journal. It ran as follows :—

"Died, on the 16th of this month, Dr Robert Gordon, of Castle Dawson."

Such is the brief obituary of one of Nature's noblemen—upright, single-hearted as a child—of the truest and most unvarying philanthropy. He was rich, indeed, in the possessions of the heart and intellect; but, as to material wealth, his was the scant reward which awaits the hard-worked, toil-worn, but greatly-useful country practitioner in medicine and surgery. His days were spent in the exercise of his noble profession, in acts of charity that never tired, and were only limited by his means. Dr Gordon's attainments were of a very high order. . . . He placed the deepest and most reverend trust in the wise and good providence of God, and it may be truly said that his life was one long exercise of re-ligious faith carried into righteous action. . . .

Many years later, in May 1884, a pleasant surprise awaited Ferguson. Two numbers of the 'Irish Monthly' Magazine were anonymously sent to him containing critical papers, signed O., on his poetry. The articles were most gratifying to the poet and to his wife; and each, independently of the other, surmised that the appreciative critic would prove to be Mr Justice O'Hagan. When it was ascertained that this conjecture was right, Ferguson wrote to his friend :—

3^d May '84.

MY DEAR O'HAGAN,—I am gratified and comforted in a high degree at finding myself so appreciated by such a mind. My wife too is delightfully surprised, for she, I imagine, had come to look on " Congal " as more than half forgotten. This notice gives her renewed, and gives me continuing and strengthened, confidence in the belief that a national literature is still possible for our country, and that I, even I, have had a hand in laying its foundation.

<blockquote>
Lord, for ae day o' service done her !
Lord, for ane hour's sunlight upon her !
Here, Fortune, tak' warld's wealth and honour,
    I'm no' your debtor,
Let me but rive ae link asunder
    O' Erin's fetter !
</blockquote>

> Let me but help to shape the sentence
> That puts the pith o' independence,
> O' self-respect in self-acquaintance,
>   And manly pride
> Intil auld Eber-Scot's descendants—
>   Take a' beside!

So sang I, my dear O'Hagan, in our native Doric, forty years ago, and the song still finds a faithful echo in my heart.

A year later, in reply to a letter from Judge O'Hagan, Ferguson wrote :—

Some time ago you asked me where some lines came from which I had introduced into a note to you. They belong to a rhymed epistle, in our own dear North Country dialect, which, forty years ago, I addressed to my late friend Gordon of Bellaghy. We were very intimate, and the topics such as would not then have been proper for the public eye. At the end of the half-century—if anybody then should care to know what were the dreams of two young Protestant Irishmen, or at least of one of them—these objections would hold no longer. It is not probable that I shall see the fiftieth anniversary of the rhymes ; and I present them to you, who, please God, will do so, in order that you may then make any use of them that you may judge right.

To this the Judge replied as follows :—

MY DEAR FERGUSON,—I receive from you with cordial thanks the copy of verses addressed to your friend forty years ago, of which I so much admired the stanza you cited in a letter to me some time ago. Whether I shall live to see their fiftieth birthday is indeed more than doubtful, but I accept the trust notwithstanding. They are in the true vein of the Muse of Coila.

> "Kyle Stewart I could hae bragged wide
>   For sic a pair."

I trust you yourself will be spared for the ten years, or a great part of them, to add much to what you have already done. Θάρσει!

Your silent inestimable services to Ireland will be remembered in the days of light and peace which, in spite of everything, I cannot but believe God has in store for us.

A year or two after the death of his friend, Judge O'Hagan republished his articles in the 'Irish Monthly' in a small volume entitled 'The Poetry of Sir Samuel Ferguson' (M. H. Gill & Son, 1887), and asked Lady Ferguson's consent to include in his preface a few stanzas from the "Epistle to Robert Gordon." This poem she had never seen, and the Judge sent it for her perusal. Before returning the MS. she copied, so far as she could decipher, the very illegible writing. The Northern or Scottish dialect added to the difficulty, the words being unfamiliar. Unfortunately the MS. so copied was lost.

MY DEAR LADY FERGUSON [wrote Judge O'Hagan on the 15th August 1887],—I am very sorry for the accident which happened to your dear husband's MS. poem. It was very fortunate that you had taken a copy, which is substantially complete.

How well I remember that last scene to which you so touchingly refer! Thanks for Faber's poem, which I really did not know, and which is very beautiful. I will keep it along with your husband's letter which you have returned to me.

God be merciful to him (if you will not be offended at a Catholic's prayer for his friend) and comfort you.—Believe me, dear Lady Ferguson, ever faithfully yours,

JOHN O'HAGAN.

In his preface to the volume published in 1887 Judge O'Hagan observed :—

Little more than a year ago, Sir Samuel Ferguson entrusted

to me a poem never yet published. It was an address to a dear friend ·of his, Dr Robert Gordon, now long dead. It is written in the style and language of Burns—a dialect as native to many Ulstermen as to the inhabitants of Ayrshire itself. . . . On the very day before his death I recalled it to his recollection, and he pressed my hand in token how well he remembered it. I was under the impression that he had given me full discretion as to its publication after his death ; but, on reperusal of the letter by which it was accompanied, I find that he wished the publication to be delayed till further on in the century. However, with the full assent of Lady Ferguson, I can give three stanzas, indicating how strongly the pulse of his heart beat for Ireland, and how keen was his desire to serve her.

In literature, as well as at the Bar, John O'Hagan attained a high position. He was placed at the head of the Land Commission with the rank of Judge, and in poetry he achieved a marked success by his spirited version of the "Song of Roland," translated from the *Langue d'oïl* in 1880. "It is at least something to aid in making known to the English public a poem of such genuine beauty and poetic power," wrote the Judge— "a poem which the world of letters in France and Germany are almost agreed in admitting to a high place among the masterpieces of human genius." The lay is said to have been chanted on the field of Hastings (or Senlac) by the. bard Taillefer, who accompanied William of Normandy on his invasion of England in 1066.

The "Song of Roland," and an essay on Joan of Arc, were later works of their gifted author; but his early contributions to the 'Nation,' in which paper he wrote under the pseudonym of Sliabh Cuilinn, are perhaps more familiarly known by his countrymen. "Dear Land" and "The old old Story" touch the Irish heart.   His generous appreciation of other writers was a marked characteristic of his fine nature.

My dear Lady Ferguson [he wrote on Christmas Day 1888],—My wife and I join with all our hearts in wishing you all the blessings of this holy time, though thoughts of sorrow and bereavement must be inevitably mingled.

We thank you very much for your gift of your husband's book on St Patrick, which is admirably brought out, and for the kind inscription you have placed in it.   I have been re-reading the poems with great interest, and reading the notes, which are a wonderfully clear and condensed summary of all that has been gathered and conjectured upon a subject so difficult in an historical point of view.

He married Frances, youngest daughter of Thomas, Lord O'Hagan, a wife worthy of him, and to whom he was devotedly attached.   He died Nov. 12, 1889, honoured, beloved, and lamented; a man of fine culture, of generous sentiments, of warm heart, pious and patriotic.

CHAPTER VI.

1843-1868.

HIS FRIENDS AMONG THE "YOUNG IRELAND" PARTY.

> "O Heaven! that one might read the book of fate,
> And see the revolution of the times
> Make mountains level, and the continent
> (Weary of solid firmness) melt itself
> Into the sea, and, other times, to see
> The beachy girdle of the ocean
> Too wide for Neptune's hips; how chances mock,
> And changes fill the cup of alteration
> With divers liquors! O, if this were seen,
> The happiest youth,—viewing his progress through,
> What perils past, what crosses to ensue,—
> Would shut the book, and sit him down and die."
> —SHAKESPEARE.

ON New Year's Day 1845, Ferguson, as we have seen, forwarded his poetic "Epistle" to Dr Gordon. It concluded more hopefully as regards the future than might have been expected from the self-reproachful tone of some of its stanzas. Its author had evidently resolved to work with redoubled energy. Ferguson certainly laboured indefatigably throughout the spring and summer of 1845; for, in addition to his professional work, he wrote in 'Blackwood,' and contributed numerous articles to the 'University Magazine.' Towards the autumn a great sorrow came to him in the unexpected death from fever of Thomas Davis, on the 16th of September in that year.

Sir Charles Gavan Duffy, in his Memoir of Davis, his 'Young Ireland,' and his 'Four Years of Irish History, 1845-1849,' has paid a high tribute to the friend whose career had been thus prematurely closed :—

The Whig and Conservative press did him generous justice. They recognised in him a man unbiassed by personal ambition, and untainted by the rancour of faction, who loved but never flattered his countrymen ; and who, still in the very prime of manhood, was regarded not only with affection and confidence, but with veneration, by his associates. . . .

It was a fact of great significance that the Irish names best known to the empire and to Europe in the peaceful professions, Stokes and Anster, Kane and Burton, were found on the committee to commemorate Davis's career by a public statue. They did not, any of them, share his political aims, but assuredly no one who had held and preached the same opinions since the Union would have been selected by them for such a distinction. And Ferguson, who lay on a bed of sickness when Davis died, impatient that for the moment he could take no part in public, asked me to come to him, that he might ease his heart by expressing his sense of what we had lost. He read me fragments of a poem written under these circumstances, the most Celtic in structure and spirit of all the elegies laid on the tomb of Davis. The last verse sounded like a prophecy ; it was at any rate a powerful incentive to take up our task anew.

The poem here referred to, "Thomas Davis: an Elegy —1845," appeared in the 'University' two years later:

I walked through Ballinderry in the Spring-time,
    When the bud was on the tree ;
And I said, in every fresh-ploughed field beholding
    The sowers striding free,

Scattering broadcast forth the corn in golden plenty
    On the quick seed-clasping soil,
"Even such this day among the fresh stirred hearts of Erin,
    Thomas Davis, is thy toil!"

I sat by Ballyshannon in the Summer,
    And saw the salmon leap;
And I said, as I beheld the gallant creatures
    Spring glittering from the deep,
Through the spray and through the prone heaps cleaving on-
      ward
    To the calm clear streams above,
"So leap'st thou to thy native founts of freedom, Thomas
      Davis,
    In the brightness of thy strength and love."

I stood on Derrybawn in the Autumn,
    And I heard the eagle call,
With a clangorous cry of wrath and lamentation
    That filled the wide mountain hall,
O'er the bare deserted place of his plundered eyrie;
    And I said, as he screamed and soared,
"So callest thou, thou wrathful-soaring Thomas Davis,
    For a nation's rights restored!"

And, alas! to think but now, and thou art lying,
    Dear Davis, dead at thy mother's knee;
And I, no mother near, on my own sick-bed,
    That face on earth shall never see:
I may lie and try to feel that I am not dreaming,
    I may lie and try to say "Thy will be done";
But a hundred such as I will never comfort Erin
    For the loss of the noble son!

Young husbandman of Erin's fruitful seed-time,
    In the fresh track of Danger's plough,
Who will walk the heavy-toilsome, perilous furrow,
    Girt with Freedom's seed-sheets, now?

Who will banish, with the wholesome crop of knowledge,
    The flaunting weed and the bitter thorn,
Now that thou thyself art but a seed for hopeful planting,
    Against the Resurrection Morn?

Young salmon of the flood-tide of freedom
    That swells round Erin's shore,
Thou wilt leap against the proud opposing torrents
    Of·bigotry and hate no more!
Drawn downward by their prone, material instinct,
    Let them thunder on their rocks and foam:
Thou hast sped, aspiring soul, to founts beyond their raging,
    Where troubled waters never come.

But I grieve not, eagle of the empty eyrie,
    That thy wrathful cry is still;
And that the songs alone of peaceful mourners
    Are heard to-day on Erin's hill.
Better far if brothers' war be destined for us
    (God avert that horrid day, I pray),
That ere our hands are stained in contest fratricidal
    That warm heart should be cold in clay.

But my trust is strong in God, who made us brothers,
    That He will not suffer those right hands,
Which thou hast joined in holier ties than wedlock,
    To draw opposing brands:
Oh, many a tuneful tongue that thou mad'st vocal
    Should be cold and silent then;
And songless once again should often-widowed Erin   .
    Mourn the loss of her brave young men!

Oh, brave young men, my love, my pride, my promise,
    'Tis on you my hopes are set,
In manliness, in kindliness, in virtue,
    To make Erin a nation yet;
Self-respecting, self-relying, self-advancing,
    In union or in severance, free and strong;
And if God grant this, then, under God, to Thomas Davis,
    Let the greater praise belong!

This poem, with its peculiar and characteristically Irish rhythm, has, for one who never saw Davis, associations not to be forgotten. It brings before that " inward eye which is the bliss of solitude " many lovely pictures: a morning in spring, the larks singing overhead, while the husbandman, tramping through the furrows, scatters the precious seed: a summer evening by the falls of the Erne; the setting sun about to dip into the Atlantic, penetrating with its beams the clear copious waterfall gliding smoothly over its ledge of rock, while the salmon spring aloft gloriously touched to still richer and more vivid colour: the mountain solitudes of Glendaloch, an autumnal storm swaying to and fro its tallest trees; the eyrie bereft of its eaglets, and the wrathful cry of the parent birds re-echoing from the hills around.

> " They that stand high have many blasts to shake them,
>   And if they fall they dash themselves to pieces."

It was not surprising that, when, on the first day that Ferguson dined at her father's table, and she, his destined wife, though she knew it not, learned in casual conversation that he was the author of the admired poem, he should forthwith have a new attraction in her eyes, and that she should feel herself free to praise the lyric which had haunted her memory before she knew the writer.

The ' Spirit of the Nation,' a handsome volume given by Davis, with an inscription in his free and vigorous handwriting—preserved by Ferguson " as a memorial of friendship and an incitement to love of song and country "—has on its fly-leaf the following sonnet from Ferguson's pen :—

TO THE GENTLEMEN OF THE 'NATION' NEWSPAPER,
ON THEIR BEING CENSURED FOR WANT OF SECTARIAN ZEAL.

> Brave youths, though much I prize the Union Act,
>   And warm resent some marchings for Repeal
>   Which I deemed menaces, no less I feel
> How loving-brave, with manly minds erect,
> Ye toil to give the people self-respect ;
>   And therefore now, when in fanatic zeal
>   Bigots assail you, that the stake and wheel
> Ye love not, I would cheer you so attacked.
> Discussion follows Freedom : difference
>   Of thought is Thought's prerogative : let none,
> Even hating Discord, wish Opinion hence :
>   But let him who would see all hates undone,
>   And Erin's day of happier note begun,
> With you teach national self-confidence.

The present writer was intimate with many of Davis's friends, who all bore testimony to his noble and disinterested character; and she admired and loved the accomplished and beautiful girl who was about to be married to him when death interposed.

Many years afterwards, writing of the Ireland of 1845, Ferguson observed :—

Other young spirits came into contact with me at this period in the outer circles of Dublin society such as it was forty years ago, destined afterwards to be poetically famous as the singers of the 'Nation,' and politically conspicuous as the leaders of the party known as "Young Ireland."   .   .   .
Here was the spark destined to kindle the souls of these fiery young men who thought to guide the destinies of Ireland by

making her ballads. Davis and Duffy, Mangan and MacCarthy, and later on Thomas D'Arcy M'Gee, the greatest poet of them all, burst into song, and while I followed up the endeavour to elevate the romance of Irish history into the realm of legitimate history in the "Hibernian Nights' Entertainments" in the 'University,' awoke the whole country to high and noble aspirations through their fine enthusiasm in the 'Spirit of the Nation.' I did not at that time sympathise in their political views, but applied myself steadily to the prosecution of my original design to keep the Irish subject up to a higher standard, and to discountenance that helotism which has so often vulgarised the efforts of Irish writers, seeking to gain the ephemeral applause of the magazines and newspapers of the metropolis.

Duffy in his 'Memoirs of Thomas Davis' quotes a letter of Ferguson to his friend, which is thus introduced :—

Samuel Ferguson, who was gradually approaching nearer to Davis in opinion, acknowledged a copy of the quarto 'Spirit of the Nation' in terms which must have been very gratifying to his correspondent.

"Accept my best thanks for the 'Spirit of the Nation,' which I will preserve as a memorial of your friendship and an incitement to my own love of song and country. When I see how we are all working, I hope soon to see Dublin at least a better Edinburgh. A sentence of Bishop Parry's, addressed to Sir James Ware, is perpetually sounding in my ears : '*Diu nimis obscurata tenebris delituit Hibernia, nec sibi prorsus cognita nec aliis. Diu satis eclipsim passa est, rudis admodum et indigesta ; filiisque suis peregrina, se ne fuisse hucusque dubitavit. Tandem vero, tanquam vero ad augendam Caroli gloriam, calamique vestri in honorem reservata, novos induit spiritus formamque venustiorem.*' The contribution to Charles's or Victoria's glory is a secondary matter. These efforts are serviceable to ourselves, and will redound to the service of those who come after us. God knows our self-reliance is all in all ; and, with the growing self-reliance of the young men, wider prospects may open. In the meantime I am satisfied with the progress we are making, even though it aim at no greater result than literary and intellectual supremacy."

From the portrait-sketch of Thomas Davis which appeared in the 'Dublin University Magazine,' February 1847, extracts are given, not only for the light thrown on the character of the man so suddenly called away in his prime of manhood, but also on the views and opinions of his biographer :—

The year 1843 was a remarkable epoch in the social history of Ireland. The Repeal agitation, up to that time, had been conducted as a means merely to an end. . . .

But, in the latter end of 1842, the agitation assumed quite a new character; and it became apparent that Repeal had been taken up by men who, believing the measure desirable and practicable, agitated it for its own sake, and were evidently ready to make great sacrifices for its attainment. The first-fruits of sincerity were respect and attention. . . .

It very soon became apparent that the new teachers were also earnestly bent on teaching them generosity and justice, and on stimulating in all their hearts the noble sentiments of self-respect and self-reliance, without which the liberty they demanded would amount to no more than a licence to put themselves into the hands of new masters. They also observed, concurrently with these manifestations of a lofty and sincere morality, in the organ through which the leaders of the new school expressed themselves, a surprising development of intellectual vigour in almost all departments of literature, and a keen and generous appreciation of genius, from whatever quarter it might present itself. Inquiring to whom they were indebted for changes so salutary, they learned that the leader of these brave and sincere spirits was Mr Thomas Davis, a Protestant, a man of spirit, and an ardent lover of Ireland, like themselves, and who differed from them mainly in believing that it would be for the advantage of Ireland to separate from the Imperial Union, while they believed that it would be inestimably more for her advantage to remain with and participate in the power and freedom of our great and free united Empire. And when, in addition to these grounds of sympathy, they found Mr Davis himself a gentleman of most unaffected charming deportment, a poet, a judge and lover of art and elegant literature, exceedingly well read, and of a character and temper the most genial and humane, it is not surprising that affection for the individual supervened on respect for the politician, and admiration for the man of genius, and that he speedily became the friend and favourite of the *élite* of the intellectual world of Dublin. . . .

The young mind of the country starting as from a trance— or from that fabulous spell which our legends tell us keeps Finn's mighty youths asleep under the green hills, waiting the advent of an Irish Arthur—came out from its forgotten recesses strong and eager for any achievement to which he might desire to guide it. Song, the instinctive expression of generous emotion, gave the first indication of reviving power. He had sounded the intellectual *réveillé* of a whole people; and, if they had slept long, they awoke refreshed. . . .

To amend the habits, as he had awakened the mental energies, of his countrymen, was now the noble duty of Mr Davis. To teach them justice, manliness, and reliance on themselves; to supplant vanity on the one hand, and servility on the other, by a just self-appreciation and proper pride; to make them sensible that nothing could be had without labour, and nothing enjoyed without prudence; to teach them to scorn the baseness of foul play, and that if they were to fight, they should fight like men and soldiers, — these were the lessons which he now appeared a chosen instrument for imparting; and in fulfilling this mission, while Providence left him with us, he did toil with faithful and unremitting energy. . . .

Multitudes of well-bred and worthy Irish people, who probably had never heard the name of Mr Davis, found themselves spared the pain of listening to old prerogative contempts against the country, on the stage, in the press, and even in the thoughtless conventionalisms of society.   But it needs a long and continuous effort to remove an old-rooted prejudice, especially when it flatters the self-love of those who entertain it ; and we have still to regret the frequent provocations to resentment which the self-respecting gentry of this part of the Empire receive from the insolence and folly of writers in the metropolitan press.   We would beg leave to remind these gentlemen, that every petulance which they indulge in against the Irish generally, is resented by those on whose continual good temper and forbearance the maintenance of the integrity of the Empire depends.   For if the Conservative gentry of Ireland thought fit to invite their friends and tenants to meet them at a new Dungannon, there is no power in Britain which could prevent the severance of the two islands. And there can be no more fatal delusion than to suppose that Irish gentlemen, because they do not profess the Roman Catholic religion, are insensible to contemptuous language against their country, or that they are disposed to rest satisfied under any social inferiority whatever to the rest of the United Kingdom.   By their loyalty and forbearance, as well as by their intellectual culture, they are entitled to the enjoyment of every social advantage that the Union can afford ; and were the depression of a temporary calamity gone by, we are sanguine enough to believe that the social losses caused by the Union would be retrieved, or at least in some measure compensated, by the habitual presence of the Royal Court amongst them.   Mr Davis was by birth a gentleman, and both in feeling and in judgment opposed to all designs for destroying the legitimate power of the gentry. He would, if he could, have won them to his opinion, and through their agency have sought "to mould, to multiply, and to consolidate" the brute mass beneath ; but he never lent himself to the anarchical project of exterminating because he could not influence them, and of reducing all society to one base level of peasants.   Had he lived to witness the servile war made on the Irish gentry since his death, none who knew him can doubt that he would now be found a generous volunteer in their camp ; and we do not say but that their camp would be stronger, and their cause more hopeful, if they had received even a further infusion of Mr Davis's characteristic national spirit, which, as we have said, operated with many of his Conservative friends as one of the strongest inducements to seek his personal acquaintance. . . .

We have dwelt on his services in imparting a spirit of independence and manliness to the people; in calling forth their genius, and enlarging their intelligence. But his influence, on the other hand, among the upper classes was even more remarkable, and perhaps not less useful. Their great fault had been a want of just national sentiment. . . .

We hear now, in all directions, a better and more hopeful tone among those to whom society must be indebted for its improvements; and, in their unceasing attachment to pursuits connected with the past and present condition of their country, see new, and heaven knows, at the present time most needful, guarantees for the stability of the whole social edifice. . . .

Another field of patriotic exertion in which Mr Davis did great service was that of our national history and antiquities, which had long, indeed, been diligently and well cultivated before his time, and still is; but, as we have said, by labourers comparatively unknown to the people. No one could be more aware of the value of the materials which these worthy men and great scholars had accumulated; for in their stores he had himself found much of the information which he communicated with so happy an effect to the people,—an obligation which he always gratefully acknowledged and worthily repaid; for he ever used his information with a view to availing himself of the tastes which it excited, to promote further accumulations. In this way he rendered great service to our Archæological Society, and justly participates in the honour due to it and to the Royal Irish Academy, of having made Dublin by far the foremost school for original research in Western European archæology. . . .

But the great essential service which Mr Davis personally effected among the better classes of his countrymen was the diffusion of amicable feelings among those who differed in politics and religion. Wherever he went, he was surrounded by an atmosphere of goodwill, which hostile politicians could not enter without mutually conceding "the right to differ," and agreeing to do something together for the common good.

Sir Charles Gavan Duffy, the survivor and historian of "Young Ireland," was himself a poet, as well as a politician and a man of undoubted genius. In Australia, where he spent his manhood, he attained high position, and when he retired from public life at an advanced age he revisited Ireland, and wrote that portion of her history in which he was himself an actor. He has described with a graphic pen his fellow-workers on the staff of the ' Nation,' and in the extracts given from the Cahirmoyle Correspondence—letters written chiefly by himself and Mr William Smith O'Brien—has thrown a vivid light on the events which preceded and followed the rising of 1848.

At the time of Sir Samuel Ferguson's death he wrote from his home in the Maritime Alps to Lady Ferguson :—

August 14, 1886.

May I offer you my sincere sympathies ? Your bereavement is the bereavement of Ireland ; she has lost the most distinguished man of letters among the few who remained true to her—who was Irish in every fibre of his nature and every flower of his intellect. As the country grows in strength their love and knowledge of him will grow, and his example and teachings will help, I trust, to cure the national sins which keep us weak and poor.

I trust you will write his life. It is a task which will console you, because it is the greatest service you can now do for one who had to thank you for so many.

Mr W. Smith O'Brien, descended from the chiefs of Thomond, was a gentleman of birth and position. He was brother to the late Lord Inchiquin, and was a man of fine presence and of chivalrous honour. Feeling that his words had incited the people to open rebellion, he considered himself bound to share its perils. Though his property and life were at stake, and he knew the hopelessness of a rising followed by a handful of undisciplined peasants only, O'Brien did not shirk the responsibility. He went "out" in the summer of 1848, and a few days later surrendered to the authorities. "His purpose was to die—there being no longer, he believed, any other honourable issue from his unhappy position." O'Brien was tried, and convicted of high treason. The wise clemency of the Crown changed the sentence to exile. After a brief captivity in Australia he obtained his freedom on parole. He refused to escape when sympathisers who had fitted out a vessel for the purpose afforded him an opportunity. Others availed themselves of the chance, but O'Brien remained a prisoner on parole. When her Majesty Queen Victoria graciously granted a pardon to the political exiles, O'Brien returned a free man to his native land and his home at Cahirmoyle. He lived for some years, honoured and respected even by those most opposed to him in politics, "for his word was sacred, his friendships steadfast, and his life unstained by guile or selfishness."

Thomas D'Arcy M'Gee, among the "Young Ireland" writers, was in Ferguson's judgment "the greatest poet of them all." When a mere boy, M'Gee became a writer for the 'Nation,' and has been portrayed by Duffy, who knew him well, as he was in early life:—

If we were to begin our work anew, I would rather have his help than any man's of all our confederates. I said he could do more things like a master than the best amongst us since Thomas Davis [wrote Duffy of M'Gee]. Since he has been in America, I have watched his career, and one thing it has never wanted—a fixed devotion to Irish interests. . . . His face was odd, and might even be considered ugly; but it had what is better than comeliness in the face of a man—plasticity and expression. . . . It changed suddenly to correspond with the sentiment he was about to utter, and, in addressing a public audience, helped wonderfully the purpose of his speech.

Ferguson—who met M'Gee first at the Irish Council in 1847—was similarly impressed by the animation and fire which lighted up the face of the "inspired" youth, and by M'Gee's power as an orator.

A few citations from Duffy's works bear testimony to M'Gee's subsequent career:—

M'Gee "in wide sweep of imagination, in the persistency and variety of his labour," in everything but in qualities where Davis was unapproachable, closely resembled the master who was lost. . . .

In Canada he became the leader of the Irish immigrants, a great parliamentary orator, and one of the founders of the New Dominion. As the Minister of a free State he developed unexpected powers, and was universally recognised as a gifted and original statesman. Success did not wean him from his early labours. While he was a Canadian politician he produced a careful and sympathetic history of Ireland, and constantly wrote verses as racy of the Irish soil as while he was a contributor to the 'Nation.'

No man ever had distinguished services more grudgingly admitted.   He had gifts which placed him on a level with the best of his associates, and for years he applied them exclusively to the service of Ireland.   As a poet he was not second to Davis, as an orator he possessed powers rarer and higher than Meagher's—persuasion, imagination, humour, and spontaneity.

So spoke Sir C. G. Duffy of M'Gee, who has left a record of his attachment to the comrade whom he was not to meet again on earth, in the following lines :—

> "Oh ! for one week amid the emerald fields,
>   Where the Avoca sings the song of Moore ;
>   Oh ! for the odour the brown heather yields,
>   To glad the pilgrim's heart in Glenmalure !
>
>   Yet is there still what meeting could not give,
>   A joy most suited of all joys to last ;
>   For ever in fair memory there must live
>   The bright, unclouded picture of the past.
>
>   Old friend ! the years wear on, and many cares
>   And many sorrows both of us have known ;
>   Time for us both a quiet couch prepares—
>   A couch like Jacob's, pillowed with a stone.
>
>   And oh ! when thus we sleep, may we behold
>   The angelic ladder of the patriarch's dream ;
>   And may my feet upon its rungs of gold
>   Yours follow, as of old by hill and stream."

From the time of his arrival in America M'Gee sedulously devoted himself to the task of benefiting the condition of his countrymen in that continent.

He wrote, he lectured, he inaugurated the Buffalo Convention. This committee of gentlemen took into their consideration the circumstances of their countrymen in the States, and proposed many valuable projects for their amelioration. The Irish emigrant whose previous training generally fitted him for agricultural work, was urged to settle in the Western States as landowner and tiller of the soil, and to avoid the demoralising influences of the great cities. Warnings such as those uttered in the columns of the 'American Celt' were needed, and in its editor the Irish in America found a friend ever interested in their moral and social wellbeing. M'Gee urged on them the duty of self-respect, thrift, sobriety, and the value of education, while he aided largely in the establishment of night-schools. He recommended to the Irish to be the subservient tools of no political party, but to be honest citizens of the country which afforded them a home and a career. His teaching on this point was alike given to the Irish in the States and in Canada. He narrated for his countrymen the story "of the dear ancestral island," and his history is written in a spirit of truth and candour, and displays great literary merit. "No one is more sensible of its many deficiencies than I am," wrote M'Gee, "and if I live I hope to remedy some of them; but it certainly was to me a labour of love, and I believe it is the first time that a history of Ireland has ever been commenced and completed by a person situated as I was at the time, in a distant colony, after his personal connection with the mother country might be supposed to have closed for ever." Other books on the subject may have more value for their reference to authorities, but as a readable and interesting narrative M'Gee's work has never been surpassed.

During these years—from 1850 to 1857—M'Gee's political views became largely modified. What he had seen of the corruption and tyranny of mob-rule in the United States revolted him; and democracy ceased to be, in his eyes, the highest form of government. The revolutionary ardour so natural to a young mind had yielded to a riper experience of life. This change of opinion was altogether uninfluenced by personal considerations. It was natural, gradual, disinterested, entirely the result of conviction, openly and frankly avowed. But in M'Gee's case it was cruelly misrepresented. It made him unpopular in the States; it made him still more unpopular with a certain section of his countrymen, who loudly accused him of betraying the national cause. He who loved Ireland with a passion which never through life abated, who watched and laboured for her honour, whose pen was occupied with her story, whose muse was inspired by the memory of her greatness, her history, and her scenery —who, in the practical business of life, never omitted an opportunity of using pen and speech in strenuous endeavour to raise and elevate Irishmen and Irishwomen,—this man was called a traitor to the Irish cause! His life paid the penalty of this delusion, when in after-years he became a mark for the bullet of the

Fenian assassin.   But Time remedies injustice and misconceptions.   His memory, despite a passing obloquy, survives in the hearts of his countrymen even as he himself passionately desired.

AM I REMEMBERED.

I.

"Am I remembered in Erin—
    I charge you, speak me true—
Has my name a sound, a meaning,
    In the scenes my boyhood knew?
Does the heart of the Mother ever
    Recall her exile's name?
For to be forgot in Erin
    And on earth is all the same.

II.

Oh Mother! Mother Erin!
    Many sons your age hath seen—
Many gifted, constant lovers
    Since your mantle first was green.
Then how may I hope to cherish
    The dream that I could be
In your crowded memory numbered
    With that palm-crowned companie?

III.

Yet faint and far, my Mother,
    As the hope shines on my sight,
I cannot choose but watch it
    Till my eyes have lost their light;
For never among your brightest,
    And never among your best,
Was heart more true to Erin
    Than beats within my breast."

After he had settled in Montreal, M'Gee wrote thus of his earlier career :—

My native disposition is towards reverence for things old, and veneration for the landmarks of the past. But when I saw in Ireland the people perish of famine at the rate of five thousand souls per day; when I saw children and women, as well as able-bodied men, perishing for food under the richest Government within the most powerful empire of the world, I rebelled against the pampered State Church — I rebelled against the bankrupt aristocracy—I rebelled against Lord John Russell, who sacrificed two millions of the Irish people to the interests of the corn-buyers of Liverpool. At the age of twenty-two I threw myself into a struggle—a rash and ill-guided struggle I admit—against that wretched condition. I do not defend the course then taken; I only state the cause of that disaffection, which was not directed against the Government, but against the misgovernment, of that day. Those evils in Ireland have been to a great extent remedied, but those only who personally saw them in their worst stages can be fair judges of the disgust and resistance they were calculated to create. I lent my feeble resistance to that system, and though I do not defend the course taken, I plead the motive and intention to have been both honest and well-meaning.

M'Gee has expressed his "profound respect for the great scholars" who had worked for Ireland, among whom he included Ferguson, the "mighty master who voiced our grief o'er Davis lost." On his election as member of the Royal Irish Academy in 1864, which he considered the highest honour he could receive, he wrote to his friend, who had proposed him as member :—

I have to thank you for this, which I do most heartily. It is, I repeat, almost the only honour left in Ireland—except the honour of having such friends and backers as those whose names I find among my proposers, which is, indeed, the higher honour of the two. You will find enclosed a P.O. order for the subscription, which you were so kind as to pay for me in advance.

I beg you to thank in the warmest terms the Very Rev. President, the Rev. Dr Reeves, Mr Gilbert, and Mr Hardinge, for me. MacCarthy, as an old personal friend, I must write to myself.

DEAR MRS FERGUSON [M'Gee wrote from Ottawa, June 16, 1866],—The recollection of your kind Cardigan letter has been haunting me like a remorse for months past. Why I did not lay the ghost was that I intended to do so, with immense effect, in full pontificals, on some day which I could dedicate to you and that duty. For I do not like short letters shot across the Atlantic. It is all very well for the two ends of Dublin to correspond in half note-sheets, for the writers may meet any day and talk it out; but a letter launched on the Atlantic should not be a cock-boat of a letter, but of a size and strength equal to the voyage.

Now having laid down my theory, like most other dogmatisers, I am going forthwith to depart from it, by not writing a three-decker. Truth to tell, what with Fenians and Confederation, the Department of Agriculture and the Provincial Parliament of Canada, one is kept so distracted, if not actually busy, as to be unfit for anything else.

In the first place, I write to beg your forgiveness for my ingratitude; in the next, to ask how Ferguson is, and what he is doing. If you can find heart for the first, and time to tell me all about the latter, I promise faithfully, when our border troubles are over, and the union of these Provinces achieved, which I look upon as a certain entry in the calendar of 1867, I promise then and thereafter to be a punctual correspondent.

Will you also tell me, if you know, whether any one is interested in putting up some memento to O'Donovan and Curry in Glasnevin. If a couple of Celtic crosses are to be erected, I should feel it my duty to contribute my mite to each or to either. I know no one in Dublin except MacCarthy of whom I could ask the question, and he, poor fellow, I suppose lives out of the world.

I have from time to time sent Ferguson some papers and pamphlets, which I hope he has received. They were intended apologies for autographs and reminders of the existence of one who would be very truly sorry to slip from either your or his memory, and who is, and always must be, very truly yours and his, T. D. M'GEE.

I have just had a gratifying letter from my Lady Governess (Lady Monck), now in your neighbourhood : if you meet her, mark her,—she is one of my best friends.

The Hon. T. D. M'Gee became Minister of Agriculture in Canada, and also of Emigration. He was President of the Executive Council, and assisted to frame the Federal Union which constituted the Dominion of Canada. In 1865, and again in 1867, he was its accredited Commissioner to Europe, and in these years he was for a short time the guest of Ferguson.

While in England in 1865 he was struck by the apathy of its politicians and their indifference to the question of the Federation of the provinces in Canada, and thus expressed himself :—

Really what brought these four gentlemen here (my respected colleagues, &c., &c.) seemed in so fair a way of being overlooked, that I began to feel uneasy, and I am not up till this moment reassured as to their errand and its results. The government of this world, at which certain old hands are playing like, as it were, a game of whist, is so wretchedly carried on, that the fate of one-third of the American continent, and a population equal to Scotland, hardly excites an emotion of interest or surprise.   To me, in all humility be it said, this is simply shocking, and I cannot tell you by what Carthusian self-denial I am able to keep down my ever-ready tendency to blaspheme against the great men of England, as I am told these are.   .   .   .

While in Ireland, in a public speech he said as follows :—

If I have avoided for two or three years much speaking in public on the subject of Ireland, even in a literary or historical sense, I do not admit that I can be fairly charged in consequence with being either a sordid or cold-hearted Irishman. . . .

I will only say further, on the subject of Ireland, that I claim the right to love and serve her, and her sons in Canada, in my own way, which is not by either approval or connivance with enterprises my reason condemns as futile in their conception, and my heart rejects as criminal in their consequences. . . .

As for us who dwell in Canada, I may say finally, that in no other way can we better serve Ireland than by burying out of sight our old feuds and old factions—in mitigating our ancient hereditary enmities—in proving ourselves good subjects of a good Government, and wise trustees of the equal rights we enjoy here, civil and religious.   The best argument we can make for Ireland is, to enable friendly observers at home to say,—See how well Irishmen get on together in Canada.   There they have equal civil and religious rights ; there they cheerfully obey just laws, and are ready to die for the rights they enjoy, and the country that is so governed.

M'Gee visited France in 1867, and wrote from Paris :—

71 AU CHAMPS ELYSÉES, PARIS,
March 29, 1867.

MY DEAR FERGUSON,—Here I am in character of Chief Canadian Commissioner to this "Exposition," and here I shall be all April! probably. I hope to face homeward early in May, making a flying. visit to Ireland, and sailing either from Cork or Derry as the time-table suits.

Who is to represent the R. I. Academy here? or, is there any likelihood of you and Mrs Ferguson coming over? The Exhibition itself will not be worth much till the 20th of April, and, indeed, it would have been better if it were not opened till the 1st of May. At present it is all litter and confusion. I got here on Tuesday last from Rome, which I saw for the first time. I am having the frescoes in St Isidore’s Chapel photographed, and the inscriptions there and in St Pietro in Montorio (where “the woman of the piercing wail” wept “so alone”) transcribed. Do you think the matter would make a paper fit for the Academy? and if I undertake to write one before I return, will you read it for me in due season? The topics are rather Roman and Ecclesiastical, but the names of Wadding, Colgan, and the fugitive Northern Earls are national as well as Church property. Tell me frankly, as I am sure you will, your judgment hereupon.

Would it be proper to ask you for a line of introduction to your Breton friend Villemarqué? Is he, or is he likely to be, in Paris? Does he *parley Anglaise*, as my French hardly carries me through *cafés* and railway carriages?

Give my best and most grateful remembrances to Mrs Ferguson, and Dr Todd when you see him, and believe me, my dear Ferguson, yours very truly, T. D. M‘GEE.

71 CHAMPS ELYSÉES, PARIS,
April 16, 1867.

MY DEAR FERGUSON,—Many thanks for your kind notes, with the two introductions. Miss O’Mara I have seen twice, and dined with on Sunday. She is really unequalled. I don’t think I ever met so fine a blending of Celticism, Catholicism, good sense, good-humour, and good taste. For making her acquaintance I am indebted to you, and we talked ourselves into familiarity by the use of your name.

The Vicomte de la Villemarqué is not in Paris, but is expected, so I hope to see him before I yet leave.

There being an election toward in Canada, under the new Confederate Constitution, I must shorten my stay here as much as possible. This will oblige me to leave for home about the first of May, when I hope to have three or four days in Dublin, and shall not forget your and Mrs Ferguson's kind invitation. Should I be able to make those days, you shall know a week in advance, and I will look forward with great interest to hearing those new lays which, since I last saw Ireland, you have evoked from the heart of the Celtic forest.—With very sincere regards to Mrs Ferguson, believe me yours always,   T. D. M'GEE.

After his return to Canada, M'Gee wrote as follows:—

For the first time in six months I got out last week. . . . I have been at death's door, but did not go in. On the contrary, I hope and trust I have got a new lease for some years more. I have done nothing the last few days but write Gaelic ballads, of which you shall have a sample or two shortly.

One of these was forwarded from Ottawa on St Patrick's Eve, with an intimation that by next post others should follow.

To-morrow, St Patrick's Day [he adds], I am to be dined here by certain leading citizens, Irish Protestants and Catholics, at which (as on every other occasion) I intend to say something on the always agreeable subject of our recent national literature. . . . I wish to heaven it was in my power to draw the minds of a few hundreds or thousands of the Irish on this side the sea to the duty and wisdom of encouraging native writers.

The speech alluded to in this correspondence was delivered at Ottawa on the 17th of March 1868. In it he thanked his hosts " for the opportunity afforded me of saying a word in season on behalf of that ancient and illustrious island, the mere mention of which, especially on the 17th of March, warms the heart of every Irishman."

In the following month—the 7th of April 1868, a few days before M'Gee had attained his forty-third year—he was shot by a Fenian as he was returning to his temporary home, at midnight, from the House of Representatives at Ottawa. Before leaving the House, he wrote and posted two letters—one of them addressed to the present writer. He had told her that 'The Irish before the Conquest,' which she had sent him, had stirred up all his rhyming faculties, and he sent as a sample a poem on St Patrick, soon to be followed by one on St Columba. A few stanzas from this, the last effort of his genius, will show how tenderly the exile's heart clung to his native land:—

IONA TO ERIN!

WHAT ST COLUMBA SAID TO THE BIRD FLOWN OVER FROM
IRELAND TO IONA.

I.

" Cling to my breast, my Irish bird,
　　Poor storm-tossed stranger, sore afraid !
How sadly is thy beauty blurred—
The wing whose hue was as the curd,
　　Rough as the sea-gull's pinion made !

II.

Lay close thy head, my Irish bird,
　　Upon this bosom, human still !
Nor fear the heart that still has stirred
To every tale of pity heard
　　From every shape of earthly ill.

III.

For you and I are exiles both—
  Rest you, wanderer, rest you here !
Soon fair winds shall waft you forth
Back to our own belovèd North—
  Would God I could go with you, dear !

.   .   .   .   .   .

XI.

Thou wilt return, my Irish bird—
  I, Columb, do foretell it thee ;
Would thou couldst speak as thou hast heard
To all I love, O happy bird !
  At home in Erin soon to be ! "

Canada accorded to him who had served her so faithfully a public funeral. It was a homage well merited, for M'Gee had worked strenuously and successfully to achieve the federation of her provinces. His execrable murder was an irreparable loss, not only to the Dominion of Canada, but also to his "dear ancestral island." He had attained that time of life when, in minds like his, experience ripens into wisdom. He had become a statesman, and took his place in the counsels of statesmen. What might he not have accomplished had life been prolonged, in the full maturity of his powers, not only for the empire, but also for Irishmen on both sides of the Atlantic !

CHAPTER VII.

1846.

A YEAR ON THE CONTINENT.

> "I cannot rest from travel : I will drink
> Life to the lees ; all times I have enjoy'd
> Greatly, have suffer'd greatly, both with those
> That loved me, and alone.
>
> .   .   .   .   .   .
>
> Much have I seen and known : cities of men
> And manners, climates, councils, governments,
> Myself not least, but honour'd of them all.
>
> .   .   .   .   .   .
>
> I am a part of all that I have met :
> Yet all experience is an arch wherethro'
> Gleams that untravell'd world, whose margin fades
> For ever and for ever when I move."
>
> —TENNYSON.

AT the time of Davis's decease Ferguson was seriously ill. Dr Stokes, his physician and friend, prescribed complete change of scene. This breakdown of health appears to have been the first of many attacks of illness from which he subsequently suffered.

A student, rarely taking exercise, a bookworm who, like Milton, " oft outwatched the Bear," must sooner or later pay the penalty. Ferguson recognises this, yet deliberately prefers to "strictly meditate the thankless Muse."

We sedentary men, I suppose, must all lay our accounts for these drawbacks on our other enjoyments [he writes to a friend]. You and I have both had our share of the pleasure that work which I continue to think patriotic confers on the labourer. If we had spent the same time in hunting, we would, I daresay, have fewer attacks of the gout and of the megrims, but we would not give up what we have done to escape from what we have suffered.

Years afterwards Ferguson, speaking of this period of his life—1845-46—observes,—

Soon after this, my state of health obliging me to give up professional work, I went abroad for a twelvemonth, and utilised my travels by a diligent examination of the museums, libraries, and architectural remains of the principal places where traces of the early Irish ecclesiastics might be found on the Continent. Nothing came of these observations at the time. In fact, the more I saw of these representatives of the learning of the *Insula Sacra* the less was I disposed to sympathise with them. The drawings and collections I brought back have only as yet yielded some architectural observations, including illustrations of a proximately perfect ecclesiastical round tower of the Irish type at Epinal, exhibited at the meeting of the British Association in 1857, and certain curiosities of symbolical sculpture in which the Deity is represented under animal forms, affording a key to much that has hitherto been regarded as the merely capricious fancy of the carver, communicated to the Royal Irish Academy within the last session [1877].

When Ferguson's project of a foreign tour became known to his friends, letters of introduction to distinguished *savants* on the Continent were freely offered. Among his papers are letters which apparently were not presented, and also many cards and notes of invitation, the results doubtless of those which had been delivered. Some of these bear distinguished names: Chateaubriand; Prosper Mérimée, Membre de l'Institut; M. L'Abbé Gañmo, Doyen de la Faculté de Théologie à la Sorbonne. Dwarkanauth Tagore, then residing in the French capital, urges Ferguson to accept his invitation, as affording "the only means of becoming acquainted with the friend of Sir James Murray."

The following introductions—one to the Archbishop of Rouen, and the second to the Abbé La Chaise— were given by the Rev. Dr Moriarty, then Vice-Rector of the College of Foreign Missions at Drumcondra near Dublin, and subsequently the wise, patriotic, and venerated Roman Catholic Bishop of Kerry :—

MONSEIGNEUR,—Monsieur Samuel Ferguson, membre de l'Académie royale Irlandaise et un des premiers hommes de lettres de notre pays, aura l'honneur de présenter cette lettre à votre Grandeur.

Monsieur Ferguson, quoique Protestant, a conçu la belle et Catholique pensée d'étudier l'action de l'ancienne Église d'Irlande sur la civilisation de l'Europe ; et dans cette vue il va visiter sur le Continent tous les monuments religieux érigés sous l'invocation des saints Irlandais, et fouler dans les vastes Bibliothèques de la France pour les monuments historiques de leurs travaux.

Ce projet sera pour votre Grandeur un indice du mouvement vers l'antiquité Catholique qui agite à présent les esprits les plus savans de ces royaumes. . . .

Dr Moriarty commended Ferguson to the good offices of the Abbé La Chaise :—

Bien cher Ami,—Je vous recommende très particulière-ment Mr Ferguson, membre de l'Académie Irlandaise, et publiciste très distingué. Le but de son voyage en France est des plus patriotiques; c'est pour étudier l'action de notre ancienne Église d'Irlande sur la civilisation Européenne. . . . Il désire surtout connaître les lieux et les églises dont les saints Irlandais sont patrons.

Sir Robert Kane wrote to Professor Liebig at Giessen as follows :—

My esteemed friend Mr Samuel Ferguson, who presents this letter to you, is travelling upon the Continent in order to carry out some historical and antiquarian investigations with which he is occupied. He is anxious for this purpose to examine the various libraries in Universities or elsewhere. Although his pursuits are not scientific, he is full of appreci-ation of all that is real progress in Science, and I am sure that should there be in your University Library books or manuscripts that could illustrate the subjects on which he is engaged, you will procure him access to them. Had you visited Ireland lately you would most probably have already known Mr Ferguson as one who has added most valuable contributions to our literature, and from whom we expect to receive important information as to the early history of our country.

Dr Romney Robinson gave his friend Ferguson some practical advice, and an introduction to the " Illustris-simo Cavaliere G. B. Amici " at Florence :—

My dear Ferguson,—My acquaintances on the Continent are few, and the only one with whom I became intimate is Amici at Florence, astronomer, botanist, optician, a perfect and real gentleman. To him I have given you the enclosed, which you may read. His son is a Professor at Pisa. Let me hear from you, when you can spare time. Two hints. If you are not gone from London, get a general passport from the Foreign

Office, and have it signed by the Ambassadors in London, especially the Prussian, Austrian, and Sardinian and French. It costs more, but, *experto crede*, the difference it makes abroad over Consular passes is immense.   2d, *Never* talk politics in Austria, Germany, or any part of Italy ; on that head remember Wotton's counsel to Milton, "Lingua stretta pensiere sciolti." God bless you, and (if, as I fear, you are not well) keep you safe and restore your strength.—Yours ever,

T. R. ROBINSON.

In this was the following enclosure :—

OBSERVATORY, ARMAGH,
Dec. 30, 1845.

MY DEAR FRIEND,—Permit me to introduce to you the bearer of this, Mr S. Ferguson, one whom I value highly.   He is rising rapidly at his profession, the Bar ; but has (in my estimation at least) achieved much higher distinction by being one of the first poets of my country, and one of its successful antiquaries, being a member of that section of our Royal Irish Academy's Council which is charged with such pursuits. To this let me add that he is a *gentleman*, and of political opinions like myself.

After all this you will easily guess that I entreat for him some of the kindness which you showed to me, and which was the secret charm that made Florence not merely the most delightful spot which I visited, but the one whose remembrance continues the most vivid in my mind.   May you long continue to adorn it is the hearty wish of your attached

T. R. ROBINSON.

Dr Petrie wrote to John Hogan, the Irish sculptor, then resident at Rome, to introduce Ferguson :—

You may be surprised, I am sure you will not be displeased, to receive a line from a friend and brother artist in the West— "our own native Isle of the Ocean."   The object of it is to introduce to you my valued friend Mr Samuel Ferguson, who visits Rome for purposes connected with our ancient History and Antiquities, as well as to gratify a love for the Fine Arts, which he adds to his many other valuable qualities. I am sure that his being an Irishman, and a distinguished one, would be a sufficient recommendation to your kind reception. But I shall, moreover, feel deeply grateful for any services or attentions which you may be pleased to show him.

Sir C. G. Duffy, in his 'Four Years of Irish History,' gives in the letter of a correspondent the impression Ferguson made on the writer, who saw him as he passed through London :—

One may catch in the London correspondence a glimpse of a man who has been dear to his countrymen since they came to understand the silent patriotism of his life—a life like Hudson's, with the larger scope and deeper insight which belong to a man of genius.

Sam Ferguson has been here on his way to the Continent. He spent about four hours with us on Sunday. Poor fellow, he looks very ill. What a terrible feeling of doubt and insecurity one gets about our true men. Rome, I trust, will bring him round—not to Romanism, but to health. He is going stocked with introductions to cardinals, legates, and other great dignitaries of the Church, who, I hope, for the honour of the religion, will treat him well. I never happened to meet Ferguson before, and I was excessively pleased with him, and, with all my previous opinion of him, was scarcely prepared to find him so very national. He is hopeful beyond measure for the country—says there is a strong manly intellect growing up in Ireland.

Ferguson's note-books—crowded with observations, extracts from MSS. taken in libraries, and sketches— afford material for an itinerary of his year on the Continent. To Round Towers a large sketch-book with chequed pages was devoted. He drew to scale: each square represented three feet; positions of doors, windows, &c., being carefully noted. Other note-books include studies of cathedrals, and churches dedicated to Irish saints. Their architecture, stained glass, and symbolic sculpture received special attention. Military fortifications, swords, and other weapons appear in his sketches. The condition of the people, their physique, the productions of the soil, and the landscapes through which he passed, were noted with an observant eye.

A letter written to his mother from Paris, February 13, 1846, tells of Ferguson's improved health and impressions of France so far :—

My dear Mother,—My health is now, I may say, quite re-established. During the first month of my tour the weather was very unpropitious, and nothing but the fortunate circumstance of my having a taste for books and antiquities could have reconciled me to the northern towns of France, in which I passed several weeks. I landed at Boulogne, where Napoleon made his preparations for the invasion of England; went thence to Montreuil, where you may remember Sterne in his 'Sentimental Journey' met with some adventures; thence to Arras, a great flourishing strongly-built city which formerly belonged to the Spaniards, and was defended by an Irish garrison in the service of the King of Spain, commanded by Owen Roe O'Neill, in 1640—just before O'Neill (who had been a colonel in the Spanish army) came to Ireland to take the command there. I then visited Douay, where they printed that well-known edition of the Bible, and where there is a great college for English priests. Thence I went to Amiens, famous for its great Cathedral, considered the finest specimen of Gothic architecture in France. It, as well as all other Gothic edifices I have seen, disappointed me. Gothic architecture is not the style of civilisation.

The way in which they construct these buildings is this: there is a great lofty vault in the centre, and arcades of less height at the sides, and the beauty of the buildings is thought to consist in making the supports which sustain the roof of this vault as slight as possible, so as to leave the upper part of the hall a sort of lantern of stained glass. If the walls alone had to sustain this weight, they would have to be made of great thickness and solidity, and the light effect could not be obtained. The plan they resort to, therefore, is this: they prop up these walls on the outside with what are called flying buttresses, or arches of stone spanning the external galleries on either side, so that in fact the roof is upheld not by the columns which one sees inside, but by these external props which are hidden from the sight by the stained glass of the windows. Thus an effect is produced on the mind which, being the result of a trick, is displeasing to me; for I like in architecture, as in everything else, to see what the result (whether it be a conclusion in an argument or an architectural effect in building) is supported by; and therefore I have conceived a degree of contempt for Gothic architecture, as not expressing the sincere sentiment which reasonable men ought to embody in their works, as well as cherish in their breasts. The flying buttresses, however, have a very beautiful appearance outside, especially round the eastern end of the churches, which are usually rounded. The little pinnacles at the end of each act as counterpoises to the height of the roof, which but for these would burst the side walls. The plan of the building is usually in the form of a cross, and the transepts have usually a beautiful round window of the richest stained glass over the doorways. . . .

From Amiens I went to Abbeville, in the neighbourhood of Crecy and Agincourt; and thence to Château d'Eu, where the Queen visited King Louis Philippe. The château is an elegant mansion in the French taste, all the walls covered with paintings, all the ceilings covered with gildings, and all the floors inlaid with polished woods of different colours, and shining like marble. The patron saint of Eu is the Irish Lawrence O'Toole, whose tomb I desired to see for the sake of the costume, in order that we may know how to dress his successor in the See of Dublin, Archbishop de Londres, for whom, you probably have heard, I have obtained a niche in the new House of Lords.   They had excluded him because he was not an English prelate, although one of the most active in procuring Magna Charta; but I came out in his defence in a letter to Mr Hallam, who had the manliness to acknowledge that he had been wrong in not selecting him with the others, and our poor old Archbishop is to have his niche as well as the rest.

From Eu I went to Dieppe, and thence to Rouen, where I stayed a week, enchanted with the old capital of the Normans, with its churches, its libraries and museums.   I then came to Paris, where I now write.

At first, on my arrival, it rained incessantly, and the city looked dismal enough; but for the last two or three days the sun has shone on us, and I am delighted with the magnificence and splendour of the place.   The most beautiful spot in all this beautiful city is (you will be surprised to learn) the Place de la Concorde, where, you remember, they cut off the heads of the King and Queen, and of such multitudes of other victims, in the great Revolution.   It is now laid out in broad terraces and esplanades, dry and smooth as the floor of a drawing-room, surrounded by gilded columns, and adorned with great fountains which shoot the water aloft in prodigious abundance and force.   Standing here you have (if you turn your face westward) the bridge leading to the Chamber of Deputies, and the part of the Chamber itself in front; the rich buildings of the Place de la Concorde, with the majestic portico of the Magdalene Church, behind; the long vast alleys of the Champs Elysées, terminated by a triumphal arch of unrivalled grandeur on the right, and the King's Palace and garden of the Tuileries on the left: all glistening in the sun with a mellow rich lustre which the atmosphere here imparts to any object.   Though the trees are leafless, the scene even now is enchanting.   .   .   .—I am, my dear mother, your ever affectionate son,   SAML. FERGUSON.

The primary object of Ferguson's journeyings was,

as we have seen, to follow the footsteps of the Irish
saints who in the seventh and succeeding centuries
carried the lamp of Christianity and of learning to
the peoples of Europe.   While in Paris he spent much
time in the Bibliothèque Royale, making a study of
their lives and writings, and taking extracts in Irish
and in Latin.   Many visits were paid to the Museum
of the Louvre, and its treasures carefully examined.
Nor were social recreations—the result of the introductions with which he had been furnished—neglected.
Many of the friendships which Ferguson formed with
distinguished foreigners date from his sojourn on the
Continent in 1846.

On the 1st of April Ferguson started for Lagni,
associated with the Irish Saint Fursey.   As he passed
the barrier he met a grand cavalcade in attendance on
King Louis Philippe, returning from Vincennes to
Paris.   Meaux, Soissons, Laon, Rheims, gave him
the opportunity of comparing the magnificent cathedrals of eastern France.   He gives, on the whole,
the preference to Laon :—

I prefer [he remarks in his notes] the façade of Laon to
Rheims.   The sculptures of Rheims are too elegant, its towers
too fine.   Laon has rude severity, force, and boldness, and
I think greater bulk.   But I prefer before both the portal of
Notre Dame de Paris. . . . No interior seems to me more
suitable than that of St John of the faubourg of Laon : plain
and strong, self-supported.   The mind is satisfied.

Chalons-sur-Marne, Metz, Nancy, St Dié, Epinal,
brought him to Luxeuil, the monastic home, among

the Vosges, of the Irish Saint Columbanus. From thence he journeyed to Besançon, and entered Switzerland at Basle. At Zürich he made the acquaintance of Dr Ferdinand Keller, whose investigations into the lake-dwellings of Helvetia have given him a European reputation. Eighteen years later—in 1864 —Ferguson received the following letter from the venerable antiquary, whom he visited, in company with his wife, at a still later period at Zürich :—

It afforded me great pleasure [wrote Dr Keller] to receive your friendly lines of the 2d inst., and to hear that you now enjoy good health. Be assured that I have not forgotten our agreeable and instructive intercourse during your brief stay at Zürich. I hope I shall have the pleasure of again seeing you at a future and not very distant period, when I may have the opportunity of laying before you many objects of interest, and communicating many new discoveries which I have made during the eighteen years that have elapsed since you were here. My excursions during this period have not been extended beyond the limits of Switzerland. Every summer I have been in the habit of spending a few weeks in one or the other of our valleys, making researches and increasing my store of antiquarian information.

As regards your inquiries concerning megalithic modes of sepulture, you are quite right in supposing that we have none in this country. . . .

In the neighbourhood of the lake-dwellings which have been discovered in our country there is no completely ascertained evidence of their existence; but were this the case, I should assign them a later construction than that of pure stone-period lake-dwellings.

I am very glad that you still take a great interest in historical and archæological questions, and that you have found an agreeable relaxation from your professional duties in the field of poetry and literature.

In his wanderings on the Continent in 1846 Ferguson appears to have been specially interested in the career of St Columbanus and his disciples, whom he followed from France into Switzerland and Italy. The founder of Luxeuil, Anegray, and Bobbio—a man of remarkable personality—had been a pupil of St Comgall of Bangor in the county of Down, whose school is said to have had three thousand scholars. Before the close of the sixth century Columbanus had founded his monasteries in the Vosges. When expelled by Queen Brunehildis he established himself at Bobbio among the Apennines. His disciples became the evangelisers of Helvetia and Rhetia. The fame of St Gall survives in the Swiss canton called by his name, and in the extant Irish MSS. penned in his monastery. Sigisbert founded Dissentis in the Bishopric of Coire. St Columbanus died at Bobbio in Italy in 615.

Miss Margaret Stokes, the eldest daughter of Dr Stokes, published in 1892 'Six Months in the Apennines: A Pilgrimage in search of Vestiges of the Irish Saints in Italy.' In this delightful book she also—as Ferguson had done forty-six years earlier—has traced the wandering footsteps of these early missionaries, and has illustrated with pen and pencil the localities associated with St Columbanus in France and Italy.

On his journey thither, Columbanus left in Switzerland his disciple St Gall, of whom the Comte de Montalembert gives an interesting account in 'Les

Moines d'Occident,' written some years later than the time of Ferguson's visits to Zürich, St Gallen, Schaffhausen, Reichenau, Dissentis, and Coire.

The materials collected by Ferguson in 1846 for a work on the Irish evangelisers of the Continent were not utilised by him.   The bent of his mind was not ecclesiastical, and the legendary accretions were distasteful to him.   Happily for the fame of Ireland, the work that he ultimately abandoned fell some ten years later into most competent hands.   It was from Schaffhausen and Reichenau that the Irish MSS. were obtained which his friend Dr Reeves used as the basis of his edition of Adamnan's 'Vita Sancti Columbæ.'

" I have long wished," wrote Dr Reeves in 1849, "to see that unique specimen of ancient ecclesiastical biography placed before the antiquarian public in an accessible and inviting form."   The wish was achieved by him, and his monumental work, published in 1856, was at once recognised as "the most valuable contribution ever made to the history of the early Celtic Church."   On perusing it the Comte de Montalembert recast his biography of St Columba in ' Les Moines d'Occident,' and acknowledged his obligations to the ' Vita Sancti Columbæ.'   Dr Reeves in a letter (4th March 1857) states :—

I have mentioned to Dr Todd my intention to read a paper at the next meeting of the British Association on the vestiges of the Irish over the Continent.   This will be the opening of an elaborate and detailed examination of that extraordinary tide of religion (*ut illo tempore*) which rolled eastward from this little spot, and sprinkled over the east of Europe and its mid-regions such a deposit of salt in full savour that to this day its seasoning remains fresh, at least in the memory of the recipients.

To this labour that eminent scholar was stimulated by his ecclesiastical superior, Lord John George Beresford, then Primate of all Ireland.

It appears to me [he wrote to Reeves] that a stigma attaches to the literature of our country, on account of our having neglected to bring forth to view in a complete form the missionary labours of the Irish Church on the Continent in the middle ages. It is a department of ecclesiastical history deeply interesting not only to us, but to those nations that benefited by the labour of Irish bishops and ministers in former times. I am not aware of any work that gives a connected view of this portion of our history and that of Switzerland, France, and Germany.

Adamnan, the biographer of St Columba, was his ninth successor in the Abbacy of Iona, and wrote about one hundred years after the founder's death. Dr Reeves's edition was pronounced to be "one of very uncommon interest and value, throwing light on the topography and history of Scotland as well as Ireland, and settling many questions hitherto deemed doubtful or unknown."

In these days, when every one travels abroad, it would be wearisome to follow Ferguson through Germany and Austria, and over the Brenner Pass into Italy. He lingered for some time at Trent. Its Cathedral, where the Council had held its sittings, with its symbolic sculpture, which he carefully studied, had endless attraction for him. Nor was he less charmed with Verona. Its Roman remains, its churches, especially that of San Zeno, its picturesque bridge over the rushing Adige, delighted him; and at Verona, Ferguson, an enthusiastic lover of art, embraced the opportunity of studying the works of Paolo Caliari in his native city. He had a special admiration for the fine works of this master preserved in our National Gallery and at the Louvre. The great "Cena" in the French collection is an admirable example of Paolo's style. What Sir Frederic Burton wrote of it is true, and applicable to all the work of the Verona artist.

The famous "Marriage at Cana" [observes Burton] offers to the eye a grand summing up, as it were, of his [Paul Veronese's] aims and his powers. Stately architecture, brilliant daylight, dignified men and beautiful women, infinite variety united to perfect harmony of colours, all combine to form a scene of festive splendour and enjoyment, in which the miracle, the main incident in the story, becomes an episode merely. The frank introduction of the costumes of the painter's own time, clothing the fine race to which he belonged, gives to his pictures of this class a living interest that more than compensates for any anachronism.

The opportunity for more extended study of Paolo's works in his own Verona was eagerly embraced by Ferguson. Here, as he stood one day entranced before a "masterpiece of cool arcades," his rapt attention attracted the notice of a nobleman of Verona, the Marchese Carlotti. The courteous old gentleman accosted him, and, charmed with his appreciation of the Veronese, invited the stranger to his palace, and during his stay at Verona showed him true kindness and hospitality. Ferguson alludes to him in the following sonnets :—

PAUL VERONESE.

THREE SONNETS.

To the Memory of the Marquis Carlotti.

I.

Paul, let thy faces from the canvas look
Haply less clearly than Pietro's can,
Less lively than in tints of Titian,
Or him who both the bay-wreath chaplets took ;
Yet shalt thou therefore have no harsh rebuke
Of me whom, while with eager eyes I ran
O'er painted pomps of Brera and Vatican,
The first delight thou gavest ne'er forsook.
For in thy own Verona, long ago,
Before one masterpiece of cool arcades,
I made a friend ; and such a friend was rare :—
For him, I love thy velvet's glorious show,
Thy sheens of silk 'twixt marble balustrades,
Thy breathing-space and full translucent air.

II.

Loved for themselves, too.   Oft as I behold,
Adown the curtain'd gallery's sumptuous gloom,
A separate daylight shining in the room,
There find I still thy groupings manifold
Of holy clerks, of nobles grave and bold,
Swart slaves, brave gallants, maidens in their bloom,
With what of Persian and Ligurian loom
May best consort with marble dome and gold :

There find thy dog, whose teeth Time's teeth defy
To raze the name from less enduring leaves
Of loved Canossa : there, in cynic ease,
Thy monkey : and beneath the pearly sky
See lovely ladies wave their handkerchiefs,
And lend sweet looks from airy balconies.

III.

They err who say this long-withdrawing line
Of palace-fronts Palladian, this brocade
From looms of Genoa, this gold-inlaid
Resplendent plate of Milan, that combine
To spread soft lustre through the grand design,
Show but in fond factitious masquerade
The actual feast by leper Simon made
For that great Guest, of old, in Palestine.
Christ walks amongst us still ; at liberal table
Scorns not to sit : no sorrowing Magdalene
But of these dear feet kindly gets her kiss
Now, even as then ; and thou, be honourable,
Who, by the might of thy majestic scene,
Bringest down that age and minglest it with this.

These sonnets, published many years later, were sent to
Sir Frederic Burton, who thus acknowledged them :—

Thank you for the charming sonnet on the Veronese.
Paolo takes one into a fine healthy atmosphere, gives one
breathing-space, and makes one know a race of manly and
womanly beings. I regret your not having seen a picture
of his we have just got. Only one figure, barring two *putti*,
but so fine !

Burton touches in his letter on another painter with
whose works Ferguson was in full sympathy :—

Francia's " Annunciation " is full of beauty : one of his
best things. But I wish you had seen his altar-piece in S.

Giacomo Magg. at Bologna. That is his finest work, and beyond comparison better than anything else he has done, for it has none of his weaknesses. But to come back to Veronese. His picture at Turin, although a wonderful piece of art, is not to me captivating. The chief group is a mistake. It was above his calibre to make it what it should be, and even its colouring, whether from any retouching I don't know, is out of harmony.

How much I should like to have been with you both in Italy!

I have only this moment seen the Sonnet II. . . . This sequel was necessary to complete the thought, which is quite beautiful. And although I have entered above on a dull technical criticism of the picture, yet it takes away nothing from the justness and beauty of what you say or sing. The very same thought suggests itself before an exquisite little picture by the late W. Dyce, an artist too little appreciated here. Christ alone, and in sorrowing thought, with hands clasped on His lap, sits on a heathery bank, which recalls *our own* mountain scenery. I have heard wits sneer at the absurdity of seating Jesus on a Highland hillside. To me, and I have no doubt Dyce meant it, there was a deep and touching significance in the conception—that which would have been absent if, after the manner of the modern pedants, the scenery had consisted of palms and cactuses. Dyce was a man not only of thought but of education, and knew perfectly well what he was doing.

Without any doubt one of the causes of the powerful effect that "Christian art" in Italy and the Low Countries had upon the people was just that the pathetic scenes of Scripture were brought home to their very doors and hearths. But now we are beyond that, of course!

From Verona Ferguson journeyed to Vicenza, where he was much impressed by the architectural work of Palladio. He visited Padua, and was amazed at the vast span of the roof in the great hall of its Palazzo della Ragione. He delighted in the works of

Giotto, Donatello, and other early masters in painting and sculpture. Venice, that unique city, full of charm for the cultured traveller, the " eldest child of Liberty," which for so many ages " held the gorgeous East in fee and was the safeguard of the West," was intelligently explored; and Ferrara, Bologna, and Imola also visited.

Ravenna had great fascination for Ferguson. Its round towers, its Eastern type of architecture, its mosaics, as brilliant as when executed in the sixth century, the historic associations recalled by the city of Honorius, Galla Placidia, and Stilicho, and the Gothic Theodoric, with Justinian, Narses, and Belisarius, all exercised a strong attraction on Ferguson's mind. On future visits to Italy he planned a long sojourn in the city for purposes of study, relieved by the rides in the *pineta*. But Fate willed otherwise. On one occasion when he found himself in Italy, and was on the eve of starting for Ravenna, a threatened attack of fever made it dangerous to venture into that swampy district, and a sudden recall homewards on another occasion made his first visit to the city of the Round Towers his only one.

When he left Ravenna he journeyed by Rimini, Pesaro, Macerata, and Foligno to Rome, and looked for the first time on the Imperial City in the month of July of that year.

The impression Rome produced on his mind is expressed by Ferguson in a poem which he wrote nearly a quarter of a century later, when he found himself at Oxford in mid-winter, about the time when the Vatican Council was holding its sittings in Rome.

"By the Isis" was addressed to a young relative, the Rev. A. G. Livingstone, then resident in Oxford. From it a few stanzas are selected which describe its author's emotions on entering Rome:—

Isis, by thy frozen marge,
  So to ask did once betide me;
Many souls had he in charge
  Who, that morning, walked beside me,
And, as town and tower he eyed,
Gazed on all with loving pride.

But, for me, past Magd'len tower,
  Radcliffe dome and roofs Bodleian,
Even in that wintry hour,
  Mounting up the empyrean
Rose the vision of the dome
O'er the palace-tops of Rome;

Such as from the Pincian height,
  Past the broad-eav'd roofs Borghesan,
Dawns it on the pilgrim's sight,
  Robed in morning's amber blazon,
With its wide-armed colonnade
For mankind's embracing made.

Such as from the Martian vale
  Oft aloft I've seen it swelling,
Grave, serene, majestical,
  O'er the mundane High Priest's dwelling,
He who binds, in judgment strong,
True and false, and right and wrong.

Yea, and to my visioned eye,
  Where the half-thawed lock did bubble,
Very Tiber darted by,
  Like a topaz, like an opal ;
Even as when its lustrous wave
These once-sinewy shoulders clave ;

While, above, the Archangel's tower,
  With brazen clang and detonation,
Answered to the words of power
  Of the Dogma's proclamation ;
And the kings, with widening ear,
Leant from all their thrones to hear.

Ferguson did not leave Rome in 1846 till late in August. On reaching Bobbio he found himself attacked by fever and seriously ill. Happily he recovered, and spent some time in this nook among the Apennines, studying the MSS. left by the Irish monks. These are now removed to the Ambrosian Library at Milan. During his convalescence he made many sketches of the place, with its picturesque bridge through which the Trebbia flows, and towards the close of the year found himself once more in Dublin, with restored health, new knowledge, and varied experiences. But on the country dear to him beyond all others a fearful calamity had fallen—the potato disease had destroyed the food of its people.

CHAPTER VIII.

1848-1882.

DOMESTIC AND FAMILY LIFE—LATER YEARS.

> "Serene will be our days and bright,
> And happy will our nature be,
> When love is an unerring light,
> And joy its own security."
> —WORDSWORTH.

> "It ne'er was wealth, it ne'er was wealth,
> That coft contentment, peace, or pleasure ;
> The bands and bliss o' mutual love,
> O, that's the chiefest warld's treasure !"
> —BURNS.

ON Ferguson's return to Dublin in 1847, he took rooms in 11 Henrietta Street, and applied himself once more to his profession.

It was at this time that he made the acquaintance, at a dinner-party, of his future wife. They had an animated conversation on the labours of those pioneers of civilisation and Christianity on the Continent, the Irish monks. Before the party broke up she had sung Irish melodies, "No, not more welcome," and "At the mid-hour of night,"—melodies from henceforward associated with that eventful evening on which Ferguson made his election of "the wife to choose."

Several months elapsed before he had again an opportunity of meeting her. At last he made the acquaintance of her family. As soon as he obtained admission to her father's house he used his opportunities, and in due time pressed his suit. He found it hard to persuade her he sought to win that she might trust in the sincerity and permanence of his attachment, and allow herself to return it. She had yet to learn the constancy and tenderness of his nature, though realising its nobility, and to a considerable extent the congeniality of their tastes. At length he was encouraged to speak to her father, and resolved to ask an interview with him as soon as he had made his first political speech on the 9th of May 1848.

Mr Guinness was no less surprised than his daughter had been when Ferguson asked for her hand in marriage. He had read his speech, differed from his views, and considered his means inadequate. But when he learned that the young people were attached, and willing to begin life on modest means, he, like the good and kind parent that he was, made no further objection.

The lovers became engaged on the 10th of May, "this happy tenth of May," as Ferguson wrote in a copy of ' Bunting's Irish Music ' which he gave to his betrothed. She had previously arranged to visit a married friend and former schoolfellow in Scotland, and it was decided that this engagement should be fulfilled.   The month of August was fixed on for their union, at the commencement of the Long Vacation.

In June Mr Guinness left his daughter on the steamer, and finding the Rev. Tresham Gregg on board bound for Greenock, gave her into his charge.   Dr Gregg spoke to her of a lecture he was about to deliver; but she listened with scant interest, as she had hoped her lover would come to say farewell.   Ferguson had been detained in court, but dashed along the quay on a car just as the ship moved slowly alongside.   He leaped on board, and after a few words with his betrothed, had to spring back to *terra firma;* but he followed its course while the vessel skirted the quay. On rejoining Dr Gregg, to whom she felt some explanation was due, she asked if he knew Mr Ferguson, to whom she was engaged to be married.   "Indeed!" he rejoined.   " I know him to be a man of mark, but I had no idea that the poet was such a handsome fellow."

Ferguson was then, in truth, "a handsome fellow." In the prime of manhood, he was clear-complexioned though somewhat pale; with a lofty and intellectual forehead, good eyes, dark-blue in colour, well-chiselled nose, and singularly sensitive and expressive mouth, and his smile was indescribably sweet and winning. About the middle height, well formed and broad-shouldered, he looked every inch a man, and one of marked distinction.   Though in later life his shoulders became somewhat stooped, he never lost the air of refinement and high breeding, nor the benignant smile and courteous manner, which attracted all who met him. It was as conspicuous in his intercourse with subordinates as with the highest in the land, for his courtesy was inborn, the outcome of personal dignity, absence of self-assertion, and consideration for others.

During their separation a close correspondence—still lovingly preserved — ensued between the betrothed, soon to be united in holy matrimony. These letters are too sacred for citation; a few extracts only may be given to illustrate what Ferguson was at this time, and later letters will show him as a husband. For a man's public life cannot give a full insight into his character apart from his more personal and domestic life. His works—the writings he leaves behind him— testify to mental power and genius; but the little, nameless, unremembered acts of kindness and of love tell of the qualities of the heart. The spiritual emotions —still more divine—testify to its religion. All these, in combination, go to the evolution of that noble product described by our greatest poet: "What a piece of work is a man! how noble in reason! how infinite in faculty! in form and moving how express and admirable! in action how like an angel! in apprehension how like a god! the beauty of the world! the paragon of animals!"

HOWTH, *June* 29, 1848.

You will receive with this a newspaper containing another speech of mine, probably the last one on the subject which I shall make during the present year. I do not think it ought to offend even the prejudices of our most Anglican friends; if it do, I cannot help it. I enclose a letter received this morning from an old acquaintance in the North, which will show you how feeling spreads, and how little any reasonable Conservative ought to be offended at me for trying as I do to moderate it, and to guide it in safe channels. Gordon, whose letter I enclose, is a poet, a man of letters, and a skilful physician; a Northern, a Protestant, and by his marriage lately, connected with some of the most prescriptively Tory families in Antrim and Derry. Yet you see what thoughts are at the bottom of his mind; and I have no doubt there are many others whose real sentiments are very much the same. If I have been able to act in any way as moderator among these conflicting and antagonistic parties, I shall think myself very well repaid for any exposure to the frowns of any or all who may look coldly on me in consequence, provided always you, dear Mary, reward me with your smiles.

July 5, 1848.

These are delightful letters you have written me in pencil. In a few days more our converse shall not be merely by spiritual companionship. Yet even by one another's side our tongues will but half express the love and peace which will speak still spiritually from heart to heart.

I have all your letters here in one mass, before me. What a correspondence already! What will it be if we continue to delight in one another's thoughts as much as now, all our lives, and should ever happen to be separated so long again? . . .

So, my dearest friend, discharge for me my obligation of gratitude to Mrs Rowan for her kindness. Tell her, in being so kind to you she has won my kindest regards, and that if I can ever serve her, or any one she loves, I shall endeavour to show myself not ungrateful.

Now—To Business.

Circuit will go out on the 10th July, and will end about the first week in August. . . .

If you, my dearest love, will fix on some or any day after the 10th of August for our marriage, I expect to have all the arrangements necessary for our humble commencement of the world effected by that time.

So I shall await you by the steamer which will leave Greenock on the 7th instant. You will write to me at what hour the vessel will sail, and at what time you expect to arrive here; and please God, I shall clasp your dear hand again in mine before you leave the ship. Praying God to bless you, I am, dearest, your ever affectionate   SAML. FERGUSON.

Oh! Mary dear, here is the first original MS. of "Thomas Davis," written in pencil. How it has turned up I cannot tell; but as you first knew me and comprehended me (worthily indeed) through the medium of this little poem, keep the MS. as a souvenir. And now

> Oh blaw, ye norlan' winds, blaw saft,
> Abune the brimming Clyde—
> Wi' favouring gale to Inisfail
> Bring hame my bonny bride!

Farewell till Saturday.   S. FERGUSON.

Ferguson met his betrothed on her return from Scotland, and accompanied her to her father's house. He told her that he had been retained as counsel for Richard Dalton Williams, a young poet, proprietor of the 'Tribune,' about to be tried for treason felony, and that their honeymoon must be passed within reach of Dublin, as it was uncertain when Williams might be called on for his defence.

The marriage was solemnised in Stillorgan Church on the 16th of August, in the presence of a large gathering of relatives and friends. On the departure of the newly wedded pair the postilion was instructed to drive first to Kilmainham. Ferguson had an interview with his client in the prison before proceeding to Slane on the Boyne. Here he introduced his bride to the charming scenery through which flows the " deep, full-hearted river, broad and brown," which he afterwards described in his " Burial of King Cormac." They inhaled that

> Breath of finer air
> That touched the Boyne with ruffling wings,
> And stirred him in his sedgy lair,
> And in his mossy moorland springs;

and wandered along "the grassy marge of Rossnaree," where Cormac was interred.

> A tranquil spot: a hopeful sound
> Comes from the ever-youthful stream,
> And still on daisied mead and mound
> The dawn delays with tenderer beam.
>
> Round Cormac Spring renews her buds:
> In march perpetual by his side,
> Down come the earth-fresh April floods,
> And up the sea-fresh salmon glide;
>
> And life and time rejoicing run
> From age to age their wonted way.

Brugh-na-Boine was also visited, with its sepulchral tumuli of New Grange, Dowth, and Knowth. After a short sojourn in Meath, the newly wedded pair established themselves at Howth, and remained within reach of Dublin for the rest of the Long Vacation.

The promontory of Howth, which forms the northern boundary of the Bay of Dublin, was dear to Ferguson, as it had been of old to St Columba. "It is quiet, and it is delightful, delightful!" wrote Colomb of the Churches, and, while wandering here thirteen hundred years later, Ferguson, in his "Aideen's Grave," reached "through pangs of keen delight the gift of utterance"—

> To speak the air, the sky to speak,
> The freshness of the hill to tell.

In various aspects he has, in this and in other poems, described it.   Lying on its cliffs, amid the heather and the golden furze, he has surveyed

> The wide pale-heaving floor crisped by a curling wind,
> With all its shifting, shadowy belts, and chasing scopes of
>   green,
> Sun-strown, foam-freckled, sail-embossed, and blackening
>   squalls between,
> And slant, cerulean-skirted showers that with a drowsy sound,
> Heard inward, of ebullient waves, stalk all the horizon
>   round ;
> And——haply, being a citizen just 'scaped from some disease
> That long has held him sick indoors, now, in the brine-fresh
>   breeze,
> Health-salted, bathes ; and says, the while he breathes reviving
>   bliss,
> " I am not good enough, O God, nor pure enough for this ! "

During the autumn of 1848 many friendships were formed and cemented.   The family connexions of both husband and wife came frequently by early train to Howth, there to " blithely spend the golden day, 'mid joys that never weary," and inhale fresh sea-breezes in genial companionship, interrupted for a time by the trial of Williams.

The agreeable picnic life at Howth had to be exchanged on the approach of winter for a house in Dublin.   9 Upper Gloucester Street was taken for a year, and when money to furnish had been saved, Ferguson settled permanently in 20 North Great George's Street, a house which he subsequently purchased.

Ferguson speedily installed his wife as chancellor

of the exchequer. He was by nature careless of money, prone to give, lend, and so often lose it. It was her study to fulfil the trust reposed in her, and free him from pecuniary cares, so that he might pursue untroubled his intellectual and professional labours. Both were resolved to incur no debts.

An unexpected difficulty arose when, a few years later, Ferguson decided that the work he had in contemplation when he went abroad in 1846 must be abandoned by him. He had traced the footsteps of the Irish missionaries on the Continent, had sympathised in their pious devotion and varied learning, yet had revolted from the accretions of superstitious and puerile legend which overshadowed their fame. He had received while abroad remittances from his publishers on account of the contemplated book. These sums had now to be refunded with compound interest. On ascertaining his indebtedness, he was dismayed at finding how considerable was the amount; nor was it possible to pay it off otherwise than by instalments. To do this he strained every nerve, and, in addition to his professional work, had recourse to his pen: till the debt was discharged in full, he laboured indefatigably. The struggle was, for one of his temperament, no doubt an excellent discipline, correcting as nothing else would have done his *insouciance* and optimism in money matters.

Notwithstanding these early difficulties, the domestic life of husband and wife was truly happy. He loved his home, his wife, his friends, his work. His tastes were simple. He was habitually cheerful, easily pleased, open-hearted, confiding, generous, and affectionate. His temper was singularly sweet and equable. To be in his genial society was a perpetual feast, to converse with him a liberal education. He was unaffectedly pious, with a heart full of gratitude to God for the blessings of his life.

As a master and head of his household he was just, kind, and considerate. His servants pronounced him "a perfect gentleman," and the description was a true one. He was as courteous to them as to those of exalted station. "I am sending a little present to my dear old master; ask him to accept it, and my life's gratitude. It is a tribute of respect, and a token of the high esteem we entertain for you both," wrote former domestics; and many similar testimonies exist, proving how much he was esteemed by those well qualified to judge of character.

The happiest years of life are often those of which there is little to record. Ferguson worked steadily at his profession, went Circuit regularly, and spent his vacations at Irish seaside resorts, such as Howth, Kilkee, Bundoran, &c., and sometimes crossed the Channel to England, Wales, or Scotland. Fortunately his income at the Bar steadily advanced, for unexpected family claims pressed heavily on his resources. Owners of land, crushed by bad times, had in many cases to part with their property, and Ferguson's elder and only surviving brother resolved to emigrate. John Ferguson was well versed in the Spanish language and literature, and the possession of this accomplishment decided him to settle in South America. He sailed for Buenos Ayres, leaving his wife and children to follow after the arrival of an expected addition to the family. Mrs Ferguson did not long survive the birth of her fourth son and seventh child. Two of the boys who were of an age to attend school had already been inmates of their uncle's house, and eventually all the family were domesticated in North Great George's Street, which was their home until the eldest daughter was of an age to undertake the management of her father's house, when she rejoined him in Buenos Ayres, accompanied by her sisters and two of her brothers, the youngest, whom his father had never seen, being then nearly four years old.

In a letter written to his nephews from Circuit, Ferguson tells the little fellows of a lecture he had delivered in Monaghan :—

First of all, my dear boys, I am glad to hear of your being all well, and to tell you that I am very well myself. I delivered a lecture to the Young Men's Society at Monaghan. The meeting took place in the Methodist Meeting House, and I spoke from the pulpit. You would have thought me a clergyman, only I talked about the sun and the stars and the moon, and the tides and winds and clouds, and the way they are caused by the heat and attraction of the sun, and about the rules and laws which regulate their motions, and the beauty and simplicity of the ways that God has taken to produce them all ; and then I talked to them about the way plants grow, and living creatures breathe and move; and about men, who are the first of living creatures, and have minds capable of reasoning, and souls which will live hereafter in another world ; and about the various races of men, black and white and red men, and their different places of habitation in the world; and also about ourselves, and that we ought not to be ashamed of being Irishmen, as some foolish people are, who think it better to be considered as Englishmen or Scotchmen who have only come over to stay for a while in Ireland, but would not get leave to call themselves anything else than Irishmen if they went into England or Scotland; and I advised them to study the history of their own country, and to read good books of poetry, like Homer, to make them able to enjoy the beauty and grandeur of Nature, and to make them brave and generous. And I told them that it was better to be good men than even to be good scholars, but that both was best; and they were all pleased with what I said, and although I did not say it very nicely, I was well pleased myself. So now, little boys, God bless you all, your own uncle,   SAML. FERGUSON.

On another occasion, when Ferguson was absent on Circuit, two of his nephews were attacked by fever. His wife, while nursing them, sickened also. She made an effort from time to time to write; nor did he learn, till the danger was past, what would have caused him great anxiety. When he heard of the illness in his home he replied as follows:—

I rejoice to hear of your being out. My poor dear, what a time of trouble and danger you have had! What you tell me of poor Bob makes me very uneasy. Is there any way, dearest, in which you could keep out of the way of further infection? I would wish dear Bob to have the best attention we can bestow, but I see no use in your exposing yourself when a nurse-tender could do all that is necessary. Do, pray, send for a nurse. Don't mind a little expense. . . .
I have a wholesome sense of responsibility, which indeed, dearest Mary, weighs on my mind day and night, in connection with the remembrance of you. If constant love for you and thought of you can compensate for the anxieties you have had,

the anxieties are not standing against me in our marriage account without a little set-off. I grow professional. I must go on to be unprofessional and volunteer an opinion—that having the best of wives and not the worst of prospects, I would be the greatest of ingrates if I were not on the whole a tolerably happy fellow, and absolutely yours.—Ever, dearest, faithfully your own,   SAML. FERGUSON.

And again :—

Thank God, dearest wife, that our danger is past. What a sad time you have had—three of you at once in bed! I am more thankful to Alicia [a faithful servant] than I can tell you. Pray, dear, let her know how much I am obliged. Send me a blank cheque, which I'll fill up for the Doctor and remit it by post. Robert's escape so far has been very lucky. Your own attack must have been comparatively mild to enable you to write to me as you did.

My case has not yet come on, nor is it likely it will be tried till to-morrow. So I possibly shall not see my poor dear wife till Thursday next. God bless you, my love, and long keep you to cheer and comfort your own husband,   S. F.

Ferguson's kindness of heart and readiness to aid a friend in trouble will appear in the following letters written to his wife from Circuit :—

How grieved I am to hear a report of ——'s failure. I daresay you have not heard of it, or you would have mentioned it to me. The poor fellow! Now is the time for us to show any kindness in our power, and possibly we may be of some use to him. At least we will be able to offer him the resources of our table and some conversation to beguile an occasional evening's vexations. If he be left without means, I hardly know what he can do in his present state of health. As yet I know no particulars, but fear from what I hear that the failure is a bad one. If you see him, present him my kindest remembrances, and say I shall be in town, ready to give a hand at anything that may be necessary, by Monday next.

And again in 1862:—

I have sent —— cheque to ——. Enter it in the block cheque-book. God help her, poor thing! I give her any help I can willingly, though it just uses up the profits of the Circuit so far.

In Ferguson's nature there was a readiness to spend and be spent for family and for friends, combined with an ever-grateful sense of kindnesses received, which was very endearing. In the spring of 1876 he was at Oxford, while his wife visited her brothers, at Leicester and in London.

I have your news of safe arrival [he wrote to her], and send loves all round to the family group in Leicester. You will not see me in London, I think, till Wednesday morning at soonest. Affairs accumulate as Easter approaches; but when I get again under your government, I shall rest and be thankful. I got everything I wanted at Corpus College yesterday, and hope to get all I want at the Bodleian in the forenoon of to-morrow. By an exceptional favour of fortune I have found Dr Acland [Sir Henry Acland], and shall go, as soon as I post this, to dress for dinner at his house. Dr Acland has done everything to secure me the earliest possible access to my work. Nothing could be more obliging than his reception of me. Livingstone [the Rev. Robert G. Livingstone, Fellow and Tutor of Pembroke College, Oxford] has made me free of the Union reading-rooms and library, where I spent most of the post-lunch hours. I lunched with him. Nothing can exceed the kindness I have received. As I cannot see you, do you put your heart in your eyes for me, and give a glance of affection all round.—Ever your own,   S. F.

Ferguson made a digression to South Wales to re-examine an Ogham monument which he had previously visited in company with his wife. He wrote describing his reception at Pyle Hotel, where they had then so-journed :—

I never longed to have you beside me more than yesterday, and the day before. You will guess that I had got down again to the vale of Glamorgan. All the faces at Pyle beamed with goodwill when I appeared among them, and many were the kind inquiries for you. John Thomas in especial came up from the garden to pay his respects. The garden is now in better order and the house more animated ; but the beauty of the surroundings is not to be put in words. Before coming away I drove down to Sker, the home of the " Maid," a most delightful region of sand-dunes blowing ferny and fresh to perfect exquisiteness. Twenty times I uttered the wish that you were with me, and refused the temptation of spending another day at Margam until I should have you to enjoy it; so you may make up your mind to see Winny Jenkins and the rest of them, some day or other. . . . About Monday morning I would suppose my advent might be looked for, but the servants could take very good care of me till the afternoon, when it would be a great delight to wel-come you with Robert, Grace, and the little ones to dinner.

The strong and mutual attachment which subsisted between Ferguson and his wife's family, and between her and his relatives and friends, was a potent factor in the happiness of their wedded life. The " Robert and Grace " whose arrival with their little ones was so desired at North Great George's Street, was the Rev. R. Guinness, his wife's youngest brother, and his wife, daughter of the late Dean Butler of Lincoln. The " Richard and Lizzie " of the letter to Ferguson's mother was her eldest brother and his wife, whose home in London was ever hospitably open to him. So also was the residence of her brother Henry and his wife. To all the dearly loved nephews and nieces

Ferguson was devotedly attached, and they reciprocated his affection.   He could invent and narrate tales of entrancing interest to the little ones clustered around him to be caressed by the dear uncle and fascinated by the stories he told to them.   As they grew up, it was his delight to see their bright faces in his home, and to enjoy their companionship when a visit to the Continent promised instruction as well as pleasure.

The following stanzas from a poem, " Bird and Brook," written at Aix-les-Bains, and inscribed to the eldest daughters of R. Seymour Guinness and Henry Guinness, then the companions of their uncle and aunt on their foreign tour, thus speaks of these dear young girls :—

BIRD AND BROOK.

Bird that pipest on the bough,
Would that I could sing as thou ;
Runnel gurgling on beneath,
Would I owned thy liquid breath :
I would make a lovely lay
Worthy of the pure-bright day.

Worthy of the freshness spread
Round my path and o'er my head,
Of the unseen airs that rise
Incensing the morning skies,
As from opening buds they spring
In the dew's evanishing.

Brighter yet, and even more clear,
Than that blue encasing sphere,
Worthy of the gentle eyes
Opening on this paradise,
With their inner heavens as deep,
Fresh from youth's enchanted sleep.

Worthy of the voices sweet
That my daily risings greet,
And, to even-song addressed,
Ere we lay us down to rest,
Lift my spirit's laggard weight
Half-way to the heavenly gate.

I would make it with a dance
Of the rhythmic utterance,
With a gambit and retreat
Of the counter-trilling feet,
And a frolic of the tone
To the song-bird only known.

With a soft transfusing fall
Would I make my madrigal,
Full as rills that, as they pass,
Shake the springing spikes of grass,
And that ample under-speech
Only running waters reach.

I would sing it loud and well,
Till the spirits of Amabel,
And of Ethel, from their nests,
Caught with new delicious zests
Of the soul's life out-of-door,
Forth should peep, and crave for more.

But, because I own not these,
Oh, ye mountains and ye trees,
Oh, ye tracts of heavenly air,
Voices sweet, and sweet eyes fair,
Of my darlings, ye must rest
In my rhyme but half-expressed !

Yea, and if I had them all,
Voice of bird and brook at call,
And could speak as winds in woods,
Or with tumult of the floods,
Yet a theme there would remain
I should still essay in vain.

For my soul would strive to raise,
If it might, a song of praise,
All unworthy though it were,
To the Maker of the air,
To the Giver of the life,
Breathing round me joyous-rife.

Giver of that general joy
Brightening face of girl and boy,
Sender of those soul-reliefs
Hidden in our boons of griefs,
Lest with surfeit and excess
We surcharge life's blessedness.

The little poem, " To a Lady, with Edward Dowden's Poems," gives a true portrait of the features, the mind, and the character of a dearly loved sister-in-law :—

Henrietta, in whose face
We a soul's experience trace
Through the working lines of grace,

Here is one in words who tries
To express the ecstasies
That inform your cheeks and eyes ;

Springing ecstasies, controlled,
Lest the world too much behold ;
As befits one of the fold.

I would think, if I might guess,
That this holy rapturousness
Which both he and you express,

He with words, and you with looks,
Drawing, as with shepherd-crooks,
Thirsty souls to living brooks ;

> Though from one same fountain sent,
> And with one benign intent,
> Comes through channels different.
>
> God is one.   His gifts of grace
> Flow to man through countless ways ;
> So the greater be His praise.

These lines, "To Amabel Mary Guinness, with Stone's 'Book of Flowers,'" were inscribed in the volume given to a much-loved niece :—

> The sponsors at the font, dear Amabel,
> With hopeful prescience named the infant well.
> Infant and child that presage you've approved,
> Now grown a damsel, lovely and beloved,
> Accept this ' Book of Flowers,' an offering meet
> For such a Flower, fresh-blooming, pure and sweet.

In the autumn of 1876 Ferguson was for the first time left alone in his home. Another sister-in-law, then in delicate health, had been recommended change and sea-air, and his wife accompanied her to the North of Ireland. Although dependent in many ways on his life's companion, he was ready to submit to solitude and inconvenience that she might be of service to her family and friends. He took the opportunity of her absence to make some additions to their house, and endured the consequent discomforts with exemplary patience, as will appear from the following letter :—

My darling Wife, dearest and best of Friends,—I trust you will enjoy your coast-tour. You will be interested in visiting Mount Sandal, thought to be the old *Dun-da-Bann* whence Cuchullin and the intoxicated Ultonians issued on their raid into Munster—the *Mesca Ulaid*, which will give material for a grand poem some day or another. I think there might be a chance of an Ogham at the grave of Bishop Cadan, close under east gable of old church above Bellarena. On the hill to the north are the remains of *Dun Cruithne* associated with Columba;—see tracing [a tracing of the district enclosed in the letter]. If you can take your month of sea and country air, do, my love, with all my heart. I am full of occupations. All goes fairly well in the way of work, but much remains to be done. Judge how I am provided as a man of letters, by this pencil-written scrap. I write with books on the ledges of my brief-stand. All this will have to be set right by the great reformer. She's coming frae the north that's to "redd-up" me! The British Association will meet in Dublin in 1878. We will then have full employment for all our new means of reception, and I hope, my darling, that you and I may assist in keeping up our city's credit for hospitality.

I read with real concern in the paper this morning that Sir Arthur Guinness is ill with inflammation of the lungs at Ems. I send to inquire at Leeson Street. Heaven grant that the poor fellow may not be cut off from his career of honourable usefulness!

I enjoyed vicariously the fine weather and beautiful exhilarating scenes through which you passed yesterday, and if I could feel the full beauty of the virtuous hours and wholesome shocks of cold sea-water, I would, I am sure, have cause for continued sympathetic pleasure. But it does not require more virtue than I possess to share with you, though at a distance, the satisfaction of being in such rare good company. I hardly know whom to put first, and will best convey all I desire by a God bless you all! I wish you were with me, and I wish you to stay away.—Ever, dearest wife, your own

S. Ferguson.

It was ever Ferguson's delight to make his house a centre for his friends, and "The Ferguson Arms"—for so 20 North Great George's Street was called by them—

was generally well filled with guests. "Plain living and high thinking" was all he aimed at. It was a large and spacious house, and its simple and unpretentious hospitality was readily accepted by the good, the intellectual, and the young. For the little ones there was an annual Christmas-tree, frequent visits to the Zoo, frequent gatherings for "Bees," and games. Expeditions to the country, picnics, dances, and musical parties made life pleasant to the young. Conversaziones, Shakespearian Readings, and occasional dinner-parties, brought together for social enjoyment those distinguished for their attainments, however divergent might be their creeds or politics. A genial host, an atmosphere of friendliness and of literary culture, made intercourse unconstrained and agreeable.

Few of the social reunions in Dublin were more agreeable than those for the study of Shakespeare, inaugurated by the Rev. R. P. Graves. Friends met periodically in one another's houses. The host and hostess of the evening selected the play and allotted the parts. These were announced beforehand, so that the character assigned might be studied by the reader. It was found desirable to shorten some of the plays. Ferguson prepared a book which indicated the scenes to be read, and told in terse verse the story of the scenes omitted. This little volume, 'Shakespearian Breviates'—an adjustment of twenty-four of the longer plays of Shakespeare to convenient reading limits—was published in 1882. In earlier years he wrote these merely for use in his own house. We give as a sample some extracts from

A SOUVENIR OF TUESDAY EVENING, 19TH JAN. 1869.

PROLOGUE TO LAST THREE ACTS OF "CYMBELINE,"
WITH A LIST OF READERS.

Cymbeline	Dr STOKES.
Cloten	Professor (now Sir ROBERT) BALL.
Posthumus	Rev. R. P. GRAVES, LL.D.
Belarius	Sir SAMUEL FERGUSON.
Guiderius	Mr PALMER, F.T.C.D.
Arviragus	Professor EDWARD DOWDEN.
Iachimo	Mr THOMAS FERGUSON.
Lucius	Rev. Dr SALMON (Provost of T.C.D.)
Senator	Mr A. P. GRAVES.
Captain	Mr JOHN CLARKE.
Pisanio	Dr INGRAM (President R.I.A.)
Cornelius	Rev. J. P. MAHAFFY, F.T.C.D.
Queen	Miss STOKES.
Imogen	Miss LAURA DARLEY.
Lady	Mrs MAHAFFY.

The prologue written for the occasion by Ferguson commenced thus :—

Ye lovely ladies, and ye men of might,
'Tis "Cymbeline" shall be our play to-night;
But since at large to read the text were long,
Our gentle Shakespeare will forgive the wrong,
If I the fore-plot of the piece rehearse
In lines foreshortened and shortcoming verse.
Know, then, till perjured Iachimo appear,
We all, to-night, are Ancient Britons here;
And this room, England, ere the English name
And tongue of Shakespeare with the Saxons came.

.   .   .   .

So stand the actors, 'mid their joys and woes,
Their crimes and passions, at the fore-plot's close

Which, had you heard from Shakespeare's living line,
Not from these frigid breviates of mine,
Long before now your eyes had overflowed;
Your hearts beat thick; your cheeks had paled and glowed
With alternation quick of every mood
That pity, sorrow, soft solicitude,
And generous indignation kindling high,
Can call from depths of human sympathy.
Oh! mighty genius who with magic pen
Can lead us thus at large through hearts of men,
And make us, as each fresh illusion's wrought,
Blameless partakers in all human thought,
Forgive the hand, that, having dared intrude
This patch on thy majestic magnitude,
Withdraws abashed; while in the authentic scene
To Roman Lucius thus speaks Cymbeline.

The 'Breviates' were dedicated to Dr Graves in the
following lines:—

Graves, first to light the lamp that brightest burns
Amidst our City's cinerary urns,
Whose voice interpretive of every shade
Of thought and feeling, has so often made,
In Shakespeare Readings 'mongst our joint compeers,
Dublin delightful, these last twenty years;
Accept—and view it with a favouring mind—
This Book of Breviates by your friend designed
To bring the Plays you love within the reach
And compass of a two hours' reading each.

   .   .   .   .   .   .

Farewell, old friend; may many a union yet
Of gentle spirits give us to forget,
In *his* perennial youth, our weight of years,
Our cares of duty, and our country's tears.

Dublin, *10th May* 1882.

CHAPTER IX.

1838–1867.

FERGUSON'S WORK AS A LAWYER.

"Still in thy right hand carry gentle peace,
    To silence envious tongues.   Be just, and fear not:
    Let all the ends thou aim'st at be thy country's,
    Thy God's, and truth's."
                                —SHAKESPEARE.

CALLED to the Bar of Ireland in Trinity Term 1838, Ferguson thenceforward gave his chief attention to his professional work. He had, as many others, to make his way under discouragements and by slow degrees; but he attended conscientiously to such legal business as came to him. When he had cases to prepare he would sit up far into the night, never retiring to rest till his work for the next day was mastered. Not even his wedding was permitted to interfere with his engagement to defend Richard Dalton Williams, then in prison on a charge of treason felony. Before starting on his bridal tour he had, as already stated, driven to Kilmainham gaol, and after an interview with his client, had arranged to return in a few days and remain at Howth, prepared to undertake this heavy responsibility when called on.

Ferguson's speech on behalf of his client was as follows :—

I am counsel for Richard Dalton Williams, who is indicted here by her Majesty's Attorney-General for felony as publisher of the 'Tribune' newspaper. Another indictment has been preferred against Mr Williams, not by a responsible public officer acting as the Attorney-General does, openly in the discharge of an honourable duty, but by irresponsible accusers writing anonymously in the press, which is regarded as the supporters of English power in this country. The charge of felony is a very grave one; and the punishment annexed to it is sufficiently dreadful to make my client, and to make me, anxious for the result of this prosecution. But, earnestly as he repels the Attorney-General's imputation, still more earnestly does he, and still more anxiously do I, with indignation and abhorrence repel the charges of his irresponsible accusers. The Attorney-General tells you Mr Williams is a traitor; his anonymous accusers tell you he is what is called a Red Republican, a Communist, an Infidel.

Gentlemen, my client is not a Republican. He believes, as philosophic men have believed in all ages of the world, that the most perfect abstract form of Government is that of a Republic; but he also believes that such a system would be unsuitable to this country, and he can with perfect sincerity point to the throne of her Gracious Majesty, surrounded by the constitutional Estates of the realm, and say with the wise and patriotic Frenchman, when after the Revolution of the Three Days in Paris he presented their future monarch to the people, still in doubt as to their form of government, "Behold here the best Republic!" . . .

He is not a Communist. . . . If there be amongst us any who believe the theory of a community of goods capable of realisation amongst men actuated by the common motives and instincts of our human nature, they must not count on any companionship or countenance from my client. He knows perfectly well that no man would labour to lay anything by if he had not the expectation of enjoying the fruits of his toil when realised in the shape of property; he knows that the right to enjoy the results of labour is the guarantee of industry, and the first right of labour itself.   If, therefore, there be any enthusiasts—I believe there are not a dozen such in Ireland—who believe in the visionary schemes of Fourier or of Flocan, let them not suppose that their folly has any countenance from the man who now stands arraigned before you, not because he has sought to array any right of labour against the right of property, but because he has sought to array, and while life is in him will continue to seek to array, the just rights and claims of his country against what he considers the usurpation and the tyranny of a particular section of her Majesty's subjects.

He is not an Infidel.   He prays God, with the charity of a pious Christian, to forgive his slanderers that scandalous and unchristian calumny.   Gentlemen, I am not a member of that ancient and venerable Church within whose fold Mr Williams seeks for salvation, and has found tranquillity and cheerfulness under afflictions; but I would be unworthy of the noble and generous Protestant religion which I profess, if I could withhold my sympathy and my respectful admiration from those services to religion and to piety which Mr Williams has rendered, both by his personal exertions in founding one of the most efficient of public charities—I mean the Society of St Vincent de Paul—and by his pen in embodying in pure and beautiful poetry the highest aspirations of faith and the noblest sentiments of patriotism.   A reverential respect prevents me, as one of a different faith, dwelling longer on what Mr Williams has done according to the practice of his own Church in the cause of religion and for the relief of the poor; but in speaking of his services to the literature of this country, I may claim the privilege of an old fellowship with him in the delightful service of the Muses, and may perhaps be allowed to declare that in my judgment the first of our living Irish poets after Moore is the gentleman now standing before you arraigned in this indictment.

Gentlemen, it is now just five years since the readers of the 'Nation' newspaper, at that time conducted by the late Mr Davis, were made aware of the noble and graceful mind of a new writer by the appearance in its pages of the first contribution of "Shamrock," the name under which Mr Williams contributed his poems. His teaching then, as since, was such as the best friends of society might expect from a man of humanity and genius.

I open the 'Spirit of the Nation' at his first contribution, . . . and how does this accomplished gentleman, who is now arraigned for seeking to plunge his country in civil war, address his brother Irishmen?—

> " Though thy cheek insulted burn—
>   Though they call thee coward-slave—
> Scoff nor blow shalt thou return :
>   Trust me, this is *more* than brave.
> Fortitude hath shackles riven,
>   More than spear or flashing gun ;
> Freedom, like the thrones of heaven,
>   Is by suff'ring virtue won.
> Though thy brother still deride thee,
>   Yield thou love for foolish hate ;
> He'll perhaps, ere long, beside thee,
>   Proudly, boldly, share thy fate."

But although as a poet Mr Williams might have taken the highest rank in literature, and earned wealth and honour in the service of the national Muse, he preferred for his distinction in life the service of the sick and the relief of the poor, and occupied himself in the study and practice of medicine—that most humane of the learned professions ; and the fact of his being brought in the prosecution of his medical duties into continued contact with the poor and afflicted, is one which I doubt not will impress itself on your attention as affording a possible explanation for the devoted self-sacrificing earnestness with which Mr Williams has lately espoused the cause of the poor. For, gentlemen, this quarrel is especially the quarrel of the poor and afflicted. Thus it came, that having been among the

poor during the year of famine, and during the year of sup-
plemental famine, he is now here because for these two
years he has been made practically familiar with the misery
of his countrymen—has been convinced that the state of
society in which such horrors have occurred can only be
remedied by a rejection of that English legislation which
has made this, our poor unhappy country, the abode of misery,
distrust, and disaffection.   Gentlemen, in seeking a repeal of
the Act of Union in whole or in part, no subject of the Queen
is guilty of any offence in the eye of the law. . . . The popular belief that repeal means rebellion is a vulgar error, and
a man may be a loyal subject of the Queen and entitled to a
verdict of acquittal on a charge of treason, even though he
does deny the right of England to legislate for Ireland.   For,
gentlemen, the law and constitution under which we really
live—a law and constitution outraged more systematically
and audaciously by the press of England than even by what
is called the felon press of this country—is that in this United
Kingdom of Great Britain and Ireland each part is governed
by the whole, and neither by the other.   Under that constitution no free-born Englishman recognises the existence of an
Irish Crown or Irish Government; and if you spoke to him
of Irish supremacy or dominion within the United Kingdom,
if you spoke to him of an Irish garrison holding England for
this country, would stand astonished at the audacity of such
a pretension; or if you attempted to enforce such a supremacy
upon him by force, would fly to arms to repel your insolent
aggressions.   Gentlemen, just so, no free-born Irishman can
recognise any British crown or sovereignty in our United Kingdom, and knows no allegiance whatever to England or to the
English people; and if the English or any section of them sought
to enforce an English supremacy over the rest of the United
Kingdom by arms, by arms would and ought to resist that
invasion of the public liberties. . . . The people of this island,
the loyal Irish-born subjects of the Queen, and members of
the United Kingdom, have a perfect right to resent, to resist,
and to overthrow such a power, if attempted to be exercised
over them by any people on earth except the Queen, Lords,

and Commons of the United Kingdom itself. And I repeat it again and again, and I shout it into the ears of the servile traitors who are not ashamed to call themselves an English garrison in their own country, that to assert any authority in any part or section of the United Kingdom less than the whole, to make laws to bind any other section of the realm, is unconstitutional, unlawful, and not to be whispered in a court of justice. We are part and parcel with them of one Imperial body, their friends and fellow-labourers for the general good ; assuming no jurisdiction over them, suffering no assumption of jurisdiction by them over us, their equals in the eye of the law, members with them while the Union lasts of one United Kingdom ; but their slaves never ! Gentlemen, it is not my place to tell you that in point of fact such a usurpation does exist; for if it did, the corollary would be another affirmation such as neither my inclination nor my duty would permit. But what I mean to submit to you, and it is the issue tendered here by the Crown, is, whether, when speaking as the writers of these presented articles do of British and English misrule and oppression, and of the necessity of resenting it, they may not have conscientiously, however mistakenly, if mistaken, have believed that that Anglican usurpation had reached such a pitch as to call for resistance. For here you are to judge of the prisoner, as you, and he, and I, and all of us, will hereafter be judged by God, not according to the weakness or error of the understanding, but according to the purity and truth of the heart.

Williams was acquitted ; and he was the only one among the prisoners tried in the summer and autumn of 1848 who was fortunate enough to leave the dock a free man. He afterwards emigrated to the United States, where he pursued for the rest of his short life his profession as a doctor.

Ferguson has recorded an incident which occurred on the eve of Mr R. Dalton Williams's trial :—

On the night before Mr Williams's trial two gentlemen, whom I had not previously known, waited on me in my study and avowed themselves the authors.   What they stated left no doubt on my mind that they were the writers of all the articles of a similar character in the leading rebellious organs of that day.   They offered, if I thought it could serve Mr Williams, to come forward as witnesses at the trial and take his liability for the articles in the 'Tribune' on themselves.   I admired their generosity, but declined, as counsel, to advise that course ; and Mr Williams had the good fortune to be acquitted without the pain of implicating any other person.   Neither of these gentlemen has, or, so far as I know, ever had, any connection with any Government office in this city or elsewhere.   Of course I have not divulged the name or given any clue to the identity of either, and of course I never will.

This incident, which is worthy of being preserved as characteristic of the young men of that period, has been mentioned by me in private, and I am glad this opportunity has been afforded me to take a matter of so much importance to others out of the region of oral uncertainty.

It is sometimes said that Literature and Law are incompatible, and that a poet cannot make a successful pleader.   It is true that, Art being long and Time short, supreme excellence is rarely attained otherwise than by undivided devotion to one pursuit.   Energetic minds, however, can accomplish a vast amount of labour; and diversified work is restful to the brain. At least it may be allowed that the student restricted to Law only, is by no means so delightful in society as the man of wider culture.

That Ferguson devoted himself to the interests of his clients is apparent in nearly all the letters written to his wife from Circuit.   In those which are here given, he relates the details of a protracted case in

which he finally succeeded in reversing former deci-
sions, and in obtaining a verdict for the defendant,
in the case of Glasgow *v.* Sloan.

DOWNPATRICK, *July* 13, 1860.

I am delighted to know that you are so well and happy.
To add to your satisfaction I must tell you that I all but
succeeded in getting a verdict for my poor client Sloan in
the great Water-house case. The trial lasted four days, and
although there had been a verdict against us already, and
an award also against us by three arbitrators, we made so
powerful a case as to dispel almost completely the cloud
of suspicion that had rested on the defendant. I succeeded
in getting Robert Mallet to come down and give evidence;
and nothing could exceed the cleverness of his evidence: he
was prepared for everything. When, for the purpose of
showing that the defendant's standard pier had been altered,
they showed that the mortar taken from it changed the colour
of their pocket-linings and gloves, Mallet was prepared, with
samples of the same mortar taken from unimpeached parts
of the same building, to produce the same effects on calico
and leather of the same colours. When they produced their
levelling instruments, he detected their inaccuracies, blew
up their models, and really delighted us all with his readiness
and ability.

ARMAGH, *8th March* 1861.

I attempted twice to write you a line yesterday, but each
time was hauled back to the field of battle, where the fight
rages with unextinguished ardour around the Standard Pillar
of my old client Sloan. . . .

I have been desperately hard-worked. One day we began
at 9 A.M., and concluded at ¼ past 12 at night.

This, my 51st birthday—how swiftly, time!—was signalised
at 2 o'clock this morning, after a second four-day fight, by
a triumph such as rarely occurs in the progress of litigation.
I got to bed at half-past one, utterly prostrated by the work of

yesterday, which began at half-past 9 and lasted till after midnight, and this morning was rejoiced to receive the enclosed, informing me of the result.   I believe in my conscience this verdict is the very truth, and the poor old man whom it acquits, after two former condemnations by other tribunals, is righteously justified at last.   But it broke the heart of his wife.   She died a few weeks ago.   He will carry home, however, a joyful message to his daughters.   It was the hardest-fought case I ever was engaged in.   During the four days it lasted we never left court earlier than 7 o'clock in the evening, and strong as I am, I was nearly broken down.   We had also very hard work at Monaghan.   We were 15 hours in court in the last case heard there.

I got a good rest, however, to-day, and look on my remaining business here as a trifle.   I have had great enjoyment of the air and country.   On Sunday I travelled through the Bath and Shirley estates, and saw a good deal of the condition of the people; but I would rather already be back again with you, darling companion of my heart.

The weather just now is delightful, the country lovely, Circuit so far prosperous, and love for you, dear Molly, undiminished.   I hope you have as much enjoyment of the face of nature where you are. ·Go up some day among the green hills where we had our walk this time (how many?) years ago; and, if you choose to imagine me by your side, you may, and may believe my heart and affections are there at all events.

The social intercourse with his compeers of the North-East Circuit was much enjoyed by Ferguson. Many of his brethren, besides being good and pleasant fellows, possessed

"The melting voice through mazes running,"

and could evoke the hidden soul of harmony at their

evenings round the mess-table. Ferguson, in his turn, was called on to sing. He obeyed; but the performance was so unsatisfactory that it was agreed that his contribution to the jest and jollity and sport that wrinkled Care derides, should take the form of recitation of lively original verse. For some occasion of the kind he produced "The Loyal Orangeman." It at once became a favourite, for he could render it perfectly in the Northern dialect. A member of the Circuit has recorded its reception at the mess-table :—

It brought back to me, as I am sure it did to all the more senior members of the North-East Circuit still living, the most pleasing memories of its genial and gifted author, as well as of the Circuit itself, and its associations and surroundings, in the good old days when Ferguson was one of its most brilliant lights and sparkling wits. Those who remember the North-East Circuit some thirty or forty years ago, can well recall to memory the crowd of legal luminaries and distinguished orators who, after the day's fatigue from professional labour, used to assemble round the Bar mess-table in the evening for dinner, contributing their ready wit and repartee to make the most delightful "Noctes Ambrosianæ"; old Robert Holmes presiding as Father; Sir Thomas Staples, who afterwards became Father; Whiteside, after fairly laughing some dishonest or trumpery case out of court; Joseph Napier, Toombe, Gilmore, Joy, and, though last not least, O'Hagan. Then, as now, the call of the Father for a song, a sentiment, or a recitation was deemed a command, disobedience or contumacy to which was visited with the penalty of a fine, to be paid in champagne or claret; and never was the command of the Father more loudly applauded or more loyally obeyed than when Sam Ferguson was called on to recite for the benefit of the mess his "Loyal Orangeman of Portadown." He was no singer, but he made ample compensation, and something more, by recitation of some of his own compositions, and no one who

ever heard him recite "The Loyal Orangeman" can forget
its effect.

THE LOYAL ORANGEMAN.

A am a loyal Orangeman
From Portadown upon the Bann ;
My loyalty, A will maintain,
Was ever and always without stain,
Though rebelly Papishes may call
My loyalty "conditional."
A never did insist upon
Nor ask condition beyont the one—
The crown o' the causeway on road and street,
And the Papishes put under my feet !

'Twas when rebellion threatened the State
In the month of April in '48,
A mounted up upon my hackney,
And off A started to General Blakeney.
Says I, "Sir Edward, here we are,
Six hundred mortial men of war,
All ready and able, never fear,
To march from the Causeway to Cape Clear,
And drive the rebels would dar' to raise
The Irish colours, intill the says ! "

Then what div' ye think my buffer sly
Had the imperance for to reply ?
Says he, " Your offer's very fair,
And very timely A do declare,
For here we're all as one as besieged,
So for your offer we're much obleeged ;
But ye won't object, A hope, to mix
In the ranks of the—loyal Catholics ? "
There was sitting by, never lettin' on,
That rebelly Papish, Radington ;

And that other Papisher rebel still,
The fella they call Somerville :
A gave them both, as A made reply,
A look from the corner of my eye.
A said, "Make no excuse, A pray,
For asking us to serve that way,
We wouldn't think the trouble much—
For we don't allow there's any such ! "
You'd have given a pound to see the two,
And the way they looked, as A withdrew.

Well, what div' ye think, sir?   After that
A thought A might put on my hat ;
But, hell to my sowl, if they didn't send
And ask me back by a private friend.
And A seen the Colonel, and brave John Pitt,
And A got a gun, and A hev' it yit,
And if ever the rebelly villians dar'
Again to provoke the North to war,
That Radington, the Papish dog,
Is the very first man A'll shoot, by Gog!

Of the members of the North-East Circuit spoken of as forming the society round the mess-table, the seniors, Robert Holmes and Sir Thomas Staples, passed away to the "great majority," making room for other men. Sir Joseph Napier and Thomas, Lord O'Hagan sat at a later time on the Woolsack. So also did Hugh Law, Ferguson's Circuit companion. Whiteside became Chief-Justice. Joy as well as Ferguson retired as Q.C.'s from the practice of the profession. Younger men in their turn came to the front, chief among these being the present Master of the Rolls, Andrew Marshall Porter.

In a recent speech—January 14, 1895—the Master

of the Rolls, alluding to Sir Samuel Ferguson, dwelt upon "one very characteristic quality of the poet and his works—that fine, delicate sense of humour, which was out of place, and therefore not developed, in most of the bardic poems, but which was indeed a delightful characteristic of some of the shorter works of his pen. Any one who had read 'Father Tom and the Pope' and 'The Loyal Orangeman' knew well what a master humorist he was."

The "Loyal Orangeman" had been no less acceptable to the uncle of the Master of the Rolls, the Hon. William Porter, for many years Attorney - General at the Cape of Good Hope, who returned to Ireland in 1863, and during his stay in Dublin renewed his friendship with Ferguson and made the acquaintance of his wife. Mr Porter revisited at this time his native county of Antrim, from whence he wrote to Mrs Ferguson to ask a copy of her husband's unpublished *skit*. Of this he acknowledged the receipt in the following letter :—

BUSHFOOT, 11th July 1863.

MY DEAR MRS FERGUSON,—Your kind note, with its enclosure, only reached me to-night. When or how it managed to preserve itself since it was written I cannot tell, but I am thankful that it came at last.

I began to fear that you could not send me the "Loyal Orangeman," and now that I have got him, I know better than before how great would have been my loss had you failed to comply with my request. Nothing more fresh, racy, and original has come my way for a long time. The language and the sentiment are North Country Orange all over. I am really obliged to you for the trouble you have taken. . . .

I need not send any message to your worthy husband, for he, of course, is out on Circuit, where I trust he is full of business. It was, I can with truth say, a real pleasure to me to see him in his silk gown, and to hear him so highly spoken of in many quarters. And it was a greater pleasure to see him happy in his own house, and to see, what was plain enough, to whom he owes his happiness.—Believe me, my dear Mrs Ferguson, yours very faithfully,   W. PORTER.

Henry Joy, Q.C., settled in Leamington. His health was not robust. A delicate literary taste gave zest to his leisure, and he printed for private circulation in 1873 a book which enshrined the thoughts of many minds, 'Horæ Otiosæ.' This he sent "To S. Ferguson, Q.C., LL.D., from one who appreciated his learning, courtesy, and cordiality on the North-East Circuit in bygone days." His old friend thanked Mr Joy in the following letter:—

I am glad to know where to address my thanks for your very welcome volume [wrote Ferguson]. I cast wistful eyes on Leamington when passing through to Banbury on a recent visit to my wife's brother, Robert Guinness, who is Vicar there. We also sought the address at Cheltenham, whither we had an invitation to another relative, but without avail. Now I thank you truly. In your book I have my old friend beside me; because, though the words are not yours, the wisdom and the goodness they breathe are part of yourself. Your daughter's lines are full of the rhythm and of the emotion of Elizabeth Barrett Browning, which is praise I would not accord to many. I have the most affectionate remembrance of Stanford, though the constitution—imperfect I am sure— of my own mind prevented my sympathising fully with him in the leading subjects of his thoughts. I have not for many years seen the 'University' or written in any Magazine. I aim, before the fire goes out, at doing something that may

bid at least for endurance; and, *eheu Posthume!* I feel I
had need to make haste.   My occasional work is archæological.   Here I have a motive, to particular research which
entertains the holidays wherever I go.   Last August I made
a neat little discovery of an Ogham inscription which completed the identification by the "Rosetta Stone" process
of the last unascertained letters of the Ogham alphabet.   I
enclose a paragraph about it cut from a newspaper.

I had a very agreeable time with friends in Devonshire,
and afterwards in Cornwall, where I corrected—I am vain
enough to think—some erroneous readings of certain inscriptions celebrated since the days of Gough and Borlase; for,
you must know, I have devised manipulative methods of
making casts of such objects, which I practise with excessive
enjoyment.

Others among the juniors of the North-East Circuit
who attained the rank of Q.C. were Randal M'Donnell,
handsome, accomplished, happy in his wife, his children, and his surroundings, till his health compelled
him to winter in a southern clime, from whence he
returned to die.   His memory " smells sweet and
blossoms in the dust."

Another is now Recorder of Dublin.   In those early
days he was always spoken of by Ferguson as " dear
Freddy Falkiner."   And now the Recorder writes
(1895) of "the beautiful life-work of a very well-
beloved friend," for which he has " the sympathy and
appreciation it deserves."   Mr Falkiner is a man of
warm heart, ever active in the cause of the poor.

Last, but not least of the younger members of the
Circuit to whom Ferguson was attached, was Henry
FitzGibbon, Q.C., now Recorder of Belfast.   He was
a next-door neighbour for nineteen years, and the

families naturally became very intimate. The Recorder of Belfast, now resident in the county of Antrim, within reach of his judicial work, has approved himself a man of clear, calm judgment and unswerving probity.

Such were the members of the North-East Bar while Ferguson went Circuit. With the heads of his profession, from Lord Chancellors to puisne Judges, he was popular and respected.

Many cordial letters from these, chiefly on legal or social matters which it would be tedious to quote, show how highly they esteemed him. He retired from his practice at the Bar at the conclusion of the Summer Circuit 1867, having accepted the office of Deputy Keeper of the Records of Ireland, offered to him by Lord Naas, then Chief Secretary for Ireland.

Ferguson was subsequently entertained at a dinner by his legal brethren, who proposed his health with all the honours. He returned thanks as follows:—

I am very grateful to you for inviting me to sit as your guest at this board when I am no longer entitled to address you as brethren; and the cordial reception you have just now given to my name fills my breast with sincere pleasure. It is a pleasure not the less appreciated because it is not wholly unmingled with regret. A connection such as mine of wellnigh thirty years' standing with a body such as yours is not sundered without a pull at the heart-strings. Everything here reminds me of scenes and associations which have become very dear to me. The genial gathering at Dundalk—the walks compensating the absence of business at Monaghan—the arrival of the reinforcements from Dublin, with the day mail's contingent of jovial good-humour, of music and learning, at Armagh—the ripening hopes, even, that time will yet ripen our old port at Downpatrick—the week's hard work merging into the judicial hospitalities, and the final relaxation and the glad return to our homes from Belfast,—all these crowd upon my recollection standing here on the eve of the Spring Circuit, and bidding good-bye to them all. And far above any amenities of place or circumstance was the daily intercourse, the habitual open-hearted interchange of thought and feeling, with men whom I have learned to esteem, and many of whom I have come to love, which I must also forego. The parting from such scenes and such companionships is not a thing to be thought of without a pang even in our most joyous moments. However, my fate has cast me not far from you. I can see you from my windows passing to and fro on your daily avocations, and as often as I recognise one of the well-remembered figures, I can breathe you an aspiration that your facts may be clear, your authorities weighty, your conclusions sound, your equanimity, come what will of the case, unaffected, and that in your hands may long remain unsullied, if possible gathering increased lustre, that precious deposit of professional honour which has been handed down to you through a long succession of illus- ' trious predecessors. Again I thank you from the bottom of my heart, and to the bottom of my glass I drink—with a full appreciation of the value of what I wish—to all your right good healths.

Ferguson made a considerable pecuniary sacrifice in retiring when he did from his practice at the Bar. But he felt the strain and anxieties of the profession, which told seriously on his health; and not having a family to provide for, he was indifferent to wealth, and was well pleased to accept a secure though moderate income. Not that he sought for inaction. His mind was never unoccupied, nor his pen idle. In a letter written in 1875 to a former client he thus expresses his feelings :—

I sometimes long for the excitement of a good speech—I mean good in the sense of vocal exercise—and the strategies of the consultation. But, on the whole, I am well content with my duties. I have a staff of excellent officers, and of workmen not to be surpassed; and I reign supreme among them, whether palæographers, smiths, or carpenters. What more could a man of sixty-five reasonably desire? My heart suffers a wound sometimes when I see men, as much in advance of me in legal learning and ability as they are, alas! in seniority and standing, still engaged in the routine of Court practice. I fancy some might almost sigh for the retreat *ubi sæva indignatio cor ulterius lacerare nequit.* I ought to thank God I am out of the way of ambition and disappointments.

CHAPTER X.

1849.

A TOUR TO KILLARNEY—IRISH FAMINE.

> "Alas, poor country,—
> Almost afraid to know itself!   It cannot
> Be call'd our mother, but our grave ; where nothing
> But who knows nothing, is once seen to smile ;
> Where sighs, and groans, and shrieks that rend the air,
> Are made, not mark'd ; where violent sorrow seems
> A modern ecstasy ; the dead man's knell
> Is there scarce ask'd for who ; and good men's lives
> Expire before the flowers in their caps,
> Dying or ere they sicken."
> —SHAKESPEARE.

IN the summer of 1849 Ferguson and his wife had a delightful visit to Killarney in company with English friends, Mr Charles Knight and Mr Douglas Jerrold.

Mr Knight, a charming old gentleman, winning and genial in manner, was a pioneer among those bene-factors of mankind who have given to us pure and good literature in a cheap and accessible form.   He was the author of 'Studies of Shakspere,' 'The Popular History of England,' and many other interesting works.   Mr Jerrold was not only a witty writer and constant contributor to ' Punch,' but a man of brilliant intellect united to much kindness of heart.

The weather at Killarney on this occasion left nothing to be desired. The scenery, always lovely, and already familiar to Ferguson and his wife, but now looked on for the first time by their English friends, appeared to the greatest advantage. Days passed rapidly; driving, boating, mountaineering on horseback or on foot—not a spot was left unvisited. The brilliant wit of Jerrold stimulated the ever-ready Irish humour: guides, boatmen, and buglemen responded to his puns. The kindly, genial nature of Knight, thoroughly happy in his surroundings, and Ferguson's poetic raptures and ecstatic delight in scenery, made this sojourn among the loveliest scenes of Nature a memorable one. On subsequent visits to Killarney—for Ferguson and his wife again and again, and at all seasons, revisited these beauteous lakes—they found that the tour of 1849 had not faded from the memories of the people of the district.

The last day of their stay at Killarney was devoted by Ferguson to the ascent of Carran-Tual, the most lofty mountain in Ireland. The rest of the party did not attempt so arduous a task, but spent the day on the lakes, fishing, and visiting the islands. Towards evening they rowed to the head of the Upper Lake to meet the absent one and his guide, who had started early, and expected to descend the mountain on that side about sunset. They were true to their appointment, had landed from the boat, but the " gloaming

and the mirk " had been succeeded by moonlight before
their anxieties were relieved.   On reaching the boat,
Ferguson threw himself down in an exhausted condition, and so remained till the Lower Lake was reached.
The food he had carried with him had been shared
with the starving people he met, for famine was sore
in the land.   Mr Knight has described this evening :—

One more day at Killarney, and then farewell !   How shall
that day be passed by us?   In perfect repose.   One of our
companions has gone to perform the difficult feat of ascending
Carran-Tual.   We are to meet him with the boat long before
sundown at the head of the Upper Lake.   We are true to the
appointment.   There is one with us watching for him with
some anxiety;   but the scene is so glorious that anxiety can
scarcely find a place even in the breast of a loving wife.   The
mountains are lighted up with all the most gorgeous hues of
heaven.   The full moon is up—we wander on, far away from
the lake, through the Black Valley.   Solemn and more solemn
grow the shadows of the mountains.   The sun is altogether
gone.   Then the rocks begin to put on mysterious forms.
Not a sound falls upon the hushed air.   A footstep ! one of
our friend's guides is come to beg us yet to wait.   It was a
needless message.   But that poor guide—he has fallen in his
rough descent, and is badly wounded.   Fear then begins ; but
at length the wished-one comes, worn out, but safe.   He has
beheld sights from Carran-Tual which we would see ourselves
if we were twenty years younger.

And now, one sight that all Killarney visitors should behold,
if possible, at the risk of some inconvenience—a row of twelve
miles under the light of the summer moon.   As we came up
the lake, four hours ago, we marked every form of hill and
island.   They are now all blended in one faint tint, when

" A sable cloud
Turns forth her silver lining on the night ; "

or suddenly touched with the partial light of the full orb,

which renders them even more indistinct in the unshadowy splendour.   In the evening glow we saw the heron fishing. The owl now flaps by us, startled.   We rest under Glena; and there, in the deep silence of midnight, we hear the mountain echo to the bugle in a voice which seems unearthly.   A night ever to be remembered.

It was midnight when the Victoria Hotel was reached.   It was illuminated in every window.   Boats were out on the Lower Lake to search and rescue, for it was feared that some mischance had happened. But we were safe, and full of thankfulness.   Yet the memory of that night remains.   Its silent beauty, the soft splendour of the moon, the exquisite scenery through which we passed, the magical effects of mountain - peaks and jutting crags as they revealed their outlines touched by her beams.   The immeasurable heavens above, the placid lake below ruffled only by the boatmen's oars, impressed on our spirits a sense of quietude, solemnity, and peace indescribably sweet.

The charm of Gansey's performance on the Irish pipes has been described by Mr Knight:—

A night is before us such as we cannot forget.   Gansey, the famous piper of Killarney, gives us the pleasure of his company.   A venerable man, blind; a man of real genius — a gentleman.   All the old traditionary music of Ireland is familiar to him.   He has his modern ballads for those who want an ordinary pleasure; but if he have " audience fit though few," he will pour out strain after strain, wild and solemn, gay or pathetic, with a power that seems like inspiration.   Never heard we such effects from one instrument

since the days of Paganini's violin.   Midnight was past
before we ceased to listen, enraptured, to

> "Many a winding bout
> Of linkèd sweetness long drawn out."

The enjoyment of this tour, in such congenial companionship, would have been perfect, had it not been for the evidences everywhere painfully visible of the terrible effects of famine.   Mr Knight's sympathetic words in his paper on Killarney in ' The Land we Live in ' may again be quoted :—

Two emaciated little girls, preternaturally pallid, have watched the arrival of the stranger, and are come to offer their gleanings of the woods—a hart's horn—a wild nosegay. Poor wretched children, all mirth of childhood is vanished from their faces.   In the mountain-hovel where they crouch there has been grievous want.   They have become acquainted with the bitterness of life very early.   And we are pleasure-seeking !   We are surrendering ourselves to all sweet thoughts and influences !   "The sunshine of the breast" is driving out all remembrances of fear and trouble.   But *now*, when we think of that quiet place in the luxuriant woods, the faces of these poor children still haunt the spot and make us sad.

If such impressions as these were produced on English visitors by witnessing misery resulting from famine, what must have been the anguish of Irishmen, fellow-countrymen of these hapless victims of the mismanagement of Government !   For if the failure of the food of the people in 1846-47 was rightly viewed as the visitation of Providence, the starvation of 1848-49 may be laid to the account of the *doctrinaires* who prohibited the reproductive expenditure of relief-funds, which they insisted must be laid out on road-making—more truly described as road-marring. It will be remembered that when the public calamity first showed itself, the Irish Council made a genuine attempt to deal with it. In the words of Sir C. Gavan Duffy—

They thought that under the Union such a visitation of Providence ought to be treated as the common responsibility of the United Kingdom; but this [writes Sir Charles, with a not unnatural tone of bitterness] was the proverbial oversight of reckoning without their host. The stronger member of the partnership had determined that, though there should not be a separate kingdom of Ireland for the purpose of self-protection, it must be peremptorily isolated in its afflictions.

. Many thoughtful Irishmen, of whom Ferguson was one, were convinced that if the representative men then assembled in Council, who knew the needs of their country and its people, had been listened to, the added misery of 1848-49 might have been averted.

Moreover, at this very time it was reported that the Viceroy had been commissioned to prepare the office he held to be "despised and abolished." It was rumoured also that the removal of the Irish Courts of Law to Westminster was about to be effected. Of this centralising policy Ferguson was "an implacable enemy." He opposed throughout life the schemes "of those projectors and centralisers who keep society in Ireland from consolidating into a settled strength and refinement." Acting on these convictions, he proposed a resolution at a public meeting in the Rotunda, from which a few passages are quoted here :—

The resolution which has been committed to me will weigh with all who will recognise the deduction from undoubted truths, of sound conclusions.   It is in these words :—

"That we are determined, by all constitutional methods, to resist the further progress of centralisation—of which this proposed measure is a part—and which we consider unjust, offensive, and contrary to true economy; that it costs the State more to repress the discontents caused by past metropolitan plunder of local institutions than would support all our civil authorities in dignity and peace ; and that a prudent economy, while it would find ample occasion for its exercise in other branches of the public expenditure, would respect those institutions through which the Irish people have, since beyond the time of legal memory, participated in the splendour and emoluments of the State, and which cannot be wrested from them without the perpetuation of a deep and just sense of national wrong."

This resolution, my Lord Mayor, affirms that, in the opinion of this meeting, we cannot accept the declaration of Lord Clarendon, that the progress of centralisation is not hereafter to be carried out by any further attempt upon our existing institutions.   Perfectly satisfied as I am that a nobleman in the position of Lord Clarendon would not pledge his word to anything but what he believed to be true, I must declare that I find it utterly impossible to believe that the system of centralisation begun by the Union, continued by the transfer of those institutions which since then have been taken away, and now intended to be carried this step further, will stop here or even cease, until London shall have grasped to itself the dignity and the endowments of our courts of law and equity.   My Lord, both countries unfortunately have had occasion to understand how little dependence can be placed on the promise of any minister or statesman in respect of the maintenance of an interest such as this.   However honest, however generous or upright, the minister may be, who declares there is no intention of taking this or that step in matters of public policy, they are all equally subject to the coercion of public opinion ; all are equally drawn onward in the irresistible current of public interests and national instincts : and I tell you now, that if this flood-gate be once opened, the current that it will set in motion can never cease — let statesmen make what pledges of finality they will—until it shall have absorbed all your remaining institutions. . . .

Remembering that in 1824, in an official publication prepared under the direction of the Commissioners of Records for England in the 'Liber Hiberniæ'—a vast collection of official and statistical State Papers—all our civil, all our ecclesiastical, and all our legal offices are marked out for successive absorption into London,—and considering the terms in which the compiler of that work expresses himself, I must believe Lord Clarendon as a nobleman and a gentleman, but I cannot credit him as a statesman. I shall read for the meeting an extract from this compilation :—

"It is good to repeat here, once for all, and for the last time, a truth which ought not for a moment to be dissembled or overlooked : 'That until the Law and the Church departments are incorporated with the parent ones in England, the Union is but half accomplished.' Nor should there remain any office of Lord Lieutenant, or any separate State department at all. While to administer the national law and religion of England impartially in Ireland, English judges only, English high clergymen, and bishops should be commissioned in ordinary."

Let not, then, Lord Clarendon suppose that we offer to him any personal affront in assuming in the resolution, on grounds higher than any statesman's promises—on considerations of the necessary tendency of human affairs, and judging from the past, of what will be the probable progress of future events—that this proposed measure is a part of this same predetermined and pernicious system of centralisation which the resolution affirms to be unjust, offensive, and contrary to true economy. With regard to its injustice, I shall say no more than that we understand the definition of injustice to include the act of taking from another that which is his, without consideration of the offensiveness of the proposed invasion. But on the point of its being opposed to true economy the resolution contains something, and I shall suggest something further, which this meeting will do well deliberately to consider, and if it be of the same opinion, emphatically to affirm. The resolution declares that it costs the State more to repress the discontents caused by London's past plunder of local institutions than would support all our civil establishments in dignity and peace. . . .

But I put it on higher ground than a mere money question, or than a mere tradesman's question. Political economists define wealth to be that which has an exchangeable value. Refined society, intelligence, virtue, patriotism,—all these bear an exchangeable value—all these are wealth, even on the low ground they put it on. It is not a mere annual sum of money of which they would deprive us, but of our higher, richer, social privileges. It is not because the Viceregal Court sets the fashion in taste or in manners—the best taste and the most amiable manners are found in circles not within its immediate influence. It is not on that account that we reckon it among our social commodities bearing a high exchangeable value, and of which we cannot be deprived without deep and lasting injury, but because it brings under one head and into one focus all whose position in society affords *prima facie* presumption of social worth, and gives us the opportunity of making our social selections from the whole body of the rich and educated classes. . . .

The Viceroyalty is coeval with the constitution in this country—it is the same office, under another name, that was filled by De Courcy and De Lacy. I ask the people of England, Do they view this question as mere economists, or as men and brothers? I believe that, in point of mere money-saving, the English people are totally indifferent to this question. I believe that outside of London there is no feeling for the abolition of the Irish Viceroyalty which would not be removed by a five minutes' candid consideration of the reasons offered here to-day. . . .

But if it be neither to gratify their pride nor fill their pockets that they demand this abolition of the Irish Court, then it is confessed that they have no interest in the matter save for our advantage; and if that be so, then we, and we alone, are the proper parties to judge the question, and pronounce upon it as we have pronounced, and now again pronounce, our unanimous disapproval.

It was in 1849 that Ferguson published in the 'Dublin University Magazine' his poems, "Inheritor and Economist," and "Dublin: A Poem in imitation of the Third Satire of Juvenal," utterances of the *sæva indignatio cor lacerans*, and from these we extract a few powerful passages.

"Dublin," the satire in imitation of Juvenal, is the supposed utterance of an emigrant about to transfer himself from the Irish capital to San Francisco. The miseries of Ireland, the narrow views of the political economists of that day, the insults of the London press, and still more the galling thought that these contempts were sometimes penned by Irishmen, embittered the tone of the writer, to whom his country was so inexpressibly dear.

> Yes, I confess that crew degenerate
> Are they of men I most abominate;
> Nor shall one touch of tenderness debar
> My painting them the rascals that they are.

The intending emigrant thus states his grievances :—

> What should I do in Ireland?   I can't
> Play cosmopolitan court-sycophant:
> I, I admit, make not the least pretence
> To frank the fallacies of "common-sense";

Can't comprehend, and truly never could,
How absenteeism does any good ;
Nor how, just now, if Court and Parliament,
Lords, ladies, commoners, and madams went
To live at Petersburg, the Cockney folk
Should take it as an economic joke.

.   .   .   .   .   .

Worse still, I never yet could bear the jest
Would make me " evil bird " in my own nest,
Nor simpering cry, " How Irish ! " when some fool
Has haply broken Hoyle's or Priscian's rule :
Therefore, I'm no man's eligible guest
On no commission, and in no request.

In Ireland now would Irishmen advance?
Who but your supple servile has a chance?
And in the struggle for the helot's goal
Your foremost runners still the servile *drole ;*
For British patrons owe you nothing, till
You've made your Celtic selves contemptible.
Then view your efforts with approving eyes,
When they by contrast adequately rise,
And chiefly feel themselves exalted thus,
When most you make yourselves ridiculous.
But thou,—let not the uncounted treasures rolled
In yellow Sacramento's sands of gold
Tempt thee, young Irishman, while health is spared,
And strength, for winning honest sweat's reward,
To rise, howe'er the eminence be prized,
On helot arts, applauded and despised.

.   .   .   .   .   .

Ah, youths, before the gifted hand you lift
To strike your Mother, think who gave the gift ;
Nor scorn the land, though poor she be, and far,
That nursed the genius makes you what you are.
Far better ere to crime like this it come,
Live all your days in Dublin here at home ;

Your lives and virtues, as your works, approved,
Like Burton, self-respecting and beloved;
Or, though one sordid act might wealth secure,
Like patriot [Petrie] honourably poor.
Still, howsoe'er the sycophantic trade
Profane the pencil, or the pen degrade,
At least the Irish chisel shall be known
In noble and in lovely forms alone;
Thanks, Hogan—thanks, MacDowell; Foley, thine
Be all the grateful Graces' thanks, and mine!

.   .   .   .   .   .

Here men of feeling, ere they yet grow old,
Die of the very horrors they behold.
'Tis hard to sleep when one has just stood by,
And seen the strong man of sheer hunger die;
'Tis hard to draw an easy, healthful breath,
In fields that sicken with the air of death;
Or where relief invites the living throng
To see the withered phantoms flit along,
Hunger impelling and exhaustion still
Leaving the weak limbs baffled of the will.

.   .   .   .   .   .

Sure for our wretched country's various ills
We've got, a man would think, enough of bills,—
Bills to make paupers, bills to feed them made;
Bills to make sure that paupers' bills are paid;
Bills in each phrase of economic slang;
Bills to transport the men they dare not hang
(I mean no want of courage physical,
"'Tis conscience doth make cowards of us all").

.   .   .   .   .   .

But one short bill that served so well before
To keep us quiet, we're to have no more.

The painful, powerful picture of an afflicted country in the throes of famine describes—

> The weakling infants' moans,
> The mother's sobs, the maddened father's groans,
> The evicted cottier's shrieks ; the thousand cries
> That swell the ruined nation's obsequies ;
> And, 'mid the hubbub of our woes and crimes,
> The daily prate complacent of the ' Times.'

" Inheritor and Economist " is chiefly concerned with the case of the landlords :—

> To Erin once, ere yet disaster's list
> Was quite filled up, sailed Sir Economist ;
>
> .   .   .   .   .   .
>
> Here saw the squire, a wealthy magnate made
> By laws impolitic, that fettered trade
> (That fettered England's dearest trade), and there
> One asking alms yet free to take the air :
> " This land," quoth he, " is in a piteous plight,
> But haply I've been born to set it right."

"Economist" enunciates the doctrine of Free Trade, beneficial, no doubt, to a manufacturing country like England, but bringing down the price of agricultural commodities, which are those alone that Ireland can produce :—

> " For who would live, in careless ease, content
> With crops deficient, though redundant rent,
> When double crops, as good at half the price,
> Would reinstate our workshops in a trice,
> Would, with the loaf, bring wages down as well,
> And, underbought, leave free to undersell ;
> Till, spread o'er all the earth by steam and wind,
> Our British calicoes clothed all mankind,
> And science hailed the spectacle sublime,
> Of mighty England working double time ?
>
> .   .   .   .   .   .

Undo your selfish toll-bars with a grace,
And call the nations to your market-place ;
So shall your hapless island soon be made
Great, glorious, free, and fruitful by Free Trade ! ”
“ Sir,” said Inheritor, for such the name
By which our Irish squire is known to fame,
“ I bought this land when beef and corn were high,
Assured by law of your monopoly ;
And, trusting in your market still to get
Like preference, am something gone in debt.

   .   .   .   .   .   .

But still, I hope, the land itself secures
My mortgagee—a countryman of yours.”
“ Yes,” quoth Economist, “ ’tis justly said ;
Your mortgagee must first of all be paid.”

The Poor-Law is introduced, and the burden falls
on the land :—

“ Assuming, then, that ’tis the wiser way
To have a Poor-Law—pray, sir, who’s to pay ? ”
“ What ! who support the land’s neglected poor ?
The land that breeds the beggars, to be sure ! ”
“ Then,” said Inheritor, “ if that be so,
And if a portion of the rents must go
In poor-rate, still you’ll lay the burden on
Proportionately as the rents are drawn ;
Thus Mortgagee, who yearly skims away
The cream of mine, his quota, too, will pay.”
“ What ! charge the interest of Mortgagee ?
Sir, let me tell you, that’s flat burglary !
You promised Mortgagee his six per cent,
Whether from greater or from lesser rent.
You share no profits if your rents go up ;
He shares no losses, *contra*, if they drop.”
“ But when the contract for this loan was made,
· We neither of us dreamt the beggar’s trade

Would thus be undertaken by the State,
Else we'd have bargained to divide the rate :
And sure on one the charge unjustly bears,
When both are purchasers at unawares."

Such was the land's and such the ruler's plight,
When heaven at length, in anger, sent the blight.
With silent swiftness, in a mildew blast,
O'er Erin, in one night, the mischief passed :
Where eve had sunk in shining emerald track,
Morn showed the green potato-ridges black ;
And all the air, as with a sick man's breath,
Stunk o'er a waste of vegetable death.
Oh, God of Heaven ! it was a dreadful sight,
To see the mighty multitude's affright,
Who'd gone to rest, secure of food, when dawn
Showed, at a glance, their year's subsistence gone.
.   .   .   .   .   .

Deem not, O generous English hearts, who gave
Your noble aid our sinking isle to save,
This breast, though heated in its country's feud,
Owns aught towards you but perfect gratitude.
For every dish retrenched from homely boards,
For every guinea drawn from prudent hoards,
For every feast deferred, and jewels sold,
May God increase your stores a hundred-fold ;
Grant to you health and wealth, and love's increase ;
Here, and hereafter, Christ's eternal peace ;
Long keep your realm from discord unembroiled,
Your arms triumphant, and your flag unsoiled !
But, frankly while we thank you all who sent
Your alms, so thank we not your Parliament,
Who, what they gave, from treasures of our own
Gave, if you call it giving, this half-loan,
Half-gift from the recipients to themselves
Of their own millions, be they tens or twelves ;
Our own as well as yours : our Irish brows
Had sweated for them ; though your Commons' House,

Forgetting your four hundred millions debt,
When first in partnership our nations met,
Against our twenty-four (you then twofold
The poorer people), call them British gold.
No; for these drafts on our united banks
We owe no gratitude, and give no thanks,
More than you'd give to us, if Dorsetshire
Or York a like assistance should require;
Or than you gave us, when, to compensate
Your slave-owners, you charged our common state
Twice the amount: no, but we rather give
Our curses, and will give them while we live,
To that pernicious blind conceit, and pride,
Wherewith the aids we asked you misapplied.

 . . . . . .

Poor native land! poor withered breast of earth,
That once exuberant nourished love and mirth,
Now tugged at empty dugs by woe and hate,
Hungry and bare, how changed is thy estate!
Yet dry Jerusalem grew in an hour
A nursing-mother by God's timely power;
And Christ, whose Death should yet redeem the dead,
Like thee, had oft not where to lay His head;
And persecuting Diocletian showed
Christ prostrate under Jove, on medals broad,
Even when the heavens, to give mankind the sign,
Were labouring with the cross of Constantine.
Thy day prefixed in God's eternal doom
May long be longed for; but the day will come
When heaven shall also give its sign to thee,
Thy Diocletians fallen, thy people free.

CHAPTER XI.

1847–1886.

A PATRIOT POLITICIAN, NOT A PARTY-MAN.

> " Breathes there the man, with soul so dead,
> Who never to himself hath said,
>   This is my own, my native land !
> Whose heart hath ne'er within him burned,
> As home his footsteps he hath turned
>   From wandering on a foreign strand ? "
> —WALTER SCOTT.

FERGUSON was not at any period of his life a " party "-man. As an intelligent student of history, past and present, he held definite views as to the policy, foreign and domestic, of the empire. Of its greatness he was proud, as well as of its position as a bulwark of the cause of man, a planter and buttress of Freedom. The foremost place in his filial love belonged, however, to Ireland, the land of his birth, that " illustrious Innisfail," that

> "Green land, still sparkling fresh and fair
> With morning dew of heroism dried up and gone elsewhere ! "

whose story he had studied; whose heroic legends he

had told in verse; whose holy men he had followed in their missionary wanderings; whose kings, and chiefs, and heroes, and bards were familiar in his mouth as household words; and whose wrongs and sufferings wrung his heart. Nor could he tolerate the English policy of centralisation which sought to deprive his native land of its local institutions. How strongly he felt on the subject will appear in the speech recorded later on in this chapter.

The people of England hardly realise how much of what is recognised as Irish disaffection is the result of the insulting—or still more of the patronising—tone of a portion of their press. It has been reformed of late, but we may say with Hamlet, "O, reform it altogether." Ferguson's thoughts on this topic have been temperately expressed in the following words :—

Those who see in the stability of Governments the guarantees of peace and freedom, regret that the consolidation of the United Kingdom should be impeded by any cause however trivial. It is therefore that we notice a characteristic of the press of London which, trifling as it may seem, and merely a *façon de parler*, exercises, we are assured, a very injurious influence in preventing that full understanding and goodwill which all lovers of settled institutions would desire to see subsist between Queen Victoria's English and Irish subjects. We allude to the habitual and too often contemptuous assumption of superiority which marks the language of the London newspapers whenever they speak of Ireland. We would submit to these journals whether it would not be wiser to adopt a phraseology which would not excite invidious comparisons, and which would be consistent with the theory of the Union which they support. In that theory England and Ireland are alike portions of one United Kingdom, neither ruled by the other, but each by the whole. A numerous and powerful body of the Irish are attached to this Union, and it is in a great measure to their support that the empire is indebted for the peaceful maintenance of its integrity.

But while the tone of the English press would lead careless observers to suppose that these Irish adherents of the Union took a morbid pleasure in avenging their quarrel with Mr O'Connell on their common country, the reverse is the fact. For it may generally be said of these Irish Unionists, that while becoming every day more sensible of the advantages of connection with Britain, they are also *pari passu* becoming more attached to their own country and more sensitive to every reflection on her honour. Habitual contempts of a country where the nobility and chief gentry, as well as a large proportion of the professional and commercial classes, are animated by sentiments such as these, cannot be indulged in without the excitement of irritation and the creation of danger.

The deportment of the Irish Unionists at the present moment commands respect. An agricultural community, they have cheerfully submitted to a change in the laws affecting agriculture, detrimental to their own immediate interests, but necessary for the commercial advancement of their English fellow-subjects. With strong temptations to the gratification of selfish ambition by assuming their natural place as leaders of the Irish masses, they adhere devotedly to that connection on which they feel the general welfare of the empire to depend; and—which is perhaps as creditable to them as anything else—they have, with little or no Government aid, and without even the encouragement of one generous notice from the capital, laid the foundations in their own country for schools of science, of letters, and of arts, which bid fair to replace Ireland in her old eminence among the homes of learning in the West of Europe.

It is unbecoming as well as impolitic to use language derogatory of a country preserved from total alienation and hostility by the presence of such a class. But what is indiscreet and even unbecoming in journals written by Englishmen, justly proud although perhaps thoughtlessly boastful of the superiority of their portion of the empire, becomes culpable and shocking when it proceeds, as unfortunately the most offensive of these follies have proceeded, from journals edited by natives of the injured country. We can conceive of nothing more calculated to pain the loyal Irish gentlemen, or to excite feelings dangerous to the peace and stability of nations, than the repeated infliction of wounds thus doubly dishonouring.

These Irish gentlemen, scholars, artists, and men of taste and letters, who are engaged in the generous task of making their capital a home for the quiet pursuits of intellect, deserve well of the lovers of peace and order throughout Europe. . . .

In their efforts for the legitimate elevation of their country, the men in question have all made serious personal sacrifices. They have preferred remaining poor and almost unknown in their own country, to accepting the invitation to wealth and fame which London holds out to the talent of the rest of the empire. May they soon begin to reap the reward of their generous efforts in winning back their own nobility and gentry, whose wealth would be amply sufficient, if spent at home, to create as great inducements to the cultivation of all the higher arts of life in Dublin as now exist in most of the capital cities of Europe.

These sanguine expectations have not been realised. The lack of patriotic feeling has made too many of the gentry absentees. Agitators in Ireland have contributed to this undesirable state of things by bringing about strained relations between landlord and tenant. Many things have contributed to keep Ireland poor. The wealth which, if expended at home, would circulate, and return in great part into the pockets of the producers, is spent out of the country. Poverty thus increased naturally leads to discontent, and so the evil circle completes itself.

> "O wad they stay aback frae courts,
> And please themselves wi' country sports,
> It would for every one be better,
> The laird, the tenant, and the cottar!"

But men, till they attain to a high sense of duty, cannot claim the patriot's boast—

> "His first, best country ever is at home."

Ferguson never undervalued the advantages to Ireland of its union with Great Britain. He saw that the antagonism between Protestant and progressive Ulster and Catholic and Celtic Ireland would not improbably result in the calamity—which of all others he most dreaded—of civil war, were that Union to be severed before the animosities of centuries had disappeared in an atmosphere of mutual understanding and goodwill. He has recorded his convictions on these topics:—

In politics I am Conservative, but always was and am a great detester of Party and Faction, and an implacable enemy of those projectors and centralisers whose schemes appear to me to keep society in Ireland from consolidating into a settled strength and refinement.

From these opinions he never swerved, although in the speech which he made in May 1848, which will be given *in extenso*, he spoke in favour of a repeal of the Union. He was then convinced that the gross mismanagement of Irish affairs, and the centralising policy which Lord Clarendon—the Viceroy at that time—was understood to have in hand—namely, the abolition of the Lord Lieutenancy, and the transfer of the courts of Law to Westminster—would be ruinous to the interests of his country. He held that the project of eliminating from society in Ireland the upper and the professional classes would make the country a mere "draw-farm" for England. He had no doubt that this was the design aimed at, though not openly avowed, by the party in power at that time. These convictions were re-enforced by his heart-breaking experience of the miseries of the land and people whom he passionately loved. When Ferguson left Ireland at the close of 1845, the population exceeded eight millions, and her natural leaders—gentlemen of honour and position — seemed to be aroused to a keener sense than formerly of their public duties. When he returned a year later, he found famine and pestilence rife, and the people decimated by starvation.   In obedience to the mistaken views of political economists, food - supplies still in the land had been exported, and advantage taken of the awful visitation to attempt schemes of spoliation which he abhorred.   We give in the words of Sir C. G. Duffy his sketch of the afflicted land at that time :—

The immediate future became more and more menacing. Two facts of fatal significance had by this time become certain.   More than a third of the potato crop throughout the island was gone, in some districts more than half; and at the same time the bulk of the remaining supplies, cattle and corn, butter, beef, and pork, which would have fed all the inhabitants, continued to be exported to England, to pay the rent of farms which no longer yielded the cultivators their ordinary food.   Deaths from starvation were reported from

North and South, and the actual nature of the danger when the food of a country is withdrawn began to be dimly foreseen. It was essentially a remediable calamity, for, as Berkeley had taught of old, if the island was fenced off from the rest of the world by a wall of brass, it produced food enough to support its population.   Measures of precaution were again urged on the Government.   .   .   .

Other practical suggestions were equally disregarded.   Sharman Crawford, being himself a man of large estate, recommended a property tax, to be spent on employing the people ; Smith O'Brien suggested that railways, docks, and canals, and the improvement of the waste lands, would constitute national reproductive work.   But the established practice at that time, which has not, as far as I know, undergone any substantial change, was to despatch Englishmen to a country of which they knew nothing, and intrust them to determine questions requiring minute knowledge and long experience.   The English officials determined that work simply, irrespective of its reproductiveness, was the proper system, and that not railways and canals or transforming the wastes into corn-fields, but a prodigious extension of highways, was the legitimate application of the national strength.   Half a million of people were soon employed on this basis, and nearly twelve thousand persons paid for overseeing unproductive labour.   Serviceable roads were torn up that they might be made anew, and new lines were projected where there was no traffic.   .   .   .

The condition of Ireland at the opening of the year 1847 is one of the most painful chapters in the annals of mankind. An industrious and hospitable race were now in the pangs of a devouring famine.   Deaths of individuals, of husband and wife, of entire families, were becoming common.   The potato-blight had spread from the Atlantic to the Caspian, but there was more suffering in one parish of Mayo than in all the rest of Europe.   From Connaught, where distress was greatest, there came batches of inquests, with the horrible verdict, "Died of starvation."   In some cases the victims were buried "wrapped in a coarse coverlet," a coffin being too costly a luxury.   The living awaited death with a listlessness which was at once tragic and revolting. Women with dead children in their arms were seen begging for a coffin to bury them. . . .

It was a fearful time for the men who loved their country not only with deep affection, but with a wise and forecasting interest. A revolution of the worst type was in progress. Not the present alone, but the future, was being laid waste. . . .

The gentry, who were responsible in the first place for the protection of the people, from whom they drew their income, insisted that the calamity was an Imperial one, and ought to be borne out of the Exchequer of the empire. It was an equitable claim. If there was no irresistible title of brotherhood, at lowest the stronger nation had snatched away from the weaker the power of helping itself, and still drew away during this terrible era half a million of pounds every month in the shape of absentee-rents. The demand was put aside contemptuously. . . .

All the nations of the earth were appealed to, and they gave generously; but the result was far from being proportionate to the need. During the year just ended the contributions fell short of £2000 a-week. And it was not forgotten that after the great fire of London, when the citizens were in deep distress, the Irish contributed 20,000 fat cattle for their relief, which at their present value would amount to a sum greater than England and Europe sent to the aid of Ireland in 1846.

I have written this book [writes Sir C. G. Duffy in his preface to 'Young Ireland'] in the intervals of a busy life, because I believed it was the best and last service I could render to Ireland. . . . My first aim was to make a new generation familiar with the truthfulness, simplicity, and real moderation of the men with whom, it was said, "a new soul came into Ireland." . . .

Another aim, if I may venture to say so, was to appeal to the conscience of the best class of Englishmen. If they should think proper to study, with reasonable pains, the brief period embraced in this narrative, they will have no difficulty, I am persuaded, in understanding a problem which has sometimes perplexed them—why Irishmen not deficient in public spirit or probity were eager to break away from the Union and from all connection with England. At present they see with amazement and dismay a whole people who profess to have no confidence in their equity, who proclaim that they do not expect fair play from them, and who fall into ecstasies of triumph over some disaster abroad or embarrassment at home which endangers or humiliates the empire; and they will not take the obvious means of comprehending this phenomenon. For whoever desires to understand why Ireland is distressed and discontented, while England is prosperous and loyal, must assuredly seek the causes in history: to-day is the child and heir of yesterday. . . . I am convinced that confusion and disaster will continue to mark the relation between the islands, till Englishmen confront the facts courageously, and with a determination to discover the springhead from which discord flows.

Irish gentlemen of all conditions, creeds, and politics met in Dublin in 1847 to consider what ought to be done in the emergency caused by the failure of the potato. This "Irish Council" had for its honorary secretaries Sir Colman O'Loghlen and Samuel Ferguson. The advice tendered by the Council was disregarded by the Government. The condition of the starving multitudes became month by month more disastrous, the experimental legislation from Westminster more futile. Many among those who knew the country were disheartened by, and indignant at, the impotent attempts to cope with the exigencies of the position. They were convinced that Ireland would have weathered the crisis more successfully if she had been legislated for by a native Parliament.

This condition of mind is indicated in the speech

which Ferguson made at the Protestant Repeal Association in May 1848, here given as reported in a local newspaper :—

Mr Samuel Ferguson then came forward amid loud and long-continued cheering, and said :—

"Mr Chairman and gentlemen, I am a Protestant and an inhabitant of Dublin, and I desire the restoration of a domestic Legislature.   Coming thus within the terms of your invitation, I have felt it my duty to present myself amongst you.   I have obeyed that feeling of duty notwithstanding a good deal of social coercion, and I have done so under the penalty—which however, in the discharge of such a duty, I do not shrink from incurring—of encountering cold looks from many whom I esteem, and from some whom I love.

"Your committee, sir, have done me the favour to place in my hands a resolution which I have great satisfaction in submitting to the consideration of this assembly, for I believe this resolution expresses a truth of the highest social import at all times and in all communities, but particularly important for us to understand at a time when a proposition directly the reverse is very generally put forth by those who profess to express the opinion of educated persons in England and in Ireland, and also by those who claim to be the exponents of the will of our governors.   The resolution is this : ' Resolved—That national prosperity is based on social confidence, and that social confidence in Ireland cannot be expected to exist while the Government is conducted and the laws are made by strangers to the Irish people.'

"I am convinced that this proposition is true and just, and that the adverse proposition which, as I have told you, has been supported by influential exponents of the opinions of our governors, not only through their own press but through that over which they exercise a control in France, is untrue and unjust—viz., that what the people of Ireland require is a material and not a political change.   I have the utmost esteem for those who tell us we do require material changes.   I am perfectly aware that we are in a condition which requires not only the production of greater wealth, but also a more just distribution of our public expenses and taxation ; but I believe such a change as that cannot be brought about so as to make it permanently conducive to the prosperity of this country, unless it be based on such political reforms as will bring the body of the Irish people to be friends with their laws.

"It has been repeatedly declared by the representative of her Majesty in Ireland, for whom I have much respect, that we ought not to ask for political changes, but be satisfied with changes in our material condition.   I wish here to say, that I am very sorry the abilities of a nobleman so highly accomplished as Lord Clarendon should be engaged in carrying out, and inculcating on the Irish mind, a proposition the effect of which would be, to divert us from that which it is of most consequence for us to attain, and to induce us to rest satisfied with something that would be transitory and of little avail.   I have taken the liberty, sir, to say that I entertain great respect for Lord Clarendon as an eminent statesman.   I believe, sir, that no reflecting man will condemn him for having, in the execution of his duty, taken care that the public peace should be preserved, and that the inhabitants of a great city like Dublin, who are so much divided in their opinions, should be protected from those horrors which must ensue on any outbreak of armed rebellion.   But, sir, while it is quite true that the preparations made by the Government to preserve the peace — preparations in making which they were discharging their duty, and are entitled to our thanks—have averted from our eyes that spectacle which, please God, I and you shall never have to recoil from—the spectacle of mutual butchery among our fellow-citizens,—there has resulted from these preparations a great loss, in the loss of that social confidence which the resolution affirms to be the true basis of national prosperity.   I deplore the necessity—I lament the evil consequences which have ensued.   I believe that it is mainly owing to the want of profitable employment, arising from the want of confidence, and the consequent fear of men to embark their money in mercantile speculations, that we are brought here to-night; for when I look around me, and ask what it is that has assembled so great a multitude, I feel that the same impulse which has brought me has actuated you—namely, that we find our affairs are not prosperous, that we want profitable employment,—that industry is deadened and enterprise at an end, and therefore we have come together to seek the best remedy that we can find, consistent with our duty to one another, to the laws, and to our sovereign.   I believe that although the remedy which we look to may not be immediately productive of the brilliant results so many of us expect, yet that the foundation of the future amelioration of our state in Ireland must be looked for in the establishment of our own Legislature.

"Gentlemen, that conviction has arisen in my mind of late, and I am not in the least ashamed to come amongst my fellow-citizens and confess that I believe in so long rejecting that conviction I have been in error.   I have been always aware of the fact that prior to the Union this country enjoyed a great degree of what is called material prosperity, and that our society was much further advanced in the arts of life and of civilisation than it has been since.   I believe, in point of fact, that since the Union this country has retrograded both in the elements of material prosperity and in the tone of its society.   However, sir, I had believed that the advantages— and no doubt they are great — attendant on the unity of government and the efficient administration of law, which are secured by having the Legislature and Government located in one part of the empire—I believed that these, and the advantages we derive from a Union with England, would have more than counterbalanced those evils.   I have, however, seen reason lately to believe that the disadvantages of the Imperial connection greatly outweigh any advantages we might derive, and infinitely outweigh those which we hitherto have derived, from that source.   I have seen that the people of this country, having their minds fixed on this great national question, to which the mass of the upper classes have been hitherto averse, social disunion has resulted, and the effect has been that our representatives in the Imperial Parliament have consisted mainly of members of either one or the other extreme party in politics. I have seen that the representatives elected by the popular constituencies—who would not seek for their members of Parliament amongst those who rejected the question of Repeal—have generally been men who did not represent the intelligence or property of the country. On the other hand, I have observed that the few members whom the upper classes, holding aloof from the people, have been able to return, have gone into the House pledged in all things to dependence on England, and by reason of that dependent position incapable of expressing the opinions of their own part of the United Kingdom with spirit or effect. I have thus taken notice of an increasing inefficiency of our representatives from year to year, in proportion as society has been more widely divided; and, concurrently with that deterioration in the character of our representatives, I have seen the growth in Parliament of a spirit of contempt, and even of hostility, towards this country, which render the services even of those who are best disposed, of no avail for our benefit. And although I can well understand how it is that English gentlemen might excuse themselves for having given way to a petulance which was not without its provocation, I must own that I have felt the utmost indignation at the unworthy manner in which this ancient kingdom—this loyal, great, and peaceable people—have been spoken of by English representatives in the House of Commons—spoken of with ribald insolence, which, if we had been represented by Irish gentlemen of independence, would never have been ventured on, much less permitted, and repeated. While our members have been thus inefficient, and while persons, unknown for property, for intelligence, or for genius—unknown for anything that should make men conspicuous—have been suffered to indulge in the utmost insolence unreproved by the Speaker of the House of Commons——"

A Voice. "Smith O'Brien."

Mr Ferguson. "No; that was not the case with Mr Smith O'Brien. But before Mr O'Brien went there, and told them his mind, like the brave gentleman he is, when the slightest attempt at expostulation was made — when a gentleman respected by us all, and whom I greatly esteem, appealed to the Speaker of the House of Commons, in terms infinitely less strong than he ought to have used, that gentleman was told that he was out of order—and that a Mr Wakley—no, not Wakley (a voice—'The editor of the "Times"')—no; the gentleman to whom I allude has not the ability to do more than utter scurrilous invectives.   But the one gentleman was told that he was out of order, when he commented on the improper language of a Mr Walters, who declared, without any interference on the part of the Speaker, and with the apparent sanction of the rest of her Majesty's advisers, that 'If Nigger were not Nigger, Irishman would be Nigger.'   I believe, gentlemen, that the House is perfectly well aware that in suffering one of their members thus to inflame international hostilities between two great sections of her Majesty's subjects, they are grossly deserting the duty which they owed to both. I believe that the House are now desirous to make reparation, and that no man in the House is more aware that he has failed in the duty which he owed to her Majesty and to her Irish subjects on that occasion, than the Speaker.

"It is not on account, however, of a mere passing cause of irritation of that kind, that I would deem myself justified in wishing for the change which I now desire to see effected. But, whilst they have exhibited this contempt for us, and this hostility towards us, they have also exhibited great ignorance of our affairs, and utter incapacity to make laws salutary for this country.   What impresses this on my mind with particular force is, that when, by the occurrence of the calamity that has lately visited us, it became essential that we should make large provision for the support of the poor of this country— when that necessity arose (and here I speak from personal experience) fifteen months ago, parties representing all sections of Irish politicians—representing both creeds and all classes in the community—saw what the difficulty was with which we had to contend, and clearly saw what was the remedy.   It was perfectly evident that if, on the first of January 1847, we had had a local Legislature in this country, not only would moneys have been raised adequate for preserving the lives of all her

Majesty's subjects who, since that time, owing to the mismanagement of the Imperial Legislature, have lost their lives, but that in apportioning the taxation for that purpose, under any Act passed in an Irish Legislature, no one class in the community would have been made to suffer more than another.   It seems that our governors at that time—and it was proclaimed by their authoritative organs in and out of Parliament—were glad to take occasion of the affliction with which the Irish people had been visited, in order, by accumulating the whole of the taxation necessary for the relief of the poor on one particular set of proprietors, to exterminate and put out of their way altogether the class of resident Irish landlords.

"I believe, sir, that the extinguishment of the Irish landed proprietors is only one part of a design, the scope and object of which is to eradicate out of Ireland all classes of gentry, to make this country what is vulgarly called a draw-farm for England, and to centralise in London all the wealth, refinement, and social attractions of the empire.   That policy has been openly avowed, and for the purpose of reconciling us to a change so great, writers have been hired at the public expense, in order to persuade us that we ought not to apply ourselves to any of the higher departments of industry, and to tell us that the existence in this country of any other class except the mere tillers of the soil is quite unnecessary.   They cannot even bear the presence of an affluent clergy among us. They would confiscate their incomes twice as fast as those even of the landlords, for they impose a double amount of poor-law taxation on them.   In the prosecution of the same plebeianising policy, the executive Government here have sought to hire the services of the most accomplished medical gentlemen, as they would hire the services of menials or mechanics ; and, to complete that policy, they have brought in a bill, now pending before the Legislature, the object of which is to transfer our superior courts of Law from Dublin to Westminster. It is impossible for one to observe what is going on, and the consistent manner with which these designs have been prosecuted, without being perfectly conceived that the object that all these people have been about is, to extinguish out of this country whatever a gentleman of education, spirit, or honourable ambition would deem best worth living for.

"But what I regard as the great and characteristic evil of this state of things, and what, in my mind, has weighed more strongly than anything else to induce me to entertain the opinion which I now hold, is this—that amongst the upper classes, who particularly look to England for support and protection, there has been propagated an anti-national and servile spirit, which is wholly inconsistent with social consolidation, dignity, or progress. I believe that if the patronage of the empire were divided in the most equitable terms amongst those who submit to this humiliating allegiance, in reward for their supposed services, such benefits would be dearly purchased by the loss of self-respect and social confidence which must attend the keeping up of such a class of mercenaries. But when I see that in return for this humiliating servitude they are only repaid by the meanest offices, whilst all offices of dignity and trust are conferred on Englishmen, I feel that we must put an end to this state of affairs— if we would not see the race of gentry (not to speak of the spirit of gentility and honour) eradicated for ever from amongst us.

"For those reasons I desire, and am willing to encounter, the dangers and the risk of the changes you contemplate. I beg to say, in reply to the question of 'What do you mean by a Repeal of the Union?' that I am prepared to declare, and in all its details, what it is exactly I desire. Details, however, are not for your meeting to-night. You are now met to affirm the broad principle of self-government. But with reference to details, I may now say that in the reconstruction of whatever legislative body we may procure to be again established in Ireland, I would seek to obtain no power inconsistent with its continued independent action ; and I agree in the sentiments of those who have originated this movement, that we ought not to seek any control outside the limits of our own country. But within the boundary of Ireland we claim the exclusive right of taxing ourselves, and of regulating and administering our own affairs.

"I am aware that such a change is not to be effected without

difficulty, nor can we contemplate those difficulties without
perceiving that those who continue averse to such a change
are not without reason for some of their objections.   There
is one objection in particular to which I wish to reply.   They
say to us, 'Look to your constituencies, see what representatives you have in Parliament and in your corporations—are
you willing to put your affairs exclusively into the hands of
such persons?'   It is my firm persuasion that immediately
on the removal of the present cause of contention, the people,
in exercising their franchises, would look for the ablest servants
they could find, and that our affairs, instead of being managed
as they are at present, would be put into the hands of the best
gentlemen in the country.   On the other hand, I believe that
there are some who warmly advocate the restoration of her
Legislature to this country, who are carried away by expectation of greater benefits and more brilliant results than can be
rationally hoped for ; but the advantages of bringing the people
to be friends with the law would go a great way in creating
respect for the law, and inducing enterprise, by the certainty of
contracts being enforced.   I believe that it would be impossible
for us, if governed by moderate and reasonable men, to go
on without great and immediate improvement.   It will appear,
therefore, that in taking this step, and in admitting those
convictions, I have not been actuated by any romantic, or
dazzled by any brilliant, picture. . . .

"I know of no spectacle nobler or more gratifying to the
friends of freedom and humanity than was presented in London,
when its citizens, including the highest nobility, arrayed themselves in defence of the public peace, threatened by some who
did not know the value of public order.   Yes, it was a spectacle
truly gratifying to all, save men carried away by factious feelings.
On witnessing that triumph of the good sense of the English
people, and contrasting her state with that of neighbouring
nations, I could not avoid exclaiming, in the words of England's
national anthem—

"'The nations round less blest than thee,
Shall see their thrones successive fall,
But thou shalt flourish great and free,
The boast and envy of them all.'

(Cheers.)   I rejoice to hear that cheer: nothing can be more gratifying to me than to find such a sentiment elicit such a response among those whom the English Government has so long wronged.   But to the English, as a people, we must be ever grateful for their magnanimous benevolence to us in the time of our distress.   As far as concerns England herself and the colonies she has created by her industry, the dependencies she has won by her arms, I say, with cordial sincerity, 'Rule Britannia.'   But we are not a colony of Great Britain—we are an ancient kingdom, an aristocratic people, entitled to our nationality, and resolved on having it; and I trust the day is not far distant when Irishmen will be able to say in reference to their country, as well as to England, in the words of the same noble composition I have already quoted—

> " ' *Thee, haughty tyrants ne'er shall tame ;*
>   All their attempts to bind thee down
>   Shall but increase thy generous flame,
>   And work their woe and thy renown.' "

When Mr Gladstone's Home Rule Bill occupied the public mind some forty years later, Sir Samuel Ferguson was asked to state his views on the subject.   He wrote in 1885 and subsequently the following letters :—

I sympathised with the Young Ireland poets and patriots while their aims were directed to a restoration of Grattan's Parliament in which all the estates of the realm should have their old places.   But I have quite ceased to sympathise with their successors who have converted their high aspirations to a sordid social war of classes carried on by the vilest methods.   I was comrade in that sense of Davis, and possibly, but with far less sympathy, of some of his companions.   But it was in sympathy only.   I never wrote in the 'Nation.'   To say that I have upborne their banner, therefore, is more than I would like to vouch.

I agree with our friend in thinking that the Irish of our day

will not give attention to any other political project save that
of Home Rule.

I think that the safest form of Home Rule—if we are to
have it—that can be adopted is that of a restoration of the
Parliament of 1799.   County Boards, in my judgment, if only
able to impose without apportioning taxation, would not in any
degree satisfy the longings of the people; and if authorised to
apportion, would become instruments of uncontrolled oppression and plunder.   I think a Parliament controlled by a House
of Lords and the Royal Prerogative would be much more likely
to end discontents, with comparative safety to property and
social security.   The proposed abolition of the Lord Lieutenancy would, in my opinion, be merely a further step in
centralisation, and would be socially injurious in depriving the
better classes here of the advantages of a Court.   These
advantages now extend to a large class of our community
who could not seek admittance to a Royal Court, even if we
had the assurance of such a substitute.   I ascribe much of
the good tone and polish of our unpretending Irish society to
the influence of successive Viceregal hospitalities, but consider
the office chiefly valuable as affording local administrative
government.

As a public servant it is not my function to interfere in
politics; but I am at liberty to form my own opinions, which
I believe are dispassionate and know to be the result of long
observation.   In my capacity as President of the Academy,
also, I know no distinction of creed or politics, all reference to
both or either being forbidden in our meetings, but the position
gives me a wider view of what is going on around me.

Ferguson, ever zealous for the honour of Ireland
and its people, was inexpressibly grieved and shocked
at the crimes which disgraced the country during the
latter years of his life.   He wrote in 1882 a powerful
poem, " The Curse of the Joyces," in which he dwells
on those " three awful years of idleness, disaster, want,
and tears," and expresses his loathing of the " sordid

gang," the "panders and apologists of crime," whose lessons had degraded and sullied the character of Irishmen. It is here published for the first time:—

THE CURSE OF THE JOYCES.

GALWAY, 15TH DECEMBER 1882.

Oh! ye poor wretches who to-day must hang,
Curse, with your latest breath, the sordid gang
Who led you on, and now have led you in
Where deaths of shame must end your lives of sin.
Curse, while your sentence yet leaves breathing-time,
The panders and apologists of crime,
Who've shown you, daily, these three awful years
Of idleness, disaster, want, and tears,
In every cunning form of speech abused,
Crime hinted, crime applauded, crime excused ;
Who've told you, plain as nod and wink could tell,
"Shoot on, brave boys, we'll see you through it well ;
Shoot landlord, agent, bailiff, working man
Who dares to earn what daily bread he can
From boycotted employer : never fear,
We'll back the good deed up, and see you clear.
We'll fill the jury-box with leaguers good,
Friends to the cause, and connoisseurs in blood,
Who'll only ask that willing lips supply
The formal features of an *alibi*.
Or, if a weak Executive take heart,
And bid our minions from the box depart,
As slaves, for Freedom's offices unfit,
God help the doomed successors they admit !
We'll show them up, we'll treat them to some tricks
Reserved for Saxons of their politics ;
Placard their businesses, and let their wills
To keep their oaths, react upon their tills.
Mark every gesture : if a note be sent
To say 'I can't come home,' record the event :

For, though the sheriff read it, was it not
A noted loyalist the missive got
As messenger?   Be sure, we'll watch them well;
And when, at night, brought down to their hotel,
Good patriot spies shall wait them there, and note
What stint of liquor goes down every throat;
Each glass of whisky, as it leaves the cask,
That bailiff, or that bailiff's man, may ask,
Sheriff or sheriff's visitor, see scored
Against the unconscious twelve men round the board.
Heaven help near-sighted juror who may trip
Over the tin-bath, for the foot or hip,
Placed in his way to bed.   With morning cries
Of 'drunken verdict!' we'll affront the skies;
And if we can't get off our guilty man,
Convict and damn his judges if we can.
Who knows, but some one whom we do not know,
(Oh! far from us be that!) by some shrewd blow,
Better than twenty challenges, may strike
Terror in judge and juryman alike?
If Justice Lawson (which the heavens avert!)
When walking after dusk, should—catch—a hurt,
If Foreman Field so—cautioned—we should see,
Shall we be blamed for that? oh no, not we."
  Curse them, while yet your windpipes are unstretched,
And breath from living lungs can still be fetched
To speed the malediction; and, then, say,
"Adjust the knot, good hangman, let's away
And leave a world where greater villains far
Than even we poor guilty miscreants are,
Live to enjoy the profits they have made
Of us and other victims of their trade.
The world we go to hardly can be worse;
Let them live on, *and bear the Joyces' curse!*"

On the 6th of May 1882, in the Phœnix Park, in
open day, a deed of shame was wrought which filled
all honourable men with horror.   The murder of Mr

Burke and Lord Frederick Cavendish by four ruffians armed with knives, and hounded on by miscreants still more guilty than those butchers, as being of somewhat superior position and education, shocked not alone Dublin, but the empire. Carey, who gave the signal, while waiting for the appearance of the unsuspecting victims was an onlooker at a game of polo then being played in the Park. His supposed meditations are analysed by Ferguson in a poem written partly to show how readily Browning's mannerisms might be imitated. " At the Polo-Ground " was a new departure, differing altogether in style from any of Ferguson's previous compositions. The analysis of Carey's hesitancies before he had given the fatal signal to the assassins is quite in Browning's manner :—

AT THE POLO-GROUND.

6TH MAY 1882.

Not yet in sight.   'Twere well to step aside,
Beyond the common eye-shot, till he comes.
He—I've no quarrel under heaven with him :
I'd rather it were Forster ; rather still
One higher up than either ; but since Fate
Or Chance has so determined, be it he.
How cool I feel ; and all my wits about
And vigilant ; and such a work in hand !
Yes : loitering here, unoccupied, may draw
Remark and question.   How came such a one there ?
Oh ; I've strolled out to see the polo-players :
I'll step across to them ; but keep an eye
On who comes up the highway.
                                                  Here I am
Beside the hurdles fencing off the ground
They've taken from us who have the right to it,

For these select young gentry and their sport.
Curse them!   I would they all might break their necks!
Young fops and lordlings of the garrison
Kept up by England here to keep us down:
All rich young fellows not content to own
Their chargers, hacks, and hunters for the field,
But also special ponies for their game;
And doubtless, as they dash along, regard
Us who stand outside as a beggarly crew.—
'Tis half-past six.   Not yet.   No, that's not he.—
Well, but 'tis pretty, sure, to see them stoop
And take the ball, full gallop; and when I
In gown and cocked hat once drove up Cork Hill,
Perhaps myself have eyed the common crowd,
Lining the footway, with a similar sense
Of higher station, just as these do me,
And as the man next door no doubt does them.
   'Tis very sure that grades and differences
Of rich and poor and small men and grandees
Have all along existed, and still will,—
Though many a man has risen and thriven well
By promising the Poor to make them rich
By taking from the Rich their overplus,
And putting all on a level: beggars all.
Yet still the old seize-ace comes round again;
And though my friends upon the pathway there—
No.   Not he neither.   That's a taller man—
Look for a general scramble and divide,
Such a partition, were it possible,
Would not by any means suit me.   My share
Already earned and saved would equal ten
Such millionth quotients and sub-multiples.
No: they may follow Davitt.   'Tis Parnell
And property—in proper hands—will win.
But, say the Mob's the Master; and who knows
But some o' these days the ruffians may have votes
As good as mine or his, and pass their Act
For every man his share, and equal all?

No doubt they'd have a slice from me.   What then?
I'm not afraid.   I'll float.   Allow the scums
Rise to the surface, something rises too
Not scum, but Carey; and will yet rise higher.
No place too high but he may look for it.
Member for Dublin, Speaker, President,
Lord Mayor for life—why not?   One gentleman,
Who when he comes to deal with this day's work—
No: not in sight.   That man is not so tall—
Will find, to his surprise, a stronger hand
Than his controls the rudder, sat three years
And hangs his medal on the sheriff's chain.
Yes; say Lord Mayor: my liveries green and gold,
My secretary with me in my coach,
And chaplain duly seated by my side.
My boy shall have his hack, and pony too,
And play at polo with the best of them;
Such as will then be best.   He need not blush
To think his father was a bricklayer;
For laying bricks is work as reputable
As filling noggins or appraising pawns,
Or other offices of those designed
For fathers of our Dublin swells to be.
  'Tis twenty minutes now to seven o'clock.
What if he should not come at all?   'Twere then
Another—oh—*fiasco* as they call it,
Not pleasant to repeat to Number One,
But, for myself, perhaps not wholly bad.
For, if he comes, there will be consequences
Will make a stir; and in that stir my name
May come in play—well, one must run some risk
Who takes a lead and keeps and thrives by it
As I have done.   But sure the risk is small.
I know those cut-throats on the pathway there
May be relied on.   Theirs is work that shuts
The door against approval of both sorts.
But he who drives them, I've remarked in him

A flighty indecision in the eye,
Such as, indeed, had I a looking-glass,
I might perhaps discover in my own
When thoughts have crossed me how I should behave
In this or that conjuncture of the affair.
Him I distrust.   But not from him or them
Or any present have I aught to fear.
For never have I talked to more than one
Of these executive agents at a time,
Nor let a scrap of writing leave my hand
Could compromise myself with any one.
And should I—though I don't expect I shall—
Be brought, at any time, to book for this,
'Twill not be—or I much mistake—because
Of any indiscretion hitherto.
But, somehow, these reflections make me pause
And set me inly questioning myself,
Is it worth while—the crime itself apart—
To pull this settled civil state of life
To pieces, for another just the same,
Only with rawer actors for the posts
Of Judges, Landlords, Masters, Capitalists?
And then, the innocent blood.   I've half a mind
To trip across this elm-root at my foot,
And turn my ankle.
                   Oh, he comes at last!
No time for thinking now.   My own life pays
Unless I play my part.   I see he brings
Another with him, and, I think, the same
I heard them call Lord—something—Cavendish.
If one; two, likely.   That can't now be helped.
Up.   Drive on straight,—if I blow my nose
And show my handkerchief in front of them,
And then turn back, what's that to any one?
No further, driver.   Back to Island Bridge.
No haste.   If some acquaintance chanced to pass,
He must not think that we are running away.

I don't like, but I can't help looking back.
They meet : my villains pass them.   Gracious Powers,
Another failure !   No, they turn again
And overtake; and Brady lifts his arm—
I'll see no more.   On—by the Monument.
On—brisker, brisker—but yet leisurely.
By this time all is over with them both.
Ten minutes more, the Castle has the news,
And haughty Downing Street in half an hour
Is struck with palsy.   For a moment there,
Among the trees, I wavered.   Brady's knife
Has cut the knot of my perplexities ;
Despite myself, my fortune mounts again.
The English rule will soon be overthrown,
And ours established in the place of it.
I'm free again to look, as long as I please,
In Fortune's show-box.   Yes ; I see the chain,
I see the gilded coach.   God send the boy
May take the polish !   There's but one thing now
That troubles me.   These cursed knives at home
That woman brought me, what had best be done
To put them out o' the way ?   I have it.   Yes,
That old Fitzsimon's roof's in need of repairs.
I'll leave them in his cock-loft.   Still in time
To catch the tram, I'll take a seat a-top—
For no one must suppose I've anything
To hide—and show myself in Grafton Street.

"At the Polo-Ground" was followed by another poem in the same manner—a Dublin eclogue—dated February 18, 1886, "In Carey's Footsteps."   In this the speculations of another stroller in the Phœnix Park are imaginatively dissected.   The supposed thinker would appear to be an ecclesiastic who finds himself near the spot where the former tragedy had been enacted.

IN CAREY'S FOOTSTEPS.

A hideous thought.   I'll walk a while in the Park
And rid my mind of it.   I wish to God
I had not said it : though no man can say
I counselled or advised it : only this ;
I did not, as I ought, advise *against*—
Express some detestation—say, at least,
Such crimes are cowardly, and Irishmen,
Having the true faith, should be bold to act
The manlier part.
                  Yes, here I'm in the Park.
The People's Garden ?   No.   Let dull Carlisle
Set out his leg among the nurserymaids :
I'm not for statues nor for works of art
Reminding one at every step he takes
In his own grounds, at home, that some one else
Confers his culture on him from outside.
I want brisk walking.   Ay ; there's General Gough,
Some little off the perpendicular,
Astride the gingered bronze.   They set him up
To show us how our masters know to ride
Over us rebel Irish ; and Lord James
And General Sir Thomas Steele, I'm told,
Made capital speeches at the ceremony.
And all the Civil Service and its wives
Sat and applauded when the Board of Works
Rigged up their platforms, either side the road ;
While the town blackguards and the ragged boys
Stood silent in the background, jeered or hissed
According to their distance.
                     To the right
I'll here turn off the highway, on to the grass.
A lovely dell : these elms, 'twould seem, escaped
The storm of Thirty-nine.   The former road
Ran here.   'Twas afterwards the Works laid out
The broad raw-margined highway—get ye gone,
Ugly associations !—that now leads
Hence to the Phœnix.   Now I feel the air

Fresh and refreshing.   Here I cross the road
That to the Zoologic Garden grounds—
Where Haughton's monkeys crack their Sunday nuts,
As he his eggs and jokes on Saturdays—
Conducts the city mothers, when the treat
Familiar brings its buns and happy hour.
Here, cross again the avenue that leads
To Lodge Viceregal, sacred to the wheels
Of folks of station driving to inscribe
Names and addresses in the Visitors' Book.
Well, say they do; what harm?   Why, by-and-by,
They'll pay the same respects to some one else;
Prince Cardinal, mayhap, or Archbishop.
Why not?   The stabling's good, and rooms of state
Lofty and spacious, and an extra wing,
For chapel, easily added.   And methinks,
Seen winding through these glades and shrubberies,
A good procession carrying the Host,
Say, to sick gardener, while our athletes there
Dropped bat and cricket-ball, and, down on their knees,
Adored at distance, were a pretty sight.
    What's here?   A fence of hurdles.   Oh, I see.
This is the Polo-Ground.   But, what, what, what,
I'm here in Carey's footsteps!—Yes, 'twas here,
This very spot, I'm certain that he stood
Waiting,—foul images, I say begone!
Why should ye haunt my mind?   What hand had I
In Carey's plot or Brady's butcherings?
I do detest them; and I ask myself
Pardon for words of question, where all's sure.
But, 'tis the mischief of such thoughts as these—
Of fire, assassination, dynamite—
One can't allow them entrance in the mind,
But straight the mind will turn to speculate
How this thing might be managed and how that,
And none the wiser.   Carey thought himself
So safe, he laughed and puffed his cigarette
Leaving the prison van.   Well, what he did

At last was right.
　　　　　　　　And what were right for me
To do at this conjuncture ?　Openly
Avow my sorrow that untimely words
Escaped me which some miscreant might wrest
To implication of assent to crime ?
That were heroic, that were right indeed ;
My conscience so inclines.　I would not bear
The blame of giving entrance, thoughtlessly,
To wicked thoughts in other minds.　For none
Amongst my hearers, thinking I approved,
But well might set his wits imagining
How he would carry on his private war
Were he Avenger : how he should procure
His stuffs ; how keep a good face to the world ;
And think it easy since a single man
Risking no more than his particular life,
With fairly even chances of escape,
Might carry half a town's destruction packed
In greatcoat-pockets or a Gladstone bag ;
Or dowdy woman drop her petticoat
And wreck a nation's palace, and walk off
Slim and secure ; or gleeful speculate
What were the outraged Briton's sentiments
And attitude regarding Ireland's right,
Should some fine morning show Westminster Bridge
Half discontinuous, or Victoria Tower
Hanging side-rent and ready to come down
Lengthwise along the roof of the House of Lords ?
Or should some *quasi* city shopkeeper
Have tunnelled till he got below the Bank,
And sent the gold he scorned to touch sky-high
Far as the Strand ? and think within himself
That Pharaoh, when he heard the mourning cry
For Egypt's first-born, were not more in haste
To let the Jews go than the Irish they.
　More I could fancy ; but immoral thoughts
Fancied in others might infect myself

And that were what our guides in ethics call
Morosa delectatio, and a sin :
Sin's punishment, besides ; for greater pain
Hardly attends the damned than have their minds
Compelled to dwell, whether they will or no,
On thoughts they know are evil.   What to these
Were Carey's worst imaginings ?   Two or three
Men in high office, well-instructed men,
Who knew the perils that attend on place,
And, haply, were not wholly unprepared—
What these, compared with casual multitudes
Of young and old sent indiscriminate
To death and pain ?   Or what the finished Law
On those poor self-imagined Brutuses.
To rage of angered cities, when the arm
Of civil power is impotent to stay
A people's fury bent on massacre,
On bloody vengeance, fire and banishment?
   Yes, here he waited till the man in grey
Should show himself approaching.   Here his fate
Turned on the central pivot, once for all.
Had Carey, then, but walked the other way,
And meeting Under-Secretary Burke,
Said, " Sir, I would not have you walk alone
Further, just now," it might have all been stopped,
And no blood spilt, and no necks stretched over there.
But here he stood, and had his chance, and chose
To walk in front and show the handkerchief :
And, in his pausing footsteps, here stand I,
Still free to turn whichever way I will."

Still, even in those awful days of shame, Ferguson
did not despair for his country. He knew that the
disgrace brought on her fair name by crime, cruelty,
and dishonesty was the work of a few miscreants only.
He believed that the better nature and religious principles of the people at large would reassert themselves,

and the "lessons of hell," enforced as they had been by intimidation, tyranny, and terror, would be in due time not only execrated, but sternly repressed.

Yet it must be admitted that the close of his long life of patriotic endeavour to raise and elevate his countrymen was saddened by their evil‑doings. "There have been men," wrote a distinguished author, "who have felt in their country's humiliation and loss a far sharper pang than in any personal suffering." These words express Ferguson's feelings. All his correspondence at this time evidences the grief and pain which filled his heart. To "wait and pray," to hope and trust that the virtues of "truth and manliness" would reassert themselves — these were his consolations.

CHAPTER XII.

1848–1885.

SOCIAL DUBLIN IN FERGUSON'S DAYS.

"Benedice la nobile anima nella vecchiozza li tempi passati, e bene li può benedire, perocchè per quelli rivolvendo la sua memoria, essa si remembra delle sue diritte operazioni."—DANTE.

SOCIETY in Dublin, agreeable at all times, becomes brilliant during winter and early spring, when the hospitalities of the Viceregal Court attract to the city many of the nobility and country gentlemen and their families. A succession of estimable noblemen, courteous and gracious, and liberal in expenditure, have as Lords Lieutenant represented her Majesty the Queen with dignity and splendour. Receptions, dinners, balls, and concerts promote gaiety and circulate money, and are gratifying to the populace, lessening the drain of absenteeism, which so seriously impairs the prosperity of Ireland.

After Easter the Synod of the Church of Ireland meets in Dublin. Hotels and private houses are refilled, and a period of clerical sociability ensues, the palace of the Archbishop being a truly hospitable centre of general as well as clerical society.

Of the few Peers who have residences in or near Dublin, two—Barons Ardilaun and Iveagh—were connected, by his marriage, with Ferguson. Following in the footsteps of their father, the late Sir B. L. Guinness, who restored the cathedral of St Patrick at his own expense, they have made munificent gifts to the community. Lord Ardilaun has presented to his native city St Stephen's Green, beautified and adorned, a boon to the poorest as well as to his comparatively wealthy fellow-citizens—"common pleasures, to walk abroad and recreate" themselves; and he has built, at his own expense, a beautiful church at Raheny. Lord Iveagh has allocated £250,000 to erect dwellings for the poor in London and Dublin. The late Lady Plunket, wife to the Archbishop of Dublin, was the only daughter of Sir B. L. Guinness. Her gracious manners, her kind, unselfish, and considerate nature, fitted her to be, what she was while she lived, pre-eminent as a hostess, beloved by all who knew her, untiring in her services to her fellow-creatures, and deeply and practically interested in all the charities of Dublin.

The officials—Chief Secretary, Commander of the Forces, Chancellor, and Judges—dispense hospitality at all times, as well as private individuals; and although Dublin has comparatively little wealth—perhaps because of that—it is a pleasant place to live in. Its environs are charming, half an hour by train or carriage bringing its citizens into contact with beautiful scenery and fine sea or mountain air.

It has been observed by an eminent classical scholar familiar with the habits and modes of thought of the ancient Greeks, that a dinner-party in Dublin resembles the *deipnon* of the Athenians more nearly than a similar social function elsewhere. The resemblance consists chiefly in the animated interchange of ideas, quick and versatile wit and humour being characteristic of both races. However that may be, social intercourse in Dublin is very agreeable.

Musical parties, meetings for the study of foreign literature, as well as Shakespearian Readings, were popular among the intimates of Ferguson and his wife. Evenings so spent have been already described. The honoured head of the University, the Rev. George Salmon, D.D., now Provost of Trinity College, great as a theologian and mathematician, is also great as a humorist. He is inimitable as an interpreter of such characters in Shakespeare's plays as Sir Andrew Aguecheek, Dogberry, Bottom, and Touchstone. Even his most learned books overflow with a quaint humour peculiarly his own. The late Vice-Provost, Dr Moore, was an admirable reader of grave and dignified parts. So also was the late Dr R. P. Graves. Lord Chancellor O'Hagan and Dr Ingram rendered, with sympathy which touched the heart, the characters of great men fallen from high estate, such as Wolsey and Antony; and Dr Tisdall, Chancellor of Christ Church, was a masterly interpreter of Falstaff, Macbeth, and

Coriolanus. These and other dignified parts were admirably sustained by the Rev. Robert Guinness, who, like Dr Tisdall, possessed the advantage of a voice of great compass, rich in tone and power of expression.

The Irish Judges as a class are noted for genial humour, and are credited with many good stories.

Of them and others Mr Le Fanu, a descendant of the brilliant Richard Brinsley Sheridan, in a recent volume has chronicled many lively anecdotes. Some also of the legal dignitaries are men of letters. The late Chief-Justice Whiteside published 'Early Sketches of Eminent Persons'; Mr Justice Lawson, a dainty volume of hymns which he rendered into Latin, 'Hymni Usitati Latine Redditi.' He sent to Ferguson some Latin verses with a beautiful rhymed translation, which the latter acknowledged in a poem of which the first lines only can be recalled :—

> Methought the verses clothed in satin
> Were Tennyson's in Lawson's Latin.

To which the Judge replied—

> " Your rhymes would make me, my dear Sam,
> Appear much better than I am,
> And though I fain would 'forge an anchor,'
> For plumage forged I do not hanker ;
> So, warned by mean Bathyllus' fate
> In 'Vos non vobis,' let me state
> 'Twas John O'Hagan clothed in satin
> His brother Lawson's ruder Latin."

" Bathyllus was the fellow who claimed Virgil's verses

'Nocte,' &c., &c., and drew forth the lines 'Sic vos non vobis,'" added the Judge in a postscript.

Of Ferguson's own "doggrel" verses and humorous pieces he has said a few words in the autobiographical fragment already quoted :—

Various unpublished pieces will float about when a man of ordinary observation with a faculty for casting his thoughts in rhyme, lives, as I have done, to a good age in one social sphere. My sentiments on various matters of permanent as well as passing interest may be found, here and there, sometimes in verses which I would call doggrel, but which may claim to be considered Hudibrastic; sometimes in sonnets of more regular structure, in the hands of my friends. Take this one on the last subject under notice, my distaste for the Ruskinite influences in architecture, written to a lady in the North of Ireland whose windows commanded a view of Down Hill, one of the grand old mansions of the epoch of Irish independence :—

> Yes, Down Hill was founded
> When builders were grounded
> (Let Ruskin go lecture !)
> In sound architecture ;
>
> .   .   .   .
>
> And the men who were able
> From state-room to stable
> To roof and to wall so,
> Could found a State also.

In matters of taste [he continues] I am more an admirer of the Regular than of the Romantic school of architecture, and of the Post- rather than of the Pre-Raphael school in painting. A lecture on Architecture which I delivered during the " Afternoon " series in 1864 is a defence of the Regular style against the current charges of unreality and constructive concealment, in which the argument *Tu quoque* is, I think, not unreasonably retorted on the Gothic.

In constructive art, as in literary construction and ideas of social order, my primary aims—whether they have reached the mark or not, others must judge—have always been strength, coherency, and endurance.

Another sample of "doggrel" had its origin when Mr Gladstone proposed to create an Irish University from whose curriculum theology and history should be excluded :—

Come, scholar, come, and see my latest rarity,
My Dublin University behold with pride.
A *Universum* framed with such particularity,
It leaves one-half the circle of the sciences outside.

For so long as the segment shall equal the periphery,
So long as the part shall be greater than the whole,
That youth will best be qualified for wearing manhood's livery
Who knows nothing of his country, or his Maker, or his soul!

This *squib*, "illustrating the views of an Irish gentleman on what University education ought to be, in contradiction to——" Here the MS. abruptly ends, but the sentence, if continued, would doubtless have named the then Prime Minister, whose occasionally vague yet magniloquent utterances have been quizzed by others besides Ferguson. Yet he was by no means insensible to the eloquence and genius of Mr Gladstone, but cordially recognised the gifts of one with whose views as a statesman he was compelled to differ.

Ferguson's versatility was remarkable. From youth upwards he composed in widely differing styles. Here is an early evidence of his rhyming powers :—

OPENING STROPHE OF THE GODODIN.

Young, yet manly he,
Braver warrior none might be ;
Red, spread, the mane did fly
Of the fleet bay steed beneath his thigh.

> Light, large, the buckler lay
> Across the croupe of the bright fleet bay ;
> Great the weight of the blue blade cold,
> And a flash of light from his spurs of gold.
>
> Oh no ! ne'er shall I
> Lays, praise, to thee deny ;
> Still will heart and voice
> Celebrate the hero of my own heart's choice.

The "outrageous extravaganza," as its author called it, which appeared in 'Blackwood' in April 1838, attained wide popularity. "Father Tom and the Pope" has been frequently reprinted; and more than once pirated in America. In one of these editions it is ascribed to Dr Maginn; and as Ferguson did not append his name to his lively *brochure*, others have believed it to be the work of that witty writer. The question is, however, set at rest in the following letter :—

45 George St., Edinburgh, *Nov.* 24, 1894.

Dear Lady Ferguson [wrote Mr Blackwood], — I have much pleasure in giving you the assurance that "Father Tom and the Pope; or, A Night at the Vatican," was by Sir Samuel Ferguson, and not, as is erroneously reported, by Maginn. This authentic statement in the Life you are preparing ought to be sufficient, and you can quote my authority.

The preface to the edition published by Moorhead, Simpson, & Bond, in New York, 1868, contained the following passage :—

It may have been written by Maginn, who was a good Catholic, but it may truly be said of him, that although he loved the Church much, he loved fun more. As a work of mere wit it must take its place with some of the brightest efforts of Rabelais, of Montaigne, or of Pascal.

In an ante-preface, signed F. S. C., the error which ascribed it to Maginn was corrected, in consequence of a letter " written by a personal friend of the author of ' Father Tom and the Pope.' "   This letter contained the following passage :—

The *brochure* was not written by Lord Brougham, nor by the Duke of Wellington, nor by Maginn, but by Samuel Ferguson, Esq., of Dublin, barrister-at-law, author of the " Forging of the Anchor " and other poems. I have my information from Dr Ferguson himself [he was created an LL.D. by the University of Dublin in 1865], whose acquaintance I formed during my sojourn in the medical school of the Irish metropolis.

With all these links of circumstantial evidence before me [continued F. S. C.], I wrote to Dr Ferguson himself for " more light " upon the subject. . . . In a letter to me he says :—

" My friend Dr Smith has informed you correctly as to the authorship of ' Father Tom and the Pope.' It was written by me in the summer of 1838, just about the time of my call to the Irish Bar. No one else had any hand in it, and, like the ' Forging of the Anchor,' it underwent a rejection before its appearance in ' Blackwood.' I am flattered by its having been ascribed to Maginn, for whose genius I entertain a high admiration. I have never made any secret of the authorship ; but as I have constantly endeavoured in any literary work I have been able to do for many years back to elevate the Irish subject out of the burlesque, I have an indisposition to place my name on the title-page of so very rollicking a piece as ' Father Tom.' "

I send you a copy of " Father Tom," which I find is now to be had at the book-stalls [wrote Ferguson to the Rev.

Edward Spring, February 6, 1879]. When I reflect that forty years have passed since I wrote it, I am forced to conclude that it must have some stamina of common-sense in it to have survived so many winters.

Mr Falkiner, now the Recorder of Dublin, has recalled his first meeting with the author of "Father Tom," then a Queen's Counsel and one of the seniors of the North-East Circuit :—

The first time I met Ferguson was when I joined the North-East Bar at Armagh. It was the Spring Circuit, and the weather was severe. I found myself after my journey comfortably seated with a brother barrister in the bar-room. I had been much amused on my journey by "Father Tom and the Pope," and spoke of it as Maginn's witty *brochure.* "You are mistaken," said my companion ; "our own Circuit has the honour of numbering the author among its members." At this moment the door opened and a gentleman appeared on the threshold. He paused to shake off the snow on his coat. "Come in, Ferguson," cried my companion. "Here is a heretic who asserts that 'Father Tom' is written by Maginn. What have you to say to that?" "It was written by a lively young fellow," replied Ferguson, "many years ago. But he exists no longer. Let the outrageous extravaganza of his youth be forgotten."

The "Loyal Orangeman," already given in connection with the North-East Circuit, is a perfect presentment of a bigoted Ulsterman, nor is his mental attitude exaggerated. "He's as honest a poor fellow as the sun shines on, whether it shine on him or not," wrote Ferguson. The late Bishop Reeves told the following story of one belonging to his diocese. The man was a farmer who, in returning from a fair, somewhat unsteady from his potations there, stumbled and fell, in crossing a bog, from its causeway into a lower level of slush and *débris*, in which he was wellnigh suffocated. His cries for succour were heard by a neighbour, who hastened to his rescue, and with much difficulty and some danger extricated the tipsy man. Once more on safe ground he blessed his preserver, but on recognising him, exclaimed, " Put me back, put me back; I would not be beholden to a Papist!"

Another witty friend and occasional guest has attained of late great and deserved popularity under the *nom de plume* Ian Maclaren. The Rev. John Watson, minister of Sefton Park Church, Liverpool, is a man of wit and genius, whose character, attainments, and brilliant conversational powers make him a delightful companion. He is one of the ablest preachers of the day, eminent as a theologian, and a writer on spiritual subjects. His recent book—1895 —'The Upper Room,' has great depth and tenderness, as well as charm and freshness. He is author of 'Beside the Bonnie Brier Bush' and 'The Days of Auld Langsyne,' both full of humour as well as pathos. A visit from him and his wife—a kinswoman of Ferguson's — was always hailed with delight, and that Mr Watson on his side enjoyed it is apparent from the following letter :—

Sefton Drive, Liverpool, March 13, 1884.

Dear Lady Ferguson,—Janie has, I know, written to thank you for the great kindness we received both from yourself and Sir Samuel; but even at this late date (I have been loaded with work since my return, 32 letters waiting an answer!) I must add my humble thanks. With your gracious hospitality and delightful society, I have never enjoyed a visit more, and I find my mind has been wonderfully quickened. To use the words of an American essayist, "I am full of eggs"— strange fellows those cousins of ours across the water. So I expect to have out some dozen good sermons, all owing their inspiration to Dublin.

The passage was not the best; the motion of the boat was steady—that is, from side to side with unvarying regularity— and we—sympathised.

Please tell Sir Samuel the following, which I heard this week. The Emperor of Russia and the King of Prussia were some years ago staying at St Cloud with Napoleon, and took a walk one evening. They met an Englishman who asked them to show him the way. They did so, and walked a little with him. On parting he asked their names. "I [bowing] am the Emperor of Russia"; "I am the King of Prussia"; and "I am the Emperor of the French." And "I," said our compatriot, bowing lowest, "am the Emperor of *China*"!—With kindest regards for you both, yours very sincerely,

JOHN WATSON.

In no house in Dublin was social intercourse more agreeable, the guests more thoroughly at home and at their best, than in the stately home of Lord Chief Baron Pigot, 52 St Stephen's Green. The dignified, gracious, and kindly bearing of host and hostess and their family, their courteous and cordial welcome, the tone of refinement and culture blended with simplicity, and the entire absence of all assumption, made an atmosphere in which every one felt at ease and happy. It is hard to say what it is that creates this atmosphere; it is *felt*, though difficult to define. Speaking generally, it is made by a hostess who truly makes her friends welcome. They are instinctively aware that their presence is considered a pleasure, and the entertainment not the mere performance of a social debt or duty.

In the days when Ferguson was a working barrister only, the Lord Chief Baron did not disdain to share his simple hospitality. The courtesy, untainted by condescension, which characterised the Chief Baron, is apparent even in the following brief notes of acceptance and of invitation :—

MY DEAR FERGUSON [he wrote on the 6th of February 1867],—I hope to have the gratification of dining with you on Monday. I hope also that I shall be able to go with you to the Academy. I shall be very anxious indeed to hear your paper on a subject *so* interesting, and upon a subject, too, which you are so qualified to deal with.

Pray present my best respects to Mrs Ferguson. I should regret very much indeed if I did not make one among friends who regard and prize you, on such an occasion, and thank you much for offering me the opportunity of so doing.—Ever faithfully yours, dear Ferguson,   D. R. PIGOT, C.B.

MY DEAR FERGUSON [wrote the Chief Baron, when illness had compelled Ferguson to refuse his invitation],—I am very glad, indeed, to hear of your amended health : I had not the least idea, until I learned that you had left town, that you had been so ill.

Pray give my best respects to Mrs Ferguson. What an anxious time she must have had of it !

When the 11th arrives, come to me if you are well enough. *But on no account do so if you are not*—your place will be ready for you, all the same, with a hearty welcome if you fill it, and regret more for the cause, even than for your absence, if you cannot. I expect the Master of the Rolls, and some— not many—other friends of yours and mine.—Ever, dear Ferguson, faithfully yours,   D. R. PIGOT, C.B.

During the lifetime of Mr and Mrs Thomas Hutton their home was a delightful social centre. Mrs Hutton was an accomplished artist. She had herself decorated her charming house at Elm Park, a few miles from Dublin, with elegant designs from Pompeii. There and elsewhere she diffused around her an atmosphere of goodness and refinement. Even in her old age—for she long survived her husband—she promoted the artistic culture of her sex by a series of Readings on Italian Art which she gave to the young lady students of Alexandra College. These were so highly appreciated that she was induced to continue the subject by six lectures on German Art. When an accident had destroyed a large portion of her manuscript Mrs Hutton, notwithstanding her advanced years, had the energy to re-compose and deliver them to a sympathetic audience. Mrs Hutton was very noble and dignified in appearance as well as in character. She was the mother of the beautiful and accomplished girl previously spoken of as the betrothed of Thomas Davis, who died of fever a few weeks before the time fixed for their marriage.

In my necessarily anxious and much-alone life [Mrs Hutton wrote to Ferguson], I cannot express how gratified I am by the assurance that friends of earlier and happy days keep me in their kind memory, as I do them. You will be pleased to know that when I showed your beautiful volume to Mr Hutton he said, "You must let me hear it ; I value everything from him."

When I next see Mrs Ferguson I shall be able to tell her how we have enjoyed this new fruits of a taste and genius we have not to learn to appreciate now.

And again, at a later period, when her children had married and she had lost her husband, Mrs Hutton expressed her sentiments to Ferguson's wife :—

I do feel truly gratified by your unfailing kind remembrance of me. To a person at my age standing alone, after so many years of uninterrupted tender care for my every wish and want, you can scarce think how grateful it is to the heart to find valued friends so unchanged as you are.

Another Dublin resident whose receptions were very agreeable was Mrs Parnell, mother of Charles Stewart Parnell, then too young to give indication of the career which afterwards made him memorable. Mrs Parnell, daughter of Admiral Stewart of the American navy, and widow of an Irish gentleman of position, was in manner quiet and ladylike. Its refinement and repose concealed a tenacity of opinion very characteristic of her son also at a later period. At the time of the Fenian agitation she called one day on Ferguson, and in the calmest tone, yet with a suppressed undercurrent of indignation and vindictiveness, asked for his advice under circumstances which she detailed.

"My house was visited yesterday," she said, "by emissaries from the Castle. They opened my desk, examined my papers, and even read a letter—a proposal for my daughter's hand in marriage. How can I punish them for this insult?" "These are disturbed times, Mrs Parnell," replied Ferguson. "It is the duty of the Government to take precautions. It is rumoured—I do not inquire if it be true, but the rumour is a full justification of the act of which you complain—it is said that you have had Stephens, the Fenian Head Centre, concealed in your house. Remember you are an alien accepting the hospitality of the British Government. It is your duty to abstain from all political intrigues. I strongly urge you to do so in future. You have nothing to complain of, nor any claim for redress." Mrs Parnell was unconvinced, and no doubt imparted her hostile feelings to her children. The policy of Charles Stewart Parnell in later years was due to hatred of England quite as much as to love for Ireland,—a sentiment probably implanted in him by his mother, and dating from the time when she sustained what she conceived to be an outrage on the part of the constituted authorities.

Among those who have contributed to the enjoyments of literary society in Dublin, a few not previously named may here be mentioned : Mr W. J. Fitz-Patrick, recently deceased—December 24, 1895—biographer of Lever, and of Father Thomas Burke, and author of ' Secret Service under Pitt,' an important contribution to a dark period of Ireland's history; Dr Joyce, who has done much for Irish music and history, and has written a valuable work on ' Irish Names of Places'; Dr Todhunter, whose ' Life of Sarsfield, Earl of Lucan,' is a recent addition to the New Irish Library; Mr Standish O'Grady, whose ' Bog of Stars ' has appeared in this series, and whose ' Red Hugh ' is an interesting biography of Hugh Roe O'Donnell; and Mr J. T. Gilbert, who has written the ' History of Dublin,' ' Lives of the Viceroys,' and other important works.   As editor of 'The National Manuscripts of Ireland,' Mr Gilbert has rendered valuable services to his country.

In February 1878 a personal letter from the Duke of Marlborough, then Lord Lieutenant of Ireland, conveyed to Ferguson the offer of a Civil Knighthood "with the Queen's permission, a distinction which I trust you will find it consistent with your inclination to accept."

"There is not one in all Ireland so well entitled to the distinction," wrote Sir Bernard Burke, with his official communication.

The congratulations which Ferguson received were warm and cordial. Lord Waveney observed that the "'gowd has got the guinea stamp,' with Burns's reservation as true as ever." It was accepted as an honour "done to his country as well as to himself," a "recognition of Irish genius."

I congratulate you [wrote Robert Mallet] upon this recognition of the services which you have conferred upon the department over which you preside, as well as of the noble and stainless position which you have achieved for yourself in the Republic of letters.

I must congratulate you on the spurs [wrote Sir Thomas Larcom]. I love to see honour awarded to Science, Literature, Art; most of all, when a dear friend is the recipient.

It stamps the Royal impress on metal already sterling—at once recognition and reward—a double compliment *in atroque felix*.

I congratulate you with all my heart on the well-won distinction you are so soon to receive [wrote Lord O'Hagan]. Assuredly, of the multitude who will applaud it as a recognition of rare genius and distinguished worth, not one will rejoice in it with more earnest sincerity than your old and ever affectionate friend   O'HAGAN.

It will be a gratification to you to know that I am about to receive the honour of knighthood [wrote Ferguson to his friend Burton].   It will be conferred at the coming St Patrick's ball on 18th March.   I suppose the main ground is official service, but it is also regarded as a literary recognition, and in that view is especially grateful to me.   I adhere to my old-fashioned notions of what they call objective work in poetry, the plainer (almost) the better; I don't despair of living to see them again in the ascendant.   The "Widow's Cloak," to be sure, is cut to a very homely pattern, and must not be too bold to be matched with "white samite, mystic, wonderful." . . .

If the old Sage be able for the journey, the Armagh Observatory party will be with us at the meeting of the British Association in August.   Will you be among their companions at North Great George's Street?   It would be a great delight to us to have you with us.

The "old Sage" was the revered Dr Romney Robinson, whose wife's felicitations had taken the form of congratulating the Duke of Marlborough on his selection of her friend as recipient of honours.   These Ferguson, with characteristic generosity, desired to share with Mr James Owen of the Board of Works, who carried out his designs in the internal arrangements of the Record Office :—

It will, I think, give you pleasure to know that I am to receive the honour of knighthood at the St Patrick's ball on the 18th.   The distinction is, I believe, in part put on literary

deservings; but the powerful ground for it is no doubt my
work here, and, I daresay, a desire to place the service on as
honourable a footing here as elsewhere.

You have done so much to help me in the practical part of
my undertaking—have shown so much consideration and, at
times, so much forbearance—and have transacted every detail
of business with such care and forethought for me, that I
would be the most ungrateful recipient of benefits if I did not
long ago feel, and continue to feel, truly thankful to you; and
it seems to me that I can take no fitter occasion for saying
what I feel in that respect than now, when, thanks in so great
a measure to you, I am about to have so acceptable a
reward.

It was said of Ferguson by one who was a frequent
guest in his house, that he lived " in a very atmosphere
of kindly friendship." This was true, and extended
to the young, for whom his companionship had great
fascination. His delight in children and tenderness
to them has already been touched on. Here is a
letter to an American child whom he met at Vichy.
Dr Evans, father of little Joseph, was an invalid, and
Mrs Evans much engrossed in attending to her suffering husband. The boy had no companion in the
hotel, crowded with inmates, and would have been
very lonely but that Ferguson took him out to walk,
and was gentle and encouraging to the little fellow.
Many years later the Evans's were again in Europe,
and Ferguson wrote to Joseph inviting him to his
house. He came, and had developed into a bright
and intelligent youth, who thoroughly enjoyed the
society he met during the meeting of the British
Association in Dublin in 1878 :—

20 NORTH GREAT GEORGE'S ST., 30*th* *July* 1878.

MY DEAR JOSEPH,—We are about to have a meeting of the British Association in Dublin which will attract many notable people during the week beginning 14th August. Will you gratify us by being our guest during the meeting, and as much longer as Dublin may have attraction for you?

It would be a great pleasure to me to see again the boy with whom I used to walk and talk at Vichy long ago, now that he is a young man, and engaged in pursuits for which his tastes and disposition then promised so well to qualify him; and I believe I am not wrong in thinking that little Joseph—I speak of you as I remember you—would also be pleased to see the old friend who often drew him his pictures of ships and of trees, and gave him his hints of perspective by the banks of the Luchon.

Pray make my kind regards to Dr and Mrs Evans, and believe me, very sincerely, your old friend,

SAML. FERGUSON.

That faithfulness in friendship so characteristic of Ferguson, extended to those separated by distance, circumstance, and the lapse of years. To an old friend long resident in Milwaukee, U.S.A., he wrote in 1885 :—

We are glad to have you and Mary Anne recalled to kindly remembrance by your Christmas cards. We are growing old, but find our hands still full of work and our hearts as sensible as ever to kindness. I advise my wife to give up some of her pursuits which entail the personal labour of keeping the accounts and writing letters on affairs. But she drudges on in the service of the poor, and still finds time for her social duties, which do not decrease. I am engaged in the affairs of my office, and in my duties as President of the Academy, which occupy my time pretty fully; but whenever I am free to follow my own impulses, I am at my old literary pursuits, prose and verse, and, I daresay, will continue to find my chief solace in them as long as I live,—I am now as old as Mr Gladstone, but I do not repine in admitting that I could not now cut down a tree. I do not expect ever to be in strong health, but may see a good many summers, and maybe write some words that may live after me yet.—With kindest wishes for yourself and Mary Anne, affectionately yours,

SAML. FERGUSON.

Ferguson was not fated to see more summers; but the words which Dean Stanley wrote of Dean Ramsay may also be applied to him :—

> "Not in vain hath he lived who by innocent mirth
> Hath lightened the frowns and the furrows of earth ;
> Not in vain hath he lived who hath laboured to give
> In himself the best proof how by LOVE one may live."

CHAPTER XIII.

1847–1886.

HIS VIEWS ON ARCHITECTURE AND ART, AND FRIENDSHIP WITH SIR FREDERIC W. BURTON.

> "Heaven doth with us as we with torches do,
>   Not light them for themselves; for if our virtues
>   Did not go forth of us, 'twere all alike
>   As if we had them not.   Spirits are not finely touch'd
>   But to fine issues; nor Nature never lends
>   The smallest scruple of her excellence,
>   But, like a thrifty goddess, she determines
>   Herself the glory of a creditor—
>   Both thanks and use."
> —SHAKESPEARE.

FERGUSON was much interested in Architecture and Art.   His delight in Westminster Hall and Abbey, and in the more modern erections of Inigo Jones and Sir Christopher Wren, as well as his contempt for much recent building in London, has already been expressed, as well as the enthusiasm with which he studied the architecture of the Continent — its cathedrals, churches, and secular buildings — during his tour in 1846.   On his return, in a review of the life of Gandon—'Dublin University Magazine,' June

1847—he dwelt, with no stinted admiration, on the chief public buildings of the Irish capital, some of the first of them being the work of that architect.

The age in which he lived [wrote Ferguson] was eminently averse to mysticism: all the monuments of our grandfathers' and great-grandfathers' civilisation, both here and in Great Britain, are designed on classic models adapted to the requisites of a Northern climate, and to the wants of modern life. You will find among them neither crockets, nor finials, nor the affectation of monastic seclusion, or of feudal rudeness; but an elegant simplicity and fitness everywhere united with forms of stability and grandeur.

It is evident that he entirely approved, for modern purposes, of the Roman Doric, and was enraptured with " those beautiful columns, those graceful cupolas, those airy and commodious porticoes, which embody the mind and genius of other days."

We have long desired an opportunity [he wrote] of expressing some opinions on the state and prospects of our public architecture, and now avail ourselves of this Memoir of a really great architect, to say what we hope may prove publicly serviceable. The buildings erected by Gandon have, for the last half - century, been the principal evidences of national taste and civilisation to which the Irish could refer. Since his time a great deal of public money has been expended — and we all feel the expense — without the production of anything to sustain even the most modest pretensions of that kind. On the contrary, our public edifices, of recent erection, very generally indicate a barbarian insensibility to fitness and beauty, and truly enough tell the stranger that this country, from whatever cause, is not now the home of refinement and intellectual culture that it once was. This mischief has flowed, to a great extent, from the administration of public affairs by Commissions, the members of which have, naturally enough, been appointed as men of business, but without the least reference to their capacity in matters of taste or elegant learning. The Board of Works are able to organise and put in operation a prodigious machinery, requiring great ability in that department; but a board of as many ploughmen could not have sanctioned more inelegant buildings than have arisen, all over the country, at our expense, both in pocket and in character, under their superintendence. The Commissioners of National Education have succeeded, against great opposition, in extending and administering their system of instruction, in a manner which shows them very capable of communicating both the rudiments of book-learning and the virtues of moderation and perseverance to the people; but they have suffered edifices to grow up for the reception of their classes which are offensive to educated eyes, and detrimental to our character as an educated people. The Board of Ecclesiastical Commissioners, while it has not gained even the reputation due to the others for administrative success, rivals and even exceeds them in the odium of having lowered the standard of the public taste; for, not content with erecting its tasteless buildings on independent sites, this corporation employs our money and compromises our character in pulling down our most valuable historic monuments to make room for its spurious and insignificant creations. . . .

We deem it more the expedient of a barbarian than the policy of an educated man to destroy evidences of past civilisation in order to reconcile men to the notion that they are "a people without a history," who ought, of right, to occupy an inferior position, and learn contentedly the lesson of dependence. . . .

Let us proceed from our paid boards of Commissioners to the more constitutional bodies consisting of the unpaid magistracy and gentry, who, in their grand juries, have the direction, to a considerable extent, of the local architectural ability of the country. Here the selectors of the designs to be executed are themselves contributors to the cost. They are disposing of their own money, and have a direct interest and a just pride in beautifying the districts where they reside.

Besides, there are generally to be found in bodies of this kind gentlemen of cultivated tastes, acquainted with the best models, and familiar, from residence in the country, with all the requisitions of climate and situation. It is not, therefore, surprising that the duties of taste entrusted to these bodies are better performed than those committed to the paid non-resident and non-competent functionaries who constitute our extra-constitutional boards. . . .

No Government Commission was ever yet created from which so great a variety of elegant and suitable designs has emanated as there did from the unpaid good taste of our native nobility and gentry during the latter part of the last century. The private mansions alone of the great Irish residents of that day are amongst the most beautiful and stately edifices of the world. Few Continental princes can boast more elegant or suitable mansions than Castletown. Carton excels the best of the Italian villa-palaces. Castle-coole, Russborough, Bessborough, are structures which, in their class, can only be matched in that true rural paradise, England. . . .

It was one of these epochs which has left characteristic marks on the face of the country; not like the present age, in which, incapable of striking out a style of our own, and arrogantly despising that of our immediate predecessors, we revive the obsolete modes of past barbarous epochs, and cover our land with motley plunder from the fourth to the fourteenth century. Architecture is as much an exponent of the intellectual condition of the immediate period as literature. To see our public edifices affecting this variety of obsolete styles, is much the same as if we beheld the principal literary organs of the age go back to the black-letter and the quaint spelling and language of the corresponding periods. . . .

What have the Irish to boast of? The answer is short but comprehensive : their music and their architecture of the era of independence. Their music is wholly and exclusively their own, and is wholly beautiful. Their architecture of the palmy period referred to belongs to the transplanted civilisation of England. The architects principally employed were natives of that great nurse of excellence in so many arts. The taste and magnificence which invited them hither, and directed their efforts here, were Anglo-Irish. We now speak merely ethnographically; for the patrons, from whatever quarter of the world they might draw their original lineage, were in feeling and affection, as well as by long naturalisation, altogether Irish, and whether the executive ability was derived from England or from Italy, the monuments themselves equally belong to the country whose liberality and taste appropriated them. .   .   .

All the best porticoes of that day are of plain shafts, and still delight the spectator with that combination of breadth and gracefulness, of elegance and solidity, which is so charming to the cultivated eye. Need we instance the porticoes of the Bank? Surely architecture never produced a set of forms more completely gratifying to the sense, and satisfactory to the understanding. Whether by daylight or moonlight, in rain or in sunshine, with shadow or without (and indeed it is one of the special advantages of the plain shaft, in this climate, that it takes just enough of weather-staining to supply the place of shadow in dark weather), seen through clouds of dust, or over a watery waste of mire, it is still the most beautiful portico north of the Alps, a permanent source of blameless gratification, and of just pride to its possessors.

In July 1849 Ferguson reviewed in the 'University' Ruskin's 'Seven Lamps of Architecture,' and sub-sequently his 'Stones of Venice,' books which he held in high estimation for their beauty of style, their intense love of Nature, and their moral teachings. But he dissented from the medieval leanings of the impassioned and eloquent author, as will be readily inferred from his observations on the 'Seven Lamps of Architecture':—

Of man's works on the globe which he inhabits, the greatest

beyond measure are those effected by the husbandman. If all the structural works of mankind were brought together in one place, they would not make, on any broad prospect of the earth, so considerable a show as the altered surface of one well-tilled province. But after the husbandman, the builder is the greatest of workmen. If he builds well, he builds for both profit and delight; for uses intellectual and moral, as well as for the purposes of practical utility. Every excellence in his art associates itself with feeling and sentiment. Whether he raise the towers or bastions of the fortress, or the spires or pinnacles of the temple set apart for the worship of God, he deals in forms and proportions, combinations and symmetries, which, with every purpose they subserve, speak a poetic language of their own, intelligible, impressive, and almost as lasting as the divine utterances of the poet himself, dealing in the unencumbered expressions of speech. How to build, so as to attain this utterance, is a more difficult inquiry than how to compose an epic or a tragedy. For the poem is a work wholly intellectual; but the building must first be useful, and is only collaterally capable of this sort of expression.

Ferguson observes in this essay that Mr Ruskin draws his illustrations entirely from medieval works.

His love of the delicate, the picturesque, and the mysterious, here gratifies itself in congenial forms of fretwork, of irregular arcades, and half-discovered vistas. The solemn roof, suspended from its unseen external props, fills him with a pleasing awe; the inlaid patterns and variegated courses and diamonds of different coloured masonry, delight his sense of colour; and the venerable air of the twelfth century inspires him with a dreamy sentiment of Anglican catholicity, and of Anglican progress in religion and virtue, most humane and amiable, and blamelessly patriotic. For our part, we discard sentiments and associations of the medieval kind. We desire light and distinctness. We wish to see the roof over our head supported by walls or pillars evidently adequate to the burthen. We admire stateliness, regularity, and spaciousness. We wish to breathe the free air of the *Stoa;* and amid gardens and fountains, and broad balustraded terraces, to ponder the lessons of Greek and Roman wisdom. . . .

It doubtless contributes much to the stability of society, and to the virtue and happiness of men, that they should be bound, one generation to another, by transmitted institutions and monuments; of which latter, the domestic monuments of the halls and hearths of our ancestors are surely most conducive to the perpetuation of pious and reverent feelings; charging us, as it were, with the preservation of the heirlooms of our race, and continually reminding us that we are but trustees and transmitters of the noble inheritance which civilisation entails on man, of truth, freedom, and social order. . . .

We cannot, however, even though with a prospect of soon returning to it, take leave of our subject or of its illustration, without again acknowledging our obligation to Mr Ruskin for the moral treat, far more valuable than any architectural analysis, which his present essay has afforded us. He writes with even more feeling than sentiment, and with philosophic meaning more profound than either. Human life and destiny are his subjects far more than any art of construction or decoration. As an essay on the critical principles of design in building, the work will be permanently known as containing the first systematic exposition of the beauties of barbaresque art. But there are none of us, in however fastidious an Augustan school we may have been educated, or however little we may care for the *rationale* of a style which we deem unsuitable for any purpose of present use or ornament, who will not also recognise and prize it as the work of an interpreter between man and nature, making us acquainted with many unnoticed signs and tokens of the divine love which surrounds us, and while bringing our faculties of perception into harmony with a novel and interesting class of beautiful objects, bringing our hearts and minds also into harmony with truth and virtue.

In 1864 Ferguson delivered in Dublin one of the "Afternoon Lectures on Literature and Art," and chose for his subject "Our Architecture." In his address he reiterated his preference for that adaptation of classic architecture termed "Regular," "Renaissance," or "Palladian," thus named from the Italian architect who accommodated it to modern use. His address contained the following passages :—

Our generation has gained for itself an eminent place in the history of literature. It has stamped its impress on a National School of Painting; but, after a long period of indecision, it has as yet come to no determination on the form to be permanently assumed by its most lasting and characteristic material exponent. It is only by the control of educated judgments that the public taste in such a period of irresolute and tentative selection can be restrained from caprices which might constitute a permanent reproach to our century. . . .

To be original is a privilege rarely vouchsafed to the architect. The laws of epic or dramatic unity impose no shackles on the man of letters at all to be compared with the rigour of those which bind the artist who must express himself Regularly in stone. If he can impress with a sense of majesty, if he can elevate and at the same time expand the soul, if he can communicate a perception of elegance, grandeur, and harmony, these will be his triumphs; but in proportion as he rises towards these heights of his art, he will leave individual peculiarities behind, and in the attainment of perfection pass far beyond the reach of any influence of egotism. If he have a style by which his works may be known from those of other men, it will be felt in their general impression, not offered to attention in their details; for of so universal and absolute a character is architectural perfection, such as we may conceive it, that, as in sculpture, the very test of excellence might be that the masterpiece should seem worthy to be the work of any master. But as there is no art in which excellence more demands of the master that he shall mortify the egotistical sentiment, so there is none in which the temptation is greater or the way more easy to mannerism. . . .

The Palladian method had indeed been adapted to our

conditions of society and climate in a form delightful to the eye and satisfactory to the understanding. Men even of moderate ability as well as of great genius had shown practically in their works that material existed for abundant variety in the combination of those forms and features on which the public taste was agreed. A British style had in fact been established, as characteristic as the national styles, growing out of the same Palladian revival, of Italy or France. We see it here in the civic buildings of our own city in as high a state of advancement as anywhere in Great Britain. We live indeed in Dublin, in the midst of great but unnoticed beauties. If our Custom House stood on the Grand Canal at Venice, we should soon see something in the windows of our photographers that would strike every eye as a lovely novelty. I do not dwell on other architectural features of our city familiar to all eyes, but which I wish my words could render more familiar to public perception and appreciation. For all our works of that period are those of an intellectually advanced and intellectually consistent people; and no better answer could be given to those who make the charge of tameness and monotony against Regular art than the variety, the freedom, and yet the fitness, strength, and dignity of the public buildings of Dublin of the last century. Nor is there really any want of variety in the works of the Regular school in its better days in London. Every composition of Wren, if we except alone his greatest and his least successful one, is an original conception. Gibbs's church of St Martin's-in-the-Fields is rich and harmonious as an Italian interior of the best Roman epoch, yet it is wholly and proudly English. The river front of Somerset House affords a source of endless pleasure to all who care to receive its successive impressions of solid grandeur, and open, airy magnificence. Such a style in the hands of men of ability, gifted only with the modesty of genius, might well have satisfied the æsthetic wants of an intellectual and magnificent people. But no style can endure the mischiefs of affectation. . . .

If I have led you fairly to the point of selection, I have accomplished my principal purpose. I do not seek to disguise my own preference for the Regular, which I am persuaded is

just as capable of new forms of beauty, in combinations as yet
unimagined, as it was in the days of Palladio; but whether the
public taste shall ultimately fix on one or the other, or possibly
on some of the many rivals of both, I shall discharge a wish I
have long entertained, if, by this review of our position, I shall
have turned other minds to the clearer contemplation of a subject delightful in itself, and valuable to society, in proportion
to its power of exalting the soul and refining the intellect.

Ferguson took intense delight in Art, and had a fine
appreciation of the works of the great masters both
in painting and in sculpture. He had visited and
revisited with enthusiastic admiration the galleries of
Great Britain and the Continent, and such private
collections as were accessible at home and abroad.
He had a fine eye for colour, and on entering a gallery
instinctively sought out the pictures of highest excellence in tone and colouring. But still more attractive
to him was the spiritual in art, and perhaps he derived
the purest delight from a small work of Francia's in
the Brera at Milan. "I would rather be the painter
of the angel in Francia's 'Annunciation' than any
picture I know," he exclaimed; "the awe and mystery in
the face of Gabriel as he looks at the simple young girl
and thinks what he has to say to her, is so powerfully
expressed." Fra Angelico's pictures enraptured him,
and so did the glorious colourists of the Venetian
school. When in London he never failed to feast
his eyes on Titian's "Bacchus and Ariadne," and on
Paul Veronese's "Family of Darius at the feet of Alex-
ander," as well as on the Raffaelles, Francias, and
Peruginos, the Claudes, Ruysdaels, and Hobbemas,

in our National Gallery. How greatly he delighted in Paolo's colouring he has expressed in the sonnets already cited, inspired by the Veronese pictures.

These tastes were strengthened by his long and intimate friendship with Sir Frederic William Burton, who in March 1894 retired from the office he had held for twenty years, as Director of the National Gallery. It is acknowledged by all competent judges that Burton's services to the nation while he held that important post have been of inestimable value. We have now a collection of works of art which in magnitude, value, and arrangement holds a proud position among the Galleries of Europe and the World.

Burton resided in Dublin during the lifetime of his widowed mother; and some of his choicest works in water-colour are to be found in the Irish capital, chiefly in the houses of his friends. He lived there while she was spared to him, as Ferguson has told, "honoured and beloved"; a man of singular refinement, delicate sensibility, and true and faithful heart. After his removal to the wider sphere of London, he returned from time to time to visit his native land, and the friends from whom his affection never swerved. His correspondence reveals his wide culture and generous heart :—

MY DEAR FERGUSON,—Mrs Ferguson will have communicated to you some ordinary kind words which I left for you, but these were words, and she could not tell you all I feel towards you and her, and what a debt of gratitude I am conscious of for all the thorough kindness which you two friends showed me during my stay in Dublin, and while we were thrown together in the unforgotten Isle of Aran. I shall not go into flourishes about the "happiest hours of my life" and so forth, but if ever there was a man who was made happy by the constancy and warmth of his friends, their forbearance and generosity, I was that one while in Ireland, and amongst the foremost and most prized of mine were you and your affectionate wife.

Burton was also the intimate friend of Stokes and Petrie, and of their children. One of his best-known and most touching pictures—"The Blind Girl at the Holy Well"—contains the portrait of Petrie's daughter, who sat to the artist for the suffering peasant who seeks the restoration of sight from the sacred waters. "The Aran Fisherman's Drowned Child" is another picture by Burton associated with the islets of the saints.

In the glimpse which I caught of Dr Stokes when he was in London lately [wrote Burton to Mrs Ferguson], I heard that you and Ferguson were remarkably well, and Whitley told me that when he last saw Sam he was in great force and spirits. The Doctor sees from a moral and physical point of view. Whitley takes generally a purely intellectual one, or something near it.

So that between both, my conception of the true state of things is probably not far from the correct one, and if it be so I have no reason to wish it otherwise than it is. It presents me with a picture very welcome to my sight.

Although I so seldom make a sign, you must not think, dear friend, that I am the less true, or that I ever can forget your incredible kindness to me when I was last in Ireland. . . .

And when you have time to throw away, dear Mrs Ferguson, will you not vouchsafe me a friendly line? When all the "hurly-burly's done" of this exigent time, I shall not dare to ask S. F. for one, knowing what work he has to do, and hoping that all his spare hours are spent upon the completion of the "Battle of Moira," which I was rejoiced to hear from my friend Whitley was making rapid progress towards it. For that reason also I do not write to him too, because I know that Sam cannot find time for everything, and that Mrs F. can find time for everything and something more. Good-bye, dear friends. Believe me ever yours affectionately,

F. W. BURTON.

MY DEAR FERGUSON,—You can scarcely think how deplorably disappointed I was last Wednesday when, on returning from town, I found that you had been here about a quarter of an hour before. I can safely say there is no one in the world whom I should have more heartily welcomed, and my pain at missing you was aggravated by the fact that you had been that day, and for two or three previously, especially in my thoughts, and that I was really on the point of writing to ask you whether there was any chance of your and Mrs F.'s coming through London this season, so that I might have a hope of seeing you. . . .

Nothing is more hateful to me than the way in which life passes by, year after year, without true friends meeting, until the sudden doom comes on one or the other, and the survivor has another fertile seed of sorrow sown in his heart, that most dreary of all kinds of sorrow which involves a regretful retrospect, without a hope. . . .

I wish you and Mrs F. a pleasant trip in Brittany. How very much I should like to be there with you ; nor is there any man but yourself, save perhaps dear old Petrie, with whom I should thoroughly relish a visit to Carnac and Locmariaquer, if you go so far south.

I would give much to hear the poem of which R. Mallet tells me; the subject must be fine, and your treatment of it evidently such as no man but yourself could have originated.

Mr Robert Mallet, whose name often occurs in this correspondence, was Burton's cousin. He was a man of Science, and had resided for many years before he settled in London, at Delville, Glasnevin, a house which had belonged to Dean Delany, and had been decorated by his accomplished wife, whose published 'Letters' give an animated picture of Dublin society in pre-Union days. Swift was a frequent guest at Delville, and in a summer-house yet standing in its grounds printed the 'Drapier's Letters.' Mr Mallet, whose work on Earthquakes established his reputation in science, had a fine literary taste. His house in London was hospitably open to his friends, and to it his conversation was a strong attraction.

Burton was urged by the Fergusons to accompany them to Brittany; but being unable to leave London, wrote to express his regret :—

My dear Mrs Ferguson,—I do not lose a moment in answering your kind letter, which I have just got, and offering you and Sam my heartiest thanks for your friendly wish that I should join you in your trip through Brittany. Beyond all question I would do so most gladly if it were in my power. Neither is there anything that could afford me greater pleasure. To travel with two such friends as you through a country of such deep interest as old Armorica, in which I have never yet been, would indeed be something too good for me to hope for. . . .

I hope you will have fine weather in Brittany, although a grey day at Carnac and Morbihan,—for the sun shines ill upon these ancient and mysterious traces of an unknown time and people—excepting, perhaps, that hour when the level rays from the west seem to light them up with a dreamy life, and to cast us with them into the remotest time. But only to think of them makes me so long to be there, that I grow impatient at the hindrances which stand in my way.

When Ferguson published in the autumn of 1864

his 'Lays of the Western Gael,' he sent a copy to his
friend with the following lines :—

TO FREDERIC WILLIAM BURTON,

WITH A COPY OF THE 'LAYS OF THE WESTERN GAEL.'

Burton, whose works, in rivalry of Art,
Fall second only to the pictures wrought
By your own Fancy on the inward chart,
Wherewith, at first, compared, you deem them nought,
Which yet, when for a season set apart,
And from the glowing tablets of the mind
The prototypes departed, glad, you find
So fair the world may take them to its heart :
I also failed, in numbers, to come near
Some strains my Fancy lately heard, so sweet
It seemed at first I laboured to no end ;
Yet now again I read the verses here,
A twelvemonth old, I deem them not unmeet
Even to be offered to my glorious friend.

The little parcel brought me by the post a few days ago
[wrote Burton] has made me prouder than anything I can
recollect. And you cannot know how deeply I thank you
for it. . . .

The honour you have shown me in those lines raises me
from my painful brooding. The affection they evince recalls
me to the fact that life is not worthless, and that such friendship is more real than our bodies themselves.

It is wrong to forget this even for a time. But there are
hours when no stars shine and the chill and palpable darkness
closes in upon us. . . .

I accept with the gift the words from your true and manly
heart as they are offered, whilst I feel how little I deserve
them, and how far short falls all I have done in my own art
of the greatness, the beauty, the pathos, and the fire that glow
in every page of this precious little volume. Only to have
been linked with him whose heart and brain have begotten

such children of light, is to have had a desert conferred which has no indigenous existence.

I argue that you and your wife are well.   Give to that other dear friend my heartiest regards, and always continue to look upon me as you now do, as amongst the foremost band of your most thorough friends.

I long to hear you read some of these verses, both those I already know and those hitherto only longed for. . . .

When you asked me about my relative views on the Lays, I had not considered them so much in that light, having been satisfied with enjoying the individual beauties of each for itself. I recollect that I spoke strongly of the " Burial of King Cormac," but it was, in truth, more that it happened to be most in my mind at the moment.   On re-reading the longer poems with the idea of comparison, I really feel it difficult to make any choice — so thoroughly fine is each of them, and so peculiar in its stuff and its treatment.   Putting aside the splendid " Welshmen of Tirawley," I now rather incline to think the " Tain-Quest " the most rounded and perfect of all. The theme is a fine one, fitted especially to poetry, the metre well chosen (though indeed that is to a quite extraordinary degree the case with all the Lays, and shows the true *œstrus* that produced them), and there are stanzas in it that, according to my feeling, have never been surpassed, and very seldom equalled.   You already know what I feel about the " Healing of Conall Carnach."   "Aideen's Grave" I knew before, but cannot know it too well.   " The Fairy Thorn " and " Willie Gilliland " are exquisite ballads, and I particularly admire the " Death of Dermid" and "Deirdré's Lament."   To the minor poems I have not yet done justice, for the grand imagery of the longer ones has captured my fancy and kept me dwelling upon them.

How fine the delivery of the Tain to Murgen is !   It is really a stupendous picture.   And in Murgen's invocation nothing can be finer than the use you have made of that strange and mystic conception as to Conor's Shield.   This is highly oriental in its character, and is one of those remarkable births of Celtic poetry which make us regret beyond all things that that poetry is not preserved to us in its original purity. . . .

Good-night, dear Ferguson. I hope you have given my kindest remembrances to Mrs Ferguson. Now I wish you and her the happiest New Year. Would to God I could hope for it for our country! And am as ever, affectionately yours,

F. W. BURTON.

P.S.—With respect to criticism on poetry in general, the whole tone of the English press is one-sided, and its views narrow.

The exquisite polish and elaborate refinement, and I may venture to say sometimes cloying sweetness, of Tennyson, have taken captive the whole nation, and manly force is generally counted as ruggedness. This is a fashion which will run its course. And indeed the seed sown by Tennyson is already degenerating and smothering its very self. As to the *animus* towards Ireland and all that is Celtic, that, I fear, is not so likely to die out. And how can it until Irishmen learn to be truer to themselves?

I am indeed glad to hear from you [wrote Burton to Mrs Ferguson]. For although I did not just think you had quite forgotten me, and am too bad a correspondent myself to dare to cast reflections, yet I was long in hopes of getting one little line from you to acknowledge the safe receipt of the "Lectures," which I forwarded to you simultaneously with the note you now make such kindly mention of.

The evil news of our common great loss I had already heard the day after it fell upon us. But I had been prepared for it in some degree, by having heard the evening before (when truly all was already at an end) bad accounts of the state of our beloved friend. I cannot say that I now first know how I loved him, for I knew it well before, well enough to make the mere anticipation of the end as painful as the end itself. If there be any poor comfort left, it is that his spirit glided painlessly away, and that he himself could not see how weary the blank he leaves behind him.

The death here referred to was that of Dr Petrie,

who passed away, leaving a blank in the hearts of his friends not to be filled up, on the 17th of January 1866. The " Lectures " returned by Burton was the volume containing Ferguson's address on "Our Architecture" in the Dublin 'Afternoon Lectures on Literature and Art.'

My native air has done me good [wrote Burton in November 1868 to Mrs Ferguson]. I am able to work again, as indeed what I above told you implied.

I cannot tell you the sort of delight I felt when again on Irish soil, nor was my regret to leave it one whit less. There is a sort of *Zauber* about it, to us at least, which cannot be described, but which we well comprehend. All the more does its sad fate press upon us. The measure of wrong and injustice, intentional and unintentional, kept up for long centuries, is now about to be filled up, and the curse lies still heavy on the country of being made the battle-ground of English political quarrels. For beyond doubt this is the main sense of the present enthusiasm for " Justice to Ireland."

In the summer of 1868, Ferguson, whose health was seriously impaired, went with his wife to the baths of Wildbad Gastein in the district of Salzburg, and so lost the happiness of seeing his friend during Burton's visit to Ireland.

The benefit derived from change of climate, and from thermal waters, induced him to spend many of his vacations at health-resorts. He visited repeatedly Gastein, St Moritz, Wildbad in the Black Forest, Homburg, Wiesbaden, Vichy, as well as Buxton, Harrogate, and Lisdoonvarna nearer home.

One of the enjoyments of Continental Spas consists of the conversation or even the sight of the distinguished people who frequent them. During their sojourn at Gastein in 1868, the Fergusons found themselves for some weeks daily seated at table beside Count Von Beust, then the Austrian Prime Minister. He had the air of a man greatly overworked and wearied; so his neighbours never accosted him unless he first began the conversation. His three secretaries sat opposite to him at table. Just as the early dinner concluded, the postman usually passed the windows of the *salle-à-manger*, and the secretaries and others who expected letters met him at the door. The Minister from his seat watched the result. If a large packet was delivered he would groan audibly. He was on such occasions no more seen for the rest of the day. And when they revisited Gastein some years later, the German Emperor William I. and Count von Moltke were taking the baths there, and were encountered daily in walks and drives. The Emperor, a courteous old gentleman with one attendant only, was quite simple and unostentatious in manner; but when the time came for his departure, he left in state with a great retinue. Von Moltke, "silent in seven languages," had a weather-beaten visage, a lofty forehead, and a thick head of short bristling grey hair.

On another occasion, at Wildbad in the Black Forest, Prince Gortschakoff was staying at the same hotel as Ferguson and his wife, — a tall, slight old man with white hair, but brilliant dark eyes, full of life and fire. To meet these great personages, and occasionally to converse with them, was an agreeable experience; and a chance encounter with the Queen of Würtemberg, daughter of the Emperor Nicholas I. of Russia, at the castle of Hohenschwangau, is recalled with pleasure. When journeying in a beautiful region, the Fergusons often engaged a one-horse carriage by the week, and proceeded in leisurely fashion, stopping for meals and for the night as chance might direct. On one of these occasions, when referring to their guide-book, it appeared that this hunting-lodge of the King of Würtemberg, decorated by modern artists with scenes from medieval romances, was within reach, and open to the public on the following day. This day was to be the last of their *vetturino* wanderings; they were to leave the district by train in the afternoon. But before parting with their carriage they made an early start for Hohenschwangau, and reached the castle about 9 A.M. To their surprise the door was opened by a domestic in brilliant livery, who informed them that they were an hour too soon. The castle was not to be seen before ten o'clock. He held the door open while they debated whether time would admit of their waiting till the appointed hour, or whether they should abandon the attempt to see the frescoes of the Munich artists. They did not observe that an inmate of the castle had descended the stairs which crossed the hall, till a simply attired lady of middle age addressed them in English. "Pray come in," she said: "you must not leave without seeing these works of art. There is no difficulty whatever; you are quite welcome. I shall send for a cicerone who will conduct you through the apartments." She turned to the servant, and sending him for the cicerone, remained in conversation during the footman's absence. She spoke English with perfect fluency and without a trace of foreign accent; and inquired what had been seen of the country, and how we were impressed by it; and spoke of the artists whose works we were about to see. By this time the cicerone appeared, and the lady bowed graciously and went on, doubtless to her breakfast. We proceeded in an opposite direction through a long suite of rooms, and heard the legend of the Knight of the Swan monotonously mumbled in German. It was all but impossible to ask a question. We had reached the bedroom just vacated, before we could inquire who was the lady who had befriended us. "The Queen," he replied: "she arrived unexpectedly yesterday." He resumed his monotonous narration explanatory of the frescoes, while we, passing through her Majesty's bedroom, reached a turret just large enough to hold a *prie-dieu* chair, and a small table on which stood a photograph, a beautiful head lying on a pillow, evidently taken after death. It closely resembled the fine profile of Clarence Mangan, by Burton, now in the National Gallery of Dublin—also taken after death. "How comes Mangan's portrait here?" we exclaimed, but on looking closely discovered our mistake. It was the likeness of the Emperor Nicholas of Russia, father to Olga, Queen of Würtemberg.

Mangan's portrait recalls us from foreign scenes

back to Dublin, and to the artist who portrayed "the rapture of repose" on the finely chiselled features of one so storm-tossed and shipwrecked on the waves of this troublesome life as the poor hapless poet.

Burton's letters touch on many subjects of interest. Music and musical instruments; his appointment as Director of the National Gallery, its pleasures and its pains; the rejoicing which filled his heart when the honour of Knighthood was conferred on his friend; the grief which patriotic Irishmen could not but feel at the demoralisation of the people,— all these are frankly expressed.

MY DEAR FERGUSON,—I hope another Easter may not come round without my seeing you somewhere or another, and that I shall then be an eyewitness of the change for the better which by all accounts has taken place in your health since last we met. All that Burchett has told me was fully borne out by the later testimony of Haughton, whom I met at R. Mallet's last Sunday, and who gave me a most cheering view of your state, showing that best sign, that your bellicose instincts are in full play when occasion calls for their action. I trust, therefore, that you are well up to your work in every way. How much I should have liked to be with you and Mrs Ferguson and the Burchetts when you were rambling about last autumn! But it was necessary for me to pin myself to my work here; and happily I was able for it, my health having been wonderfully restored by my long stay abroad, though I did not feel the difference until after my return.

Seeing that I may believe you to be so well, I am the less reluctant to trouble you for a bit of information and advice on behalf of a friend of mine here, a most interesting and talented man, Carl Engel, the author of a good deal of matter upon the subject of music (a musical composer too), amongst the rest, of two works, one on National Music, and the other, earlier, on Assyrian music (!), really a most interesting, ingenious, and instructive essay, though *a priori* one would not expect much could be told the world on that point. He is now engaged on a very elaborate ' History of Musical Instruments,' which I have no doubt will be carried out with thorough German patient enthusiasm, and exhaustion of all possible sources of information.   He has a wonderful collection of musical instruments, which I may tell you begins with a whistle of a raindeer's digital bone from the caves in Perigord (given him by Christie); and although there is a pretty wide gap, chronologically, between that work of art and the next earliest one in the collection, still he can boast of some curious things. A good portion of his collection is on loan at S. Kensington, and he has made a valuable catalogue of the whole of their collection.   To make the matter short, however, he has heard of the Indian musical instruments which were, and I suppose still are, in the Museum of the R. Irish Academy, and about the nomenclature of which Meadows Taylor read the paper some few years ago, published in the ' Proceedings R.I.A.' These instruments seem to have been presented to the Academy by Colonel French.   Mr Engel is very anxious to get some outline drawings of some of these things, and he was about to see whether S. Kensington could procure him what he wants.   I ventured to offer my interposition, and I want you just to tell me to whom I had best apply to get the drawings made.   Clibborn, or Gilbert, or who would manage the affair for Engel?   Of course he wishes to pay for the drawings.   The only needful thing next to getting leave for the copier, is that *he* should be able to do them accurately.   When I know to whom to apply, I can give the particulars of what is required.

MY DEAR FERGUSON,—I was glad to get your letter yesterday, and I thank Mrs Ferguson heartily for the gift.   .   .   .

Sir W. W. Wynn is going to send his rich collection of ancient Welsh musical instruments, here on loan exhibition. Engel builds much on seeing and examining them.   And

I should not wonder if they throw light on Irish matters of the sort.

I hope, dear Sam, that your not very cheery account of yourself is but the result of a passing fit of unusual depression —not unnatural in a man of such active habits of mind and body as yourself. Both Burchett and Haughton gave me so good an account of you that I almost venture to come to the above conclusion. I am glad to find you, nevertheless, speculating on the continuance of your creative works, and I do yet hope to live to see your great poem in type. It is a miserable business that men of kindred thoughts and aspirations should be so often isolated entities in this queer random system of the world. There they stand, each for himself, without a chance of that electric contact which might kindle the damped and smouldering coals into flame. I lately met Campbell of Islay ("Islay"), the author of 'Tales of the Western Highlands.' Besides what he has published, he has ponderous piles of Gaelic MSS., which will probably never see the light, but which some strong sympathetic mind might urge his indolence to publish. You know by his "Introduction" that this disinherited chieftain is no narrow Albanach, but a wide-spirited Gael. But here he is a cool diner-out, wasting his talk on fools, and limiting it to their capacities. By the way, an article in the 'Times' a week or so ago, *apropos* of Clerk's 'Ossian,' was doubtless his. . . .

I often have a hankering after old Dublin, though its air never well suited me; but often I wish to be near you and one or two still surviving friends there. Ah! that common wail of poor humanity, if one could only begin life again! I know where my heart would lie, and whither my flight would tend and my efforts.

I won't bother you with more now. Give my heartiest remembrances to Mrs Ferguson, and ever think of me as your affectionate friend, F. W. BURTON.

MY DEAR FERGUSON,—Your letter gives me the heartiest pleasure—I wish I could convey to you how much. Above all things else it tells me unmistakably how well you feel, and shows that it was not alone the elation caused by unexpected good news of a friend that sent the pulses of health through your true and affectionate heart, but that you were already in your native vigour and capable of enjoying what you heard without mitigation or drawback. I should have known, indeed, without your writing, what delight you would feel at the honour that has been done to your old friend [Burton's appointment as Director of the National Gallery, 1874], and that it would banish, for the time at least, all your own cares from your mind. . . .

I know, too, very well, that Mrs Ferguson is as well pleased as yourself, and thanking you both is out of the question. One might as well thank the sun for shining or the rose for blooming. But one feels none the less of gratitude to both, or to Something that made both, for all that.

It would be affectation to say I do not appreciate what has come to me, or feel great pleasure at it. If I did not, I should not have accepted it. It is the greatest honour by far that could have been conferred on one of my calling and position, and being entirely in harmony with my tastes, and probably not likely to hinder my work altogether, it ought to afford scope for great enjoyment, and, what is rather to be thought of in the first instance, for promoting the great work for which the office was created. This, indeed, shall be my prime endeavour. I only pray that my capacities and opportunities may not fail in the arduous task.

But, like all earthly things that contain good, it has also its bitter ashes contained within it potentially ; sometimes, perhaps, to come disagreeably between the teeth of the taster. My nomination will have made me many enviers, and therefore enemies, and no opportunity will be let pass to smite me in darkness and daylight. Besides, the " public " are ever on the look-out for wonders. Every man who has to cater for the nation, and consumes the money of the taxpayers, is expected to be a thaumaturge, and there are always lots of art penny-a-liners and dilettanti members of both " Houses " to find either that money has been squandered on trash or that nothing is being done for the income. All this I don't like ; but I have made up my mind to bear it, and hope I may have strength and self-reliance to do so with some equanimity. I am alone responsible for anything that may go wrong. So there is no want of perils in the path. . · . .

You and Mrs Ferguson must come see my domain when next you are in London, and give me the joy of leading you over it. Allingham congratulates the "ould country" or one of her children getting the control of what scores of the natives here looked for, and upon, as their right, each one for himself. Well, I am pleased at it too. It is not the least of the pleasures the thing brings with it.

Remind me affectionately to Mrs F., and ever think of me, dear old friend, as yours while life lasts,

FRED. W. BURTON.

On the 7th of January 1878, Burton and Ferguson lost a dearly loved friend by the death of Dr Stokes, a loss keenly felt by both.

But what is to be said of this last sad scene and all that it means? [wrote Burton.] Another old and dear friend carried to the grave. One of the very, very few until now to be counted amongst those with whom so much of our happiness was associated. Such a friend, and such a man too, as none of us may ever hope to see again.

This fidelity of heart was a marked characteristic both of Burton and Ferguson. It shows itself again and again in their letters.

You ought not to have thought it necessary to assure me of your and your wife's regard [wrote Burton]. I believed and believe in it, and it is one of the not numerous precious things left me. I have not yet found that my affection and esteem for my old friends has cooled in any case. On the contrary, it ever seems to grow warmer. Nor does distance of time and place affect it.

The following letter, written a few months later, is

more cheerful in tone, its object being to congratulate Ferguson on his Knighthood :—

I must thank you for your warm-hearted and welcome letter. I am rejoiced to hear of the distinction about to be conferred upon you, both because you yourself are pleased at it, and because it is grateful to me to know that those whose duty and right it is to mark merit are taking the only means in their power to do so, and spontaneously too; for I know you are one of the last men to covet or care for such things in themselves. But you may justly feel that you have earned this public sign of recognition, without seeking for it, and that in its bestowal upon you the country is honoured in your person. I congratulate Mrs Ferguson too. It will add to her happiness for your sake.

I have read the "Widow's Cloak" with delight. It is beautiful in itself, and a fair act of homage gracefully rendered to a Queen and woman who deserves all the praise and love that can be given her. Theodore Martin tells me that she was highly pleased by it. It seems to me that in the vii. stanza you have struck a key-note which ought long since to have been struck by other hands. It is only the want of imagination amongst English statesmen generally, and the contempt of its use and the want of recognition of its power as a popular factor in the art of governing, that have hindered full use being made of a fact which might have been a powerful influence against discontent, and an antidote to specious agitation and hopeless aspirations.

You may be sure I agree in almost all you say about art matters in Italy and here. As to architecture, *we* are at the lowest point. That shapeless pile in Piccadilly is a lasting monument of jobbery and ignorance, and I may add impudence. But what can be expected?

How much I should like to be with you on your Ogham-hunting expedition! Few things would give me greater pleasure or so great. But I know that I must not think of it. I hope the game may prove plentiful and sound. If you can bring out the results which are the objects of your long re-searches, you will have added a large stone to the slowly growing monument of the ancient European world.   Never forget that many are strenuously working at that monument, and we never can tell what discovery, and in what remote corner, may furnish the key-stone of its dome.

My dear Ferguson,—You will certainly have thought me to be "a friend of an ill fashion," never having vouchsafed you one word of thanks in return for two gifts, two tokens of your unfailing affection, so long since sent me.   I might, I ought, to have at least acknowledged the safe receipt of them, and at once.   But I vainly hoped to find a leisure hour to absorb myself in "Deirdré" or the Poems, so as to be able, when writing, to say some few words of appreciation and sympathy. The hoped-for leisure and peace of mind has not yet come.

The arrival of the books found me in trouble, hardly yet at an end; and now that I am on the eve of a journey to Italy on business, I feel how wrong I was not to have sent you a line of thanks at the proper time.   Pray draw upon your inex-haustible store of forbearance, and forgive me.   I recollect, too, that you and Lady Ferguson were expected here, and in fact looked forward for some time to your coming, and to the opportunity of thanking you in person.

The advent of the present Government brought trouble to me as well as to many more.   Movements made in every direction to satisfy or to anticipate any real or pretended popu-lar cry did not leave even the National Gallery out of their scope; and by way of gaining popularity, motions made in the House were only too readily listened to by our new masters, without any inquiry into the merits of the case, without a care or a thought for the safety and preservation of the precious collection itself.   The pain and anxiety caused me by these things, the labour in writing and by other means seeking to avert what I considered a serious danger and most needless and unwise innovation, I cannot describe to you.   For about two months my days and nights were spent in such work.   But I trouble you with the affair only to explain how it was I had neither time nor quiet for reading, or for communion with my friends.

I was greatly disappointed at your not putting in an appearance here this summer. But I daresay you found pleasanter and more health-bringing work to do at home—some site to be explored, some Oghams to be copied, or perhaps some old friends to be visited.

I will not touch upon affairs in Ireland, all the less that I do not know well how you look upon them. To me, and from this side of the water, their aspect is deplorable and hopeless.

A bright gleam shows me yourself still active, and engaged in your life-long work. All else, on every side, is a cloud of gloom, and a distant roar of coming evil, and of the upturning of the foundation of society, without a stone ready to erect a new edifice with, or an architect to devise it. We shall go down with the things that are, and I, for one, do not care to live to see the chaos that will follow. Out of it may come something better. But whether from the effect of gathering years, or from an unsanguine temperament, or from a want of deeper insight, I feel no hope for humanity. . . .

I hope you and Mary (I venture to call her so) are well and fortified for the winter. I have been detained here until the late splendid weather has changed to torrents of rain. But I am pledged to go, and perhaps may find things better in Italy. Anyhow, the change will be agreeable.—With affectionate regards to my other old friend, your wife, yours, my dear Sam, ever sincerely,   FRED. W. BURTON.

Ferguson and his wife spent the autumn of 1880 on the Continent. He took the baths at Wildbad in the Black Forest, and afterwards descended the Danube to Vienna; and having explored the Salzkammergut . and the Dolomites, revisited Trent. They sailed up the Lago di Guarda, breaking the journey at Malcesine to visit its castle, and after wandering through a lovely but rarely visited region, found themselves at

Venice.   There he took his wife to a room in the
Doge's Palace devoted to maps, globes, &c.,—generally
passed over by tourists,—where, by ascending a ladder, ·
it was possible to examine closely the great globe
which records all of the earth's surface known in the .
sixteenth century to Italian, Spanish, and Portuguese
geographers.   On it are indicated the lakes of Central
Africa, the falls of the Zambesi, facts then known
though subsequently forgotten, and rediscovered by
David Livingstone, Sir Richard Burton, Captains
Speke and Grant.

At a distance of some fifteen miles north of Treviso
is a villa built by the great architect Palladio for the
Doge Barbaro, and decorated with frescos by Paul
Veronese.   The subjects are classical, and they are
as fresh and glowing with colour as the day he painted
them.   When in Italy in 1880, Sir Samuel was desirous
to see these paintings of a master he so much admired.
He went to Treviso, and drove from thence to the
Villa Mazar on a lovely autumnal day.   The villa
was open on payment of a few lire.   As we moved
from room to room we became aware that the apartments through which we were guided by our cicerone
were vacated on our approach.   It is not a pleasant
sensation to be conscious that the occupants are disturbed to gratify the artistic curiosity of the tourist.
We made no unnecessary delay, and as we parted on
the steps with our gratified guide, having inscribed
our names in his book, and moved down the avenue
towards our carriage, we became aware that the lady

of the house was following to overtake us. We stopped, and a dignified and beautiful woman, who had thrown a light wrap over her head and carried a bunch of large keys in her hand, joined us, and proposed a visit to the chapel situated in the grounds and built by Palladio. As she escorted us thither, she observed that as we were Britons, and appeared to have been charmed with the Villa Mazar, she would be glad if we would purchase it. She said that her means were no longer adequate to keep up the place; that she and her daughter were the last of the family, and that it would suit them better to live in an apartment in Rome. Her noble bearing and charm of manner, and the pathos of her story, touched us deeply. We explained to her that we were not wealthy English, nor able to purchase such an artistic gem as her villa; nor did we think it would suit the habits of a *milord Anglais*. But we suggested that it was admirably fitted for preservation as a national museum or monument of the glorious days of Venice. Sir Samuel wrote to his friend Sir Frederic Burton on the subject, being aware that he was about to proceed to Italy for the purchase of pictures for the National Gallery, and would be in communication with the Ministers of the King of Italy.

I have a good deal to say if we were together, but what I write about is this. When at Treviso in September last we visited the Villa Mazar, and there saw the lady of the house—Countess Barbaro, I believe—who told us the villa is for sale. What occurred to me at the moment, and what

I wish to put before you, is that—however expert artists may be in detaching fresco paintings or even in transporting entire edifices—any purchase of the villa which would lead to a dispersion of its decorations would be undesirable, indeed calamitous.   If Vicenza and Verona could buy and preserve it as a memorial of the fame of Palladio and Paul Cagliari, it would be an undertaking worthy of these renowned and still noble cities.   If their municipalities would take the matter in hand and appeal to those who have visited North Italy and carried away the charm of beauty and splendour suggested by the works of these great geniuses, I really think the purse-strings of the whole world would be opened to them. I would—poor as I am—be a subscriber, and so I am sure would many English and American people of culture whom I could name.   You would be one of the best qualified men in the community to take this matter up.   The Italian Government would, doubtless, help; and the compliment paid to Lombardy and Venetia would, I am sure, be gratefully remembered by these good and noble people.

I have been travelling in Italy since the close of September, and letters from home have often been long delayed in following and reaching me [wrote Burton from Rome].   Yours of the 22d Nov. came into my hands only yesterday, with several others bringing the most chequered news.   I wish all had been as pleasant to me as yours, which shows me yourself in your seventieth year, still vigorous in mind, fresh in heart, and capable of interest and execution in the cause of all that is noble and beautiful.   I believed I had heard of the villa which captivated you.   But my plans, which were regulated by business, have not allowed of my getting to Treviso on this occasion.   How pleased I am to find any one giving Palladio his due: I lingered in Vicenza some weeks ago enjoying the city which he did so much to make what it is.   What a fine spirit, what a sense of the beautiful he had!   What a feeling for line and rhythm!   I do fear it would be difficult to move the Italians, who probably for the most part know nothing of the existence of that villa, to do aught for its preservation.   And to say the truth, they are so oppressed by taxation that I believe few of them could afford to do anything.   But if I can see Morelli, who is now here, and who is deeply interested in the preservation of national monuments, I will consult him on the subject.   He is a Bergamask, and is "Senatore del Regno," and if any one took up the question it would be he.

Burton's next letter informed Ferguson of the serious illness of Mr Mallet, who passed away in November 1881.   The letters which follow it, written a few years earlier by Ferguson and Mallet, will evince how cordial were their mutual relations :—

Two of the letters which reached me with yours yesterday were from Mrs Robert Mallet and Robert's daughter Constance.   They had of course been directed to my house, as the writers supposed I was at home, and told me of what I fear must be poor Robert's mortal illness.   The nature of it was not mentioned.   But the doctors were of opinion he could last only a few weeks at the utmost.   I am deeply sorry to be away from home and unable to see him.   The letters were dated the 22d and 23d of Nov., and I fear that even by this time all may be over.   It is pretty sure to be so before I return, which will scarcely be within a fortnight hence.   I am abroad on affairs of National Gallery.   Another link with the past severed.   There comes a time when a man would live no more.   I begin to feel it.   .   .   .

I will write to you again on my return.   Meantime give my love to Mary Ferguson, whom I shall not be able to call Lady F.

My dear Robert [wrote Ferguson to Mallet on the 10th January 1877],—Your remembrance of me is truly grateful to my heart.   It is vain to wish for what is denied us ; but if wishes and a good deal more could do it, your letter should not miscarry for want of a well-seen direction.   "Man never is," &c.; and I look forward for my coming hours of blessedness here to the sight of old and good friends' faces, when perhaps the meeting of the British Association, perhaps some earlier occasion, may give me that opportunity.   I would like to see Robinson, Larcom, and yourself together.   God knows, God send! is all that the uncertainties of this existence allow me to add to the expression of the wish.

Now I address myself to Mrs Mallet.   The last day I saw you, dear friend, I was by no means as vigorous as, thank God, I feel myself to-day.   My wife, too,—and again I am full of thankfulness,—is at last able to go about her usual pursuits, after a long lying up from a sprained ankle.   I have put up a little conservatory for her, where I trust she will find occupation and pleasure during many summer days.   We lately saw our friends the Armagh Robinsons.   The old giant is strong enough to make an earthquake if whelmed under a mountain, still; but, unlike his cousin Titans, is full of sweetness and placidity.   Take, both, the hearty salutations of your affectionate friend,   SAML. FERGUSON.

ENMORE, THE GROVE,
CLAPHAM ROAD, S.W., 2d July 1878.

MY DEAR FERGUSON,—My wife and I have received your own and Mrs Ferguson's very kind invitation to become inmates of your house during the approaching meeting of the British Association at Dublin.   It is never pleasant to say "No"; it is least of all when the "No" must be said to old and highly esteemed friends, and with respect to kindness offered which, if possible, we should gladly accept. It would be tedious were I to try and explain all the reasons which oblige us to give this decisive "No"; it is enough that you and your kind wife will, I hope, know that though unable to accept, my wife and I are deeply sensible of your kindness in remembering us.   We shall be with you in remembering thought during the week in which you will entertain your learned guests, amongst whom will no doubt be some whose hands, like that of Doctor Robinson, I should have liked to clasp in mine.   I am glad to find that you have been able to make a long tour abroad this year, from which you have no doubt returned in reinvigorated health. I quite agree in your notion as to river-courses, the cutting back of the beds of cataracts, and so forth. Geology in our day would present a more hopeful outlook if a larger number of its professed cultivators were better acquainted with mechanics, physics, and chemistry. The subject is, however, too big for note-paper.—I remain, my dear old friend, sincerely and gratefully yours,   ROBT. MALLET.

The next two years were, to all true lovers of their country, the darkest and most discouraging in recent Irish history. How Ferguson reprobated the crimes of 1882 may be read in his poems—notably in his " Curse of the Joyces," given in a previous chapter. Sir F. Burton's despondency is expressed in his correspondence during these years of national dishonour :—

Dark days are passing over the land which is our common birthplace, and neither of us is likely to live to see the advent of much brighter ones. How you feel on the great problems which now seem to admit of no happy solution, I do not know. But for me the one blighting thought is that a total demoralisation of the country has come to prevail, and that right and wrong, good and evil, end and means, cease to be distinguished. Ay, that even that last sentiment, that survives among men in the wildest state of society, and in the darkest periods, that of *personal* loyalty and gratitude, seems to have disappeared.

MY DEAR FERGUSON [wrote Burton in March 1883],— I have found time to read your address, in which I was deeply interested. Every word of it comes home to me with an echo of the past, and a joyful sense that so much still remains with us in you. It is a noble record of what some of Ireland's best sons have done for her, and a proof of what such might do if they were only allowed opportunity to do it. It is even hopeful, which I am not. Would that your words of wisdom

and good sense and true patriotism might prevail.   But the
last is just what is most wanted and least to be found.   The
country is at the mercy of blatant beasts, to no one of whom
can a particle of sincerity be ascribed, and who recklessly
foster every bad passion, as if in doing so they could raise
the character of their countrymen and make them fitter for
self-government and enlightened freedom.   As if the true
way to make men worthy of the human name was to debase
them first below the brutes.   But I will not go on with
that theme. . . .

I have a remarkably fine tawny flint spear- or javelin-head,
found in the north of Ireland, and got by my brother, who
sent it to me, from the farmer who unearthed it in making
a drain.   It is quite perfect, and beautifully made.   Franks
knows of only one like it, which is in the British Museum.
I should be glad if it were in the R.I.A. collection, and if you
think it worth acceptance there, I would send it to you. . . .
—My affectionate regards to Lady Ferguson from yours ever
steadfastly,   FRED. W. BURTON.

MY VERY DEAR OLD FRIEND,—I do earnestly hope you
will not have misunderstood my silence since you last showed
your affectionate regard for me more than a month since. . . .

These were the causes, and not even a moment's forgetful-
ness of such a lifelong friend as yourself, that delayed my
writing to you.   You can understand them, and if a shade of
disappointment crosses over your mind, I trust you will accept
my explanation.

And now I hear you are not well.   Sad news it is to
me. . . .   So I will hope your indisposition is only a temporary
one, aggravated by the severity of the season, for I hear it has
not prevented your active mind from working.

Your paper [the Patrician Documents] is a most valuable
one, reasoned out with all the acuteness of a judicial mind and
training.   And the translations in verse of the ' Confessio '
have all the beauty and vigour of your earlier work.   This
essay will add some solid stones to the monument you have
raised to our country and yourself.   That unhappy country !

But I will not trust myself to talk of it here.   Only when I think of the men and women it has brought forth, if but of those whom I myself have had the privilege to know, I stand more and more in wonderment that such a leaven could not save it.

I believe Lady Ferguson—let me call her Mary—is well.

I do not need to tell her that my heart is where it ever was. To me the past is much nearer than the present.   How should it be otherwise?   Daily I realise the thought and words of Goethe.   And now bear me in remembrance, my dearest Sam, for I am more than ever affectionately yours,

F. W. BURTON.

True love of country, no less than the warmth and sincerity of friendship, breathes through these touching letters.   The hopeful temperament of Ferguson,—

"One who never turned his back, but marched breast forward,
            Never doubted clouds would break,
    Never dreamed, though right were worsted, wrong would triumph,"—

sustained him in the doleful days of Ireland's shame. He, as we have seen, not even then despaired of his country.   Burton was less sanguine.

In the matter of personal regard, however, they were alike responsive to the ties of friendship :—

If only friends could remain with us!   It is neither work nor time that makes us old, but the sense that we are being left in loneliness, and that those better than ourselves are gone before us. . . . Give my constant affectionate regards to your dear wife, and remember that you share and will ever share them while life is in your old friend,   FRED. W. BURTON.

The heart would indeed sink, when Death deprives us of those we love, were it not for the hope that what has made life so precious, and earth so sweet, will be part of the blessedness of heaven,—

> "And with the morn those angel-faces smile
> Which we have loved long since, and lost awhile."

I have been solacing myself, when it was impossible to do anything else [wrote Sir F. Burton to a friend, after Ferguson's death], by reading John Campbell's 'Tales of the West Highlands,' a long-needed and desired second edition of which is now appearing under the care of the Islay Association,—just a facsimile of what the dear, genial, large-hearted fellow himself produced. I associate him in my mind with Sam. Ferguson. Both had much in common, and much the same aims, the same love of country and kin, the same amiability of nature and honesty of purpose. Both were men whom those who knew them can never forget.

Campbell of Islay and Ferguson were personal friends, and they certainly had tastes in common. They alike delighted in Gaelic literature, and felt the charm of intercourse with peasants of the Celtic race. It is interesting to compare Mr J. F. Campbell's opinion of the Highlanders of Scotland and the Isles with Ferguson's of the Gael of Ireland. The latter will appear in the following chapter, which tells of his sojourn on the islands of Aran off Galway Bay. The views of Campbell of Islay are thus expressed in his Introduction to 'Popular Tales of the West Highlands':—

I have wandered amongst the peasantry of many countries, and this trip but confirmed my old impression. There are few peasants that I think so highly of, none that I like so well. Scotch Highlanders have faults in plenty, but they have the bearing of Nature's own gentlemen—the delicate natural tact which discovers, and the good taste which avoids, all that would hurt or offend a guest.   The poorest is ever the readiest to share the best he has with the stranger.   A kind word kindly meant is never thrown away, and whatever may be the faults of this people, I have never found a boor or a churl in a Highland bothy.

Sir F. W. Burton expressed his appreciation of the photograph sent to him by Lady Ferguson, the latest which had been taken of one so dear to both, in the following letter :—

43 ARGYLL ROAD, *Sept.* 16, 1886.

MY DEAR FRIEND,—Let me thank you for the precious memorials you have sent me—one of them beyond expression precious, I mean the photograph.   Previously I had contented myself with the one made at Milan some years ago, which is not indeed perfect, but in which I could in imagination fill up the deficiencies and correct the errors.   But now you have endowed me with a portrait of my beloved friend which, so far as portraiture can go, leaves nothing to be wished for.   To me, at all events, it brings home the man in all those qualities and capabilities which his countenance suggested, in a degree beyond what is usual.   For from that countenance was re-flected, beyond all intellectual power and all sweetness of disposition, that absolute candour of soul which is rare and beautiful over everything else.   I cannot thank you enough for this portrait.

I did not write to you before, and I had no fear of your mistaking my silence.   You knew what I felt about *him* and for you, and I could not intrude upon the freshness of sorrow by vain offers of sympathy, still less of consolation.   Time and your own pure conscience must be trusted to mellow the keen sense of separation and loneness.   This will come.   But you have, even in the meantime, a still higher source of comfort.—Ever your affectionate friend,   F. W. BURTON.

CHAPTER XIV.

1852–1857.

VISITS TO CLONMACNOIS, CLARE, AND ARAN.

"O what a glory doth this world put on
For him who, with a fervent heart, goes forth
Under the bright and glorious sky, and looks
On duties well performed, and days well spent !
For him the wind, ay, and the yellow leaves,
Shall have a voice, and give him eloquent teachings.
He shall so hear the solemn hymn, that Death
Has lifted up for all, that he shall go
To his long resting-place without a tear."
—LONGFELLOW.

FERGUSON was eminently reasonable, kind, and considerate, singularly easy to get on with, but he had one peculiarity which in their early married life was somewhat embarrassing to his wife. It was difficult to induce him to make up his mind as to where he would pass the "Long Vacation." She was aware that at the close of Circuit all legal business would be at an end until October, and was prepared to spend their holiday in whatever manner he should find most agreeable. She only asked to know his wishes, so as to be able to carry them into effect. But he put off from day to day the task of making up his mind. If others were concerned, this procrastination was inconvenient. In the summer of 1852 they were alone, and she thought it a favourable opportunity to find out to what lengths his indecision would extend. Accordingly, having questioned him in vain as to his plans and wishes, she ceased to inquire. All needful arrangements were made, and the servants instructed that directions where to forward letters would be sent to them. Their luggage was packed, and after an early breakfast a cab was sent for. They took their seats, and when the driver asked where he was to go to, she preserved an amused silence, and Ferguson, forced to decide, looked at his watch. "We could just catch the Midland train," he laughingly observed. "What say you, shall we start for Athlone?" About noon they found themselves on the bridge which crosses the Shannon, the train having proceeded on its way. They leaned over the parapet, and saw a boat beneath. "Let us drop down the river and visit Clonmacnois," proposed Ferguson. So the boatman was beckoned, and the luggage transferred to the boat. Some nine miles or so below Athlone the ancient ruins were approached. He landed to see if accommodation could be obtained, and found an available room in a farmer's house, in which they established themselves. Some days were passed in great enjoyment, but when they desired to continue their journey they had no vehicle at command but a cart. On it their luggage was placed, and walking by it, and occasionally mount-

ing and sitting on their luggage, they made their way
to Shannon Harbour.

Youth, health, happiness, good spirits, and good
weather made the journey a joyous one. The sedgy
banks of the river, the verdure of the grass, the carol
of the larks, the delight of an adventure, and even the
terrible joltings of the cart when fatigue impelled
them to climb into it, were all elements in their
mirthful enjoyment of that journey.

" Clonmacnois, Clare, and Aran," two papers
which appeared from Ferguson's pen in January and
April 1853, in the ' University,' describe this visit to
the Shannon :—

I had been under the impression that the banks of the
Shannon, immediately below Athlone, offered nothing to the
view but a dreary expanse of bog, and was prepared to see a
succession of level, black peat-banks at either side, as I descended the river to Clonmacnois. It is true, these banks of
the Shannon are low; and stakes, erected at different points,
show that in flood-time the channel has to be marked out
from lateral inundations. With the exception, also, of the
flight of wild birds, the occasional passage of a turf- or hay-
boat, or the appearance here and there of a solitary angler,
there is little to vary the monotony of the scene; but on the
clear and serene September day on which I descended the
Shannon from Athlone to Clonmacnois, it was a monotony of
verdure and beauty that surrounded me. The banks are continuous meadow, and as our little bark was wafted along, the
breeze came deliciously scented from the harvest of the after-
grass. The skies were of a pearly lustre; the river was just
heard to murmur among the beds of sedge and bulrushes that
occasionally fringe its banks. Where the greensward, at any
point, rose a few feet above the level of the water, the banks,
through a distance of several miles, were seen to consist of a

white stratum of marl, supporting the vegetable soil; but in general the emerald carpet of the meadows extends to the water's edge. Without timber, without any diversification of surface, without edifices, even in ruin, the scene was fresh, sparkling, and delightful. Shall I ascribe all those agreeable impressions to the sky, and air, and the smooth motion with which I was carried along between continuous green meadows and whispering reeds? The gentle reader will probably guess that other influences contributed to the charm, and that such pleasures as the scene could afford were enhanced by being shared with a sympathising companion. . . .

At first sight [on coming into view of the towers and gables at Clonmacnois] the long line of buildings appears as if rising from the water; but on a nearer approach, the ruins are seen to stand on a green acclivity rising from the river, and sloping backward to another series of romantic *eskers*, which overlook the left bank of the river, through a distance of about two miles. On the opposite side, beyond the margin of meadow, lies the vast flat of red bog so conspicuous in all Petrie's drawings of the locality. But to imagine that Clonmacnois stands immediately in the midst of bogs would be a very erroneous conclusion to draw from Petrie's paintings. On the contrary, it stands in the midst of meadows, and pastoral hills, and warm village-lands, set, it is true, in an encircling ring of bogs, which surround the fertile tracts on every side; and, in truth, nothing can be more impressive than the sight of these vast deserts from the summit of any of the green heights around the ruins. . . .

The level, russet floor of the interior possesses the grandeur of the sea, and wears an air of repose that is almost sublime. Between the level, brown surface of the bog, and the undulating, verdant *eskers*, the contrast is one of the most striking that can be imagined. . . . The excellence of the soil is seen not only in the verdure of its grasses, but in the golden hue of its cornfields. Nowhere have I seen straw of so deep and florid a yellow. This combination of objects so diversified in form and colour, with the wide, blue Shannon, its course defined by those immense tracts of meadows, backed by the still more immense tracts of bog winding through the midst, would alone fill the eye of a lover of natural beauty with abundant enjoyment; but seeing in the midst of so singular a scene the remains of a place so venerable and celebrated as Clonmacnois, adds vastly to the charm, and really renders this one of the most interesting spots that can be imagined.

The objects constituting the group of ruins are of an antiquity of from six hundred to upwards of a thousand years. In crossing the stile that leads into the churchyard, you step on a tombstone of the tenth century. When Dr Petrie first visited this vast depository of historic evidences, one of the earliest inscriptions he deciphered was that of Suibhne Mac Maelhumai, one of the three "most learned doctors of the Irish" who visited Alfred in the year 891, and aided in laying the foundations of learning at Oxford. . . .

The most conspicuous objects among the ruins are the two Round Towers; and the greater of these, or O'Rourk's tower, may be said to be the most remarkable building of its kind, both as being the largest and the only one the date of which is known with absolute accuracy; for, as recorded in the Annals, it was finished by the Abbot O'Malone, for King Turlogh O'Connor, in A.D. 1127. The other, the tower of Temple Fineen, is evidently and unquestionably of contemporaneous date with the church to which it is annexed. . . .

Next to the Round Towers, the great sculptured stone crosses at the west end of the cathedral take the eye with peculiar attraction. . . .

We have here [in the Cros-na-Screaptna], therefore, a specimen of the art of sculpture as it flourished among our Irish forefathers nearly a thousand years ago. . . . The rudeness of these sculptures is barbaric, not barbarous. There is considerable grandeur in the proportions of the stone, great delicacy in its knops and interlaced pattern-work, and a sumptuous although rude beauty in its general effect. It is eminently interesting, also, as exhibiting the costumes of its period. Here we have the Roman soldiers asleep at the sepulchre arrayed in conical helmets, such as the Bayeux tapestry exhibits on the Normans of two centuries later. Here we have kings, warriors, and various orders of ecclesiastics in their proper costumes.   On the base appear horses, and chariots with very high wheels, and hunters following the deer with hound and horn.   The other cross is of even greater elegance of form, but its decorations are confined to ornamented bosses and pattern-work.   These circular-armed stone crosses are peculiar to Scotic and [North] British districts. . . .

On the south of the churches, at a little distance, stands Lis-na-abbaid, or the Abbot's fort—an earthen *dun*, surrounded with a deep ditch and lofty external rampart, and crowned by the ruins of a fine old feudal castle.   It has been destroyed by gunpowder, and its massive fragments lie and lean against one another in picturesque disruption.   The green hills, the fragrant meadows, this verdant mound with its toppling masses of masonry, the towers and ruins of the roofless churches, with their one ash-tree and wilderness of gravestones, all form a scene not to be forgotten, and, as often as recalled, associated with recollections of pleasing intercourse at the homely but genial hearth of my entertainer.

From Shannon Harbour Ferguson and his wife made their way southwards — sailed down Lough Derg, sojourned at Killaloe, and visited the site of Kincora, the abode of Brian Boru.   Again embarked on the Shannon, they dashed down its rapids, reached Limerick, steamed down the estuary to Kilrush, passing the historic castle of Bunratty, and ultimately settled for the rest of the season on the rock-bound Atlantic shore at Kilkee.

During that stay at Kilkee Ferguson visited the Isles of Aran, off the coast of Clare.   They form a breakwater for Galway Bay, and are holy ground. The Christian remains of Aran of the Saints date from the sixth and seventh centuries, and the pagan forts are prehistoric.   Ferguson has described these remains in the papers already alluded to which appeared in the ' University,' and from these further extracts will be given :—

The patches of vegetable soil which occur here and there over this rugged tract are carefully enclosed, and generally planted with potatoes. The soil is light and sandy, but owing to the absorption of heat by the rock, peculiarly warm and kindly; and the islanders here have had the singular good fortune never to have been visited by the potato-blight, never to have had a death from destitution, and never to have sent a pauper to the poorhouse. They are a handsome, courteous, and amiable people. Whatever may be said of the advantages of a mixture of races, I cannot discern anything save what makes in favour of these people of the pure ancient stock, when I compare them with the mixed populations of districts on the mainland. The most refined gentleman might live among them in familiar intercourse and never be offended by a gross or sordid sentiment. This delicacy of feeling is reflected in their figures, the hands and feet being small in proportion to the stature, and the gesture erect and graceful.

His description of the church of St Cavan on Inishere tells of the purity of the spot, and recalled to his memory the ode of Horace, which he afterwards translated, " Archytas and the Mariner " :—

> But, shipmate, thou refuse not to my dead
> Bones and unburied head
> The cheap poor tribute of the funeral clay !
>
> .   .   .   .   .   .
>
> Give—'twill not keep thee long—
> Three handfuls of sea-sand, and go thy way.

The aspect of these graceful ruins, with their airy chancel-arch and ivied gables, surrounded by a surface so pure and untrodden, is singularly impressive. On the seaside all the hillock is covered with tombs and headstones. A rugged pillar-stone, higher than the rest, marks the site of *Leaba coemhain*, or St Cavan's bed—a grave held in great veneration, which the blowing sands have risen around till it now forms a pit of about five feet in depth. An engraved cross, of very ancient design, decorates the flagstone at the bottom, but there is no inscription. The clear fine sand alternating with patches of verdure, and backed by the blue incorruptible ocean, gives an air of purity to the scene very congenial to the idea of a last resting-place for people of a simple and virtuous life. "Our island is clean—there are no worms here," were the repeated expressions of my companion ; and when, on passing a little farther on, we came to where the wind had stripped the sand from a skeleton, I could see that the cleansing, calcareous envelope had brought the bones to the whiteness of chalk. I thought of Archytas, *prope litus Matinum*, and bestowed the rites of ancient piety—*ossibus et capiti inhumato*. Old as this interesting ruin is—I judge it to be of the twelfth century—it is the most modern of all the ecclesiastical remains on the Isles of Aran. It is, at the same time, the most picturesque, and perhaps the best calculated to awaken while it tranquillises the soul.

On Inismaen, the middle island, Ferguson dwells chiefly on the great pagan fortress of Dun-Conor, and on reaching Aran Mor, the largest and most northerly of the group, on its great Gentile fortresses of Dun-Ængus, Dun-Eochaill, and Dubh-Cahir. He then describes the early Christian remains in the vicinity of the village of Kilronan :—

Next to the pagan fortresses and *clochans*, their ruined churches and sepulchral monuments constitute the main attraction of the islands for the ecclesiastical and architectural antiquary. And for any one imbued with these tastes, the way westward from Kilronan is indeed, on both sides, full of objects of curiosity. On the right, in the low tract between the road and sea, are the remains of *Manister Connachtach*, with the chapel of St Kieran. It was here the founder of Clonmacnois disciplined himself for his subsequent mission on the mainland. . . . On the left hand, at a little distance up the craggy ascent of the hill, which is crowned by the pagan fortress of Dun-Eochaill and the lighthouse, stands another of the little churches mentioned by Colgan, *Teampul Ceathair Aluinn*, the church of the Four Beautiful Saints. These Colgan states to be Fursey, Brandon of Birr, Conall, and Barchann. Fursey was the founder of the Abbey of Lagny on the Marne; and no one, certainly, walking through the beautiful aisles and cloisters of that once sumptuous establishment, could suppose that so much ecclesiastical grandeur took its rise from these little Irish *cellulæ*, scarce better at their best than well-constructed hovels. Still more surprise would the visitor of the splendid French foundation experience, were he told that Fursey's attachment to his Irish hermitage had brought him back to spend the evening of his life on those rugged crags, and to seek a grave under the rude pillar-stone which at a little distance still marks the sepulchre of the Four Beautiful Saints.

The sentiment which influenced St Fursey has not lost its strength even in our own day. St Columba expressed it in the sixth century when he wrote of Aran: "My heart is in the west with thee. To be laid in thy pure soil is, as it were, to lie in the land of St Peter and St Paul." These remote islets were sacred as Rome itself! How numerous were the holy men who lived and died there is evidenced by what Ferguson narrates of the Church of St Enda:—

Enda's original church has disappeared, and the blowing sands have quite obliterated the cemetery, famous for its hundred and twenty inscribed tombs of saints, adjoining it. The foundation of his Round Tower, however, is still visible;

and on the brow of the green eminence above, conspicuous against the sky, still stands the cell of Benignus, the most elegant and best-built as it is the very smallest cell in all Ireland. Twelve feet by eight internally, it is more like a sepulchral vault than a house of worship. Its stone roof has now nearly disappeared; but the great blocks composing its well-jointed walls and graceful Egyptian doorway defy the storms of thirteen centuries. It was evening when I visited the spot. I had come from Dubh-Cahir and the Atlantic side of the island over the intermediate tract of stone. These immense sheets of rock, ringing to the tread with a metallic sonorousness, cover all the surface with vast ridges and furrows, like the tillage of some extinct race of giants. The hollow reverberations of the Atlantic, the lonely crumbling pagan fortress, and the utter solitude of the dark marble-ribbed desert over which I passed, had combined to sadden and depress my mind; so that, when at length we came forth on the verdant carpet that fringes the eastern brow of the desert, and stood beside this graceful little temple overlooking the green slope on which the herds of the village were as-sembled, lowing in the parting sunshine, the spectacle was attended with a sense of pleasure most grateful to experience. The sun had set before I left the spot, having traced in the indistinct light on a square monumental stone under the little eastern window, inscribed in large, deep-cut Greco-Irish characters, the single word *cari*. The tomb "of the dear one" could not have been erected in a spot better calculated for serious and tender contemplation.

Deeply interested as was the writer of these de-scriptions in the scenery and the ruins, he was yet more attracted by the inhabitants of these islands, "so fine-natured, genial, and intelligent." He had also seen much to increase his respect "for the historical traditions of a people whose annals are corroborated out of every corner of their island."

The same obliging disposition that characterises the people

of the less frequented islands, shows itself in equally amiable ways among the inhabitants of Aran Mor.   In the neighbourhood of the Seven Churches they preserve a grateful recollection of the interest taken in the preservation of their antiquities by Dr [Sir W.] Wilde during a visit to these islands several years ago.   At his instance the fragments of a richly-sculptured stone cross, which had long lain scattered in different directions about the ruins, were brought together, adapted to one another, and laid in their places on a smooth, flat rock, forming part of the threshing-floor of Martin O'Flaherty, the guardian of the ruins.   The fragments have been surrounded with a low wall of dry stone to keep off the trespass of cattle, and are an object of much respect and the source of very grateful feeling towards their restorer.   I also succeeded in collecting from various quarters of the ruins and surrounding stone-wall fences the fragments of another cross of greater dimensions, but ruder workmanship, which is now laid side by side with that restored by Dr Wilde.   On one side is a sculpture of the crucifixion, of extremely barbarous design ; the other is carved with knots and patterns of interlaced work of the usual kind.

This, which was the first, was not the last visit paid by Ferguson to Aran of the Saints.   In 1857 the British Association met in Dublin, and he, as one of its local secretaries, accompanied the Ethnological Section on an excursion to these remote islands. Stokes, Petrie, Burton, Curry, were of the party, and remained behind with Ferguson, who secured a roomy cottage, and wrote to his wife to join him with their nephews, a servant, and a well-stocked hamper.   Dr Stokes wrote for his wife, son, and daughter.   The combined party chartered a hooker with its crew, and retained as guide the local antiquary.   The friends, so congenial in their tastes, passed a few weeks of entire enjoyment. They sailed from island to island, taking with them on board the hooker all the local singers of whom they could hear. The music they sang was noted by Petrie and rendered on his violin— the Irish words recorded by Curry and translated by Whitley Stokes. Burton painted the peasants and their children, and he, and Ferguson, and Margaret Stokes sketched the ruins and other antiquarian objects; while Whitley Stokes worked at the ancient inscriptions. The weather was propitious, and the friends thoroughly enjoyed the out-of-door life, the pure air, and refreshing sea-breezes.

An incident of their sojourn which might have had serious results may be recalled to memory. They had landed on Inismaen, leaving one man only in charge of the hooker, and, taking the rest of the crew on shore to carry their dinner to the pagan fort on the summit of the island, proceeded to explore Inismaen. When the meal was over and the hampers repacked, they descended, towards evening, to the place where they had left the hooker; but no boat was visible on the wide horizon. At last, at a great distance, off the coast of Connemara, the vessel was descried slowly making for Inismaen. It was apparent that many hours must elapse before the boat could arrive, and as the sun had set, and no shelter was possible, dancing for the sake of warmth was resorted to by the shivering party. At last the hooker, manœuvred by its one man, arrived. He, when left in charge, had lighted his pipe, and under its soothing influence had fallen asleep. The boat drifted with the tide, and was almost on the rocks off the mainland, when the sleeper was aroused by shouts from another vessel. With great difficulty he navigated his way back. It was almost midnight when the party were under way for Aran Mor. The ocean was luminous; the track of the curragh — a light canvas boat in which to land—was a veritable line of light. Every movement of its oars seemed to cleave through molten fire, and to reveal marvels of nature before undreamt of. The lustrous waves beneath, the silent stars overhead, the dim outline of the rocky shore, and its utter solitude, impressed and solemnised our spirits. It was an adventure not to be forgotten.

As the autumnal days became shorter, the musical *séances* were held on *terra firma* and in the evening. Dr Stokes has described the scene by the islanders' firesides :—

In the autumn of 1857 it was the writer's privilege to spend a fortnight in the islands of Aran along with Petrie and several of his friends, when he often accompanied him in his search after the old Irish music, of which not less than twenty-eight airs were collected. It will be well to describe the method by which the airs were obtained. Inquiries having been made as to the names of persons "who had music"—that is, who were known as possessing and singing some of the old airs—an appointment was made with one or two of them to meet the members of the party at some cottage near to the little village of Kilronan, which was their headquarters.

To this cottage, when evening fell, Petrie with his manuscript music-book and violin, and always accompanied by his friend O'Curry, used to proceed. Nothing could exceed the strange picturesqueness of the scenes which night after night were thus presented.   On approaching the house, always lighted up by a blazing turf-fire, it was seen surrounded by the islanders, while its interior was crowded with figures, the rich colours of whose dresses, heightened by the firelight, showed with a strange vividness and variety, while their fine countenances were all animated with curiosity and pleasure.   It would have required a Rembrandt to paint the scene.   The minstrel— sometimes an old woman, sometimes a beautiful girl or a young man—was seated on a low stool in the chimney-corner, while chairs for Petrie and O'Curry were placed opposite ; the rest of the crowded audience remained standing.   The song having been given, O'Curry wrote the Irish words, when Petrie's work began.   The singer recommenced, stopping at a signal from him at every two or three bars of the melody to permit the writing of the notes, and often repeating the passage until it was correctly taken down, and then going on with the melody, exactly from the point where the singing was interrupted. The entire air being at last obtained, the singer—a second time—was called to give the song continuously, and when all corrections had been made, the violin—an instrument of great sweetness and power—was produced, and the air played as Petrie alone could play it, and often repeated.   Never was the inherent love of music among the Irish people more shown than on this occasion : they listened with deep attention, while their heartfelt pleasure was expressed, less by exclamations than by gestures ; and when the music ceased, a general and murmured conversation in their own language took place, which would continue until the next song was commenced.

In a letter written by Dr Petrie to Edwin Earl of Dunraven he dwells on this pleasant time in Aran, and on the "noble-looking and noble-hearted race, full of lively intelligence and kindly feelings," among whom we sojourned :—

DUBLIN, 7 CHARLEMONT PLACE,
22d September 1857.

MY DEAR LORD,— . . . I returned only yesterday morning, after travelling by the night train from Galway—from

Aran na naoimh, or Aran of the Saints, where I had been sojourning for the previous seventeen days.   How happily these days were spent you will easily imagine when I tell you that I had for my constant companions my beloved friends Dr Stokes and his son; Frederic Burton, the painter; Samuel Ferguson, the poet and antiquary; and lastly, Eugene Curry, the Irish Shannachee!   Could I have wished for more, it would have been that you had been added to the party.   The weather was glorious; and we scarcely left a church, or grave, or cloghan, a saint, or a dun of a Firbolg, in the three islands, unvisited or unexamined. . . . The islanders I found to be less changed for the worse than I had expected.   They are still a noble - looking and noble - hearted race, full of lively intelligence and kindly feelings.   And I indulge the hope that these characteristics will remain amongst them after all their ancient monuments have perished.—Believe me ever, my dear Lord, most affectionately yours,   GEORGE PETRIE.

As the time approached when we had all to return to our several homes, we parted with regret from the good and friendly people among whom we had so-journed during many happy weeks. We also could exclaim, as Saint Columba did more than a thousand years before, " Oh Aran, beloved land, my heart is in the west with thee ! "

Our Aran guide, Paddy Mullan, at a subsequent period finding himself out of health, felt that he would do well to consult Dr Stokes. He got in a friend's boat to the mainland, and walked thence to Dublin, and presented himself at Ferguson's house. Here he was invited to take up his abode while under Dr Stokes's treatment. He got on well in the kitchen, from whence sounds of hilarity frequently were heard, both song and laughter. On his restoration to health, a purse was made up for him to pay his travelling expenses, and a weighty bundle of garments contributed by those who had been under his guidance on Aran. We found subsequently that he had saved the money, and had walked all the way to Galway, and on reaching Kilronan—his native village—had described our hospitality in such glowing colours — "lashin's and lavings" were among the terms employed — that another islander appeared on the scene, who had walked to Dublin to seek employment. He was a handsome youth, tall, clear-eyed, with the air of purity and honesty so characteristic of these people. A situation was obtained for him, but he pined for home. The city life bewildered him. He walked back to Galway, thence to take boat for Aran, and was no more heard of in North Great George's Street.

CHAPTER XV.

1850–1886.

FRIENDSHIPS—WILLIAM ALLINGHAM.

> " I have read in the marvellous heart of man,
>   That strange and mystic scroll,
> That an army of phantoms vast and wan
>   Beleaguer the human soul.
> .   .   .   .
> And, when the solemn and deep church-bell
>   Entreats the soul to pray,
> The midnight phantoms feel the spell,
>   The shadows sweep away.
> Down the broad Vale of Tears afar
>   The spectral camp is fled ;
> Faith shineth as a morning star,
>   Our ghastly fears are dead."
>   —LONGFELLOW.

WILLIAM ALLINGHAM, a poet from early youth, was born in that picturesque region of Ireland where Donegal, Fermanagh, and Sligo meet near the estuary of the Erne, which empties itself into the Atlantic, falling smoothly over a ledge of rock just below the little town of Ballyshannon. Mr Allingham held here an official post in the Customs. Its duties were not onerous, and he had leisure to devote to books, and to the exploration of Nature in her varied aspects—for ocean, mountain, and river were within his reach in his daily and generally solitary rambles.

Wordsworth has told us that the universal mother never betrays the heart that loves her. Whatever be the future in store for the child whose mind she has impressed with quietness and beauty, he will preserve throughout life the cheerful faith " that all which we behold is full of blessing." So it was with Allingham. The loveliness of his earlier poems, the philosophy of the later, are coloured by his communion with Nature in youth and early manhood. His Irish idyl, " The Music-Master," his pictures of peasant life in " Laurence Bloomfield," his " Mary Donnelly," show the depth of his sympathy with his humble fellow-countrymen. And the scenery of the district is truly presented to the reader in his " Winding Banks of Erne " and " Abbey Assaroe," and many other lyrics.

When Mr Allingham visited Dublin he was much with Ferguson and his wife, and was a welcome guest. They were ever ready to lend him books, and encouraged him in his literary tastes. These, as well as his observant eye for natural beauty, are evidenced in his letters, which were generally addressed to Ferguson's wife, who had more leisure for correspondence than her husband, whose time was engrossed by law and literature.

BALLYSHANNON, *8th May* '51.

MY DEAR MRS FERGUSON,—I am very much pleased indeed by your kind remembrance of me, evidenced by the two volumes that have reached me to-day, for which I thank you heartily. . . . By the way, I have not yet entered on possession of the promised MacCarthy loan.   I mention this, thinking it just possible that you may have sent the book to Morrow's, and that they may have mislaid it.

Yes, I still ramble *solus*, when weather permits—it is now damp and raw—through open field, scanty woodland, or wide warren by the sea.   This last is a fine place, with dells where all the world is shut out but the slopes around you; with lawns of yellow moss and paths of it winding among mounds full of rabbit-holes — cities, villages, and detached villas of rabbits, where the inhabitants, after a moment's stare at the stranger, vanish like optical delusions; primrose tufts and sprinklings of wild violet here and there scattered round these petty porches, and heaps of little pearly-coloured shells; and then, above all, from some cone of sand, a view of the great level sea, stretching away from this to America.   Let me not, however, in my rural raptures, pretend that I never sigh for city life.   The guests at Lord Mayor's balls and the like are not specially the objects of my envy; but I love sociability—real conversation, friendly relations with estimable people—softened and brightened with music and other fine arts; and I desiderate other advantages which are yet more peculiarly attainable in a large town.

You ask about my writing.   I have been little better than idle during the past winter, partly by reason of external circumstances.   People won't buy my last year's volume, and I must feel the result "as per account furnished"; while in other respects I am still less satisfied with my essay, and "were't to do again——"! but I was, as the Scotch say, *left to myself* in the matter, and did as at the time seemed best.   However, I should like to say to somebody—let me say it to you, for instance, to encourage myself—that there are some short pieces in the volume which I honestly expect to live; and if I thought otherwise, I would never write another line; and not one per cent of even good poetry *lives* in the sense I mean.

In the list received by our bookseller to-day I was sorry to see Leigh Hunt's Journal marked "dead."   It was not so good as I expected, yet it was, to my taste, the best of the weeklies.   But Dickens's name and practicality hit the general middle-class readers, Eliza-Cookery takes those who are a step lower down, while the mob delight in Mr G. M., W. Reynolds, and other thrilling writers.   What ruined Hunt, however, was, as I suspect, the tinge of heterodoxy, which he let appear more distinctly than usual in this his last publication.   It seems but the other day when I wrote to congratulate him on his new undertaking, and now I am about to write in condolence on its premature end.   I would willingly have done much for it with my own pen (I don't mean to insinuate that that would have saved its life!), but I hate writing for periodicals, and had little or nothing ready written.

I have not contributed to 'Household Words' for many months; but lately, from a feeling of sympathy with Mr Dickens which I had no other means of expressing, I sent a short poem called "Spring."   I offended Mr Wills, the editor, on a time, by objecting to his improving my poetry in its passage through his hands—requesting him to "take it or leave it," as it was.   He is, as regards song, a very, very—peacock, and may likely reject me altogether.   As, at all events, you do not see 'Household Words' regularly (I think you told me so), I may copy the aforementioned verses :—

SPRING.

"Ye lead the timid verdure
    Along the hills of Spring—
Blue skies and gentle breezes
    And soft clouds wandering;
The finches in the budding boughs,
    The larks in ether sing;
And Hope repeats her youthful vows
    In every living thing.

The gay, translucent morning
    Lies glittering on the sea;
The noonday sprinkles shadows
    Athwart the daisied lea ;
The broad Sun's sinking scarlet rim
    In vapours hideth he;
The darkling hours are cool and dim
    As vernal night should be.

> This world is not grown aged
>   With all her countless years;
> She works, and never wearies,
>   Is glad, and nothing fears;
> The ancient glow of earth, sky, wave,
>   In season reappears;
> And will, when slumber in the grave
>   Our human smiles and tears.
>
> O rich in songs and colours,
>   Thou joy-reviving Spring !
> Some hopes are numb'd with winter
>   Whose May thou canst not bring;
> Some voices answer not thy call
>   When field and woodland ring;
> Some faces come not back at all
>   With primrose-blossoming !
>
> The distant-flying swallow,
>   The upward-yearning seed,
> Find nature's promise faithful—
>   Attain their humble meed;
> Almighty Father ! Thou hast formed
>   These hearts which throb and bleed;
> With Love, Truth, Hope, their life-spring warmed,
>   And *what is best* decreed."

I mean to add one for a short time to the crowd in London, and hope to pay a visit *en passant* to Dublin, and to find my friends well and happy. — Believe me, dear Mrs Ferguson, sincerely yours,   W. ALLINGHAM.

Whatever may have been the cause of my rather long silence, it was anything, I assure you, rather than my not being delighted to hear from you—for I always am.

In the meantime the year has turned the point of ebb, and is flowing in again (under a new name). To-day is fine, and I am hoping for a pleasant, though muddy, walk. Our river is greatly swollen with rains, and in some houses on its bank has changed the ground-floors into water-floors, to the amusement of the children probably, and to the dismay of every one else. It has also made changes in its sea-channel, ex-

citing the townsfolk to Public Meetings with the hope of
having their bad harbour made into a good one. Ballyshannon, you must know, is a place of great "natural capabilities" (the phrase is stereotyped here), and exists, as it
were, on a reputation of the *possible ;* but in the meantime
it is very poor. My chief, or at least longest, literary productions lately have been Letters to the Board of Works and
others, as Secretary of the Ballyshannon Harbour Improvement Committee—all in prose.

A friend of mine in London, one of the originators of the
Metropolitan Rifle Club, writes to me the other day pressing
me to organise a similar defensive association in my neighbourhood, which for several excellent reasons I was obliged to
decline attempting, — though were I residing in England I
would join at once, and would obstruct an invading Louis
Napoleon to the death. Tennyson is enthusiastic about the
Rifles, I hear. He and Mrs Tennyson returned about November from the Continent to their house near Twickenham,
rather contrary to their intention in leaving home. But I
believe they will not continue to reside near London.

Thackeray's three-volume novel, long ago announced, is not
yet finished. By the way, Mr Ferguson abuses Thackeray
and Thackeray praises Mr Ferguson (tell him) ; and Thackeray
is the most admirable and lovable "man of the world" I
have ever seen, or can imagine almost.

I observed that Mr Ferguson was at Monaghan at the
absurd Special Commission, and noticed his name elsewhere
too. I fear he is going to turn a lawyer (I don't mean to say
he is not one). With my best regards to him, &c., &c.

P.S.—Can Mr F. oblige me with the loan of Hallam's
' History of the Middle Ages '?

MY DEAR MRS FERGUSON,—I do not know any one else
so provoking as you ! though I must admit it to be unintentional. I allude to your invitation—for, ah me ! I cannot go.
Of course I should know *the* young lady out of a thousand,
by poetic instinct ; and indeed, in all seriousness, it is a very

high pleasure to hear of one's poor little verses being kindly received, now and again, on their wanderings.

I hope to be in Dublin for a day about the 20th *en passant*, and to have then the always expected gratification of seeing you and Mr Ferguson again.

Again, at the close of 1859, Mr Allingham wrote :—

Many thanks for the kind remembrances and good wishes conveyed in your note ; you and Mr Ferguson have mine, with true goodwill, in return. Yes, the little volume, 'Nightingale Valley,' was from me. You will easily conceive that I was ashamed to let the title-page of it show a name which appears so often in the table of contents! Be that as it may, I am sure I made the selection as honestly as I was able (holding manfully by my self-esteem among other honesties), and that if I had listened to the opinions—all various, and all more or less valuable—of a score or two of friends, the little book would never have taken shape at all. . . .

After ten days in London, I went over to Rotterdam, saw with great delight something of the Hague, Amsterdam, Utrecht, Hanover, Brunswick, and was at Berlin (a flat, big, ugly town of mud-coloured stucco) 4 or 5 days, visiting Potsdam and Sans Souci into the bargain. At Berlin I fell in with a young Dr Rodenberg, *littérateur*, who was for some weeks in Ireland last year, and on the strength of that was writing "The Myrtle of Killarney, a Tale," for the 'Kolnische Zeitung' (a newspaper of large circulation), and preparing for press two sizable volumes, to be called 'The Holy Island,' and to include a view of Irish poetry from the earliest times to the present day. It appeared that he had translated something of mine for a Berlin paper: after telling me that, he requested me to oblige him with a short biography of myself for his book, but I respectfully declined. The book cannot fail to be a most absurd farrago ; yet the man is not without a share of reputation, and has had some travels in Wales of his translated in England. Such are the world's instructors. From Berlin I went to Wittenberg (Luther), Dresden, Leipzig, Weimar (where I had three memorable days), Eisenach (Luther again), Homburg, Frankfort, and down the Rhine to Rotterdam again.

Mr Allingham was eventually transferred to Lymington, and henceforward his home was in southern England. Here he continued his habit of walking and exploring the scenery of the district, and of recording his impressions in verse or in prose. The 'Rambles of Patricius Walker,' which, with the exception of two chapters devoted to the Erne, delightfully describes the scenery and the people of Hampshire and Dorset, was published by Allingham in 1873. Many of his subsequent poems are coloured by his English surroundings.

On receiving a copy of Ferguson's 'Lays of the Western Gael,' he wrote as follows :—

I duly received the handsome volume, have read it, and shall often return to it. Pray accept my congratulations and best thanks—why delayed so long I cannot tell, unless it be that there is a kind of tie, a kind of pleasure, in owing a friendly letter, which may be written to-morrow as well as to-day; or is this mere sophistry?

The ballads on ancient Irish subjects are very fine, and I believe stand by themselves in poetry. Of the poems new to me I think that on Brittany struck me most. The volume altogether takes a place of its own, and adds honour to old Ireland. . . .

I continue to like this place tolerably well, and see a much greater variety of people than I used at Ballyshannon ; yet I don't feel the same " nature " to the scenery and circumstances of life. Do you know W. Barnes's Dorset Poems? They have great merit. The writer, a Church of England clergyman, who lives near Dorchester, and a simple, almost quaint old man, gave us a lecture here lately on the dialect of his native district, which he maintains to be a superior old form of English, and read some of his own poems. He stopped with me. My rooms, by the way, command a very fine view of the Solent and Isle of Wight from Osborne to the Needles. Tennyson has made several thousand pounds by 'Enoch Arden,' and is for buying more land. He would like to buy the Isle of Wight and build a wall round it. I dined one day, not long ago, at Sir Percy Shelley's, Boscombe, near Christchurch, son of the poet, and sat next Miss Shelley, the poet's sister, who is still graceful and like his portraits; she is tall, very slender, and rather lively. Sir Percy short, fair, fattish, silent, a sportsman, and not the least poetic. His wife, though but a Shelley by marriage, is enthusiastic and *blue*, and has a room full of Shelley relics—MSS., locks of hair, portraits, &c.

I have been wishing ever since I heard it to write and wish you both joy on Dr Ferguson's appointment to the Record Office, as I do very heartily. The money is not much, considering; but I could not congratulate you in the same sense if he had been made a judge with £3000 or £4000 a-year. It makes me doleful and angry to see any one of the few who are distinctly fitted to serve the world in a higher way (the purely intellectual ways are the highest), fastened down by some business of petty details, no matter how honourable.

But a truce to theorising and generalising! I shall be truly glad to hear that you are both well and happy. I often think of you, and always with a warm and kind remembrance. I go on quietly—much as usual outwardly, more contentedly, I think. I hope to visit Ireland next year.

The world in general is very mobile and interesting just now.

You told me of a paper on the Brehon Laws by Dr Ferguson. Could you lend it me by book-post?—Believe me always most truly yours,   W. ALLINGHAM.

Mr Allingham was fortunate in his marriage. The lady of his choice, Miss Helen Pattisson—an artist whose water-colour paintings are much sought after and deservedly admired—made him an excellent wife, and three promising children greatly added to his happiness. The names of Gerald, Evey, and Henry William constantly occur in their father's letters. Poems were written to and for them, and their moral and spiritual training was very near his heart. This will appear in his later correspondence. He undertook for a time the editorship of 'Fraser's Magazine,' removed to London, and ultimately to Godalming in Surrey.

Ferguson wrote on the 19th March 1878 :—

My dear Allingham,—I think it will be a pleasure to you to know that I have received the honour of Knighthood, and that the distinction is given as well on literary as on official grounds. I think I shall be able to bring out another volume during the present year. I shall publish in Dublin, although the fate of other home products might be a warning to me to expect little recognition. However, I am very earnestly bent on helping, as far as I can, independent Irish publishing enterprise. I see that you also have lent a helping hand to our little venture at Belfast, where McCaw & Co. have brought out the 'Lyra Sacra' of the Irish very creditably. I have been for a long while as inert as a chrysalis on a wall; but this last year the old incitements have begun to stir again. I spent a good part of last summer in the country on an official round of duty, and got round to some of my old delight in metrical utterances. One of these, "The Widow's Cloak," I sent to Blackwood, and have had the pleasure of having it (though cut to a very homely pattern) well commended both at home and in America. One notice which was very satisfactory to me I cut from the 'Providence Journal,' 26th Dec. last. I have sent Blackwood an Irish Ballad also; I hope that the intrinsic beauty of the subject will make it acceptable.

Certainly our old Irish literature furnishes more material for poetic treatment than any other known to me, and it will not be for want of my endeavour if it be not turned to something characteristic in English.   I have hardly left myself room to say more than that my wife unites with me in affectionate remembrances to yourself and to Mrs Allingham, who, we hope, is now quite recovered.—Yours, dear Allingham, very faithfully,   SAML. FERGUSON.

12 TRAFALGAR SQUARE, CHELSEA, S.W.,
March 31, 1879.

MY DEAR FERGUSON,—It is always a pleasure to see your hand, and a still greater to touch it.   Will you not (this is to Lady Ferguson, and includes Helen's cordial wish on the matter) dine one evening in our little house when you are in London at Eastertide?

I thought and think it very hard that the Fates should not have permitted me to see a little more of you when the same city contains us both, and there was no other in the 4 millions odd whose company I so much desired.

To this hospitable wish Ferguson responded, and when next in London he and his wife spent a very happy evening with Mr and Mrs Allingham.

DUBLIN, *2d April* 1879.

MY DEAR ALLINGHAM,—Certainly we will ask you to let us sit at your board whenever we again visit London.   This Easter, however, must be spent by us here.   The Academy, in which I take a great interest, has a meeting on Easter Monday; so here I am till quieter times allow me to recreate myself with the sight of dear old friends' faces once again in London.   .   .   .

The more I see of the extreme æsthetical school the less I like it, and the less likely do I think it to survive.   One-half its utterances among our young men here is mere mouthing and gasping. We have got a call back to better things in the revived taste for original Celtic music which the Swede Sjödén excites among us with his wonderful harp. He is enchanted with an Irish air which my wife has taught him, and dines with us to-day to try how it will sing to some words of mine. I wish you and Mrs Allingham were with us. We shall have an evening of harmony and pleasure. Take a blessing with you from, dear Allingham, ever faithfully yours,

SAML. FERGUSON.

DUBLIN, 9th March 1882.

MY DEAR ALLINGHAM,—I read a curious paper lately before the Royal Irish Academy here, on a subject which, probably, has often struck you as a very picturesque though apocryphal one. I think it has more historic foundation than hitherto supposed. If I am right in identifying the scene as at Pfeffers, the circumstances of picturesqueness and grandeur will certainly not be diminished for any poet taking the "Edda" of King Dathi in hand. If you have the 'Hy Fiachra' of O'Donovan, you will find the Irish story with all its romantic incidents at p. 20, &c. I enclose a synopsis of the paper, prepared for circulation among the local Swiss clergy, in order, if possible, to obtain traces of some other localities still eluding my research. Ireland rises, notwithstanding all her drawbacks, and things of which those who love her best are most ashamed, and, I think, will have her own literature yet. A volume of 'Poems of Places,' like that edited for Macmillan by Longfellow, is projected. I would like to see "The Winding Banks of Erne" in decent company if our endeavours, so far, have provided cloth-of-gold enough for such a field. . . .

Make my kind regards to Mrs Allingham. Have the soft misty distances, the blue airy summits, the warm chimney-stacks, and golden stubbles fixed the air of the country on many more precious cardboards? Does your boy take it all in with a capillary attraction? and I think I saw, when last with you, a little girl recalling the image of another on whom the other day I composed a much-admired ode.

Wilhelmina
Is as fine a
Child as you'll see anywhere,
With her ribbon
And her bib on,
And her top-knot in her hair.

Macte virtute, senex!   When you come to us, we shall have room in space and welcome for all.—Ever very faithfully yours,   SAML. FERGUSON.

Dec. 19, 1882.

MY DEAR FERGUSON,—I am sending by post two little books, and trust they may have the same friendly and indulgent reception as others of my brain-children with you.   The subject treated of in 'Evil May-Day,' &c., one does not willingly discuss; but the spread of Atheism among all classes of society during the last 20 years is a most noticeable and lamentable fact.   The old theological weapons are powerless against it.   May not a poet direct a fresh-air current of imaginative reason against the poisonous fog?

Poor Ireland seems to be going from bad to worse.   My brother has become a hot "Home-Ruler," and thinks an Irish Parliament would cure all.   I wish I could think so.   And how could any English Prime Minister venture on the experiment (for such at best it would be) in the present aspects and prospects of public affairs?   "Politics" must be practical—that is, according to expediency—or experimental, sometimes at huge risk; wherefore I long not to meddle in them.   But, Politics or no Politics, I would give the waste lands of Ireland into toilful Irish hands, for one thing.

I hope I am right in believing that your Presidency is bringing and will bring you satisfaction and honour, at no undue expense of energy; and that the Muse is still allowed to whisper in your ear.   We are all well here—my dear Wife, little Gerald, Evey, Henry William—and find the fir-woods beautiful even in mid-winter.—With friendliest regards and best wishes to both, I am ever, affectionately yours,

W. ALLINGHAM.

The little volume, ‘Evil May-Day,’ which accompanied this letter, contained the following lines—the confession, doubtless, of the faith of the writer:—

> “What Life is I know not,
> Nor claim the right to know; but gladly accept
> The highest hints and intimations given,
> As likest truth.   I know not what God is,
> Nor count it reasonable to suppose
> A man could know; but that God lives and rules,
> My soul in times of pure and tranquil vision
> Sees without effort; which great central truth
> Sways into order all the world of thought,
> That else were chaos.   And, since I am I,
> To me, a person, He, a person, lives;
> A Living God, of power immeasurable,
> Nature incomprehensible, and plans
> Inscrutable ; of whom I know by faith ;
> A reasonable and necessary faith
> Correlative to ignorance, and yet
> Noway self-contradictory, a clue
> In a prodigious labyrinth, a lamp
> In a great darkness.
>
> .   .   .   .
>
> We must live
> In a material world, must therein work,
> Thereby be wrought upon.   I am conjoin’d—
> This personal I (invisible as God)—
> To my own bodily organs first of all ;
> Related strictly to the beast, the bird,
> The blade of grass, the clod of earth, the cloud,
> The faintest haze of suns within the sky.
> That nearest fiery orb makes flow my blood ;
> Electric ether vivifies my brain ;
> And I, made up of these, who am not these,
> Exist in personal being, think, inquire,
> Reason, imagine, feel, and nothing know;

But in my clearest moments I think—God.
Ask you, what use is Faith?   Faith is like Health,
Which if you have in full serene possession,
You feel it every moment of the day,
In every fibre of your frame, each mood .
And movement of your mind, yet for most part
Unconsciously.   Inherit health and lose it,
Then shall you know its worth.
.   .   .   .

And Faith is higher, wider, subtler health,
What ether is to air, a harmony,
A pure truth inexpressible in words,
All the great truths being measureless, and God
Greatest.
.   .   .   .

May-Day was evil when I miss'd my God :
Earth, sea, and sky fall'n empty of a sudden,
All the wide universe a dismal waste
Peopled with phantoms of my flitting self,
And mocking gleams chance-kindled and chance-quench'd,
All meaning nothing.   Natural May-Day
Revived to me when I found God again ;
World full of beauty and significance
Wisely and justly govern'd, and I too
Part and partaker of the wondrous whole ;
Made capable to feel, enjoy, adore,
To think and reason, not to comprehend."

DUBLIN, 23d Dec. 1882.

MY DEAR ALLINGHAM,—I do not wonder at your alarm at
the prospect of such teachings getting an extended hold of the
public mind.   You do your part, as a poet and as the father
of children, to stay the plague ; but I think you undervalue
the help of the received formulas and underestimate the
strength of the barrier afforded by established religion.   I
suppose it will be swept away ; and the field left open to the
forces of Newman and Bradlaugh within the present century.
I heartily hope you will have succeeded in instilling the love
and fear of God into these young minds before the social trial

comes. When it does come, God may possibly make Himself known to the human family in some new dispensation more acceptable than those which have gone before, and more conducive to virtue and happiness; and God send it may be so! But meantime what we know of God, apart from Authority, goes but a little way towards satisfying the craving of young minds. You have put it as well as any poet of our time can do, and I honestly wish your book circulation and influence. May God give your children pure, pious, and happy minds, and yourself a joyful contentment with the preparation against evil with which you will have fortified them, when your turn shall come of leaving them to face the trials of life on their own dependence. I suppose it is my own liability to local infection, but you touch me more in your home-looking verses than anywhere else in the volume. I know nothing of the management of 'Hibernia,' but see that it is a not discreditable organ, and that it might be made a really good one, if men like you contributed. Make my kind regards to Mrs Allingham. If I were near my good wife, she would join me in sincerest good wishes to both.—Ever faithfully yours, SAML. FERGUSON.

GODALMING, *Dec.* 20, 1883.

MY DEAR FERGUSON,—When this old year was new you sent me two stitched books, and I believe no one to whom they were sent received them with more gratification or read them with more attention than the seeming Ingrate who now at last writes. The paper on the Legend of Dathi is full, exact, and lucid; and the Address to the Academy seems to me truly admirable, both in matter and style, as well as in tone and temper. I rejoice to believe that your estimate of modern science and its assumption of supremacy in thought does not differ from my own. Poetic insight, not scientific, gives the widest, loftiest, deepest view of things. We will not substitute Vortex for Zeus.

> " 'Man's a machine.' Well, if we ever can
> Construct one bit by bit on some new plan,
> Be sure 'twill be a Scientific man."

On the other hand, alas! what is literature coming to?

Archbishop Whately's theological views were undoubtedly much modified in later years.

Carleton, with the "light step and huge frame," himself sprung from the people, has, beyond all other delineators of Irish character—except, perhaps, Miss Edgeworth, before his day, and Miss Jane Barlow in recent years — given truthful and touching portraits of Irish peasants, pictures instinct with humour, pathos, and vivid individuality. No reader can ever forget his " Poor Scholar "; nor Miss Barlow's " Widow M'Gurk," to whom she has introduced us in her ' Irish Idylls.' Ferguson, always ready to render such services as were in his power, was in after-years helpful to Carleton and his family. Long after her father's death Miss Carleton wrote to thank him for his " great kindness ":—

I feel it difficult to express to you how truly grateful my sister and I feel for your exertions on our behalf. We have learned from Mr Bourke how you have worked for us, but we did not need this testimony to confirm our belief in the kindness of your heart and your desire to aid us.

Dr Anster, " with the absent aspect of a man of learning," was an early friend, and in later years a very agreeable neighbour, to Ferguson. He had a cultivated wife and charming daughters, and a pleasant and hospitable home. Many agreeable evenings were passed there, and the Anster family were frequent and welcome guests when Ferguson, as a married man, could offer his friends musical parties, dances, and other social enjoyments in his own house. It is generally understood that the most poetic translation of Goethe's masterpiece would never have been given to the world but for the energy and devotion of Miss Anster. Her father wrote on scraps of paper, and it was her labour as amanuensis that evolved order and sequence out of the chaos of his literary workshop.

Although Ferguson wrote much in prose, yet it is as a poet that he hoped to be remembered. His earliest compositions were in verse. "Light and Darkness," produced at a very early age, shows traces of the influence of Shelley on the writer's mind. It deals somewhat ambitiously with "Chaos and Eternal Night," and was not included by its author in the volume of his works collected in 1864. It appeared in 'Blackwood' in 1832, after he had made his mark by the "Forging of the Anchor." The originality, vigour of expression, and imaginative glow of this latter poem are marvellous, when it is remembered that when it appeared Ferguson was only in his twenty-second year. The "Forging of the Anchor" has found its way into many anthologies, has been published with illustrations by Messrs Cassell & Co. in 1883, and some of its stanzas set to music by Sir Julius Benedict and performed at a Norwich Festival.

"Captain Bey," a humorous ditty, also belongs to this early date, and was not republished by its author. But some lively prose writings which appeared in 'Blackwood' in May 1837 and May 1838 have been again and again reprinted in 'Tales from Blackwood.'

"The Involuntary Experimentalist" narrates in a minute and matter-of-fact way the supposed scientific observations of an imaginary sufferer who is described as having fallen into a vat in a distillery during a great conflagration which actually occurred at the time in Dublin. "Father Tom and the Pope; or, A Night at the Vatican," is a humorous *skit*, suggested by a controversial encounter on a Dublin platform between Father Tom Maguire, a well-known priest of that day, and Mr Pope, a clergyman of the Church of Ireland, champions respectively of their opposing faiths.

Sir W. R. Hamilton, in a letter to Professor De Morgan, asks the mathematician—

Did you ever read in 'Blackwood' the article entitled "Father Tom and the Pope; or, A Night at the Vatican"? If so, you cannot have enjoyed it as I have done, who am an Irishman. . . . What I invite you to do is, to tell me *which* was the Protestant and which the Papist. If you had ever spent, as I once did, a night—the richest night of my life— with *Father Tom*, you could decide at once.

To these polemical contests Ferguson was carried, somewhat against his inclinations, by two lady friends, desirous of his conversion to Roman Catholicism. Mrs Fitz-Simon and Miss Mary O'Mara would take no denial, and in courtesy he felt himself bound to obey their behest, and take care of them at these stormy meetings. The married lady was the eldest daughter of O'Connell, and wife of Christopher Fitz-Simon of Glancullen, Clerk of the Hanaper. She was an accomplished and charming woman, most engaging in manner. She is said to have had more of her father's genius than any of his children. To the close of her life she was a frequent guest in Ferguson's house, as he and his wife were also at Glancullen while the agreeable and hospitable circle remained unbroken. Christopher Fitz-Simon was a genial and kind-hearted host, and in their mountain home, surrounded by their large family, there was ever a welcome for friends and relatives, and countless attractions to draw them thither. Miss O'Mara, a connection of the Fitz-Simons, was a brilliant and witty lady of the old school. She as well as others of the household were quite as much French as Irish, both in language and manner and mode of life. In the penal days Roman Catholic families of their social rank were frequently educated abroad, so great and galling were their disabilities at home. Mr Fitz-Simon's father—who had landed property in the county of Wicklow as well as among the Dublin mountains—when riding with other gentlemen of position to meet the High Sheriff of the county on some state occasion, was mounted on a very fine horse. One of the party admired the animal and asked its value. Its rider stated that he had bred it himself, and valued it at £200. The Protestant —so-called gentleman—drew from his purse a five-pound note, handed it to Mr Fitz-Simon, and said, "You are a Papist, and are not entitled to have a horse exceeding five pounds in value: that animal is

Low enough it seems to me, and still sliding down-hill.   The vulgarity of " The Trade "—to which authorship has become a mere adjunct—and the dishonesty of current criticism are incredible to any one who has not been behind the scenes. One would fain forget it all ; and ·we are pretty well out of the way here—my wife painting her landscapes and cottagers with great contentment of spirit and a still increasing skill of hand, taking no note whatever of the envy and malice raging in the world of pictorial art, there also.   Our three children, Gerald, Evey, and Henry,—a bright funny little Irishman with gold curls,—have had happy lives so far.   The two elder are able to enjoy 'The Tempest,' and make endless stories of their own.   I have a little book in the press called 'Blackberries,' aphoristic and epigrammatic, which will please nobody, and yet out it must come.

My brother has become a hot " Nationalist," and is elected Mayor of Waterford for 1884.   The Conservatives will soon be back in office here, I think.—With kindest regards to Lady Ferguson and heartiest good wishes, I am always your affectionate friend,   W. ALLINGHAM.

DUBLIN, *5th Dec.* 1884.

MY DEAR ALLINGHAM,— . . . The ballad in 'Longman' is very powerful.   You are too able and original for me to say a word against the form in which you clothe your fancies ; but differences of metre have the effect on my mind of diminishing continuity and wholeness.   Yet the piece has both in a high degree, and perhaps I am wrong.   I have just been putting St Patrick's 'Confessio' into blank verse.   It is a most interesting composition, expressed with evident difficulty in broken Latin, but full of fervour and effusion.   I propose to read it in connection with some critical papers (non-controversial) on the Patrician Evidences, at the Academy.

I wish to heaven we had a Dublin 'Fountain,' with you for editor—clear, pure, copious.   I long to see the Irish mind take the lead it is entitled to outside that arena of sawdust and word-catching.   And " sae wull we yet "; but not, I fear, while I shall be able to take part—though you may join in the chorus.

I don't despair at all for my country. Knaves, cowards, assassins, at present represent her; but this scum floats on a substratum of noble qualities. I am old, but, if I do not see it, I shall close my eyes in the faith of her resurrection.

Now for your own household: you are happy in those young creatures round you, and in the life-companion by your side. Heaven grant you may long have these reasons for "copious" gratitude. . . .—Ever sincerely yours,

SAML. FERGUSON.

SANDHILLS, WITLEY, GODALMING,
June 6, 1885.

MY DEAR FERGUSON,—I hope the inclement spring has not harmed you or yours. We are all well now, thank God, and June is glorious.

May Saint Patrick prosper and become *ter quaterque beatus* in your hands! Your undertaking this subject is all the more interesting to me inasmuch as, many years ago, I planned and commenced a poem on the Saint, in the form of a *Cantata*—

> " The mighty feast proclaim !
> Kindle its sacred flame !"

and so forth. But want of sympathy with some aspects of the affair caused this scheme to be flung aside, with a heap (alas!) of other fine intentions. You will make a noble thing of it. . . .

I confess the thought is dear to me of distinctly connecting my name as a Poet with that of the Old Country—and at the same time with *yours:* would you give me the honour and gratification of accepting the dedication? I do not ask with the selfish aim of tying my tow-rope to the ship. It would be a most genuine expression of lifelong admiration, gratitude, and friendship. . . .

When you come into my mind (which is very often, my dear Ferguson) the thought is apt to rise that hereafter, perhaps, they will be reckoned among the friends of Ireland who have done something, each in his degree, to make her name interesting and amiable in the ear of mankind. *Forsitan et nostrum,* &c.

Can you tell me how much of Petrie's collection of Irish Airs has been published, and where it can be bought ?

My wife is painting out of doors every day, to her own great pleasure as well as other people's—happy lot !—With our united very kind regards to Lady Ferguson, I am ever your affectionate friend,   W. ALLINGHAM.

20 NTH. GREAT GEORGE'S STREET,
8th June 1885.

MY DEAR ALLINGHAM,—Any dedication you may make to me will be grateful, and esteemed honourable. I think we have amongst us enough of ability to lay the foundations of such a school of letters here as will be honourable also to the country. That has been the great aim I have had in view in all my efforts. . . . A Dublin School would, I think, restore good taste and good English in our current poetry, now over-run with gaspings, affectations, pet words, and bad prosody. . . . The history of this country furnishes plenty of material ; its native literature more. But the people—idle, *feckless* as they are—are a game breed, and won't disappear before the face of any other competitors for existence here ; and they must have their history and their humanities *tolites qualites*. I trust in God they will yet recognise as friends the men who revolt against the present teachings given them by those who would make them knaves and cowards. They need strong hands over them—even Orangemen for want of better, if the Orangemen could only be made to feel Irish. I don't think the Whig Liberals will ever understand them.—Ever yours,

SAML. FERGUSON.

MY DEAR FERGUSON,—I received with much pleasure and satisfaction your gift of 'Saint Patrick.' Your version is doubtless the most perfect rendering into English of those ancient documents, and makes clear certain points which might be obscure in the original even to a good Latinist. The blank verse is lucid and elegant, but, I must own, it seems to me to carry with it modern associations. Others may not feel this. The striking passage, " And once I saw him," &c. (v.

282), comes out very finely; and altogether it is a valuable piece of work. The chances of being able to get anything published in this country, save what meets the taste of the passing day, grow less and less. I have put my poems, old and recent, together in the hope of their appearance, some day, as a whole—after my own disappearance, if it may not be sooner.

We are all well here now, thank God, spite of the countless variations of weather, and snowdrops are in blow in sheltered nooks. My wife is very busy with a series of "Surrey Cottages," which she undertook last year, to be exhibited in the Bond Street Gallery in April. I hope you will see them. There will be about fifty drawings. Many of the cottages have been altered for the worse, and some pulled down, since she began this work, even in that short time.

I wish I could get a copy of Petrie's 'Ancient Music of Ireland.' Are there six numbers or more?—With kind regards to Lady F., ever yours,   W. ALLINGHAM.

When this letter reached Ferguson he had entered the Valley of the Shadow of Death. Allingham survived him for a few years, but now he too has "crossed the bar." In a "familiar epistle" to his little son he enjoins the boy, who will ere then be fatherless, to visit when he has attained to manhood the scenes which that father loved.

> "Nor will that ghost be happy unless he may know
> Your footsteps have wander'd where his used to go
> In the spring-time and song-time—among those green hills,
> And gray mossy rocks, and swift-flowing rills,
> On mountain, by river and wave-trampled shore,
> Where the wild region nourish'd the poet it bore,
> And colour'd his mind with its shadows and gleams.
> That lonely west coast was the house of his dreams
> And his visions."

These dreams and visions he describes, with his

longing prayer for sleep—the happy slumber when *He*
giveth His beloved sleep :—

> " See Ireland, dear Sonny, my nurture was there;
>   . . . Is there sunshine elsewhere?
> Such brightness of grass, such glory of air,
> Such a sea rolling in on such sands, a blue joy
> Of more mystical mountains?
>   O eyes of the Boy !
> O heart of the Boy ! newly waken'd from sleep.
> Might I sleep again, MASTER, long slumber and deep,
> To wake rested !"

END OF THE FIRST VOLUME.

PRINTED BY WILLIAM BLACKWOOD AND SONS.

BLANAID: AND OTHER POEMS.

"Mr. T. D. Sullivan may be congratulated, without hesitation or reserve, on his success in rendering the old Irish tales into English verse. As to the literary value of the Gælic originals we are not competent to speak. But that the version before us is remarkable for melody, and beauty, and force, no one who reads it carefully will be at all inclined to question."—*The Literary World.*

"Mr. Sullivan's Irish historical and legendary poems are very readable. Mr. Sullivan at his best has much of Scott's narrative strength. . . . "The Voyage of the O'Corras" reminds us of Dunbar's great poem, "The Dance of the Seven Deadly Sins." Ossian's visit to the Land of Youth is a splendid poetical subject, and Mr. Sullivan, on the whole, is equal to it. Sassenachs will be grateful for an attractive presentation of interesting legends with which Mr. Sullivan has helped to make us familiar."—*The Speaker.*

"Mr. T. D. Sullivan has done good service to the cause of Irish literature by collecting his renderings of old Irish tales into English verse. . . . It is a noble work to perpetuate the too scanty remains of our original poetry and to present them in a suitable manner for modern readers. This Sir Samuel Ferguson did with conspicuous success, and now Mr. T. D. Sullivan offers us towards the same end a bright and welcome volume of translations from the Gælic. . . . We can only in conclusion express our desire that Mr. Sullivan's volume will have a circulation in some way commensurate with its sterling merits."—*Freeman's Journal.*

"Mr. Sullivan shows himself a very capable translator. His diction is pointed and graphic, and he shows his proper appreciation of the legends by rendering them in the simplest forms of verse. In the more impassioned scenes he rises to a dignified but never inflated style of language, and in his most simple narration he is always pointed and interesting. The book is a most acceptable addition to the by no means too large store of Irish legendary poetry."—*North British Daily Mail.*

"Mr. T. D. Sullivan's return to the pleasant but neglected fields of Gælic legend for the matter of his modern ballads is more than justified by the result. We have to thank him for an easy, melodious, simple rendering of some of the choicest, most pathetic, and most characteristic stories left to us by the old bards."—*National Press.*

"In this volume the Member for Dublin has translated into strong and vigorous English verse the old Irish legends which deal with the heroes Cuchullin and Ossian, the love-story of Ailleen and Baille, and the conversion to christianity of the O'Corras and King Connor Mac Nessa."—*Review of Reviews.*

"The subjects of these stories are in the main connected with ancient Irish legends, and they have the true stamp of fancy, simplicity, and weird grace proper to the efforts of the Gælic muse. Mr. Sullivan's verses are characterised by easy melody, and he has on the whole preserved the spirit and form of the historic ballad."—*Newcastle Daily Leader.*

"The contents of the little volume before us form a valuable addition, and in a pleasing form too, to our folk lore. In his treatment of the subject chosen the author exhibits all the qualities which have made his lyrics known and welcome wherever an Irishman is to be found."—*Belfast Morning News.*

"This little volume of Irish historical and legendary poems from the Gælic will be welcome in England to all who take an interest in Ireland, its history, and its people. . . . Mr. Sullivan has caught the spirit of those fine old romances, and in his mellifluous, graceful verse, they will find a happy entrance into many a heart."—*Northampton Mercury.*

"In Mr. Sullivan's new volume there is a charm and sweetness and simplicity in the domestic passages most winning and delightful. . . . . Ferketne's song of mourning is touching and tender, and there is in it that strange incommunicable melody of Irish pathos and poetry to which Mr. Swinburne and Mr. Matthew Arnold direct attention."—*Manchester Guardian.*

"Mr. T. D. Sullivan has never put from his always busy hand more worthy work than that which lies between the covers of the dainty little volume which, under the title of "Blanaid, and other Poems," Messrs. Eason & Son have just published."—*Irish Catholic.*

"Mr. Sullivan has done his work well. Smoothness of rhythm and simplicity of language are the characteristics of the verses which enfold five charming legends dealing with the more romantic aspect of Irish life."—*Welsh Review.*

"Mr. T. D. Sullivan has gone to the fine old tales of Ireland for the subjects of this little volume. He has succeeded in producing a body of verse of unusually high quality, rhythmical and forceful. . . . . The little volume is well worth reading for its poetical quality alone. It has of course an additional value for Irishmen who love the old tales of their country."—*Northern Whig.*

"The contents of this volume are renderings of old Irish tales into English verse. Their translation evinces merit of a high order, and the author has very successfully preserved the spirit of the original legends."—*Publishers' Circular.*

"Mr. Sullivan's spirited verses are attractive in themselves, and breathe the fire of true poesy."—*Whitehall Review.*

"Mr. Sullivan has the full spirit of the true Irish bard, and tells the old tales delightfully."—*Irish Monthly.*

"As was generally anticipated, Blanaid proves to be a charming addition to our library of Celtic folk lore."—*Cork Herald.*

"'Blanaid and other Poems' is certainly a very interesting volume. . . . Blanaid is a really pretty story of the days of Irish chivalry."—*Glasgow Evening News.*

"Five gems of narrative verse, certain to become popular, for the subjects, treatment, and versification are all good."—*Liverpool Mercury.*

"In his selections from the literature of the Gael, Mr. Sullivan has turned chiefly to the period in which Cuchullin is the prominent figure, and when Connor Mac Nessa was Ulster's King. The opening poem contains the story of the beautiful Blanaid, who dwelt on "Manan's lovely isle" (the Isle of Man), her marriage with Cuchullin, and her abduction by Caroi with its tragic ending. The history of Baille and Ailleen, "by cruel falsehood slain," is taken from Professor O'Curry's MS., and the "Lay of Ossian on the Land of Youth" from the "Transactions" of the Ossianic Society. There are five poems altogether. They are all done into metrical English of a free and fluent kind, literal translation not being attempted."—*Bookseller.*

"If some of the most beautiful traditions and legends of our early forefathers have to be presented in an English dress, we do not know by whom the task could be better performed than by Mr. T. D. Sullivan. . . . The volume he offers to the Irish public is one that has every attraction that can commend it to favour. . . . We can heartily congratulate Mr. Sullivan on having made another precious addition to Irish literature."—*Cork Examiner.*